NO

A NOVEL BY BERNARD J. PACKER

CHAPTER ONE

I felt sorry for Knocky; he comes from a scuzzy family. Meanwhile, I was jealous of the talented and sharp looking cat. Slouching around in Levis and scroungy T-shirts, the Ace shines brighter than most cruds do in brand new suits and ties. When Karl, Knocky, and I shot downtown to catch a movie it was not only girls our age staring at him, mature matrons snuck peeks his way, and whispered sly comments behind cupped hands. His exotic aura captures attention. Alexi shuffles along like a gangly Jack-in-the-box but with his bushy helmet of black curls, eyes with a Tartar glint, almond-shaped, like the eyes of the Kalmucks moving in over by Third Street, but his are a cobalt blue, he stands out like a misplaced Siberian wolf that wandered out of the woods into our neighborhood.

Knocky ignores his effect on girls, does not like to hear about it. When Karl said, "Hey, you see the way that old biddy just gulped your way? " Knocky shrugs it off. Besides, he's not much of a talker. Karl and I are the chatterboxes. Drifting along the docks, hoofing it out to Shibe Park to catch a double- header, we'd be blabbing away about the latest action films, the Tarzan novels, the latest edition of Amazing Stories, the Shaver mysteries, Alexi bobbles along, occasionally chuckling at our blah blah.

The three of us were closer than brothers. Knocky spends more time down at the Wronsky gas station, or my place, than in his own home. His scroungy family makes him a mutt in the streets. The ornerier branch was coal town trash from up in Reading, mortifying him no end during their summer visitations, arriving like a rowdy plague from God's Little Acre, squabbling, fussing and a feuding, parking out in front of his house, guzzling and brawling till the wee hours of dawn.

Oddly enough, his only relative more or less passing for normal is his Uncle Ivan, a bizarrely flamboyant magician going by the stage name of 'John the Wizard.' Ivan is a shifty sharpy with a snide Basil Rathbone accent, dashing enough to wear his

Mandrake get-ups without looking geeky. Audiences rarely suspect Ivan is a Green-horn, born in Rumania. His slick tuxedo costumes are for acts he performs in South Philly and nightclubs down the Jersey shore, where he flashes onto stage amidst bursts of green and purple smoke as John the Wizard in black top hat and scarlet cloaks. The Wizard zips around town in a polished black hearse lugging his magic equipment. According to my Dad, this is the same vintage hearse that Ivan used to smuggle his black market goods during the war.

Ivan makes a splash when he enters Dave's Pool Hall at Sixth and Girard, big hullabaloo, our local dull tools want to snip off a sprig of his classy style, because the Wizard sachets in with the wise-cracks, snappiest jokes, inside dope on high sakes poker games and sex orgies down in Atlantic City. Many say the Wizard is wasting his time in stodgy old hat Philly. They say the Wizard is ready for the Big Time, ready for New York, Broadway, Hollywood, the West Coast.

Knocky was proud of his Uncle Ivan but ashamed of the rest of his clan. His father was rummy, he'd been a stevedore, Mrs. Ratchinov kicked that boozer out of the house long ago. Cousin Rita was our neighborhood pig. Saturday matinees she stations herself in the front rows of the Astor theatre, one by one the gang dispsy-doodles down there to get a hand job while Rita obligingly hides the clammy deed beneath her sweater. Knocky rarely strolls down Oriana Street, afraid of bumping into Rita, or her Momma, his Aunt Svetlana. Svetlana has achieved notoriety due to her formidable hips, employed to bump and grind away in the Troc Burlesque chorus line under the Nome de Guerre of Trixie Malloy.

But it was his mother who was his main tormentor. What do you do when your Momma is the neighborhood sexpot? Sonya Ratchinov causes accidents when drivers speeding down Sixth Street swerve at the sighting of a statuesque red head with the sensational curves. It was not only her lush figure inducing the double takes. Mrs. Ratchinov is deliberately provocative, flaunting her charms with out-landish outfits. Evenings, she steps out as the Fiery Gypsy Dancer: clicking bracelets, gaudy beads, spiked heels, sheer paisley skirts tracing her muscular thighs through filmy gauze. For her daytime job Mrs. Ratchinov has the disconcerting habit of wearing pointy pink bras gleaming through her translucent white uniforms

The older guys say her peekaboo blouses increase her tips. She worked as a manicurist in ritzy center city hotel barbershops; everybody knew how she lost her last job. They caught her upstairs with a customer. That night Sonya got sloshed in the Golden Slipper Club on Girard Avenue, bitched to the steadies around the piano bar that the real reason for her firing was that the manager was a slimey shithead, always trying to pinch her fanny, and pissed because she had never spread for him. Her audience around the piano laughed, mostly for the comical effect of her rattling off raunchy Yankee slang in her lispy Rumanian accent. Only reason I know this, Billy Schmitz afterwards got yucks in the poolroom by repeating her complaints and imitating her production number. Two days later she plugged into a spot at a posher hotel where the tips were bigger. The gossips around our way say that women like Sonya do not go unemployed for long.

The Saturday after classes ended we were playing basketball when the taxi paused at Knocky's house on Randolph Street. June, baseball season, our schoolyard at Sixth and Thompson was too cramped, baseball we played on Sundays down at the Kearny yard. To our right was Sixth Street; broad red brick row houses three stories high, with high stone steps, and slanting attics tacked on. The Ratchinovs rent one of the dinky two story brown brick shoeboxes to our left on Randolph with a flat roof, no attic, too narrow to stick a sofa in except sideways. No steps, no vestibule, you pass directly from the sidewalk into stuffy parlors, are hit by the rankness of the cabbage cooking in the back kitchen.

The cabby began honking impatiently, we saw fluttering in the window curtains, Sonya signaling that she would be out shortly. Neighbors often criticize her for using taxis so much. Why doesn't she take the 65 trolley like everybody else? She is even too hoity-toity to walk to the cabstand on Girard; she calls to summon taxis, which costs a quarter extra. When the cab arrives, it always takes minutes for Her Highness to emerge; she's still putting on her make-up, with the meter ticking. The luxuries you can afford when you do more for the customers than clip their nails.

Again the taxi beeped. Mrs. Ratchinov opened her green door; garishly bright, not like the dull green of the other doors along Randolph. Sonya was in a black leather skirt; her waist belt was too tight, a black slip was glinting wickedly through her scarlet blouse. She could have been a brazen Balkan Daisy May. Heads twisted around to take in the cartoonish spectacle;. She seemed confused, started searching frantically through her oversized purse. She always forgets something, appears harried, flustered, lost, until men hurry in to help her. The hacky beeped at her; she motioned him to hold his horses, she would be there by and by.

Dribbling toward the basket, Knocky pretended not to see his Mom. Karl, Alexi, and I were teamed up three to three against Irv Kauffman, Burdumi, and Leon Hess: high school seniors, starters on their varsity teams, we were only fourteen but holding our own against them, because of Knocky. Alexi is a dazzling ball handler, mixing up deadly left hooks with his fade away jump shots. And, can he take it to the basket. Astute observers say that he may have inherited dark magic from his John the Wizard genes. He has an uncanny knack for plunging into traffic, penetrating defenses while being banged, clawed, bumped, clutched at, fouled, he manages to get the roll, curling reverse lay-ups into the hoop from impossible angles.

His face went blank when he saw his mother crossing Randolph, entering the yard. Onlookers playing stickball and small fry on other basketball courts paused to take in the show. Also, smell the roses. Mrs. Ratchinov sprays on potent perfumes and powerful toilet waters. Aside from her seductive acoustics; at a distance you hear suggestive serenades of rustling silks and swishy satins in counterpoint to her clicking beads and bracelets, the tension of tight garters on her girdle staining her sheer nylons. Maybe it was just me hearing that siren song.

Against the rules for Mothers to invade schoolyards; an American Mom would never pull this dirty trick. Sonya, despite her slangy cursing, does not quite catch our ways. Her brother's another matter, you might think Ivan spent his adolescence as a jive-talking drugstore cowboy in South Phillie, but Sonya's a hopeless case. After all this time in the U.S. she still comes off as a gushy Greenhorn right off the boat.

Knocky sought to extricate himself with a casual 'high' and 'goodbye' wave. She was having none of that; Sonya called to him, "Alexi! Come over here!" She added orders in Rumanian, making Knocky shudder. None of us, not the Polacks, Porto Ricans, and Ukrainians down by Spring Garden, nor the gang up here on Girard

Avenue, appreciate it when our parents call to us in their Russky, Yiddish, German, Hunky. We answer back in American.

Burdumi called a time out; we passed the ball around while Mrs. Ratchinov tortured Knocky. She chewed him out for not putting on the freshly pressed Levis she had left on the sofa. Why does he insist on dressing like a bum when she buys such nice clothes for him? She tousled his hair, looking more like a chick flirting with her date than a bossy Mom busting her sonny boy's balls. From her purse she brought out five bucks, and said, "This is for a movie, and your lunch, and supper. But make sure you eat a proper dinner at Himmelstein's tonight, Alexi: the special with the soup, meat, mixed salad, and vegetables. And don't you try to lie to me, Alexi. The waiters are all my dear friends, they will tell me what you ate."

"Yeah, Mom, sure," Knocky mumbled.

That should have been enough torture for one session but Mrs. Ratchinov smirked, put her fists on her hips, and cooed, "Now give your Momma a little kiss."

"C'mon, Mom, knock it off," Knocky moaned

She cursed at him in Rumanian again, then complained, " You poor Momma must go into work, you can't even give her one little kiss, you dumb jerk? C'mon, give me one little kiss on the cheek, and I'll stop bugging you."

We stared elsewhere while Knocky suffered the death by a thousand cuts. The troops might ogle his Mom, make jokes about her when he was not within hearing range, but Alexi occupied a unique niche in our pecking order. Respect was accorded to his athletic abilities. He was never picked on. Around our way we had sadistic bullies making life an endless torture for the porkers and pee-wees but nobody messed with Knocky. Hawaiian Jack and Billy Schmitz, the mightiest oxen around Sixth and Girard, for whatever reason, ordained that nobody lays a hand on Knocky. Alexi oscillated in a precarious equilibrium: object of pity, of envy, untouchable mascot, crown prince.

The impatient taxi driver honked again. What was his problem? His meter is running. Knocky was shying back, Sonya lunged at him. Alexi squirmed helplessly in her clutches. He might be a great athlete, but Mrs. Ratchinov, looking soft and curvy, was incredibly strong for a woman. She planted a loud smooch on his cheek, then shoved him away with an imperious toss of her hand, and haughtily hoisted her purse strap over her broad shoulder. She was well aware that she was being gawked at while she promenaded on her absurdly high heels back toward the yellow cab on Randolph Street

If I were a movie director I'd have the drummer thumping out a Strip Tease Artist Gypsy Rose Lee beat to her oom-pah- pah strut as the lady ignored the gantlet of leers and left the yard. Rubbing the blotch of lipstick from his cheek, Knocky shuffled back to us. Leon Hess tossed me the ball; I popped in a long set shot. The gang was still gaping at Sonya. What can we say about a woman blatantly ridiculous and tormentingly desirable, half goofy and half goddess, arriving in the same package. Her magnificent ass blossomed into a perfect Valentine as she bent over to enter the cab. Anguished eyes in the Ludlow schoolyard slowly rose to the heavens.

Karl Wronsky has no Mother. No Father, either. Well, actually, he had both but they were ardent Communists. Right after World War II ended they chose to return to Russia, leaving Karl behind to be raised by older brother, Dmitri. Some said that Karlie was the one doing the raising, was the only adult in the family, taking care of a shaggy, uncouth, elbow-bender like Dmitri. The Wronskys shared tiny rooms behind their gas station on the south side of Spring Garden Street between Sixth and Randolph. Karl did the cooking, opening cans of Spam and Franco- American Spaghetti. Half the time they ate sloppy Joe take-out from the Diner at Fifth Street.

Wronsky was already a man. He had been taking apart motors since he was nine years old: many o truck drivers from the terminals along Spring Garden preferred Karlie to Dmitri when it came to working on their tractor-trailers. Dmitri was a top-notch mechanic but smack in the middle of a rush job Dim could fade over to Gold's taproom on Fourth Street to down a few suds, leave it to Karl to handle matters. The Police passing by in their red cars had already pegged Karlie as a man. Any other neighborhood there might have been flack about child labor laws, cops around here had heavier stuff to worry about.

A price to pay, Karlie looked older than his years: chunky, built like a corner mailbox, teeth irregular, pumpkin-shaped head too bulky for his abbreviated trunk.

Seeing him slouch along beside a movie star like Alexi you wondered how Mother Nature could be so stingy with the distribution of the goodies, but she compensated Karlie for his dismal physical dowry by supplying him with a souped-up Mind. He was the biggest brain up at Saint Pete's, whiz at science, math. Ask him what is 693 by 492; Karl could multiply that faster between his ears than most plodders can with a pencil and paper. Karl looks like a lumpish meathead, but was multi-faceted: clever stuff pouring out of him, great with accents, hilarious imitations of Jewish storekeepers from Marshall Street arguing with Amos and Andy stock boys, Porto Ricans pleading with an Irish cop to tear up a parking ticket.

Usually Karl shot up to Girard to hang out with us but that Saturday evening Knocky and I picked him up at the station, our trio hit the Diner at Fifth. The end of June but already steaming like deep August, mashed greenish caterpillars smearing the sidewalks, mosquitoes swarming in the traffic headlights, the Diner windows were splotched with greasy streaks and splattered butterfly marks.

Betty, the waitress, bending over behind the counter, brought to mind Sonya dipping into the taxi this morning, I censored that thought. Against the rules to think about a pal's mother that way, though I'd heard other dinks in the schoolyard confess to having wet dreams about Mrs. Ratchinov. Mine was just a run-of-the-mill, widely shared, commonplace phantasy.

'Again' was playing on the six for a quarter Wurlitzer.

'Again. This couldn't happen again. This is that once in a lifetime. This is the thrill divine. What's more, this never happened before...'

"For the thrill divine," Karl said, "I use Ivory soap and a copy of Planet Comics."

Knocky chortled, he enjoys our material, rarely makes contributions. I was finding the syrupy lyrics of 'Again' to be out or sync with Spring Garden Street. Down to the river this was a grim stretch of warehouses, factories, and garages. Most selections on the jukebox, Hillbilly banjos, rhythm and blues, seemed fitting for this stark wasteland. Syrupy 'Again' sounded like a Strauss Waltz lullabying a junkyard.

The lights by the gas station suddenly dimmed, Karl groaned, "Oh, shit. Dmitri knows he shouldn't do this. Twice he's already been warned that we can lose our franchise if he keeps this crap up."

Only nine-thirty, Saturday nights the station was supposed to stay open till eleven. What the sign by the soda machine says. A minute later, still in his greasy overalls with the Esso emblem, Dmitri came bursting into the Diner like a shaggy mongrel nobody would dare take home because he would eat too much. Plopping down with us, making the whole booth tremble, Dmitri announced, "Hey, you punks, I knocked it off early because tonight there gonna' be showing hot smoker flics in Gold's. Wanna' tag along? Down a brew with me?"

From behind the counter Betty the waitress shouted to him, "You crazy, Dim? You ain't dragging these kids into no tap room. Especially not a dive like Gold's, "

"So who asked you to stick your two cents in, Miss Buttinsky? " Dmitri cooed back at her. "No beers. I'll sport them to root beers. And maybe pretzels with hot mustard. If you give me the green light, Madam Loud-mouth."

I began to rise, peeled a dollar bill out of my wallet to pay for our coffees plus the tip. Betty pointed a finger at me and snapped, "Little Doc, you ain't going into no smelly saloon. Big Doc would skin your skinny ass alive if he heard you entered Gold's. And, if he don't hear it from others, I'll be the one to call Big Doc."

I hated my nickname. I was five-ten, still growing, but because my father was six-four I will forever be Little Doc around these environs.

To tease Betty, make matters worse, Dmitri said to her, " This ain't for any booze, darling. It's educational. Hymie will be showing dirty French films. Maybe you should drop by, baby. Ooh la Lah. You could learn more advanced stuff, graduate from giving back seat blow jobs."

Planting her fists on her hips, Betty growled, "You're gonna' take Karlie and these two kids to see filthy crap like that? You ought to be ashamed of yourself, you thick, crazy animal."

"Woof-woof," Dmitri barked at her, and added, " Lighten up, bitch. They gotta' see what the real thing is like so they can stop pounding their puddings. It'll be good for their complexions. They'll start losing the pimples on their cheeks."

I dropped the dollar bill on the counter by the cash register; Betty wagged her finger at me, and said," Big Doc will hear about this first thing tomorrow. Of all the kids around here, his son, stooping to this."

A large pain in my ass, I'm supposed to be the well-behaved boy, model son of my renowned father. I never applied for this position.

As we followed Dmitri out the door Betty slipped in one last shot at him, shouting, "I may call the Buttonwood Street Station, sic the cops on you, Dim, you scummy pervert, taking kids to see crap like that."

In lieu of a response Dmitri merely gave her the finger sign, then angrily waved off pesky Kamikaze mosquitoes buzzing at his ear while grumbling. "The twats think they run the world now. This whole goddam country is fast becoming Cuntsville."

"Ah, Betty was just being motherly," I said.

"Motherly, my hairy ass," Dmitri snorted. He turned to me, a worried look on his face, asked," Hey, Little Doc, I ain't gonna' get in Dutch with Big Doc for taking you into no saloon, will I?"

"Nah. As long as I don't get arrested and booked my father doesn't ride me too much." We sort of had our family secret slogan: Don't get caught.

"How about you, Ratchinovsky? " Dmitri asked Alexi." Is your momma gonna' bustle down my way, chew me out for purr-vurting her precious sonny-boy?"

"She's working tonight," Alexi said. "Part time, hatcheck girl on Locust Street."

Dmitri rolled his eyes, limiting his commentary to that.

We headed to the corner, shot down Fourth to Buttonwood. Further down, Gold's neon sign was blinking at the corner of Noble. This area was once let rooms for the Fishcake Irish, merchant seamen, oystermen, who sailed down to Chesapeake Bay. Now it was changing, Porto Ricans, and Negroes moving in. Dmitri sniffed, and said, "Gold's bar, last outpost of the vanishing White Man in what is fast becoming the heart of deepest Africa."

"Boom bah-bah boom, bah-bah boom," Karl intoned, imitating the thumping of jungle drums. The Wronskys pay scant attention to the brotherhood posters on the trolleys showing all the mixed together: Black, White, Red, Yellow, mixed, and Brown marching off toward Technicolor Bright Horizons.

Entering Gold's I felt a zing that was not exactly the thrill divine, this wasn't the Rubicon, but it was the first time in my life I stepped into a bar. Betty's objections were nothing compared to the scowls hitting us from the proprietors. Hymie was polishing shot glasses behind the counter; Saul Gold was tinkering with a movie projector. Spotting us ducking in behind Dmitri, Hymie snarled, "Dim, what the fuck are you doing, you idiot? This ain't no goddam Kindergarten!"

"Serve 'em a lemonade," Dmitri growled back. "Know how to make lemonade? First, you squeeze the lemons. If the cops come in I'll talk to Mahann, and tell him that I'm the one responsible."

"Yeah?" Saul snapped. "And who will be responsible for you, you asshole?"

Gold's smelled of beer, sawdust, sweat, smoke, and a faint pinch of piss. The customers were toughies in their twenties and thirties: Dick Jardine from Fifth and Green, Chick Gallagher, Sibronsky, Eli, Schatz, Joe the Worm. I knew them from the Third and Brown poolroom, and the Fairmount Avenue. Police Gym. They all knew me; had been to my Dad's office for a sprained ankle, a girlfriend in trouble, or to get a shot for a case of the clap.

"We could lose our license if Mahann comes in and catches these kids in here, Hymie groaned. "These fucking kids ain't even in High School yet."

"We will be in September," Knocky said. "All three of us in September."

The crowd playing darts and the pinball machine found that to be riotous, laughed even louder when Dmitri said, " You should lose your license for watering the Wild Turkey and pissing in the draft beer. Meanwhile, serve 'em a Coke, and get off my goddam case."

A tense moment, Saul and Hymie were about to order us to amscray. To the surprise of everybody Chick Gallagher raised a finger, called over, " Saul, let the small fry stay. But they gotta' promise to keep their hands out of their pockets during the hot scenes."

Dmitri nodded in in gratitude to Gallagher, and the four of us sank down at a side table. Gall nodded back with the chilling style he uses for nodding, like' you may proceed to cut off the head, executioner. ' Difficult to tell what Gall is thinking, he never takes off his dark glasses. He is not as powerful a bull as Hawaiian Jack or Billy

Schmitz but Chick Gallagher was the hood most feared from Christ Church up to Fishtown. Dark Irish, Gall had been a paratrooper, won medals, also served time in the stockade for black market shenanigans. Now he worked for the union on the docks, though some claimed that the union works for Gall.

Hymie served Dim a double vodka and for us kiddies brought ginger ales, even decorated them with a slice of lemon as a good will gesture. We sank down and tried to blend in with the foliage. Saul was still tinkering with the projector, most of the gang was watching the game on television; the A's were losing again. Neither Knocky, or Karl, nor I would say it aloud but we glanced at each other, were digging this grungy ambience, the put downs, the razzing of the softies, the dirty gabbling about ginch; our initial glimpse into the joys awaiting us down the road. One day we would be the tough guys in here. My first time in a bar but I caught on that this was not exactly Duffy's Friendly Tavern: this joint was more a private club, unhealthy for unwary wayfarers.

Carrying his suds with mannered deliberation, Gall rose from his booth, and plunked down at our table. From the way the clientele was squinting I sensed we should feel honored. I was not sure which was more menacing, Gall's sinister dark glasses or his radiator wide shoulders in the black turtleneck black sweater. If they made a movie about him, cast Albert Dekker. After a sip of his suds Gall said to me," Paulie, it's okay for you to pal around with Karlie but does Big Doc know that means you also get to associate with a dirt bag like Dim here?"

"Hey, c'mon, get off it, Gall-man," Dmitri complained. "I'm taking these punks under my wing. Teaching them the ropes, teaching them everything I know."

"That would take thirty seconds," Gallagher said. He turned to us and asked, "High school, eh? What schools were dumb enough to admit you three Patsies?"

Woof, flattering to have hard man Gall inquiring into our academic vistas; equivalent to Lucky Luciano asking where we'll be spending our summer vacations.

Karl said, enthusiastically, "I'll be going to Roman."

Half the characters in here had attended Roman Catholic at Broad and Vine.

"You're Ukransky," Gallagher said, "Where else could you go? Now you move on from getting whacked with yardsticks by the Sisters to getting hard socks by the Jesuits. How about you, Paulie?"

"Central," I said. " I'd have preferred North-East, where I wouldn't a hada' study so hard, but my old man insisted on Central because that's where he went and starred on the basketball and baseball teams."

"Sure, " Gall said. "But Big Doc went there when Central was downtown, still had a few regular guys in the hallways. Now it's candy-ass uptown, strictly for the Bar Mitzvah boys, and they throw in a few Spades for the track team."

Beer drinkers were closing in, hovering around our table, mockery on their faces. Gallagher touched Knocky's shoulder, and said, "You, Ratchinov? Franklin? Or you gonna' skip high school altogether and go straight to the Pros?"

Sensational, Gall was clued into his rep. Not even in high school yet but Knocky was already subbing on a semi-pro team where they had starters who once played college ball, graduates from Saint Joe's, Villanova, La Salle. Wild that Gall would know about his rep. Of course, Gallagher also knew about his awesome Momma, and Aunt Svetla, the one and only Trixie Molloy.

Alexi gulped, apologetically, before saying, "Central High."

The crowd in Gold's bar cackled. Schatz called over, "Get the fuck outa' here, you ain't got the brains for Central. You sneak in up there with the Izzies and Moishes they'll stick a dunce cap on your skull and stand your dull ass in the corner. "

"Franklin's more your speed, Knocky, "Eli said. "Better program, you could be the White Flash at Ben Franklin if the night-riders don't mess up your pretty face first."

"Nah, " Dick Jardine said," Southern's the school for you, Ratcho. Where I went. You'd make out like crazy with the sweet sixteen Italian bambinas with the big bamboolas. There was one stacked fustafazoo in my math section, Beatrice Esposito, a jaw dropper, her knockers entered the classroom thirty seconds before she did."

Weird hearing these cruds arguing about our destinations and academic credentials: The gang on Girard Avenue was slicker, more with it, better educated. the crowd here, six blocks south, was cruder. Several of these shady characters were into extreme stuff like mugging drunk merchant seamen along the docks, and rolling the fairies coming out of the Fag clubs on Locust Street.

Saul was still having troubles with the projector. Sibronsky called over to him, "Hey, get a goddam technician on this case, this stumblebum can't hack it."

"If you're so smart why don't you give it a shot, ace," Saul called back to him.

Rising like a ranch hand, Sibronsky said, "Well, I may jut do that, pardner. " He sidled over to the projector, clicked buttons, lights flashed on the screen. Amidst the hooting and cheering Hymie snapped off the ceiling lights, turned down the volume on the TV. Baseball fans could still follow the game while the other customers enjoyed the pornography. At Shibe Park Elmer Valo just misplayed a ball off the right field wall, and King Kong Keller was scoring. The screen was simmering with streaky, tattered threads of light, grainy brilliant asterisks and stars, Saul finally found the focus, and we read the title:

MEE HUNG LOW, THE CHINESE COOK, VERSUS THE FRENCH

MAID, FIFI LA TAUT

A CORNHOLE KENTUCKY PRODUCTION

DIRECTED BY PETER DICKSHOT

The troops were laughing, Karl nodded to me, this was neat; we were digging this raunchy stuff, and getting to hang out with big guys. Apart from the schoolyard, that is. On Sundays there were softball marathons in the Kearny yard, game after game from morning to dusk, the age spread on the field ranging from squirts in junior high to family men, futzes in their forties with their dumpy wives showing up with the toddlers to drag hubby home for supper. I wondered if there were other towns like Philly where the boys became men early, the men stayed boys late.

On the screen a Chinese cook attired as a French Chef smirked as the waitress burst into the kitchen, wiggled, and crouched to retrieve a dropped napkin. A Cupid's bow motif decorated her ruffled panties. The gang in Gold's snickered as Mee Hung Low blew an imploring kiss at the Cupid's bow. On the TV Dimag had singled again, a clean shot to right field, the entire Yankee order was batting around.

Straddling a chair, Saul Gold sat down at our table, and asked me," So, how's your father doing, Paulie? Busy all the time?"

"Must be. His waiting room is always crowded. "

"Does he know you're in here, watching this crap?" Saul asked.

"Not unless somebody rats on me. Which I'm sure somebody will."

"Does he still do babies?" Saul asked me.

"He's trying to cut down on that side of his practice. He says most babies seem to want to be born at three in the morning,"

"Anyway," Saul said, " tell him my wife will be in to see him next week. This morning she vomited. Last night she wanted dill pickles with pistachio ice cream. "

Gallagher snorted, and said," Saul, I aint got no degree from Penn Med but it's sounding like you knocked up Arlene again."

"Sure seems that way, " Saul agreed, glumly. Then to me he said, "Your father still charge the same? For office visits and delivering babies?"

"How the fuck would I know? He hasn't raised my allowance lately."

The bunch around our table yucked and Schatz said, "Doc Burris is such a great old mule. How come you turn out to be such a snotty, worthless prick, Paulie?"

"Can't say. My dad claims the virtuous genes skip every other generation."

Dmitri grumbled," Will everybody please shut the fuck up, and let me enjoy the movie?"

"From the way you're squirming your knees together, you're already enjoying it too much," Sibronsky cracked.

The A's had finally ended the Yankee rally. Pete Suder was at the plate, missing a wide curve. Fifi La Taut was shimmering out of her panties. Mee Hung Low unzipped his fly. The audience in Gold's roared as he brought out his hose. Eli moaned, "Holy Shit! Will you look at the Schlang on that Chink?"

Dmitri shrugged, and said," Almost as long as mine."

"What did you do?" Eli asked. "Buy a new one?"

As I am secretly in training to become a journalist, I'm always composing catchy headlines in my own mind. At the sight of Fifi's gorgeous figure I registered for future purposes: STRIPLINGS SIGHT SUCCULENT STRIPPER.

Fifi sat down on the wood butcher's block, spread her legs wide. Mee Hung Low sank down to his knees, started examining her bush as if he were a Nazi U-boat commander peering into his periscope. Dick Jardine shouted out, "Hey, buddy, don't make a meal out of it." The troops chuckled, laughed louder as Karl got into the act, barking with a thick Erich Von Stroheim accent, "Achtung! Fire torpedo twei, Reinhardt! Mach Schnell!"

The laughter faded as the front door opened, the dismal glare of the corner street lamp entered Gold's, along with three cops. Mahann, we knew, the other two were new to this beat. Joe the Worm was rushing to the John to flush away the Mary Jay joint he'd been puffing on, Fifi was spreading her thighs wider, Sam Chapman was digging in at the batter's box, Hymie was rushing behind the bar to snap on the ceiling lights, Saul clicked off the projector. The scene reminded me of kindergarten classes where teacher stepped out to the hall for a moment, stepped back in, and all the naughty kiddies had to scramble back to their seats.

Dmitri muttered," Shit. Just when it was getting interesting."

The abrupt entrance was a downer. Since I had as yet to get laid, I am hardly an expert on sex but the jarring opening of the door and jangling snapping on of lights felt like a combination punch between premature ejaculation and coitus interruptus.

The cops scowled down at us, squinting ugly our way, three underage kids in a dive. We scrunched lower in our seats. For a second I thought that Betty might have gone through with her threat to sic the Law on Dmitri. Then, through the opened door, we saw flashing red lights, more cops wearing their bulletproof vests, two red cars parked out there on Noble Street. Hot action somewhere tonight. They had not sent a convoy of squad cars to apprehend three kids sipping ginger ales in a bar.

Wiping his hands on a dishtowel, Hymie Gold explained, "We were just showing a movie, Mahann. The kind of spicy stuff they don't show at the Ruby."

Mahann ignored that, turned around to face the regulars in Gold's. They were frozen into passively defiant postures, preparing to lie, offer as little information as possible. In a harsh tone, Mahann asked, "Anybody in here see Joe Spinelli tonight?"

The question triggered instant head shaking. Saul Gold said," Nope, Joe hasn't been around for days now. You guys checked by his house on Brandywine Street?"

Saul was awarded slit-eyed glances of disgust by the cops for the denseness of that question. Of course they had been by his house. Otherwise, they would not be here. Mahann opened his hands to Gallagher, like possibly pleading for cooperation; Gall ignored him, continued picking away at the label on his bottle of Schlitz.

One of the unknown cops announced, "We are worried about Joe Spinelli. We're afraid that Joe Spinelli may have been hurt."

"No shit," Sibronsky exclaimed, theatrically. "Some kind of accident, officer?" Sibronsky's *'officer'* was liltingly disrespectful.

"Turn on the radio,"the other cop said." An All Points out after a nasty Brouhaha at the Produce Terminal. Two dead. Three more shot. Joe was supposed to be a watchman on duty tonight, the word is he never clocked in, didn't show up for his shift. We're worried that Joe might have caught it before he ever reached the docks."

Schatz whistled and said, sarcastically, "Jeez, two dead? It's a crying shame the way those Dagos carry on down there."

"Maybe more than two dead," Mahann said. "Bloodstains around that don't match the dead or wounded. That's why we're looking for Spinelli. We're figuring poor Joe might have walked right into the middle of that gunfire, was hit."

The regulars in Gold's were shaking their heads, theatrically, babbling away, it appeared that one or two of them were preparing to talk, say something to the cops. Gallagher was ostensibly picking away at the beer label but he made a tiny 'down-boy' movement with his index finger, ordering the troops to 'muzzle it.' Only a tiny flick of the finger, Mahann spotted that action.

Amidst the ensuing silence Hymie Gold clucked, "Nope. We haven't seen Spinelli since Wednesday. Wednesday, or Thursday, the last we've seen him."

"Yeah," Dick Jardine added. "It was Thursday. I beat him at a game of darts."

 The police confronted a stone-faced congregation. Only a few of these buckos in Gold's had ever served time but to a man they cultivated the cast of hard-nosed, seasoned yard birds. Frustrated on the main front, Mahann gave us an exasperated toss of the chin, ordering us to get lost.

Dmitri mumbled, " Catch you punks later."

As we stood up the toughies in Gold's nodded sardonic farewells. Gall paused in his label scratching to give us the thumbs up sign. To have hard man Gall reconfirm our existence was a high honor.

Outside, the heavily armed cops blinked in amazement at seeing such underage kids emerging from this seedy dive. They were wearing bulletproof vests, packing shotguns, were ready for combat on the front lines. We hurried up Fourth, and did not break out laughing till we reached the corner of Spring Garden. We were all jazzed up, the summer only beginning but kicking off with a great evening, hanging out in a bar, catching the start of the French smoker film, getting to dig that Gang-Busters entrance by the police.

"That was nifty, "Karl said. " Straight out of a George Raft Jimmy Cagney gangster movie. Bap-bap-bap-pop-pop. 'Try to catch me, you dirty rats.'"

"I'd prefer to do the Alan Ladd roles," I said.

"But, woof, the Fuzz must think people are really stupid," Karl said. "You see what shitty actors they are? Asking dumb questions like that, so innocent?"

"How so? "Knocky asked.

"Don't you get it, numbnuts?" Karl said. "The cops weren't worried about Spinelli getting shot, they're believing he's one of the shooters. They sachet in there with their bullshit malarkey, you saw the way Gall ordered the team to zip it up."

"No, I didn't catch that," Knocky said.

"Ah, dum-dum, " Karl snapped." You've never caught anything in your dum–ass life except a loose basketball. Put 'em up, dum-dum. "

They put up their mitts, began shadow boxing as we headed up Spring Garden, knocking over trashcans along the way. We were messing around, acting silly, still giddy from the experience in the bar, and maybe because we were mostly sad. This was goodbye time. I'd be stuck here in crappy Philly the whole long hot summer, Knocky was taking the bus to Atlantic City tomorrow, had a job down the shore, Karlie would be going off to summer camp soon. The three Mosqueteers were being temporarily disbanded.

When we reached the gas pumps Karl and Alexi shook hands, pounded each other on the back with abrazos, Gilbert Roland Latino style. Wronsky said, "Our final instructions to you, Gospodin Ratchinov, Courier of the Czar, you must bust your cherry in Atlantic City. At the shore that will be your primary duty, Captain Alexi."

"I'm sure gonna' try," Knocky said. "I've heard about the Jersey girls. You pick'm up at Steel Pier, and they do it right under the Boardwalk. "

"Yes, check out those myths and legends," Karl said. Meanwhile, I'll be doing my damndest to do likewise here in Filthydelphia. My immediate problem, I must resist an overwhelming urge to covertly slip back to my marble throne, soap up, and whip off a torrid long play featuring Fifi La Taut."

"We all face that challenge, "I said.

They shook hands again, macho style, like Randolph Scott saying 'adios' to Glenn Ford after defeating the black hats, I said to Karl, "Maybe I'll catch your sorry hide tomorrow, Cossack."

"Same time, the same station, Doctor Kildare."

I never escape the hook of the sawbones clichés. Adults assure me that one fine day, when I've grown up, and have my head screwed on straight I will follow in my father's footsteps. An unpromising path, I'd look wobbly trailing in his footsteps, my big foot Pop sports a size 14-D brogan.

Patrol cars were racing up Fifth, billions of mosquitoes danced in the lamplights while Alexi and I headed up Sixth. Wronsky had not yet entered the station; he was dawdling out front, reluctant to head inside to his tiny cubicle in back, stinking of axle grease. Karl squared his shoulders, put his key in the lock. He never complains about his lot. Me, I bitch and whine though I fairly much dwell on Easy Street,

Knocky asked me," You talked to your Dad again about the shore? For maybe later in the summer?"

"Mentioned it to him several times. None are so deaf as those who will not hear."

"Really a good deal, "Knocky assured me." My Uncle Ivan has a three-month gig in the hotel, they're putting me on part time, busboy, working only four hours a day, but I can sleep in the busboys dormitory and eat in the employees cafeteria for only ten bucks a week, the rest of the time I'll be in the gym. They have this summer basketball league, lots of hotshots and hotshits from South Jersey and New York. It'll be great training for when we try to make the freshmen team in September. "

Try? There was no doubt Alexi would make it, he was a shoo-in, ready to start at the varsity level, not on any pukey freshman team. I was the dubious prospect.

"Sounds like a cushy deal," I said. "But my old man snarled a 'Nyet.'"

I did not add that Dad shuddered when he heard that John the Wizard was connected to these arrangements. According to my old man Ivan is a scummy con man, supplementing income from his shows by dealing in rigged card games: the hearse he drives is used not only to carry his gear but also furs and jewelry lifted from hotel rooms; and, when times are slow Ivan is not adverse to pimping off Wanda, the big blond he uses in his night club act.

"No way at all then?" Knocky insisted.

"My father's already secured gainful employment for me. He insists on my need to build character. I believe I ooze character out of my ears, he finds me lacking in that department, so deficient I'll be working in my Uncle Moe's deli all summer. If I'm a real good boy I may get to go to Atlantic City for the Labor Day weekend."

"That's cruddy," Knocky grunted. "Why the hell do you need to work, man? My Mom says your Dad's probably the richest professional in our neighborhood. Give it one more try. Why do you have to sweat out lousy summer jobs?"

"Could you please bring the lady around and have her explain that to my Dad?"

(I had a vision of Sonya Ratchinov unbuttoning her blouse for Dad, and cooing, 'You must let poor Paulie go to the shore this summer.' I blotted away that image.)

We were passing the Kearny Junior High at Sixth and Fairmount Avenue; I had gone to Jay Cooke, uptown, at Old York Road and Louden. Knocky had spent the last two years in this gray stone prison; they all look like Gothic correctional institutions. To show his appreciation for the education received at Kearny Knocky lifted his leg, and with his lips simulated the crack of a resounding fart.

DISGRUNTLED STUDENT CRITICIZES SYSTEM

Out of nowhere, Knocky asked, "You think I can make it, Paulie?"

"Make what, the basketball team? Sure."

"Nah, I mean Central, the academics. You saw how those crumb-balls in Gold's snickered when I said Central. They all think I'm too slow between the ears."

What to say to a buddy when you might concur in that view? Knocky was hardly Central material. Even at not overly demanding Kearny his grades had not been too hot. Rumor was, he was slated for like Dobbins Vocational, or to dumps like Gratz or Franklin, until his Aunt Trixie visited a Muckety-muck in the Board of Education.

What you say is, " I don't know what to tell you, man. You're smart enough but you'll need to study harder. And you can't rely on Wronsky to write all your compositions for you anymore. At Central they'd catch onto that fast."

"That's why I'm sweating it," Knocky said. "At Kearny I got automatic B's just for not playing hooky too much, and not calling the teachers mother-humpers to their faces. Up at Central, I'll be in a different league."

"You'll make it," I assured him, suspecting he might not. Alexi is not dumb but he is not into books. Karl and I were the voracious readers. When he wasn't pumping gas Karl was on the bench in front of the station, reading Thomas Wolfe, Phillip Wylie, Aldous Huxley, Sabatini, Graham Greene, and Dos Passos. Wronsky devoured a book a day: Alexi does the Funnies; Brenda Starr. Joe Palooka. Dr Rex Morgan.

The block between Poplar Street and Girard Avenue is by far the longest in Philadelphia, easily three times the length of a regular city block. Except for the luncheonette and Poplar Movie, near the south corner, this entire block consisted of spacious three stories red bricks designed for large families. My house was in the middle of this block, a tad wider than the others, just four feet wider, but enough of a difference to unsubtly hint that herein dwells the most well to do family hereabouts.

When we reached my steps, Knocky said, "Try talking to your Dad again, Paulie. Get him to at least let you come down in August for the whole month, tell him about the league, how it will sharpen up your game for the try-outs in the fall."

"Yeah, I'll talk to him," I said, though I knew I wouldn't. Pop gets ticked off when I broach matters that he regards as resolved. He detests redundancies.

We shook hands and I said," Knock 'em dead down the shore. And, see if you can get laid while you're at it."

"You, too, man," Alexi, said. "Have a great summer, Paulie. Work on your inside game. Right now, you've a great left hand stab, but only the potential to come in as a sub. If you ever wanna' be a starter you gotta' learn to take it to the basket."

From the war movies we learn not to be sloppy sentimental. We shook hands one more time, that was it, Knocky spun away, headed up Sixth. I lit up a smoke, stood there for a while. Knocky floated away in his sneakers. I've never seen him wear shoes. I'm sure he must have a pair somewhere, for church, funerals, but I'd never seen him in shoes. Reaching the corner at Girard, he shrugged his shoulders, looking like Karl before he entered the gas station. Should I feel a pang of guilt about the extra four feet of exterior here? My sidekicks return to crappy hovels while I enter this structure on a block of bourgeois fortresses built for families with seven children plus the grand folks thrown in, and it's Just Dad and me in here, we have this whole place to ourselves.

Our front steps are sanded a sparkling white, the black rail glistens from monthly touch-up jobs. The red brink façade is pointed in an austere auburn. The gold plaque between the front door and the frosted office window proclaims that this is the residence of;

DOCTOR DANIEL BURRIS, MD. GENERAL MEDICINE, OBSTETRICS

The first time Alexi came in here he whistled, this vestibule was about as large as his parlor. The first time I entered his house, I winced, inwardly. Their living room was too close to the street, one step away, their door was too thin a partition, all the ills and furies of the world could pour in too easily.

Sign in time. Dad is a methodical man and big believer in systems, methods, and structures. Before leaving I must jot down in his logbook my departure time plus my itinerary, upon return, the hour of return. It was now 11:17 and my official curfew was Eleven so I was only fibbing a little when I jotted down10:53. He already accuses me of being shifty in the character department.

Directly in front of me is the broad staircase where the fancy iron grille above, Arabic or Hindu, prevents patients and intruders from invading the privacy of my father's suite on the second floor. Down the hardwood floor, past the potted plants, a similar Levantine metal portal protects the sanctity of our parlor, dining room, and kitchen in the rear. To my left is the door to the waiting room, and his office, the gold plaque says ring and enter. This hallway has no odor, neither neutral, nor sterile, nor musty. Mrs. Jordan, the nurse, and Miss Pearl, our colored cook and cleaning lady, do a superb job of keeping these premises fresh, spotless. To me this hall reeks of iodine, pus, sodium peroxide, tainted tabs and swaths, ether, purple tinctures, urine samples, caca in a paper cup, sickness and decay, muffled by cleaning fluids, pine sprays, and Dutch Cleanser, the odor of pain prevails, triumphs. That is just me smelling this. As in I may be the only listener hearing the snaps on Sonya's garters straining her nylons.

Heading upstairs, one might expect to hear eerie creaking, the spectral, spooky creaking on the 'Inner Sanctum' radio show. These stairs do not creak at all, that's just me with my obtuse notions. I unlocked the Arabesque grille door; it resembles the elevator cage doors in cheaper French hotels.

Dad has this second floor suite all to himself: the library with a thousand books, the music room with his cherished collection of classical records, the Lily Pons, the Carusos, the King sized bathroom with his sunken tub. When I reached the master bedroom I saw that he was out for the evening, his pajamas dropped carelessly on the floor, an opened book on the nightstand next to a half-filled glass of Scotch, and half-smoked cigar in the ashtray. Checking, I saw that his big black Buick was still parked in the back yard. Saturday nights he is usually out for the evening, his many lady friends, or his poker, but from the evidence here he had been retired for the evening, was called out on an emergency, a baby to deliver. Dad was the only physician still left in the area making house calls with his black leather bag. He gets called when a stevedore is hurt on the docks. The red cars show up and cops rush him down to the Buttonwood Street Station when they have a criminal bleeding in the middle of the night. Dad must be off on one of his angel of mercy missions.

I have this entire third floor to myself: private bath, extra bedroom for guests, which we rarely have. My library and rec room hold the games of childhood, the chess set, Lionel Trains, Monopoly board, mechanical pinball machine, the miniature roulette wheel, a small pool table. Both Knocky and Karl were impressed the first time they came up here. Knocky checked out the pool table, Karl the bookcases.

After a shower I stretched out, wondering why Dad dashed off and had not driven his Buick. Sometimes, he walks the few blocks to the Northern Liberties Hospital on Seventh Street. Nurse Jordan and Miss Pearl beg him to not do that. Sure, he is a huge bear of a man, not for nothing is he called Big Doc, but this neighborhood is sliding downhill fast, hoods and muggers infest these streets after dark, hopheads, strangers, who don't know that he is the beloved Doc Burris, known to treat poor patients gratis, even throw in the pills and medicines for free. Miss Pearl nags him with how would he like it if the red car shows up at three in the morning to tell Paulie that his father was dead on the streets?

By house regs, even in summer time, I'm supposed to snap off this lamp at eleven thirty, but I started to read the thirty pages I had left of 'The Razor's Edge. I was restless and disturbed, recalling Mrs. Ratchinov stooping over to enter that cab this morning, Fifi La Taut shimmying out of her ruffled panties. Let us build character, Burris. No flogging it tonight. We are trying to break that pernicious custom. Still, I had one question. Did Mrs. Ratchinov add an extra wiggle to her tail when she bent over, inviting the gawkers to line up and kiss her royal derriere? Knocky died a thousand deaths when his Mom slipped into that cab.

I glanced at the framed black and white portrait of my mother on the bureau: a proud lady in the graduation ceremonies wearing her white nurse's uniform. She is young, pretty, the perfect mother. This is a Mom who will never scold me, tell me to eat my carrots, never embarrass the shit out of me like Mrs. Ratchinov did to Alexi today. My Mom will forever be a perfect Angel in the Mother of Pearl frame.

A slamming of car doors woke me. I must have slept with the night lamp on; the alarm clock on my desk said past two in the morning. From the rich resonance of the closing doors it was a luxury vehicle down there on Sixth Street. Dad probably spotted the light burning here but I quickly snapped off the lamp anyway, hoping he would not come up here to give me any guff about breaking the rules. The man is a stickler for the rules, and a bit of a hypocrite.

Peeking through the curtains I saw that Dad had been driven home in a black Cadillac. He was carrying his leather medical kit. The hulking bruisers stepping out of the Caddy to shake his hand were dressed like waterfront thugs in Levis and black leather jackets, not like the young interns who normally drove him home from the hospital, or the bridge players from his social circle. The biggest of the bruisers embraced Dad around the shoulders, patting him hard on the back, like they do in South Philly.

CHAPTER TWO

Monday I went to work in my Uncle Moe's deli on Marshall Street. Tucked out of sight between Sixth and Seventh, this was the liveliest street in Philadelphia. Down around Fourth and Bainbridge, and the Italian market by Ninth and Washington there were similar stretches but they were hardly competition for Marshall when it comes to size, bustle, verve, and aromas. From Parrish to Poplar, then the incredibly long block from Poplar to Girard, Marshall Street was a teeming Balkan Bazaar, a pandemonium of accents and spices: in the fresh fish market you select your victim from the tanks, they chop off the head, wrap it in a newspaper. Same with the live chickens in the coops, they slaughter and bleed them right before your eyes. Music blaring from the record shops clashes with the clucking of the roosters, you can almost get dizzy drunk from the heady mixture of powdered cinnamon blowing through bakery fans, pungent cheeses, tangy olives, the briny odor of sauerkraut and green tomatoes in the wood barrels. Food here throbbed with life, was not the bland mush of super markets, buried in sterile cellophane.

In front of every candy store, haberdashery, and deli there was a pushcart or stand selling fruits, bras, toy pistols, turnips, girdles, bloomers, garters. Crowds were thicker than on downtown Market Street, shoppers were brasher and poorer, mostly immigrants. In this colorful clutter of canopies and awnings you heard bargaining and haggling in half the languages of the world. This was where the ethnic stew simmers in the melting pot. With the possible exception of Orchard Street up in New York, there was no other market like this jumble on the maps, the hemispheres scrunched together into a mashed accordion, balalaika strumming refugees from Kiev arguing with recently arrived banjo pluckers from Appalachia.

I was supposed to build character here, my Uncle Moe, theoretically, in charge of the process. I've never seen a Troll or a Gnome but suspect they might resemble my Uncle Moe. Not quite five feet tall, but strong, he was always kidding around with me, putting up his fists to challenge me, goading me with, "C'mon, kid, put your dukes up. I can take you, kid, I can take you."

He probably could, at least he was always able to muss up my carefully sculpted ducktail and pompadour. My first day on the job I caught on that this deli was no Dark Satanic Mill, I'm not about to have a hellish childhood out of Dickens. If Dad consigned me to this Cavalry in order to fortify my backbone Moe and Aunt Sara were not totally aboard on the project. I was prepared to hustle, do my duty, Moe advised me to take it easy, saying, " Don't get a hernia, Nefel, I'm only paying you the minimum wage, with no intention of raising your salary this summer. "

No children of their own, Moe and Sara pawed at me affectionately. She was inordinately proud, telling the customers, "You see that boy putting the cans up on the shelf? Know who that boy is? That's Doc Burris's son, Paul, and Paulie is an excellent student. He'll be going to Central High in September. Paulie doesn't need to be working here. He could be at a fancy-schmantzy summer camp in the Poconos."

Moe called over to her, "Hey, Sara, knock it off. You gotta' tell everybody coming in here the whole story of Paulie's life?"

"Wha? You're a censor now, Moe? At least Paul will have an interesting life. He'll be a famous heart surgeon, not a Shmo in a stained apron fretting if the smoked fish is smoked enough."

No matter how often I tell people I hate medicine, plan to be a journalist, they insist on dressing me in surgical smocks. Sara was the same height but double the poundage of Moe. When it came to squabbling this was a champion couple. They bickered in front of me as if I were an inanimate object, unable to hear the awful things being said. My first days on the job Moe interrupted her fifty times with moans to shut the hell up, why must she dig up stuff that was better left alone? Sara waved him off, with Moe wincing disapproval, she plunged right back into the past.

In the Gospels according to Sara, her sister, my mother, was no Saint. Five girls in the family, consensus among them, Leonora was the pretty one, but cold, self-centered, egotistical, manipulative. The family joke: the stork delivered her to the wrong address. With her uppity airs, the stork should dropped her off on the Main Line, Bala Cynwyd, not in a cramped row house in Strawberry Mansion, smelling of borscht and seething with the noisy daughters of a Litvak pants presser.

Leonora was distant, mysterious, seemingly serene, but flying into rages at any invasion of her privacy. She had implausible social pretensions, never went to the nickelodeon movies with her sisters, or boys from the neighborhood. No, she loved the opera, only dated serious fellows who must take her to classical music concerts. Leonora was bookish and snooty, an aloof ice queen who allowed her sisters to adore her but returned little in the way of warmth.

Moe shook his head, muttered, "Why you telling the boy this? There's no call for this. Let the dead rest in peace, you should only talk about the good things."

"Hach!" Snorted back at him," she was his mother, but my sister, first. And the boy should know what she was really like. What galled us most, Paulie, she was the favorite. Leonora could do no wrong. The rest of us, we needed to find work. I found a job as a cashier in Lit Brothers, that's where I met this Schlepp, here. Leonora, she gets to graduate high school, attend a college for nurses. "

Sara said that as if it were yesterday. When my aunts offer their versions of what my mother was like back then their resentments sound like current events.

"Leonora goes off to college, the rest of us are marrying paper-hangers, cigar-makers, slaving in the Five and Ten. She graduates, a nurse, so sassy and lah dee dah in her starched white uniform. We were proud of her, jealous, too. We were sure she was going to latch onto an upcoming young internist. So, who does she take up with, Paulie? None other than your father."

"That much I had already gathered."

"Uich," Sara said. "Nobody was jumping for joy. Your father was about the last man we thought she'd bring around. Divorced. Twenty years older. She brings around this old cock in tow, and tells us this Alta Cocker is her new beau,."

"The age thing was nothing, " Moe said. "Down deep Leonora was more mature than Dan back then. More level headed, a steadying influence on an old buck."

"Shut up, Moe," Sara snapped. "I'm telling the story."

Customers entering the deli interrupted the story. Later that afternoon, in dibs and dabs, with flashbacks and leaps forward, I heard further episodes. Doctor Burris had been previously married to Elizabeth, a classy Shiksa from Bryn Mawr, a lawyer, noch. They had two handsome sons and a messy divorce. She left him because of his gambling, and his womanizing. Dan was reputed to be a real Casanova, though some said it was the other way around; he never did the chasing, the women chased him.

"Does the boy need to hear this crap?" Moe complained. "Such negative things about his own father? None of this is necessary. The boy can live without it."

"He should know, " Sara growled back." None of you bastards are plaster saints. If you don't run around, Moe, it's because no other woman would have you."

Some old married couples act like caged baboons dedicated to picking at their respective fleas and lice. I was horrified by the way Moe and Sara casually said cruel things to each other. Aunt Sara prattled on while I attempted to envision my Dad as an errant rake He was still a ladies man, had ladies chasing after him but I could not picture my Pop kitchy-cooing the rosey rumps of receptive patients. It was easier to see him as a regal British Viceroy strutting around with a swagger stick.

"Well," Sara said, "Elizabeth, the lawyer, she did a job on Dan with the divorce, plucked and fleeced him cleaner than they e er do the roosters in the poultry market across the street. With the property settlement Elizabeth moved out to California, used the big money to go into the real estate business. Dan, he went into a tailspin, it took him years to recover. With the way he was gambling, maybe he didn't care to recover, financially. If it hadn't been for Leonora, he might have never straightened out. And, to get his head above water again, your father got into things not totally on the up and up, things we can't even talk about. You'd be surprised, Paulie, at some of his connections, at some of the people your father knows."

Moe grumbled if we can't talk about it, don't talk about it. I was envying my rich half-brothers in California. Sunning themselves on their yachts in fabled California while I am condemned to shredding carrots into the coleslaw on putzy Marshall Street. According to Nate, the counterman, I was learning a highly useful trade, salad maker. Which would come in handy when they cancel my license to be a doctor. During the afternoon Sara insisted on telling me about how both families ve-hemently opposed the marriage. The poor but proud Bermans of Strawberry Mansion regarded Doctor Burris as a randy old goat, damaged goods, a stiff-necked lecher who should be taking up with matrons in their forties, not be sniffing around after their precious young daughter. The well-off Burris, of Sephardic German stock dating back to Colonial times, regarded the Bermans as insufferable Mockeys from Beyond the Pale, Yussels Come Lately. To Dan's brothers, Leonora was a snippy gold digger, pretending that butter wouldn't melt in her mouth while scheming to get her clutches on a prosperous doctor, his big house on Sixth Street, his summer home in Cape May, his properties in Florida.

"Happy now?" Moe asked her. "All that ancient history better left unsaid. You satisfied now that you've told the boy about petty quarrels none of his concern?"

"Sure, " Sara said flatly. "Both families were dead wrong. Those two were nuts about each other. That was a five-year honeymoon they had. Me, and my sisters, your aunts, were green with envy at how your father treated her. He carried that girl around on a golden tray, took her to the finest restaurants, the Academy of Music, the opera in New York, vacations in Havana. Daniel coddled Leonora on a silver cloud while I was sweating my *Toukas* off in this store to help Moe get this business off the ground."

"After all these years you're still complaining?" Moe asked her. "I'll never hear the end of the scratchy record?"

"What's to complain about?" Sara said. "It's all in God's hands. Nothing ever works out the way you think it will. They were so happy when you were born, Paulie. Your father called you his 'Winter Wheat.' And, Daniel, surprisingly, turned out to be such a down to earth humble man. A professional of his stature, a man who pals around with the big shots, but he became part and parcel of our family. Sundays, without fail, he brought Leonora and you to have lunch with us Bermans in our tiny home in Strawberry Mansion. What were we? Paperhangers and shoe clerks, lucky to have a pot to piss in and a window to throw it out of. But your father took off his jacket, rolled up his shirtsleeves, and sat down to play gin rummy and pinochle with your grandfather and uncles like one of the boys. Not once did he let on that he could buy and sell the lot of us out of petty cash, that's the kind of man Dan was."

"The kind of man he still is," Moe cut her off.

Sara could not help herself. Before I left she regaled me with more grievances that helped me understand why Dad rarely talked about his family. His two brothers had never forgiven Dad for slumming, marrying beneath his station, the daughter of a hardly literate tailor. And, their rich-bitchy wives with all the airs had regarded Leonora as 'not one of us.' Daniel was already alienated from his brothers when Leonora died, struck down by a drunk driver on Sixth Street, racing down that long block as if it were the Indianapolis Speedway. His bother, Jonathan, was vacationing in Florida at the time, and could not be bothered to fly north to attend the funeral. The older Brother, Ralph, he later died, and since the day of Leonora's funeral Daniel would not brook mention of Jonathan's name."

"Jesus Christ almighty, woman, "Moe groaned. " Did Paulie have to hear that, too? What good is it to stir up that crap? One day Paul might want to call his uncle on the Burris side. Why do you want to poison the well with crap from the past?"

"Sure, Paul should hear about it," Sara assured him. "So he learns to do the right thing at the right time. If you do the right thing at the proper moment then you don't have to crawl around afterwards, and beat your breast, and beg forgiveness. "

I suspected that I had inherited traces of snobbery from my unknown uncles. To me, every family has its distinct, peculiar odor. To me, the Bermans reeked of pickled herring and mothballs in a long locked closet. Even when they were all gussied up for social occasions and doused on their colognes and perfumes my aunts smelled like they had just wrung a chicken's neck. I had no idea what the signature aroma of the Burris family might be. The only Burris I knew was my Dad and the man was set in his ways. Maybe it was a patrician and aristocratic odor. He liked to luxuriate in long baths in his sunken tub, a cigar in one hand, a glass of scotch in the other hand, Wagner records roaring on the Philco.

Friday afternoon, two-thirty, the deli crowded with demanding customers, I'm supposed to work till five, Uncle Moe slipped me three tens, thirty bucks cash, no deductions, and said, "Go on, get the hell our of here, kid. Go play ball."

"Hey this is too much," I objected. "You said you were gonna' pay me the minimum wage. Which happens to be forty cents an hour."

"What," Moe said, "you trying to get me in trouble with the law? The State of Pennsylvania says kids your age can't work more than twenty hours a week. I got you working almost forty, so everything between us must be strictly cash, off the book. No taxes. No Social Security deductions. Got that? Now vamoose, Boichick."

"The place is still busy, Unc. I should work at least till five."

"Paul, you're doing a fine job, better than I'd thought you'd do, but it's a beautiful day out there. You should be out in the fresh air, playing ball, not shmutzing around in this dump. Just because it 's my rotten prison it doesn't have to be your jail, too."

"You're sure, Unc?"

"Go Play ball, but no poolroom. If I hear that you've been hanging out in Dave's again I'll have your skinny ass sweating in here till midnight."

"Gotcha. Thanks, Unc."

"Say goodbye to your Aunt Sara first. I'll see you tomorrow."

Before I left Sara insisted on giving me a moist smooch on the cheek. She was born here but is as mushy a Furriner as Mrs. Ratchinov. Then She handed me a baguette pastry bag containing an enormous salami sandwich on an Italian hoagie roll with tomatoes, onions, mozzarella cheese, hot peppers, and Russian dressing.

"Hey," I protested." Thanks, but I've already had lunch, a spiced beef sandwich."

"Take it," Sara ordered," or I'll give you such a kick in the ankles, it will knock some sense into you." She slipped another two bucks into my pocket.

No more disputing, I blew her a kiss as I left. For her generosity and a hoagie like this you have to forgive a Sara for her viperish tongue and mushy smooches.

Thirty bucks was a windfall. I'd been doing calculations, had worked thirty six hours, thirty six times forty was fourteen-forty, minus the expected deductions, so Uncle Moe was being super-generous to me. Given the heat, it was scorching out here, I might have instantly shot over to the cool shade of the pool hall, but I had to nix that, not break my promise to Moe. I was already feeling guilty about cutting out when the Deli was hopping busy. Sheeoo, that's no way to build character.

No pool hall, I headed south, to check on Karl at the gas station, picking my way through bumptious crowds of old Polish Babushkas with leather shopping bags, Puerto Ricans, Kalmucks, and Slovaks, fresh batches of foreign species arriving daily to this bustling circus. Merchandise costing fifteen bucks on downtown Chestnut Street runs you nine nine-five on Marshall, Boichick. We have Special discounts just for this you, Bubele.

Every store has its princess or crown prince waiting on trade, your future orthodontist and corporate lawyer, you could select a delectable harem out of the big-busted Myrnas and Arlenes helping out in these Mom and Pop shops. The indignity, I've joined their ranks. I'd always seen myself as unique but I've become one more stock boy dreaming of escaping the clutches of the clan, the customs of the tribe, longing to become my own handcrafted creation, the Man of Action, World Traveler, not woeful Little Doc, his beautiful mother died so young.

There was an upside to my downside; Moe just gave me special treatment. I've always received special treatment. Not quite the dispensation Alexi receives for his athletic prowess but around Girard Avenue I had the prestige of being Doc Burris's son. The entire Berman family treated me like a Royal Dauphin, compensating, I suppose. When I was smaller my aunts and uncles vied for my favor, taking me along with their kids to the zoo, Willow Grove Amusement Park, League Island to swim, down the Shore, Beach Haven, Wildwood. I was booked up for weeks in advance. Pop never expressed it that way but he was delighted to lend me out. And, I was the kid who was never slapped. The Bermans were always bashing around their own brats, bopping them across the skull; to this day my snotty-ass cousins resent the way Prince Paulie floated above the fray.

The hustle-bustle of Marshall ends at Parrish Street. Down to Brown Street there were three kosher butcher shops, next comes blocks of drabness, our neighborhood trapped in a time warp, houses with rusty foot scrapers by their front steps though travelers no long scrape mud off their boots. Corner groceries no longer sell kerosene, still had big green oil drums mounted outside. The war ended years back, families still have gold stars hanging in their windows. Loafers, pretending to be vets, hang out in front of the bars, wearing surplus combat boots and fatigue jackets.

At the corner of Spring Garden an oddity proves that this was once a Deutsch enclave: the ominous grim, gray German Cultural Center seemingly transported sinister stone by lugubrious stone in one fell swoop from Unter den Linden Strasse before Berlin was bombed to smithereens. This building is totally out of character with the rest of this area. We have never seen anybody enter or leave this forbidding structure. Karl swears that Adolph and Eva Braun have a deluxe bunker hideout in the basement.

The Wronskys were on their bench, both in greasy overalls, Karl reading, and Dmitri sucking on a brew. Their radio was on loud; the A's losing to Cleveland again. As I approached Spring Garden Dmitri looked up and chirped, "So, who's minding the store, Moishe?"

"My Uncle Moe left me off work early today," I said.

"I wish I had an Uncle Moe," Karl muttered.

"Ah, shaddup, " Dmitri growled at Karl. To me, he said," What you got in that long white bag, Little Doc? It looks like the old joke:' Schultz is dead.'"

"My aunt made me a super-dooper sub on a hoagie roll. I can't handle it because I already ate lunch so I brought it along for you guys. One of my fringe benefits."

"For my fringe benefits I occasionally get a stale Tastykake," Karl mumbled.

"Shut the hell up," Dmitri told Karl. To me he said, "Great. Give it over here."

Karl, at least, first dipped inside the station, and used the fountain to splash water over his hands. Dmitri used his greasy paws to tear the hoagie out of the bag, and exclaimed, "Jeez, if I had a dick this long I could retire from the transportation business. Thanks, Paulie."

He ripped the hoagie into highly unequal parts, passed the smaller share to Karl, and began munching away at the thick sandwich with the Russian dressing and salad oil spurting out and dripping through his blackened, greasy fingers. That did not seem to bother Dmitri. Karl was slightly more delicate in his table manners. Through his chewing, Karl asked me, "You heard the news about Joe Spinelli?"

"Nah, the radio in Moe's deli is tuned strictly to the music station."

"On the radio an hour ago," Karl said. "Flashes every fifteen minutes. First the cops found corpses riddled with Tommy gun bullets in the trunk of a Pontiac down by Passyunk Avenue, blood all over the place. The cops said there could be more cadavers scattered around the vicinity. Then, a shoot-out near League Island. No dead but the cops took suspects into custody. One of them was a bigmouth and squealed that Spinelli was involved in that Saturday night bang-bang at the produce terminal. They said that Spinelli was wounded in that shoot-out, and might be dead, but he was definitely hit. There's an all-points ut for Joe, as armed and dangerous."

"Yeah," Dmitri growled through his munching." You saw how those motherless cops barged into Gold's trying to get us to rat on poor Spinelli. And the bastards came busting in there just when the picture was getting good. "

Not many Italians lived around our way. Joe was originally from South Philly; he had married an Irish girl from Brandywine Street. With what Karlie was saying I had to blot from my mind images of Dad stepping out of the Caddy Saturday night.

"Crazy South Philly," Dmitri snorted, chewing at his hoagie. "Those crazy-ass Wops really go at it, pow-pow–POW, they think they're back in Sicily,"

"It's not that way at all," I said." I've relatives down that way, I'm down there often, know lots of Italians. Most are square conservatives. The streets are the safest in town because the Mob doesn't let piss-ant criminals contaminate their habitat."

Dmitri does not like being contradicted. He glared at me, and said, "You know, Paulie, some times you're too fucking smart for your own good. "

"I've been told that I'm obnoxiously precocious or precociously obnoxious."

Karl was nervous about the way this was going. To change the subject, he said, "Woha! We've other news for you, Doctor Kildare. Sensational news. "

"Like what?"

"Sibronsky and Schatz were by the station earlier this morning. They said they were down the shore yesterday, ran into Knocky on the Boardwalk."

"No shit? How'd they say he was doing?"

Karl shrugged. "From what they said-doing great. He's only been down there a week yet everybody seems to know him, popular all over the Boardwalk He's already played one game, his hotel against the Chelsea, Chelsea won, but Knocky scored twenty-two points, giving the Chelsea team fits, popping them In from the outside, then scooting in for lay-ups."

"Ach," I groaned, "I am drooling with purple and green envy."

"Hold it up," Karl said, " I ain't got to the truly sensational part yet. From what Schatz and Sibronsky were saying, Knocky was claiming he almost got laid."

"No shit? What does 'almost' mean?"

"Knocky told them she was an older girl, seventeen, Irish, from Trenton. He met her in a Pokerino Palace, they strolled around for a while, he invited her for a Coke, she was the one suggesting they dip under the Boardwalk. He said sure, thinking it was just for some regular grab-ass and feeling her up, but they French kissed for a while, she got all hot and bothered, voluntarily peeled down her panties."

"Great balls of fire," I sighed. "Next chapter, please."

"They never finished it off," Karl said. "Alexi told them that just as he was about to stick it in there a beach guard shined his flashlight on them, the girl yelped, they had to scoot ass out of there with the girl leaving her skivvies behind in the sand."

We might be the Three Mosqueteers but we were also rivals and competitors. I said, "Well, that's a relief. I'da hated to hear about a totally happy ending."

Dmitri had been listening. He let out a belch and said, "Thanks, that was a great hoagie, Paulie. But, you know, your talking about Knocky, that made me dream of being a sandwich. I'd love being pressed in a sandwich between Knocky's mother, and his Aunt. I saw Svetla shaking her Kazoo at the Troc where she is billed as Trixie Malloy. Planking that dish would be a violation of the pure foods act. Those two broads got frames that could turn cork screws into rapiers."

He was a crude, insensitive bastard. Out of loyalty to Alexi neither Karl not I commented on what Dmitri just said. A truck was pulling up to the gas pumps. With a toss of the chin Dmitri indicated it was Karl's urn to wait on trade. Then he saw the disturbed look in Karl's eyes, changed his mind. Wiping the Russian dressing stains off on his knees, and he rose and snapped, "Alright, I'll handle this. You take the fuck off for a while, Karl. But, wash up first. You look like a slob."

That's as sentimental as it gets around here. I stared out at traffic while Dmitri pumped gas. Karl went to the rear room to change. On the radio, the A's were losing again; Sam Chapman just struck out swinging. I was a Phillies fan. Fans in this town are condemned to perpetual despair. Connie Mack ran the A's like a Triple A farm team; every time a player developed into halfway decent, Mack sold him off to the Yankees. Mack was so cheap he wouldn't even hire a manager. He was the manager.

Karl returned dressed for kindergarten: baggy gray leggings, bright polo shirt with broad stripes, white socks, and scuffed brogans to match his flat crew cut.

"Well, that's an improvement, "Dmitri said, handing Karl a two dollar bill, and adding, "If I ain't here when you get back, pick me up at Gold's. I'll likely be soused by then and need a hand to guide this rusting hulk home. Last night, If I hadn't a been for my trusty wrench in my back pocket three Spades mighta' jumped me on Buttonwood Street."

"Yeah, I'll pick you up at Gold's, "Karl promised him.

"Ciao, " I said to Dmitri. He grimaced a pained goodbye as a way of dismissal.

Karl moved to head up Sixth. I pointed to Fifth, If we went up Sixth it would be just my luck to have my old man spot us as I strolled by, have him ask why I'm out early, not building character in the deli. Karl was slumping along, seemed to be mumbling to himself again, like the bums sprawled on the benches in Franklin Square do, arguing with invisible demons. Girls from around my way, nasty picky snipes, have advised me that I should not hang out with Wronsky. They say he is not cute, he's icky, but I think Karl's a nifty sidekick, loyal, funny, and smarter than I am. A sharp dresser, he was not. Across Fifth, near the corner of Spring Garden, was the Catholic Charities Center. This was where skinflint cheapskate Dmitri did most of his shopping for Karl's wardrobe, explaining why Karl comes off as a ragamuffin refugee in donated hand-me-downs, just off the boat from lower Slobovia.

Wronsky must have read my mind. When we reached Green Street he said, "You shouldn't mind Dim, Paulie. He's doing the best he can with the crappy cards dealt him. I'm one of the cards, a Joker in a stacked deck, but Dim does what he can."

"It's not for me to say, man. To me Dim is pretty much of a dingbat, but his heart seems to be in the right place, even if his head ain't screwed on too tight."

Karl shrugged. I try to avoid mawkish stuff but Karl might be worse off than an outright orphan. If your parents are dead, so be it, happens all the time, but his parents dumped him. For what, pray tell? Dreams of an abstract Utopia? Nothing on Fifth Street looked abstract or utopic: three-story red bricks, prosaic pharmacies, a printing plant, The Hebrew School, the big lumber yard at the corner of Poplar. Then this long, long block up to Girard Avenue, the parochial school, and Saint Pete's, the majestic cathedral with the golden cross gleaming in the afternoon sunlight.

Karl squinted at the gray school building. He had not been whacked many times by the nuns in there, but had told me he hated the place; I hoped he would not make a Knocky-style acoustic comment on his academic experience. Instead he said, "Tomorrow I need to go to confession, Paulie."

"What evil deeds have you done lately? Aside from your nightly roundevouz with Madam La Palm?"

"You're not my confessor but I confess that I have sure sinned in my heart and mind, man. I was jealous that Alexi might have been the first of us to score. Then glad it was spoiled for him at the crucial moment by the nosey beach guard shining his flashlight on them. Does that make me an envious prick, Paulie?"

"Yes. Though I must confess I also derived consolation from the interruption. I couldn't stand the thought of Alexi having all those bragging rights."

"Good enough, "Karl said. "Then we're both pricks. And maybe I won't go to confession tomorrow. The priest might queer the deal I have cooking with Dim. He has promised to set-up a Cherry Buster for me."

"You've something lined up?" I asked, anxiously.

"Dim promised that for my fifteenth birthday, instead of a present, he's gonna' get me laid. He won't say with whom but I've seen him chatting up a woman on York Avenue, she seemed to be agreeing. I'm suspecting it is Rosey Ivanovich. On welfare, lives next to the Russian Orthodox Church on York Avenue, she has two babies. She picks up extra bucks doing laundry and cleaning houses, cash, off the books. "

"How about the important details? Is she stacked, alluring, voluptuous curves?"

"She is a bit of a porker," Karl said with a shrug, " but then, I am not exactly Tyrone Power, so I'll be grateful to Dmitri."

"As you should be. For my next birthday my old man plans to buy me an ornate chess set. Sight unseen, I would much prefer a Rosey Ivanovich."

We both broke out laughing.

Ludlow schoolyard was jam-packed. Prospects from our courts were on teams at all levels from Frankford High up to West Chester State Teacher's College but Karl and I were not quite on the tail end when it came choosing up sides. Wronsky was no Nijinsky but surprisingly nimble for a blimp with his stocky configuration. Me, I tend to shine when Knocky is not around, toss up a deadly left hand stab. 'Thank you, Oh Lord for small gifts.' Most of our opponents were bigger and stronger though not necessarily better. Basketball is like hitting the curve, you have the eye or you don't. Older guys were actually envious of me because they might be superior athletes but they just could not put the ball through the hoop.

Near dusk a yellow cab pulled up by the Ratchinov house. Sonya slipped out, wearing her manicurist's uniform with the pink undies gleaming through. The elderly gent climbing out with her appeared to be in his sixties. In this heat he was wearing a necktie and poplin suit. With the briefcase in his hand he looked like the businessmen coming out of the downtown Warwick Hotel. He also looked nervous, uncomfortable, and queasy, about bringing out his wallet in these environs.

As I suspected, Mrs. Ratchinov adds a defiant extra waggle to her wiggle when she senses spectators are gaping her way. A smirking silence prevailed until the green door closed behind her and her new acquaintance.

Irv Kauffman murmured, "Looks like Sonya is buying a new insurance policy."

"Or, paying for one, "Buddy Baer suggested.

The older guys snickered. Karl and I did not join in the merriment.

Jack Fishman, studying at Drexel Tech, said, "This is so disillusioning. It messes up several of my more cherished Gestalts."

"Why?" Baer said. "Knocky's not around to hear squeaky bed springs. That means Sonya can bring her tricks home, avoid the squints of elevator operators."

"That's what's screwing up my cherished preconceptions, "Fishman said. "I've always envisioned prostitution as taking place in an enticing setting, the glamour of a hotel suite, seductive lighting, chilled champagne in an ice bucket, a tinkling piano in the next apartment. Not as a boff in a ratty warren smelling of musty sofas and the beans on the kitchen stove."

"Maybe she only brought her customer home to clip his nails in more cozy and comfortable circumstances," Mel Fleischer suggested.

The Troops chuckled again. College boys, I thought they should be more discreet, mature, sophisticated, than to snicker like that.

"We're not even sure that Sonya charges," Baer said. "They could be conducting a flaming, love affair in there. That could be Ronald Reagan and Gene Tierney climbing into bed on the second floor."

"True," Fishman said. "Such is the hypocrisy of our society, if she spreads for love, she could be the heroine of a romance novel, a decent woman, torn by the storm. If the John drops a twenty buck bill on the dresser to help with the groceries, automatically, Sonya's a whore."

Wronsky and I winced. There was no need to so frank about things. Why do people open their yaps like that? My aunts and uncles tore into each other, said vile stuff, some of the slop might be true, but did not need to be said.

After one more game it was too dark to play. With Karl tagging along, I headed home. As we entered the vestibule, Mrs. Jordan, the nurse, was coming out of my father's offices. She is razor-thin, albino witchy white, with the sharp features of a hawk. She looked askance at Karl because he was red-faced, sweaty, and messy.

Mrs. Jordan said," Good evening, Paul. You shouldn't be running around like this. Excessive activities at these elevated temperatures could lead to dehydration, prostration, even a stroke,"

"Yes, ma'am."

"Your father is at his bridge tournament, Paul. He left his number in case of any emergencies. He won't be back till late. You're to be in, as usual, by eleven."

"Yes, ma'am."

I did not like this prissy woman but every Eden must have its snake. Dad says she's a Cockney affecting uer nasal Cambridge accent but since she is efficient her forgives her pathetic pretensions. Mrs. Jordan was a war bride; married a GI who claimed to have his own business; that turned out to be bull. After the divorce she stayed on here but is always complaining that the U.S. is not all it's cracked up to be. As far as I'm concerned she can grab the next bloody boat back to bloody Liverpool.

"Miss Pearl left a nice dinner for you in the fridge. Boiled chicken, corn on the cob, and a green salad,"Mrs. Jordan said. "There's enough for two, you can share it with your friend."

What she said was okay, but it sounded like,' you may toss this mongrel a bone.'

"Thanks, ma'am, but we were thinking of going out to grab a bite."

"Then you should warm it up tomorrow for lunch, "Mrs Jordan Insisted. " It's a fine, nutritious meal. I had some of it today, myself."

"Yes, ma'am, I'll do that."

. Her smile of departure was sharky, slicing, hardly benign. Mrs. Jordan is no big fan of mine, either. She has been with us only a year. I liked my Father's previous nurse. Bela Spivak was with us for four years; Dad had something cooking with her. Eventually Bela grew weary of waiting for him, and married an executive from the Sixth and Spring Garden leather factory, across from the bank.

After Mrs. Jordan closed the frosted vestibule, door, Karl trilled, mockingly, "'Yes, ma'am, no ma'am.' Wow, what a phony you are, Burris. You forgot to say, 'Aw, shucks,' but you sounded more cornpone cornball than Andy Devine."

"My survival technique. I tell them what they want to hear, then ignore them."

"I try to do that with Dim but I can't snow him. He may look dumb but he always knows when I'm shitting him."

Upstairs, Karl played my miniature pinball machine while I took a shower. He balked, but I made him take a shower, too, lent him a T-shirt so he wouldn't put his stinky polo on again. Dmitri was raising him but hardly keeping him up to snuff in the hygiene department.

After I signed out in the log we hit the streets, destination, Girard Avenue, only one hundred yards from my house, no need to go further. It might be jumping down in South Philly or out in the Mansion, near Cherry's and Pat's Steaks, but we also had our lively, jazzy scene here, a mini-downtown on Girard Avenue. From Sixth to Marshall to Seventh to Franklin to Eighth: the pool hall, two movie houses, two bars, luncheonettes, a family night club, Ritzy people from uptown Oak Lane and Oxford Circle drove down here to patronize the three schmaltzy restaurants. Girard had a throbbing beat. Stationed on every corner were the drugstore cowboys eyeing the Myrnas from the Marshall Street. The Yiddishe Maidels attended the movies in protective flocks, in uniform, coordinating what to wear before assembling.

Likewise, the Irish chicks from Kensington; the Colleens arrived in brassy bunches, occupying their own spaces in the movies.

At Gansky's, corner of Franklin, Karl and I ordered the French fries and the Texas Tommies, hot dogs slathered with cheese, extra chile, and onions, deliciously spicy and greasy, not like any bland boiled chicken. Then we caught the double feature at the Astor: 'The Count of Monte Christo' and 'The Corsican Brothers.'

Our crew from the schoolyard was in attendance with the regular breakdown, boys bunched together on the right flank, the Beckies from Marshall Street and the lassies from Fishtown gathered on the left, but close enough for them to dig the obscene catcalls coming from our quarter. No official rules had ever been written down but on Friday nights we conducted impromptu contests to see who could shout out the raunchiest wisecrack at the most inopportune moment. The girls pretended to be offended, then tittered their sweet Asses off. Last week Leon Hess won the prize. During a gangster movie with Richard Conte and Susan Hayward, Conte was just sprung from prison, they're about to leave, go out for the evening, Susan says, "I'll get my wrap." Hess shouted out," Wrap it around me, baby."

Laughter ensued. Okay, it was not that funny; you had to be there.

Karl and I took the movies as seriously as we did books. Whatever happened in real life, brawls, accidents, a shrewish wife kicking her husband out of the house, we argued about what scene did that resemble from what flic or novel. So far I'd never seen a picture capturing the peculiar flavor of our particular jungle. They tried with the 'Dead End Kids,' and "Bowery Boys' flics but the endings were always maudlin unrealistic hooey- gooey. The baddy has a change of heart. The coward becomes brave. You never saw the real thing, the troops in Ludlow schoolyard narrowing their lids when Sonya pulls up in a taxi.

The double feature ended at ten thirty. Older guys were piling into cars to head up to the Hot Shoppe at Broad and Godfrey, where the main uptown action was on Friday nights. Karl and I were not yet in that league. We faded over to the poolroom. Mrs. Jordan had said that Dad would not be in till late. I figured that I could safely shoot pool until midnight, jot down eleven o'clock, and fudge a little in the logbook.

As we entered Dave's the fat manager glared at us. The sign on the door says 'You must be eighteen.' Half the cats already clicking balls in here were underage. Dave put his fist on his wide hips, gave us the kind of scowl Hymie and Saul hit us with when we slunk into Gold's behind Dim last week. He grumbled, "Does Big Doc know you sneak in here, Little Doc."

"Of course," I lied. "He says I can play until midnight. But, if you don't want our patronage we can go down to Third and Brown. "

Dave winced, doubting that I had Dad's permission, figuring that I was bull-shitting him but he shrugged, chalked up our starting time on the blackboard. He waddled back to the coffee counter, muttering about the breakdown in manners and the decline of civilization. On the TV set over the coffee counter the Phillies were losing again, seven-zip. Del Ennis just struck out.

We played One Ball. Sudden Death. Karl is better than I am, good enough to spot me a left front to a right side. One Ball is the Blitzkrieg gambler's game; the object is to put the One Ball into your designated pocket. Aside from the battle on the green felt we were digging the sleazy atmosphere in Dave's, foul cigar smoke, whoops of the winners, groans of the losers. There were often fights in here when welchers refused to pay off side-bets. Clientele-wise, this joint convened an eclectic potpourri: slickers, hoods, hustlers, gophers, numbers writers, hangers-on, this might be the only place in town where customers included the Jewish goody-goody boys from the Marshall Street stores mixing with the tough Mick stevedores from under the El Tracks. No Negros in Dave's. No sign on the door. It would just never occur to them.

A table away the hustlers were arguing about Spinelli, some saying that Joe was Mob, others claiming that Joe was part of the bunch the Mob was retiring early from duty. Spinelli had come in here not to shoot pool but for the poker in the back room, thousands of bucks changing hands. The cops never bother these games. Cops came in here only to collect their cigar money,

Chalking up again, Karl said, "Wasn't that a neat picture. I really dug that movie."

"Which? 'The Count of Monte Christo'?"

"No. 'The Corsican Brothers.' The twins separated at birth. But, it was funny. During the movie, when the twin feels a stab of pain because his brother, hundreds of miles away, is wounded by a sword, I was thinking about Alexi, wondering if he felt the jab of pain I felt today when those bastards in the yard started talking dirty about his Mom. I'll have to ask Knocky about that when he gets back in September."

Wronsky is a bumpkin with the soul of a poet.

"Yeah," I agreed. "Bad shit to be talking about mothers. But perhaps you should not mention that to Knocky as that would also inform him that the bastards in Ludlow were downing his mother."

"Oops," Karl said. "Right. I hadn't thought about that one."

There was a commotion over by the coffee counter. Leon Hess had burst into the poolroom, excited, he was flitting from table to table, jabbering about the sensational action in the parking lot at Marshall and Thompson. Pool shooters were laughing, others shaking their heads in disbelief. A few were rushing up to the cash register to pay off their time, and hurrying outside. After telling the guys at the counter what was happening Hess passed by our table and said, "How about it? You two virgins want in on this, too?"

"What's going on?" Karl asked.

"Crazy shit," Hess said. "Orgy-porgy time. Billy Schmitz and Hawaiian Jack picked up an old floozy in the Golden Slipper bar. She's pie-eyed drunk, and she said she'd take us all on, handle all the cock we will throw at her."

"Woof," Karl moaned.

"Suit yourselves," Hess said, then hurried off to extend more invitations.

Karl looked at me. I looked at Wronsky. He gave the nod. We joined the line forming at the cash register, five guys ahead of us. When it became my turn to pay, Dave growled, "You, too? Your father hears about this he will skin you alive. Run home, Paulie. Stay away from the crap out there."

"Yeah, yeah, yeah," I said, and dropped my two dollars down. How can you stay away from an interesting car wreck or a fascinating head-on collision?

Outside, Karl and I sniffed the wind, hardly necessary, all we needed to do was follow the pack racing up Sixth Street, turning the corner at Thompson. I don't know how the word got out this fast but it seemed as if the whole neighborhood was electrified, the scurrying in the darkness resembled rats fleeing a sinking ship. In this case they were charging toward a victim. A rowdy crowd had already gathered in the parking lot at Marshall and Thompson. Thirty or forty guys were milling around, laughing, creating a protective cocoon, so that passer-by pedestrians and the customers leaving Himmelstein's Restaurant up the corner at Girard would not see what this commotion was about.

We infiltrated the crowd, heard Lippy Goldfine explaining that it was Hawaiian Jack who picked up the drunken woman in the Golden Slipper. Then it was Billy Schmitz who broke open the back door of the blue butter and egg delivery truck, it was the old lady who suggested this could be a gang bang, all comers invited. More candidates were arriving from all points of the map, it seemed that the whole neighborhood wanted in on this.

Moe Tanner, he went to art school, was on top of the old lady squirming in the truck. Buddy Baer was acting as ringmaster, lining up the crowd. Mel Fleischer was holding up a stick as if it were a microphone, offering a running commentary on the action, imitating By Saam broadcasting a game from Shibe Park. Mel was saying "Ladies and gentlemen, Tanner is digging deeply into the batter's box, please limit your time in the box, Tanner, we've got a slew of hitters behind you, all of them eager to take their swings."

I suppose that was dimly witty but this scene was nauseatingly disappointing. These were college boys, I'd imagined them to be collected, levelheaded, had not expected to find them panting in this line. This Crapola you found over by the docks, down by grubby Delaware Avenue, not up here. Tanner had finished, was wiping himself off. Tim Marchand from Oxford Street was climbing onto the old lady.

Her head was flopping from side to side, and she was groaning filthy stuff. From what I could see the woman sprawled in the truck was hideous, sort of a mermaid in reverse, the slim pretty legs of a sixteen year-old girl but from the torso up she was a wrinkled hag. What sickened me most was not the laughter and the crap that the spectators were braying, but the sight of the old lady's gear on the chicken coop by her side. One tattered purse, jodhpurs, a pink polo shirt, soiled panties, broken down high-heeled shoes. Her dirty ankles and the pathetic rags made her seem too unbearably fragile, too vulnerable, like a caterpillar you could easily step on. They reminded me of why I hate medicine; I don't want to be this close to people.

I glanced at Karl; he nodded in agreement, and simulated the act of barfing. At Girard the lights dimmed, Himmelstein's was closing, customers gathering outside the restaurant, many had cars parked in this lot. The customers were hesitating, even at a distance they sensed that nasty shit was happening here, maybe only an illegal crap game, but they were leery about approaching this rambunctious crowd.

Bill Schmitz came over to us and asked, "You two here as fans or players?

Billy can lift beer kegs over his head, leap over schoolyard fences with a two-step vault, he is Decathlon material, a magnificent physique, starred at fullback with the Wilmington Clippers, even had a try-out with the Eagles. That came to nothing, as Billy is an undisciplined bum. Instead of being in Hollywood playing the Hercules roles in gladiator films Billy can barely hold onto his job on the shipping dock at the brewery. His world is the bars, the schoolyard, the poolroom.

Since I did not respond, Schmitz said, "How about you, Karlie? Want to go next? Hawaiian Jack and me did all the work of picking up this douche-bag, now all these leaches are horning in, taking over our show. You can go next, I'll give the order."

"No thanks," Karl said. "I'm saving myself for Paulette Godard. "

"Ah, chicken shit, " Schmitz taunted him." You aint a man till you've had your first case of the clap. And, if she gives you a dose Paulie's father can clean it up fast with a few shots."

It bothered me that Schmitz was trying to egg Karl into climbing on that slime pit. When I was smaller I idolized Billy but there are guys who can have the cast of mighty heroes and turn out to be mental midgets,

Burdumi had finished. The crowd whooped as Irv Kauffman unzipped his fly, climbed into the truck. Another illusion shot down. I had always seen Irv as serene, professorial, the kind to eventually be a pipe-smoking sage wearing herringbone jackets with leather patches on the elbows, not a drooling cunt hound about to dip into a cesspool. I recalled the evaluation when Dad sent me to the psychologist because I was playing hooky so much: Doctor Schwartz tagged me as the 'classic under-achiever, deliberately failing to live up to my potential.'

Billy Schmitz, Irv Kauffman with his pants down, pumping away; our whole neighborhood was densely populated by under-achievers.

Sirens screeched. The pavement seemed to shiver, tremble, as if for an imminent earthquake. The crowd in the parking lot let out wails, moans, shouts, the troops started scattering in all directions even before we saw the flashing red lights on the red cars, heard the whoops of the patrol cars racing our way. Kauffman came stumbling out of the truck, trying to run while pulling up his trousers at the same time, the old lady in the truck was groaning, "Hey! Where is everybody going?"

Pick your poison, panic time, the cops seemed to be arriving from all points of the compass, with the sirens snarling louder the troops were scattering to all point of the compass, scrambling up side alleys, climbing over back fences. Karlie and me hauling ass out of there, taking off down Marshall to cross Girard, to reach the safety of Uncle Moe's deli. Ten other cruds were fleeing along side us. As we passed Himmelstein's the old Jews in front of the restaurant were shaking their fists at us, screaming, "Run, you scum! Run, you filthy lice! Degenerates! "

Tearing across Girard we were almost hit by a swerving taxi, had to dodge the trolley clanging by. When we reached the other side merchants living over the Marshall Street stores were scraping their windows open, wondering what the police sirens and the uproar was about. A few of them shook fists at us.

To my right was the small synagogue, only structure on this block not dedicated strictly to commerce. Our escape route was to our left, Karl followed as I ducked into the unlit narrow alley feeding into Sixth Street. The bricks and cobbles were uneven; you could easily sprain an ankle running in this darkness. I never forget that Mom was supposed to have used this alley the night she was run down by the car roaring down Sixth. The stupid city should not permit blocks this damn long, encouraging idiots and maniacs to press the pedal, drive too fast.

We came out directly across from my house, twenty yards from a refuge, both of us ready to groan in relief, but then we saw the red lights flashing, a patrol car bearing down on us like an angry bear charging at prey. It halted with a chilling screech. Two cops with upraised clubs stormed out of the red car, they were eager to swing, clubs poised, at the last second they saw that we were kids.

Both cops were beefy sized extra large. One appeared to be ruddy Irish, the taller a swarthy South Philly Italian, both cops were bristling, all het up, looking for the slightest pretext or excuse to bust our heads open. No wisecracks occurred to me.

The Italian appearing cop snarled, "Where do you two think you're going? Were you two involved in that shit at the parking lot?"

"No," Karl said. " Not at all. We were nowhere near Thompson Street, officer."

Oof. For a genius Karl can pull some real bloopers.

"Then why the huffing and puffing? The Irisher asked. "What you running from?"

Before Karl could stick his foot in it again, I said, "We heard police sirens, sir, thought you might be after dangerous, criminals, so we began running, sir. We're just coming back from playing monopoly at a buddy's house on Franklin Street."

The Italian cop sniffed, "Aren't you two out pretty late? Isn't it time for your diaper change?" He was tapping his billy club in his hand, still itching to use it on us.

I pointed to my house directly across Sixth Street, the bronze plaque next to the glazed window, and said, "I live right there, officer."

Both cops frowned unhappily at the sign for a doctor's office. Down by Franklin Square cops get away with roughing up the Colored and the bums and hobos from the Eighth Street Skid Row, but they might get into trouble for clobbering the offspring of the middle class, headlines in the Evening Bulletin and Daily Noose.

"You, fatrat? What pigsty did you climb from?" the Irish cop asked Karl.

"I live down by Spring Garden and Randolph. Rooms behind the gas station."

The cops glanced at each other, stopped tapping their clubs into their palms. The Irish cop said," I know the place. Once made the mistake of sitting on the bench outside, staining my uniform."

Tossing his chin, the Italian cop said to me, " Okay, you, you get up those steps, get your boney ass inside your house." He turned to Karl and said, "You, Porky Pig, into the car. We're driving you home to get your dumpy ass off the streets."

I touched my finger to my temple as a way of nodding farewell to Karl. He was still shaking. Karl catches extras rations of crap from all quarters.

The squad car did not take off till I was inside the vestibule. It was unlikely the cops would now slap Karl around. Everybody knows that gas station, knows Dmitri.

Luckily, the Buick was not in the back yard. I had made it home before my bon vivant of a father has deigned to arrive. Wronsky still has one more hairy adventure pending. After the cops drop him off Karl has to decide whether he sneaks out again to pick up his brother at Gold's, or else he'll catch a lot of lip off Dmitri.

CHAPTER THREE

Sunday evenings my father cuts a dashing swath in the Golden Age Dances at the Broadwood Hotel. These soirees feature a quartet pounding out rollicking standards such as 'Pennsylvania Six-Five Thousand, T'zena, T'zena. Roll Out the Barrel, The Wedding Samba, and the Miami Beach Rhumba. There are almost twice as many 'Girls' as 'Boys' attending these affairs. By 'Girls' we mean widowed Bubbas, optimistic spinsters, plump divorcees. The 'Boys' are mostly creaking elder statesmen chancing cardiac arrest if they assay moves overly ambitious on Fred Astaire's turf. In lieu of the traditional 'Good Night, Ladies' as the wrap-up song the quartet occasionally plays, for comic effect, 'The Old Gray Mare Ain't what She Used to be.' 'Love Is Better the Second Time Around,' had not yet been written. I suspect that several of these seasoned vets were on their third or fourth time around. Then they all go out for a late night snack. As there are almost two chickadees for every cock who invites whom to Linton's afterwards is of transcendental importance.

Some Sundays the Girls pick up Dad with their own cars. They have told me how popular he is for his snappy jitterbugging: his divine foxtrots. Dad also participates in the Israeli Shticks, vigorous Kazatchkas; they get tres ethnic, dance 'the Hora' in circles. For the Sadie Hawkins routine where the Girls pick their partners there is a stampede of matrons seeking to latch onto Dapper Dan, particularly for tangos. He does a mean 'La Cumparsita,' hams it up a little, becomes a reincarnated Valentino dipping and half-mooning the more pliable dowagers at the Golden Age dances.

Dad also likes Italian women. He has lady friends in South Philly; one is muy simpatica. Mrs. Carla Fiore is a widow with two grown sons. She owns a beauty parlor, has her own nest egg, and is definitely no gold digger. I'd not mind having Mrs. Fiore for a step-mom; Carla kind of groovy, but she is one more of the ladies

Dad has been stringing along for, lo, these many years, hiding behind shields, telling them that nothing *'serious'* can happen until the *'Boy'* is out of the house.

Me-Boy.

When Dad told me it was time for his annual fishing vacation in Cape May I wondered whether it would be Mrs. Fiore or one of his Rifkas from the Broadwood Conga lines to share his idyll on the beach. He made the customary noises about me possibly accompanying him, knowing I'd turn the offer down, I detest worms, fishing bait, pulling the hooks out of a dumb fish's mouth. The only matter in debate was the disposition of my persona while he is off doing his thing. So far, every summer he had fobbed me off on the Berman Sisters, one of my goosey aunts, meaning two weeks of putting up with my noxious cousins. This year, since I was already working in the deli, it seemed logical that I stay with Sara and Moe; they have an unused bedroom on the third floor. I argued that I was now old enough to be left alone. Miss Pearl certainly took adequate care of the cleaning and cooking. Mrs. Jordan would be on duty half the day, referring all emergency calls to Doc Gillman.

"This can be the acid test of my maturity, Dad."

He eyed me dubiously but a compromise was reached. Pop arranged it so that Boris, our handyman jack-of- all-trades would paint the hallways, back porch, and basement during these two weeks. Boris will sleep on the premises, a cot in the basement provide security against burglars. His other duties would include reporting on me if I did not get in by curfew time or ignored the eleven-thirty lights out rule. Miss Pearl, Mrs. Jordan, Moe and Sara, were also recruited to provide surveillance and monitor my activities.

Dad probably let out a sigh of relief when he crossed the Delaware River Bridge into Jersey. Later I learned that he was not with Carla. Mrs. Maxine Barufkin was the chosen one. Also a widow, she owns a cosmetics boutique on Walnut Street. In spite of her gruff surname, enunciate 'Barufkin,' it sounds like a Siberian wolfhound sneezing; she is an attractive woman, the reigning beauty of the Broadwood dances, and a slightly more zaftig version of Ruth Roman.

Meanwhile, I sighed in relief on Sixth Street. Miss Pearl served my breakfast, an onion roll with cream cheese and a cup of hot chocolate. She said, "Now don't you go running off hog-wild, Paulie, while your father is off doing his gallivanting around."

In my mind I twirled my non-existent mustache.

"Wipe that evil smile off your face," She ordered as she returned to the kitchen.

Miss Pearl is more than our trusted family retainer, practically my real mother, raising me since I was three. She lives near the Booker Movie house in the Colored project. It wasn't supposed to be a Colored Project; it was designed to be for poor people, ended up with only the Colored over there by Tenth and Brown.

From the kitchen she was frowning my way. A hard-shell Baptist, she sings in her church choir, offers Dad thundering Jeremiads condemning his wanton ways. For years she's been noodging the man to stop playing the field, it was time to give Paul a proper home life with a mother in residence. The results of her admonitions have been palpably negligible. Dad is an unregenerate swinger. I don't know how the old boy gets away with it.

When I entered the deli that morning Uncle Moe and Aunt Sara also told me that I must behave and not take advantage of the situation. This was my chance to show that I am a responsible individual, and can be trusted to do the right thing. Then they contributed to my delinquency: at one o'clock Moe told me to get lost, go schlepp around. Aunt Sara slipped me five bucks as I went out the door.

In the clutter of stalls and booths the endless war between the shopkeepers and the shoplifters continues. I stalk down Marshall to see if I can spring Karl from bondage vile at the gas station. Bumping along through the crowds I hear language that is accented, coarse, imprecise, colorful, cruel, prejudiced. Folks here think Hoi Palloi means the aristocrats. I've heard guys accusing hypocrites of having phony '*fakades.*' Cornpone refugees from the Gulleys of West Virginia think 'Jew' is a verb. The Famous at the corner of Marshall and Poplar is the fancy Deli hereabouts. Moe survives by charging slightly less, also letting customers run a tab, a hairy way to do business, the last bill is never paid. Kitty-corner from the Famous is the noisy, smelly saloon looking like it belongs in Bucharest or Bavaria, the whiff of the beer is so overpowering it almost smothers the stink of the live chicken market, where, as usual, they are koshering a bleeding chicken.

One day I might fill in the gap, write about this neighborhood. Whenever we saw movies about Philly, it was mostly dippy doo-doo about snooty Clydes in tuxedos on the Main Line pushing prissy WASP debutantes into swimming pools. That aint Philly, McGee. Philly is Brown Street, drab row houses, empty lots with virulent weeds malignant bushes, scrofulous sunflowers, orchards of despair. Spring Garden Street is a jarring name for a wide avenue with no trees in sight, only thing green hereabouts are the stone slabs in the incongruous Fritz und Franz German Library, transplanted from a somber Strasse in Nuremberg. Every time I pass this forbidding fortress I hear Karlie swearing that Adolph and Eva are hiding in the basement. I wish I could shake these pings. The ping each time I cut through that back alley to Sixth, this was the shortcut Mom took before she was run down.

The Wronskys on their bench are part of the inventory on Spring Garden. Dmitri grimaced as he spotted me dodging through traffic. He knew I was up to no good, arriving to plead for the release of Karl from servitude. As I reached them Dmitri scowled, and asked "So, who's minding the store, Moishe?"

Certain comics have limited repertoires. I said nothing, Dmitri added, "And yeah? Where's my sandwich?"

"I ate it, amigo, " I said. "Maybe, if you behave, I'll bring one next time."

Karl said, trilling in a broad hint, "Nice day, no, Paulie? Real nice afternoon."

Dmitri scrunched his lips, thinking, unable to engage in that activity without running through a gamut of facial tics. Then he glared at his brother, and snapped, "I hear you. Get the fuck out of here. You're a pain in the ass, anyway, Karl. "

Since we now had Dmitri's blessing we immediately took off. Heading up Sixth Street we passed the unkempt garden of the big synagogue near Green Street. The plants were scraggly, the twisting vines had a leprous, sickly glow. Dad contributes one thousand dollars a year to this temple but does not attend services. He is not a believer but says religions are necessary, just as we we need dentists, plumbers, and garbage men; we need priests to help keep us bestial animals caged.

Karl said, " So you have two weeks to freely ride the range. What you gonna' do with so much freedom, Paulie?"

"I'll think of something. It's not total liberty. Dad assigned a whole team to ride herd on me. Boris, the handyman, will be sleeping over to put a damper on my nocturnal visitations. I was thinking of inviting a girl over, Anita, she comes into the deli, she says, wink, wink, she wants to learn to play chess, hoo-hoo -hoo, but damn Boris would rat on me."

"My worries are worse," Karl grumbled. "I'm leaving Saturday. Dim says it's good for me to get out of the city for the fresh air and sunshine, but it's really to get me out of his hair for a while. He knows I hate it but every summer sends me to this dippy camp where they make us pray daily, jog through the woods, we have to call these freaky counselors 'Uncle Joe' and 'Uncle Mike.' I always get stung by ten bees, return infested by the poison ivy and smeared with fucking calamine lotion but Dim insists enjoying nature is healthy and good for me."

I was not too fond of summer camp, either: handicraft classes where we learned how to make faux silly-ass artifacts like Ersatz Mohawk bracelets. Moronic songs: 'Oh, you can't get to heaven in a trolley car, cause the PTC don't go that far.' Screw Hiawatha, and Minnie Ha-ha, too. But, to be conciliator and peacemaker, I said, "Dim's just trying to be a caring brother to you."

"The bastard is blackmailing me, He swears that if he hears one more gripe about the camp he'll cancel my birthday present with Rosey Ivanovich."

"That's blackmail, "I agreed.

It was so hot we considered entering the shade of the pool hall but continued on to the schoolyard where only one of the basketball courts was being used. Is virtue its own reward? Our ranks were temporarily decimated: five of the participants in that parking lot gangbang were currently scratching their crotches with a ferocious case of the crabs, and several more were in denial and lying about it.

Near dusk the cab paused at the Ratchinov house. By now we were accustomed to seeing Sonya taking advantage of Knocky's being down the shore, arriving with doddering codgers looking Today, innovations, the John paying off the taxi looked like a Big Shot high roller. In spite of the heat he was wearing a pinstriped gray suit, a buttoned vest, uniform of a high school principal or Walnut Street Coupon Clipper. Glancing around, nervously, he looked like a priest making sure the parishioners don't spot him slipping into the bookstore with the soapy windows. The second novelty was Svetla, Sonya's sister, A.K.A. Trixie Malloy, flashing sheer nylons and powerful thighs as she also squirmed out of the taxi.

There are women so painfully beautiful they seem to have descended from a superior planet. Svetla might have escaped from a glossy cover of Amazing Stories, one of the robust Valkyries tossing the spears at the saber-toothed dragons on Jupiter. Sonya was the Amazon slaying the Neptunian Troglodytes. Both of these gorgeous apparitions were entering that shoebox of a house with that distinguished gentleman. I recalled Dmitri's phantasy, the lurid Hoagie sandwich.

Who knows what raunchy, exquisite immoral stuff transpired in that dump till another taxi showed up one hour later. Maybe they only played Parcheesi in there? All we saw was the rickety trick, wobbling out, disheveled, as if he had been churned in a fur lined cement mixer after sampling all the positions from the Kama Sutra. Sonya waved goodbye to him from the doorway. I held the basketball while all we stood there with our jaws slack, the drool dripping down into our bibs.

That week Karl and I were all over the map, shooting pool at Dave's, also the Third and Brown poolroom. Two nights we hung out in Gold's with Dmitri; Saul even laced our Seven Ups with splashes of Seagram's. As to the curfew, it was easy to bribe my watchdog. Instead of throwing Boris a bone I had Billy Schmitz buy three flasks of Slivovitz in the State Store. Billy kept one bottle for himself, for the other two Boris agreed that my cut-off would be at One AM, and I could jot down anything I wanted in the log. Dad sets up these tight control systems but as, with Moe and Sara, he cannot find reliable help to run the operations.

Saturday Karl took off for camp. That Corsican Brothers link, I could already feel his pain: dawn masses, bee stings, and poison ivy, morning jogs through the woods. I had hated the stupid songs. 'John Jacob Jingleheimer Schmidt?' How could they infect kids with that such piffle and tripe when we were defenseless tykes? Then there was 'Oh, Hogan's Goat, was feeling fine. He ate three red shirts, off my line.'

Childhood is a disease we must survive. I have been told we never get over adolescence. Such were my ruminations when at two o'clock Uncle Moe told me to take a hike, go enjoy my unblemished, pristine youth. He did not put it that way, but I'm sure that's what he intended to say. Aunt Sara, apart from my salary, slipped an unearned fiver into the envelope. I had money in my pocket, an entire city to explore, no buddies to pal around with. I thought about hanging out with the sharpies at the Seventh and Oxford luncheonette, had to drop that option; there was one crud up there vowing to punch me out. I'd taken Sylvan Gans to the cleaners at eight ball and Sylvan was a bad loser. He invited me to step outside, we had a brief scuffle in front of Dave's, I was losing but managed to clip his nose, which bled profusely, provoking interlopers to interrupt the festivities.

Sylvan vowed revenge. Eventually we must meet on the sacred field of honor, Ludlow Schoolyard, but I was in no mood for fisticuffs on this hot, sticky afternoon.

Downtown was Leary's Bookstore, my destination. Dad has his impressive library: aside from the medical texts and scientific tomes, the complete works of Henry James, Thomas Mann, Zweig, Musil, Rilke, tons of history books. By the time I finished Kindergarten I'd already read H. G. Wells 'The Outline of History,' Hendrik van Loons 'The Story of Mankind,' and was reading William Shirer's 'Berlin Diary. I knew more about the battles of World War Two, geography, and politics, than most adults around our way. Lord, I was a detestable little pecker, the kind of smug smart-ass you want to punch on general principles. At the Thomas Jefferson School, Fourth and George, they wanted to skip me from the First to the Sixth Grade. Dad would have none of that; he had me transferred to the special Thaddeus Stevens School of Practice, Thirteen and Spring Garden. Dad said he wanted me to have *a normal* childhood. Lots of luck, Dad

At Franklin and Spring Garden the Negroes were living it up brown in the Blue Room Bar, Sixty Minute Man' playing on the jukebox. A raucous crowd was digging the rhythm and blues. In a panorama otherwise dull and somnolent this joint was seething and throbbing in the sultry nothingness. I almost envied the Negroes for living in their own town, a hotter, jazzier version of Philly,.

Up Eighth Street was our festering '*Tenderloin*. In other cities they call them 'Skid Rows,' I don't know why, by us, it's the Tenderloin, from Callowhill up to Arch Street a mini-Calcomania of New York's Bowery, three blocks of puke-stained pavements, rowdy tap rooms, hock shops, dirty book stores, two-bits a cot flop houses, stinky saloons, Evangelical missions, gypsy fortune teller joints, geeky novelty stores selling exotic herbs, freaky prosthetic limbs, yellow surgical trusses, aromatic weeds, and Rosicrucian astrology pamphlets. The sidewalks were swarming with purple-nosed winos, dregs and gimps; jukeboxes were blaring with Hillbilly banjos, while the bums in the missions sing hymns to His Glory, they must praise the Lord, or else they will not get their bowl of bean soup.

Why would they call this scabby-ass eyesore '*The Tenderloin*' when *Anus* would be more appropriate? Parents up our way warn children that if we do not straighten up and fly right we will end up with the derelicts at Eighth and Race. Whenever Karl, Alexi, and I shot downtown to see a movie we never walked up Sixth, Knocky was leery of passing the benches in Franklin Square, where the bums were sleeping off hangovers, it could be his father on one of those benches. We never used Eighth, this labyrinth of bleary boozers, Knocky was afraid of running into his Old Man staggering out of one of these saloons to slobber all over him, as he had done on several occasions.

Big coincidence, I spotted Mister Ratchinov shuffling out of the Texas Bar. He was pie-eyed, as usual, dirty trousers ripped at the knees; he was shuffling around erratically, like one of those red-nosed clowns in the circus. Unsolved mysteries: How could a stunning woman like Sonya ever have co-habited with this *Wreck of the Hesperus?* Next question: How could a handsome kid like Alexi be the product of this lummox's testicles? We are not supposed to have gross thoughts like that. I wondered whether Knocky was doubling over with a stab of pain on the Boardwalk, like Karl felt the rapier thrust, our Corsican Brothers communion.

Mr. Ratchinov did not recognize me. He would not recognize his Momma at the moment. I recognized how lucky I was to have my neat old bastard for a Pop. Yes, he is stuffy, pompous, stern, more a put-upon grand-pa than a regular Pop who might take me to a Phillies game or play catch with me, but then, I am certainly no prize, and I'm the price he's paying for pleasures long past.

The hobo jungle ends abruptly. Reach Arch Street, you're back to civilization. Nothing was written down but the bums knew better than to stray past Arch. One block more to Market Street, when we turn right, down by Broad Street City Hall blocks our view. William Penn up there. In the phony movies about Philly they always show this City Hall tower, to certify that this is Philly, then the ensuing crap can be about any old burg. I crossed Market Street, and entered Leary's, tucked inside the Gimbels Department Store building, across from the Federal Court.

Dad had his excellent library but Leary's was top-notch unique, seven floors of used books in chaotic stacks, gems mixed in with the garbage, tremendous bargains, classics costing ten bucks elsewhere found in Leary's for a buck. Dad had ponderous works, I was hankering for lighter reading, spicy while we're at it, a pecker picker-upper, along the lines of 'Fanny Hill' or 'The Chinese Room.

After an hour of browsing through the jumbled stacks I bought 'The Mucker' for fifty cents, then I walked another nine blocks to leafy Rittenhouse Square.

For the next three hours I was totally absorbed. Except to occasionally glance up at the pretty girls passing by. Squirrels were begging for nuts, darling noisy brats were running around, old ladies were their walking ridiculous poodles and Chihuahuas, but I managed to finish 'The Mucker.' I had read all of E.R. Burroughs' Tarzan books, his Venus and Mars novels, the Pellucidar series, the set about the back of the Moon, but this obscure, way-out ' Mucker' was far superior to any of them. A sullen thug from Chicago is shanghaied, endures fabulous adventures on remote Pacific Islands, after fifty twists and turns the brute that started off his life as a rotten swine is a completely transformed man. Often, novels that nobody ever heard of are more gripping than the consecrated bores they ram down your throat.

Afterwards, I was spiked to the bench, analyzing 'The Mucker.' Is it possible to change that much? I did not enjoy being sardonic, flippant smart-ass me, always wising off. I'd prefer to become a laconic pistolero, a strong, silent leathery gumshoe. Was it possible to take myself apart, discard my excess snideness, and reassemble a sounder, more solid model? Did other guys think about such things? Or, are we all tetched and quirky, but condemned to skulk around portraying a standard product?

Still spiked to this bench, I lit up a smoke. Where did Paul Burris fit into this scheme of things, this equation? When William Penn planned his greene and rolling towne he established four squares as parks in the four quadrants: over by the Parkway it was Logan Square for religion and culture; the Independence Hall square was for government; over by the bridge, Franklin Square was for the bums suppurating on the benches. This was ritzy Rittenhouse Square with the upper crust strutting by. With my bummer tendencies, where do we end our story? Do I slide down the crapper, end my days crawling out of saloons over by Franklin Square or do I end up here in Rittenhouse Square, looking like one of these grizzled bulldogs intently studying the stock market tables in the Inquirer.

Weird being alone, Freedom is not all it is cracked up to be, with no buddy to talk to disturbing notions buzz in your skull. I did not care to think anymore so I went to the movies: the Stanley, on Market Street, a double feature starring John Garfield, 'The Fallen Sparrow', and 'Humoresque.' For the next few hours I was a tortured ex-agent, and a torn, tormented violinist. Then I was famished, had eaten nothing since the pancakes and sausage Miss Pearl served for breakfast. She had an argument with Boris. She knew my night shift watchdog was not doing his job; Boris was letting me get away with murder.

After gobbling down three hot dogs at Needick's I had no place to go. Allinger's was out, the best pool hall in center city but they were strict about enforcing the age rules. I thought about grabbing the 47 trolley up to Girard but if I entered Dave's Gans might be in there. Automatically it would be step outside time again. Okay, sure, but not tonight, Dear Lord, it's too hot and muggy for fisticuffs.

I don't know about other cities but if you're not out on a date, or, at least, hanging out with your buddies, Philly, on a dreary Saturday night is Desolation Junction, the pits. Sundays were not exactly a Carnival in Flanders, either, but on Saturday nights like this, the stores shut, movies all let out, deserted streets, neon lights on the signs off, you can understand where existential screams come from.

The used bookstore at Sixth and Market where I bought my Amazing Stories was closed. In the rear they have a porno section selling two-by-fours; Popeye planking Wonder Woman, the Green Hornet nailing Sheena of the Jungle. A block away from Independence Hall? Am I the oddball for worrying about such matters?

Tonight, with the headlights of the oncoming cars washing over me, though I've traversed this terrain one thousand times. I'm an explorer, mapping this route. The natives snooze early in this overgrown village. At Race Street Sixth widens, so the cars heading for Jersey can swerve the wide turn to the left. To my right the benches in Franklin Square are empty, the park guards no longer allow the boozers to sleep here; they must shell out for a flophouse or enter a mission where they must endure a sermon, are obliged to take a shower, only given a paper towel to dry off with.

Corner of Vine, the Sunday Morning Breakfast Association where the bums line up daily for their oatmeal, next, Callowhill Street, the big pharmacy, the smell of the meat packing plants, stink of an abattoir, I've never been to the Chicago stockyards but imagine they smell like this. A block further down, the cobbled train tracks on Willow Street, another lumberyard, larger than the lumberyard at Fifth and Poplar. When I reached Noble Street I saw the neon light blinking over Jakey Rubin's Bar at the corner of Marshall and Noble. According to press exposes this might be the baddest bar in the universe, averaging four bodies a year found in the vicinity. Rubin, owner of seventy tenements, is accused of being an unrepentant slumlord. The occupants of his rooms are the rural Colored, just up from Alabama and Mississippi; they pick the tomatoes for Campbell's Soups, work maybe three months a year, dedicate the other nine months to mayhem and mischief. Reformers loudly demand that Rubin's bar be shut down, and the Captain of the Buttonwood Street Police Station got in spitting match trouble with the press for saying that was ridiculous, let Jakey's be, if they shut down Rubin's the killings will just spread out elsewhere. At least here they had the contagion quarantined off.

Sociology. Adult stuff. What did I know? I knew this neighborhood. Noble Street disappears for two blocks here. I cut through back alleys behind the bronze foundry and the wood cabinet factory, circled behind the loading platform at the SKF plant to where Noble reappeared at Fourth Street. It was not yet midnight, closing time for saloons in this uptight city. Do they call them the Blue Laws because people get the freaked-out Blues on nights like this? The neon sign was blinking over Go-d's bar, the 'L' had gone stone dead. This was a hoot. Hymie and Saul were now advertising their humble dry gulch watering hole as Go-d's Bar.

There must be deep symbolism here. I now stand before the bar of Go-D.

'Are you worthy to enter, Paul Burris?'

'A heavy question, sir; I'll take the Fifth, your honor."

Peeking through the glass slot in I saw the usual crowd in there playing darts and the pinball machine: Schatz, Eli, Sibronsky, Dmitri; Gall sitting in the rear booth, looking like some ferocious minor deity. I thought about entering but, nah, they'd rib and treat me like a lost puppy, poor waif, no place to go. They'd give me a hard time for carrying a book. I'd thought about leaving 'The Mucker' behind in Rittenhouse Square, but took it with me for Karl when he gets back from camp. Books in this dive would be an intrusive object from an alien galaxy. I was in no mood to be patronized tonight so to hell with this scene.

Let us drift off into the night and the swirling fog while I tug at the lapels of the cool tan trench coat I'm not wearing. We will wend our enigmatic way down these mean streets toward destinies and destinations unknown. Actually, I am heading for the docks. Tonight I'm the private dick gumshoe Sam Spade, Boston Blacky, Carson of Napier, Mister Kean, Tracer of Missing Persons, and Chinese Gordon. Others have done batman and The Lone Ranger to death,

No other adventurers were out as I trudged down Spring Garden toward the El tracks and the Delaware River. Cars were seeping by, the truck terminals were shut tight, dim street lamps were offering a menacing glow, warnings to 'stay back, turn around, dope,' rather than helpful illumination. Business conducted around here at this hour of night would be the Devil's business.

Karl, Alexi and I came down here to watch the horses pulling the trash wagons up the ramp. When the loads were dumped there were huge bursts of sparks and flames. We came here to watch the banana boats being unloaded. When the hatches opened hundreds of scorpions came swarming out of the holds, girls screamed, ran with their skirts up, spectators scattered, the spiders spread out all over the wharf like roaches fleeing a burning house, while the sailors stomped around and stamped on the scorpions like Gauchos dancing an angry samba.

I snuck down here on my lonesome when I felt dead inside, needed my private tour of the waterfront. I never told Dad about this; the Old Boy would have fits and conniptions. I love this grim place. The heart beats faster when you pass under these dark elevated tracks, reach the ruptured cobbles on Delaware Avenue, hear the last train rumble by overhead, like a last clipper out of Lisbon. The lights blink on the masts and deck lamps of the freighters tied up at the piers, you take a magic carpet whisking us away from the chicken pluckers of Marshall Street and starched-ass school teachers. These docks are beautifully dangerous; blocks away from my smug citadel on Sixth Street is this escape valve linking us to the great wide world.

Aside from the romance, menace, and mystery it also stinks down here.

No man bathes twice in the same river. He'd better not; if it were the Delaware, he might not get a second chance. The river is polluted with industrial muck and chemical sludges. The authorities prattle away about cleaning her up, on bad days the stench can reach all the way to Seventh Street.

From my aimless meandering I was finally leg weary. Wandering thither and yon I may have clocked twenty miles today on our speedometer. The plan now was to shoot over to Second Street around Poplar, grab a donut and coffee at Dirty Gertie's. Second has its stores, stalls, pushcarts, not as much as Marshall but the same off-key touches of fey character whiffs of old world distinctness. By now it would be dark and deserted except for Dirty Gertie's, the café open all night for cab drivers and stevedores working the dead man's shifts.

A girl was leaving the rust bucket Greek freighter tied up near the Ferry terminal. She was plump, awkward, she had a hard time of it descending the wobbly gangplank. In the distance she was a barrel-shaped tub, along the lines of Knocky's Cousin Rita. I chuckled at my private embarrassment: How great of an adventure could this be If I'm sharing it with the dumpy female plotzing along the wharf over there. I'm a Walter Mitty imagining that I'm bold and brave, prowling around a sinister waterfront at this vampire hour of the night, then reality intrudes.

I thought no more about her, and lit up a smoke. Do I become a foreign correspondent or do I ship out? I also wanted to learn to play the tenor sax and become a pool shark. Besides directing movies, writing a history of my neighborhood, and maybe squeeze in a stretch in the Foreign Legion. Allons enfants de la Patrie.

The girl was heading north, in a parallel line across from me, toward Fishtown. Nearing the level of Brown Street I ducked back into an alley to take a piss. After zipping up, returning to the cobbles of Delaware Avenue, I saw two guys about a block behind me. The girl was no longer across the way, then I heard steps, thought it might be the girl, but the steps did not sound like the pitter-patter of a girl; the clopping grew louder, sounded like the gait of a mugger moving in for the kill. The notion of cutting back toward the ranch instantly seemed more judicious. I was tempted to glance back over my shoulder but if you are about to be mugged the act of looking backwards can precipitate the attack. I visualized the headline:

WAYWARD WASTREL SLAIN ON DOCKS.

Plan two: Count to three, and break into a sprint at the three.

Then I heard the call of, "Little Doc, that you?"

Once again, stabbed in the heart. One day they can be awarding me the Nobel Prize in Stockholm; some sucker in the audience will blurt out, "Little Doc?"

Turning around, I saw that it was indeed, Cousin Rita, trailing after me. The two guys were nowhere in sight.

"Paul," I said by way of correcting her. "Paulie, if you insist."

"Watcha' doin' out this time of night, Paulie?"

I might have asked her the same thing, but feared what her answer might be. She was coming off a ship after midnight. Did they have her on there to do the wash?

"Ah, just wandering around," I mumbled.

Rita sniffed. Why not? Even to me, that sounded dumb,. 'Wandering around? ' Why are you wandering around this graveyard at night, Dracula."

Falling in beside me, Rita surprised me by removing the book from my hand, and asking, "What you reading, Paulie?"

"The Mucker."

"The Fucker?"

"No, 'the Mucker,'" I said, exasperated.

Rita continued to surprise me by holding onto my book, and taking my hand, giving my hand a squeeze, as if she had squeezing rights. We had never had zilch. Years back she kicked off her career by charging boys a nickel to feel her boobs in the Girard movies. Then she took it up a notch, giving sociable hand jobs in the Astor. According to the latest scurrilous reports Rita had graduated, gone pro, was into remunerated back alley wall jobs with Swabbies. The Fuzz arrested her on Filbert Street; her name was not released to the papers, she was still a protected minor, who has latched onto my hand, without my authorization. A snapshot of this would ruin my reputation. I longed to extricate my hand from her clutches but was constrained by my good manners and breeding. Why was she cozying up to me? We slouched along in an uncomfortable silence until Rita murmured, "Alexi is down the shore."

No kidding, dum-dum. Hot news flash.

"Yeah, I know," I said. "Living it up, the bastard."

"All the girls are nuts about Alexi. But he don't play them no mind. He plays his Mister-Hard-to-Get-role."

"I try to do likewise," I said, " but they don't try to get me."

Rita grunted, affirmatively She was still gripping, having a field day with my hand. Should I stop being such a critical bastard, feel a tad bit sorry for her? Nature plays filthy tricks. Momma, Svetla is gorgeous; Rita got the smudged end of the stick looks=wise, waddling around like a soggy flour sack with grapefruits tacked onto her chest as an afterthought, and her complexion is so swarthy you'd need three slices of white bread to clean her up. Svetla must have mated with a warthog to formulate this aberration. Maybe Rita has a right to be such a rebel, always running away from home, the authorities dragged her back from unpromising locales like Camden, and Hagerstown, Maryland. Once, she made it all the way to Baltimore.

"So, are you having a nice summer, Little...Paulie?"

"Draggy but okay, I guess. Dad has me slaving in a deli on Marshall Street. At least my Uncle Moe lets me out early almost every day."

"Maybe I'll come visit you at the deli," Rita suggested. "You can make me a super submarine sandwich with extra ham and Swiss cheese."

I shuddered at the notion of Rita entering the deli to flutter her Cupid's arrows eyes at me. I could hear my Aunt Sara saying "So, you're dating Pocahontas now?"

We had drifted off Delaware Avenue, crossed under the El tracks, reaching First Street, almost back to civilization. Rita was still gripping my hand. I wanted to yank it away from her but that would have been too crass, even for me. Maybe her hand was a cursed object, like the Monkey's paw. I really did not want to think about all the action this hand might have seen. Out of loyalty to Knocky I has never once dipped down to the front rows in the Astor to experience her specialty.

To make conversation, I said, "So what were you doing down here by the docks?"

From the cunning smile she gave me she could have been Marlene Dietrich in the 'Orient Express. She said, "You don't know, eh?"

I knew. It was a tense moment. Rita had never appealed to me, but I was hearing the unsubtle swishing of her silk slip under her greasy skirt. I was afraid. Not the fear of 'let's step outside' time, but she was unknown, dangerous terrain for me.

"I didn't make much, "Rita said. " And I had to pay half to the fucking deck guard or he wouldn't let me off the ship."

"Hey, that's rough," I said, in commiseration. "That's extortion."

"I've always liked you, Little...Paulie. You're nice. You're not like all the others. You're a gentleman."

That was fairly sickening by our local standards, hardly a compliment. To be called a 'gentleman', and 'nice.' She had me sweating now.

"I usually charge seven bucks, but I like you, and since you're such a good buddy to Alexi, all you have to do is buy me a malted milk shake in Gansky's next week."

My jaw moved, my mouth opened, no words came forth. I could not say that I'd rather paid twenty dollars cash on the barrelhead than endure the mortification of being caught dead in Gansky's with Rita, the troops smirking at us.

She put out her arm to block my path. We were by a darkened alley feeding into Second Street. She put 'The Mucker' down on a trash can, and asked," You don't want me, Paulie?"

I did not want her, I wanted her Momma, while I was remembering the saps scratching their crotches from the butter and egg truck gangbang. Rita, this tramp, how many Greeks had she just boffed on that freighter?

None of that mattered as Rita deftly lowered my fly. The way she did it, this was not a first for her. She chuckled, a lewd chuckle, noting that I obviously did want her. Hiking up her skirts, she pressed against me, we stumbled around in a clumsy tango. Rita was running this show, knew what she was doing, I was the novice around here. Was it a sacrilege, showing disrespect for literature, as she planted her broad bottom on the trashcan she was also sitting on my 'Mucker,' her hand active in fitting us together, and her face became hideous with a grimace of pleasure.

CHAPTER FOUR

Dad returned from Cape May bronzed and salty. Karl returned from summer camp puffy from the bee stings, plus dripping pus from his scabby poison ivy and the calamine lotion. Shredding the cabbage for the cole slaw in the deli I was hoping that my liaison up the alley was not a foretaste of my fate. I had been fantasizing about a sublime initiation, SHE OF THE ETERNAL FLAMES inviting me to join her in the blue glow; Trixie Malloy, sheathed only by balloons, using a lit cigarette to pop all the balloons until she was stark naked and writhing on the rug at my feet. My evil gymnastics, what I did in phantasy land with Sonya Ratchinov, that will forever be a secret. And, what had reality proffered me as an introduction to the mysteries of Eros ? Rita, parked on a trashcan, "The Mucker' under her butt as we did it.

I did not mention to Karl that I was no longer a virgin. That brief encounter with Cousin Rita had been heart pounding, and terrifyingly exciting, but not exactly fun, or pleasurable. So far the hottest sex I had ever experienced was from batting it out on the sofa with Elaine Goodman from the George Street candy store.

The scalding heat of August was making Dad feel properly guilty about keeping me here in the city. It was unadvisable to go swimming; the public pools were shut down due to the Polio scare. Dad began making noises about sending me to the shore, but no Atlantic City, any contacts with John the Wizard STRENG VERBOTTEN. Dad proposed Wildwood: Aunt Roz was renting a cottage for two week in Wildwood. Ugh. That meant two weeks with her Zhlub husband, my Uncle Phil, and their unfortunate offspring, three of my more fatuous cousins. I told Dad no thanks, I preferred hustling pastrami on Marshall Street.

Meaning I endured the scorching Heat Wave. An article in the Inquirer alleged that when the temperature reaches past ninety-two degrees the murder rate soars. Maybe so, maybe no, but heat waves in Philly fuel fierce brawls in bars, assaults, muggings, punch-outs in chicken shacks, drive-by shootings, and domestic violence: husbands beat wives, wives bash husbands with skillets. Tempers grow shorter, especially among us kiddies, antsy we are as the days dwindle down to a precious few, classes will soon start; this leads to cantankerous combustion in schoolyards, minor incidents trigger major reactions. It seemed like a sponsored tournament, a fight a day. Tim Marchand pulverized Denny Ryan for suggesting that Mary, Tim's sister, wore her skirts too short. Moe Tanner, the art student, went at it with Buddy Baer when he caught Buddy messing around with his sweety, Ruthy Gilder, in the Girard movie house. Moe kicked his ass and almost threw Buddy through the window of the Ambassador Dairy Restaurant. At first Burdumi and Leon Hess were only kidding around with broomsticks, they had seen an Errol Flynn swashbuckler with pirates swinging through the rigging. It was all in fun until Hess caught a hard knock on the knuckles. Out of nowhere their playful sword fight became a ferocious duel to the death. Burdumi almost lost an eye to a sharp poke, his left eye was gushing blood. Billy Schmitz and Hawaiian Jack picked him up and rushed him to the emergency ward at the Northern Liberties Hospital.

I was in no danger of losing an eye but had a flamboyant shiner after my third tussle with Gans. Labor Day Weekend, I'm shooting pool in Dave's, Sylvan sachets in, like the bad-ass gunslinger entering the cantina in Tombstone. No need for dialogue, with a toss of the chin Gans invites me to step outside. I clearly had the better of our first go-around, left him with a bleeding nose, our second match was inconclusive, but here we must go again. The Code dictates the rules. It is step outside time.

Six spectators left the poolroom with us, Hawaiian Jack indicating he'd serve as referee. Sylvan is bigger than I am, stronger, but sloppy. What mostly saves me, I'm a Lefty, and southpaws confuse many contenders. After thirty seconds I was ahead on points, my right jab wreaking havoc with his acne, bursting open his florid collection of whiteheads. Then Sylvan caught me with a lucky barn door shot, leaving me with a purple shiner, precisely on the one night a month Dad devotes exclusively to Moi.

Upstairs, shaving, I checked the eye. Fair is fair, Sylvan lost a quart of blood when I clipped his nose in our first battle. But it was really annoying to have this telltale fluorescent shiner on the one night a month Dad reserves to cultivating our palship. Unfortunately, it is always music, music, and more music.

I don't expect him to attend Bugs Bunny Cartoon Festivals with me but I wish it wasn't inexorably the Academy of Music, the Rites of Spring, Bartok, Schoenberg, Alan Berg? Once he took me to see the ballet. I never told the gang in Ludlow about that, they'd ask when I am buying my tights and pink slippers. These cultural safaris evolve into musical appreciation seminars where Pop displays his onerous erudition and encyclopedic knowledge of the bios of the great composers, renowned perform- ances, and controversial premiers. After symphonies at the Academy he takes me for sandwiches to Lew Tendler's where he explains why Gustav Mahler is grandiose, Tchaikovsky bathetic, and Wagner's operas are better than they sound. If he notes that customers at adjacent tables are listening to his incisive critiques of the of the recently concluded concerts Dad is not adverse to augmenting slightly his volume for the benefit of his audience.

When I entered the parlor downstairs Dad flinched to inform me that he was not convinced by my sartorial selection. He shrugged to suggest that he could live with it, then handed me a pair of dark glasses, and said, "Put these on. I wouldn't want people to think that I bopped you one. Though I certainly would like to whop you one forgetting into a stupid brawl like that."

"Yes, sir, yes sir, three bags full."

Dad was Abercrombie and Fitchy tonight in a blue blazer with gold buttons, sporty white ducks, blue and white checked sport shirt. With his full head of battleship gray hair flacked with strands of silver he achieves nautical effects, could pass for the Captain of a two-master off Cape May. No doubt. To la simpatica Carla Fiore and the beguiling Maxine Barufkin he presents a dashing figure

We have our routines down pat. My assignment is to lock the gates after he maneuvers the Buick out of our yard. Most of these back yards are scraggly gardens or vegetable patches. Only three other families along this block use these spaces as garages. As we pulled out of the alley back onto Girard Avenue, Dad said, There was no way you couldn't talk to the boy, reason with him, instead of rolling all over the sidewalk like a common hoodlum and coming home with an incandescent shiner?"

"Dad, Gans is a bully. There's absolutely no way to reason with a bully. Only thing you can do is take your beating but sock him hard in the nose, make sure you hurt him bad enough that he doesn't want to repeat the drill. Yeah, I got a black eye but I bust open all his pimples, his face looked like a split-open Chinese apple, I don't think Gans will be back for another helping."

"That's your contention. How did it all start, Paul? Originally?"

"Basketball. Sylvan was pissed because I was guarding him too tightly, making him look bad, he couldn't get a shot off, started using his elbows, shoving, I had to shove back. You must stand up then and there or forever be tagged as a candy-ass. "

"Watch your language, young man. And, that's your convenient story, but it's not quite the way I heard it."

"Oh, for kicks, I started swinging at a lunger much bigger than I am?"

Dad used the dashboard plug to light up before saying; "Dave Untermeyer was in to see me about his diabetes, and his prostate. According to Dave, that scuffle stemmed from you betting on eight ball with Sylvan Gans in his pool room."

Fiddlesticks, caught again. I said," Maybe that was a contributing element but the precipitating factor was the shoving. I made him look like an oaf at basketball so he challenges me to eight ball, to prove he's better at something than I am."

"Stop quibbling with me, Paul. I say quibbling because it'd pain me too much to flat out call you a liar. Of course, I could put a stop to this immediately. One call and I get Dave's raided, padlocked for a month, but Dave's is not the problem. You, Paul, sneaking around, are the problem. From other patients I've heard that you also play One Ball at Third and Brown. I don't want to outright forbid you to enter poolrooms,

I've never gone in for strict prohibitions and Diktats with you, it's always been my goal to have you think through matters for yourself. Those two joints are filled with scum, criminals, dregs, the refuse of humanity."

Exactly what makes them interesting. This was easily the twentieth time I'd heard this particular sermon. Pop likes me to think things through for myself, as long as I reach his conclusions. I wondered whether he classifies me as a major or minor disappointment. Most fathers expect, or, at least, hope, that their sons will be better, smarter, stronger, taller than they were. I was none of those things. In his library Dad had that fading photo of himself in his antique basketball uniform, the cast iron look of resolve of the study lad who won't let earning his varsity letters interfere with his getting top grades. A flimsy goof-off like me is his punishment. I am the low-yielding paltry crop of his winter wheat.

As we crossed Broad Street Dad had finished his Shtick about how the choices I make at this point in time could affect my entire development, and he said, "I'm just throwing this out as an idea, nothing is set in concrete yet, but while we were fishing down the shore, Mrs. Barufkin mentioned Valley Forge Military Academy to me as a possible solution to our problems. There are not too many poolrooms up that way."

"No Kidding? Mrs. Barufkin? She is on your advisory board now?"

"Yes, wise-guy. That's where she sent her sons, two to Valley Forge, and one to Bordentown, to get them out of the city, at a far distance from bad influences."

Wha' happened? Her sons did not get along; she had to send them to different schools? I sank lower in my seat. Was this an implied threat, a warning shot across my bow? Shape up, kiddo, get with the program or he'll ship me off to an institution specializing in injecting starch into backbones? Where did a Mrs. Barufkin get off proposing interim or final solutions to my hide? Or was it him? Was I cramping his style too much lately?

When we reached Fairmount Park, instead of entering the woods to use the lot for the Robin Hood Dell Dad parked our Buick behind the small trolley depot near Cherry's. Then he gave me his Shpiel about how it was advisable at stadiums and cultural events to park as far away as feasible, in order to escape the throngs and traffic jams after the event concluded. This seemed sensible but why did he have to make it sound like the Wisdom of the Universe.

I carried the blanket and thermos of lemonade, we joined the crowds streaming down the dirt path to the last concert of the season, a lighter, Boston Poppy kind of affair, fripperies from Operettas, Broadway Show tunes. For a Wagner lover like Dad I suppose this was the equivalent of the Bug Bunny Cartoon festival.

"So how much money did you finally save up this summer," Dad asked.

"Last I counted, one hundred and sixty bucks in the kitty, sir"

"Hey, you're taking me to the cleaners, kid. Well, I promised that I would match whatever sum you saved up, so you'll get your one sixty on Saturday, and we'll head downtown to Wanamaker's to buy your back to school wardrobe. "

"Marshall Street," I suggested." Lots cheaper. Across from the deli there's a close-out sale at Klein's, two suits for fifty bucks."

"I've never been into 'I-can-get-it-for-you-wholesale syndrome Paul. It will be Wanamaker's. I want you looking spiffy at Central, not marked-down discounted, but top of the line. To feel classy you should look classy,."

At times the man makes me flush with shame at my own smallness. Underneath his pedantic, authoritarian, and spikey crust he was good guy, doing the best he could. I was the noodnick, picking at the threads of his minor flaws.

Inside the Dell we spread out the blanket on a grassy hillside. Dad has reserved seats in the auditorium below but for these pop concerts he prefers to remain in the background. If the music becomes too unbearable he can escape with minimal fuss. Apparently Mrs. Barufkin had given him a gift, a new silver cigarette case. I prefer Mrs. Fiore but do not get to vote in his elections. I watched him insert his Chesterfield into the type of holder FDR traditionally wave around. Dad can get away with it, as did Roosevelt. Certain men have enough flair to flaunt stylistic tics that might seem ostentatious in others, but Dad was nonchalantly in character with that holder, like a John the Wizard, in top hat and scarlet cape, a genuinely authentic phony.

Acquaintances were waving to him from the seats below. Dad sighed, and said, "Excuse me, lad, I have to do some quick politicking."

"No problem. Meanwhile, could I have one of your cigarettes, sir?"

"No, you definitely cannot have one of my cigarettes, "He harrumphed, adding a derisive snort. I watched him trudge downhill to shake hands with colleagues and bridge partners. He can smoke, but not me? We are obliged to forgive our parents for their myriad contradictions. The Dell was filling up, the orchestra tuning up, unless that was a new Chinese symphony they were assaying. It was a muggy evening; way too hot for early September, the fireflies and lightning bugs seemed to be dancing in a syncopated ballet with the swarms of mosquitoes.

Many familiar faces down there, I surveyed the audience, faces from the winter concerts at the Academy of Music, from Lew Tendler's deli afterwards, here were the same folks in their summer togs, prisoners of the routines and the seasons.

This was the sixth or seventh year in a row that Dad has dragged me to these clambakes. No matter what the program says what this audience has really come to hear is 'The Blue Bird of Happiness. ' More than a tradition, it is a ritual. It is never listed on the program. Every year when the show concludes, the audience starts stamping their feat, applauding, whistling, chanting, and demanding an encore, begging the beloved couple for their favorite duet.

'And so, remember this, life is no abyss

Somewhere there's a bluebird of happiness.'

Sure, Over the Rainbow, or in my Blue Heaven?

I'm ticketed to be one of these people, begging for the 'Blue Bird of Happiness. Four years before I even graduate high school Dad is already talking up the U. of Penn, where he went, unless I can swing Harvard. I'm Destined to be one more familiar face applauding as the maestro struts onto the stage and taps his baton. Examining the spectators in the seats below and spread out on the hillside blankets I see mothers with daughters, aunts with nieces, spot few fathers exclusively with their sons. Maybe in Montana fathers take their sons out and teach them to hunt, urban life tends to stunt father-son bonds, so we have a unique and rare relationship for this town; we get into each other's hair, like a daughter and Momma might.

The audience was applauding the familiar opening strains of 'The Magic Flute.' Dad had finished with the glad-handing, was saying farewell to his friends below.

Returning, he was detained by another group. These people were not from his Academy of Music set or his bridge partners but the faces of the men were familiar, I'd seen their photos in the newspapers. Catch this action, sports fans, the hoods were effusively were delighted to see him. My crusty self-righteous Dad was shaking hands with none other the notorious Salvatore 'Big Sal' Bonafaccio, and the equally notorious Sam 'the Clipper' Sacco. Their stout, gaudy, and heavily bejeweled wives were kissing Dad on the cheek. Now he was shaking hands with the burly bodyguards posing as music lovers tonight.

Aunt Sara had hinted about seamy stuff, never to be talked about. There were other clues, last time I was in Go-d's bar Gall said that my Dad was respected on the docks because of his discretion. I found it pretty cool; my Old Man seemed to be on howdy-doody terms with top capos of the Mob, in like Flynn, It would be hilarious if my predilection for the wild and stormy side were an inherited trait.

But I guess that goes with the turf, he blithely skates on the dark side while sermonizing at me about the dangers of seedy of pool halls.

Returning, Dad sprawled out on the blanket. I intended asking him if he should not have been coyer, reserved, discreet, about his palsy links to Big Sal and Sam Sacco with so many ritzy-titzy types observing. He put his finger to his lips, prefers no yacking when the music is playing, I go along with his fussy habits. At times I feel like an Errol Flynn is bringing me up. The Rake treats me well, I'm a pet spaniel out in the kennel, he scratches my belly before venturing out to the forays on his yacht.

After the saccharine 'Magic Flute, Dad merely arched his lashes when the next number was a medley of show tunes including a rip-roaring rendition of 'Oklahoma'. For a Wagner buff this had to be more unbearable than Blue Grass banjos banging out, 'You Are My Sunshine.' Dad was being a good sport about this, sacrificing; no doubt he'd prefer to be out with one of his lady friends, or playing poker. We never know what this guy is thinking, When he returned from Cape May I asked him about the pinochle Sundays out in Strawberry Mansion with the Bermans, where he was just one of the boys with his jacket off and his sleeves rolled up. He confessed that those were ordeals he endured for his beloved Leonora. Neither for Cleopatra nor the Queen of Sheba would he again put himself in that bind.

The kind of question you can never ask your father: Am I one more cumbersome obligation? Are these monthly cultural outings with me the current equivalent of the starchy lunches and gin rummy Sundays with the Lower Depths in-laws?

The conductor was gearing up to announce the next number; bleats, whoops, horrendous screeches raspy scratches, and raucous squawks on the loudspeaker system interrupted him. Several thousand music lovers shuddered as the message emerged with loopy noises and static: "Doctor Daniel Burris, would you please report immediately to the administrative offices behind the stage. You have an urgent call concerning a police emergency."

"Oh, shit," Dad muttered, though he rarely curses.

"Another seventh mother?" I asked.

Dad began to rise, and said, "None that I'm aware of. You stay here, and finish the concert, Paul. Grab a bite at Pat's Steak's and then take a taxi home."

He was reaching for his wallet, I quickly gathered up the blanket and thermos, and said, "No problem, sir. I'll go with you."

They had tracked him down again. This was not a new experience for us on these cultural excursions. Once at the Academy of Music and once at the Walnut Theatre Dad had been called out of the audience by his answering service.

The overly familiar lilt of the 'Merry Widow Waltz' serenaded us as we hurried down the slope. Colleagues, friends, complete strangers were nodding to Dad in commiseration. Only doctors were yanked out in the middle of a concert like this. No stage play was ever interrupted with the question: 'Is there a lawyer in the house?'

The group from South Philly waved a wan farewell to Dad, Big Sal moving his chin, expressing his sorrow that a man cannot be left in peace on his night out.

Cool, beyond words. Anybody can know our shithead Mayor, but my Dad is on intimate terms with none other than Big Sal and Sam' the Clipper' Sacco.

I asked friends in South Philly had Sacco got that nickname, 'The Clipper.' They said," You really don't want to know that, Paulie."

A uniformed usher escorted Dad to the offices. I was wondering what the emergency was: a heart attack or severe complications in the delivery of an infant?

Dad was a specialist, often summoned at the last minute, often, when it was too late, when they needed him to cover up for botches, blunders, butchery.

'The Merry Widow Waltz' had concluded, the Dell chorus was singing 'The Donkey Serenade,' the annoying, irritating Hee-Hawing part. Dad was only in the office minutes, it seemed hours, he came out and glanced up at the heavens before saying, "I'm sorry, Paul. That was Officer Mahann on the phone, with bad news; a hold-up at the gas station. Wronsky resisted and was hurt by the fleeing robbers; one shot in the head and two bullets in the chest. Dmitri is in the intensive care unit at the Hahnemann Hospital, and is not expected to make it. The Police asked Karl whom they could or should call. Karl said they should call you. And, me."

We headed for the Buick. As we left the Robin Hood Dell Dad passed me a cigarette. First time ever the man passed me a cigarette. I always look for the symbolic significance in small acts. Like, maybe, welcome to the real world, kid, where this shit happens. This year we would not get to hear the finale: No 'Bluebird of Happiness.'

CHAPTER FIVE

For the funeral I retained residues of my black eye so I was still wearing my dark specs. Dad hates funerals, rarely attends, says he doesn't even plan to attend his own: there is only dank clay in the casket, flesh past its expiration date; his spirit, if it by chance still exists, will be elsewhere, avoiding pious prayers and dreary eulogies. I'd be lying if I said I remembered much about my first funeral. I was only three when Leonora died; vaguely recall they said Mommy had gone off on a long trip. Even back then I knew that was Bull.

Our turnout was larger than might be expected for a third string bench warmer like Dmitri, easily fifty mourners assembled in this graveyard, a smorgasbord of dibs and dabs: Betty, and cooks from the Diner, wharf rats from the Third and Brown poolroom, Ukrainian refugees, buxom Rosey Ivanovich, a smattering of priests and nuns, Karlie's teachers from Saint Pete's, truck drivers from the Spring Garden garages, plus a contingent of the scrounges from Go-d's Bar, Sibronsky, Schatz, Eli,

Dick Jardine, et al. this delegation lead by Gallagher. Gall was in his black turtleneck sweater and dark glasses, chatting with Mahann. Six other police were paying their respects; the cops had used Dmitri's station as a pit stop for the pisser and free coffee. Gall, with his wry, impenetrable style, was telling Mahann that the authorities must do more to crack down on violent street crime. The other cops were nodding in agreement though from their expressions they were asking where the hell did this brazen thug get off lecturing them on street crime?

Theological sectarian undercurrents swirled around us. You didn't have to be Sam Spade to detect the tugs of war going on, peevish disputes over who threw out the first pitch, and which will get the last word in. The Irish priests handled the mass in Saint Augie's, now, here in the cemetery, a Ukrainian priest was delivering a final prayer, at length, at way too great a length, and, in Ukrainian. The crowd was impatient, the Ukrainian prelate seemed to regard their restlessness as a challenge, he could continue on till next Easter. The Irish and Ukrainian clergy were glaring at each other. When I return home I'll check this out in our Encyclopedia Britannica. If I recall correctly, the Ukrainians are called Uniats, classified as Roman Catholic, but with the variation that their priests are allowed to marry

Karl was standing dry-eyed over the coffin. Knocky had his arm draped over his shoulder. Alexi has been back from Atlantic City for three days. First time I've ever seen Knocky in a suit. Shoes, no, but he's wearing his best sneakers, the ones reserved for formal occasions. Also the first time I'd ever seen both Wronskys in suits. Dmitri returns to his maker in a double-breasted blue serge number; Karl is in a tight-at-the-shoulders cardboard horror donated by the Fifth Street Settlement House. If I'd seen Karl's get-up before these rites began I'd have donated from my summer's savings for a decent outfit from Klein's.

Present here are bureaucrats, the battle is over whose clutches Karl falls into, the social workers or the clergy. He whispered to me before the services began they're treating him like a prisoner, the state welfare agency and the two branches of the church fighting over who will handle his living remains, he urgently needs to talk to me.

Karl was glancing at robust Rosey Ivanovich; I wondered if he were entertaining impious thoughts about a certain birthday present he would never receive .I impiously recall Dmitri's bantering with Betty the waitress, the way the Russian dressing spurted from my hoagie and mixed with the grease on his dirty fingers.

This prayer in Ukrainian was really dragging out to unconscionable lengths, mourners were struggling not to yawn, display boredom. Conclusion: funerals are home movies amateur productions where even the extras are obliged to posture, play roles, act contrite, be serious, mournful, and portray grief.

Dad is not in attendance but his presence looms large as here he is picking up the tab for these festivities. Without me asking he was shelling out for the mass, the flowers, candles, hearse, headstone, plot, the whole shebang, including the reception at Slovak Hall, afterwards. Dmitri left a mess behind, no papers, no will, no nothing, There's a padlock on the gas station door, everything else is up in the air, except for Dmitri, they are lowering his casket into the earth.

 When this ordeal was finally over, Betty was crying, being consoled by Rosey Ivanovich, and I lit up a smoke. Other mourners were lighting up so I guess this was now permissible. The tug of war instantly resumed, the Irish clergy, from Saint Pete's, surrounded Karl, hustled him off to the main limo. The Ukrainian priests were waving for Karl to join them in their station wagon. Karl was waving for me to accompany him in the main limo. That invitation was instantly cancelled, the priests guarding Wronsky signaled that there was not enough room for me. None too gently, they adjusted Karl into the back seat.

It looked almost like a kidnapping as they whisked him away.

Another of my illusions shot to shingles. From the movies I expect priests to be benevolent, warm, sympathetic Pat O'Brians, genial Spencer Tracys, twinkling Barry Fitzgeralds, crooning Bing Crosbys, cuddly teddybears. This crew from Saint Pete's was a bunch of sour-pussed Simon Legrees. I thought about huffing, 'hey, who's picking up the bill for this production?' but, that's not my style, and Dad had also given me strict instructions to never toot any horns about financial contributions.

The parking lot was emptying out fast; I was lucky to grab a lift with Saul Gold. Sibronsky, Eli, Schatz, Joe the Worm were already squeezed into Saul's Plymouth, they were still arguing about who murdered Dmitri, was it the Spics, or the Spades. No eyewitnesses to the shooting had come forward but customers who came out of the Diner at the crack of the pistol shots swore that that they had spotted a green Chevy coupe speeding away, the occupants looked dark.

There had been little in the papers about the hold-up or shooting. A grease monkey or storekeeper getting shot in a robbery was practically a natural cause of death in Philly. We were driving toward Randolph Street, between Sixth and Fifth. Slovak Hall was at the corner where Fairmount Avenue cuts Randolph off for the next few blocks. This location meant that Slovak Hall was only forty yards away from the pestiferous stables housing the draft horses that dragged the local junk, milk, ice, coal, and trash wagons. Open the windows in Slovak Hall, you were hit by the stench of straw, hay, and tons of horse manure, followed by the inflow of the flies. On bad days the stink overpowered the fumes coming from the river.

When we reached Slovak hall the atmosphere was stifling, the crowd larger. Slews of mourners who never bothered to make it to the church or the cemetery were here; Knocky was doing back-up duties for Wronsky, standing firmly by his side. I hovered in the background while Karl received condolences from moochers, jackals, and Schnurers who could not make it to the heavier items on the program but did not mind swarming around the buffet tables. Karl kept on signaling me to hold on, he needed to talk to me; he looked frantic, trapped, outflanked. Both the Ukrainian priests and the Irish clerics were keeping him boxed in. The social workers also looked worried that he might try to bolt.

With one of the nuns was tugging at his sleeve Karl finally managed to slip away. Knocky turned to join us, Karl motioned Alexi to hold it up, he had to talk to me, first. While we huddled in a corner behind the bar the clergy eyed me like I might be an accomplice who would help this felon escape. Karl said, "Man, I don't know how to thank you, and your father, for all you've done for me, Paulie. "

"He's not asking for any thanks. He doesn't worry about such stuff."

"I need more help, man. I'm going fucking ape. They've got my ass in a hairy sling, pulling at me from three directions. "

"What they doing to you?"

"Hitting me with weird shit from every angle. The Ukrainian priests want to take charge of me, say they have religious families wanting to adopt me. I want nothing to do with that. Dmitri didn't even know the word but he was an atheist. The Irish from Saint Pete's want to handle me, tell me they have several fine orphanages I could be sent to. Father Mallory was talking about a seminary, me taking vows. He said a bright young lad like me could have a promising future in the priesthood. "

"Holy Mother of God," I said. I don't know where that came from, as I've never exclaimed anything similar in my life.

"Right. I've got no affinity, no vocation, for the priesthood. But they're pressuring me. I'm ready to crack up, man. There's no way I'll spend the rest of my life passing out wafers and jerking off behind the rectory."

"They can't force you," I said. "They can't ram religion down your throat"

"What I thought, but the alternatives might be even worse. I told the staff psychologists in the Child Welfare Agency that I didn't want to be assigned to any churchy institution. Sure, I'm a good, faithful Catholic, but, please, no orphanages, Guess what their solution was. They said I'm a ward of the court but not a real orphan. They said that by shipping me to Russia I can be with my proper birth parents and that could legally resolve my case."

"Russia? Are they nuts? Haven't they heard there's a Cold War going on?"

"I flipped out, but they said I'd get over it. And, I don't know what the hell they are. Maybe they're Martians. I'd suck on a gas pipe before I ever let them send me to Russia, Paulie."

"You're a hot prospect, valuable property. Everybody wants to latch onto you."

"This ain't funny, man. I'm fucking desperate, ready to slit my wrists."

"What do you want me to do?"

"Think of something, Paulie. I don't have any place else to turn. These adults, these fucking so-called adults scare me."

Two nuns came over to drag Karl away. Who was going to argue with these ladies? I faded back to my corner. More mourners who had not bothered to reach the cemetery were dropping in to express their sentiments and partake of the pirogies, sausages, blood sausages, cheese dumplings and fried pork schnitzels. Dad was paying for an awful lot of pork tonight. Total strangers were entering to scarf down the freebies, and sip the slivovitz plum brandies, wines, and Pilsner chasers. There was no guest list and they were not checking reservations at the door. I heard complaints about the lack of music. Wharf rats from the Third and Brown poolroom were telling not particularly funny anecdotes about Dmitri's mistakes and foot in the mouth errors. Scrounges from Go-d's bar were reminiscing about what a zany, goofy character Dmitri had been. The social workers were rolling their eyes in disapproval of the amount of alcohol being consumed at this rowdy Wake, also the vile language they were hearing. Time to say Shazam and get the hell out of here. I gave the thumb's-up sign to Knocky, pledging that I would talk to him later, another thumb's up sign for Karl, vowing that I would do something. He responded to my wave with opened palms, a pleading gesture. The priests around him did not seem overly distressed by my departure.

I waited till I was outside on Fairmount Avenue to scratch my nuts, expel a huge sigh of relief, snort, shake myself, and then formulated my headline:

SOUSED SCUM STAIN SACRED SACREMENT
(Inebriated mourners decry lack of music)

There was an ice cream parlor at the corner of Sixth; strangely enough, in all the years I'd lived around here, I'd never entered this place. Further up the block was the Hebrew Day Nursery where they had Victory Gardens during the War; now the gardens were overgrown with weeds and scraggly Sunflower plants. Next came the factory, a metal machine grinding plant with the sign: NUTS, BOLTS, and SCREWS. We always made jokes about this sign. On certain days, like today, no joke is funny. That wake was a downer; I'd never been a great admirer of Dmitri Wronsky, mostly remembered Dim pouting like a mutt who had his bone snatched away when they snapped off the Fifi film, but I was still irritated by the jokey crap about him in Slovak Hall. And I'm hardly an arbiter of good taste.

When I reached home Dad was alone at the dinner table, austere, haughty, solitary. When he sits alone at the long table, he looks like a King in exile who has lost his Kingdom. Miss Pearl asked whether I'd be having dinner. I touched my gut and said," No thanks, ma'am, I ate too many kielbasas at the wake. An Alka Seltzer is about all I can handle."

Dad was awaiting my report. I skipped the part about the wake becoming coarse and sloppy, and said, "The funeral was nice. If funerals can be called *'nice.'"*

"'Nice' is important, Paul. That's about all most people can aspire to. How is Karl taking it? He didn't resent me not showing up at the church or the cemetery?"

"No, sir. Karl is deeply appreciative of all you've done for him. Otherwise, he's taking things horribly. I can't blame him, they're torturing the poor fucking guy."

Dad winced. Surprisingly, he did not order me to watch my language, but said, "What's the problem?"

Miss Pearl served my Alka Seltzer, returned to the kitchen, her ears cocked. She picks up on all that's happening,, later is generous with unsolicited commentaries.

After my belch Dad grimaced as I explained, "Karl didn't have time to furnish me with the nitty-gritty details but apparently he's being drawn and quartered in a three way tug of war for control and possession of his body and soul. Governmental authorities are talking about shipping him to Russia, back to his so-called birth parents. Two branches of the church want to gather him to their bosom, whether he wants to be harvested there, or not. Karl is in agony, rejecting all these options. "

Dad lit up a smoke, then went through a series of facial contortions that almost reminded me of Dmitri when he was puzzling through problems, but Dad is quick on the uptake. After a sniff he said, "You're prodding me. Paul. What, exactly, would you propose I do?"

"You are versatile and resourceful, sir, when you choose to be so."

After scrunching his lips, Dad said," I could get him into Girard College."

That would be an elegant solution. If an orphanage could be called de luxe, Girard College was de luxe, almost equivalent to attending Phillips Exeter Academy. At least it would keep Karl in town, far from the humbling fare of a seminary, and further from the steppes of Russia.

"I thought there's supposed to be a long waiting list for Girard College, " I said.

"I can get him into Girard College," Dad assured me.

No doubt he could. I had an idea in mind but in dealing with my father I had learned not to volunteer proposals, to let him offer lists of possibilities; humbly suggest the one I wanted. Great ideas must originate with him. We'd been studying each other for a long time. Playing chess, he wears a poker face but a telltale glint flickers in his eyes when a vicious gambit occurs to him. He was particularly dangerous when he seemed to have blundered, sacrificed a major piece.

He had also been studying me for a long time. After the silence he said, "Girard College won't do it for you? What, exactly, do you want from my life? What, specific, remedy, do you require for Karlie's maladies?"

"I'll leave that up to you, sir. I have complete faith in you, sir."

Dad cracked his knuckle before looking over at me, and saying, "Wise guy."

When Dad came up with the solution I was hoping for I naturally had to ask myself-what's in it for him? Bingo! For many years Dad has been deploying *the Boy* as a foil and a barricade to ward off the ladies stalking him. Another 'son' on the premises would be useful in fending off the widows and divorcees avid to dance 'la Cumparsita' with Doctor Dan, especially if they had his ring on their finger.

Of course I could not mention my deduction to him, aloud. According to the official records a decent man went beyond the call of duty in a stressful situation. Decency doesn't do jack unless you have power, Dad had enough power to put calls through to the state government drones in Harrisburg, and hacks in City Hall. He tapped his main source of power, the wives of prominent businessmen in South Philly. Fronts were used, it was never clear who arranged the audience, Dad had a meeting in the Archbishop's chambers where he assured his holiness and his advisors that Karl Wronsky would attend Roman Catholic High, be spiritually guided by the Church with respect to masses and confessions. Eventually Karl would attend an institution of higher learning such as La Salle, Saint Joseph's, Villanova, Loyola, or Georgetown. Dad also used this occasion to pledge a one thousand dollar contribution to Catholic Charities Settlement House on Fifth Street. The prelates dropped objections to Doctor Daniel Burris being appointed the legal guardian of Karl Timoshenko Wronsky.

(Later on, when I heard about how much he promised. I asked Dad if he had not also taken a vow to only have fish served in our house on Fridays?)

There was still red tape to be cut, papers to be signed, but two days later Karl moved in with us. Miss Pearl was delighted. Since she now had more clothes to wash, an extra mouth to feed, Dad increased her salary by ten dollars a week. She was already the best paid domestic employee in the area, making as much as a skilled craftsman down at the Navy Yard, so she was happy, chattered away about how now that there were two boys to be raised Dad might stop his rutting around and bring a definitive woman into the house, it was about time.

Miss Pearl indicated that other parties were less enthralled. Karl was upstairs, Miss Pear washing the dishes, she said, "I hate it when that Mrs. Jordan woman sits down to have lunch with me. Like, she's doing me a big favor, showing me how sociable, tolerant, and democratic she is. She ruins my digestion making her catty noises about your friend moving in with us."

"Another country heard from?" I said. "Where the hell does she get off making comments about that?"

"She doesn't cotton to Karlie. Says she sees no sense to him being here."

"She doesn't have any right to stick her two cents in," I said. " She's in the office, has nothing to do with him, it's no sweat off her keister."

Miss Pearl frowned at my language, then said, "It's something else going on, Paul. That woman, believe it or not, has ambitions. Outlandish ambitions. "

"Ambitions to what, pray tell?"

"You're so smart and you don't see it, Mister Snoopy-pants? She's been eyeing your Daddy for a spell now. He pays her no mind but she has her cold, fishy eyes on him. When he gets a call from his lady friends her eyes become cold chips of ice."

"Mrs. Jordan?"

"Learn something, boy. Just because a woman is mean, skinny, nasty, and ugly, don't mean she can't have ambitions."

Mrs. Jordan? I shuddered at the notion of Mrs. Jordan rising to the second floor, taking over around here. Carla Fiore from South Philly, okay. Mrs. Barufkin also acceptable. Dad took me out to dinner with her and she had displayed a crisp, no-

nonsense attitude, neither pinching my cheek nor kissing my butt. Mrs. Jordan? That would be like bringing the Wicked Witch of the West into our castle.

The Saturday before classes started Dad sent me downtown to help buy clothes for Karl. He had shown up at our house carrying one baseball bat and one dinky cardboard suitcase containing his knickers and polo shirts. Dad examined those threadbare, sand boxy items, and ordained a total revamping of Wronsky's image. He could not accompany us, had to attend a medical conference that day, besides, he hates shopping. I'd never seen him buy any physical object except for classical records and books. Pop gave us exactly three hundred and twenty dollars to splurge on the new back to school wardrobe for Wronsky.

I appreciated the symbolic significance of the sum: my summer savings plus the matching amount he had put up for my togs. Dad was sending a clear message: we are to be treated equally as sons. I blotted away squalid thoughts about how I had worked for my one-sixty. Besides, Moe often let me leave early, and Aunt Sara slipped me unearned fivers, so be it, we are brothers.

Knocky was tagging along, telling us about his adventures down the shore. When we reached the corner of Sixth and Spring Garden the Sixty-Five trolley rumbled by, the bank was to our right, the 'I'd Walk a Mile for a Camel' sign was to our left, the gas station shuttered. In so short a time it had deteriorated, decayed, was defaced by graffiti of cocks and tits and valentines. Karl paused for a second to take the station in. I thought tears might come to his eyes. Nope. He shrugged and shook himself vigorously, like a mutt might after a hard scrubbing in a washtub. Dad's lawyer, Darmopray, was handling financial matters. Aside from the three thousand dollars that Dmitri had salted away in a rusty rural mailbox buried in back, the station will be sold, proceeds entering a trust fund.

A block down from Spring Garden is Buttonwood Street, Sam Auer's grocery on the north-east corner, across from Auer's a bizarre store, Miss Leah's luncheonette, selling not only canned foods but ceramics, art works, antiques, a mishmash of banal and esoteric items jumbled together in the front window, trays of candied apples mixing with ceramic statuettes of Blue Boys, bottles of Orange Crush next to models of Spanish galleons, Courier and Ives prints, Tootsie Rolls. On the southeast corner is the Paxton elementary school, a regular school; James Madison is the *special school* for our district, *special* meaning for retards and delinquents. Facing Paxton was an eyesore, a four-story monstrosity candidate for most ugly building in town where they had smeared a whitewash of dirty gray cement over the surface, the cement now crumbling, and red bricks peeking through the cracks. It looked like a primitive drawing by a not too talented child. Capping off the ugliness was the black, rusting fire escape out front.

Three stout colored ladies on the front steps were passing around a brown bag holding a mason jar of the Moonshine they cooked on these premises. The rusting waterspout was a part of the still. Saturdays, after the bars shut at midnight, this was a gathering place for desperate drinkers needing their White Lightning.

One lady gave Knocky an evil wink, seemed to be offering him a slurp from their jug, Knocky waved her off but the wink inspired Karl to ask, "So how many times did you score down the shore, Ace? And I 'm not talking about hook shots."

Alexi shrugged, said, "Three, but lots of almosts."

After a grunt of admiration laced with envy Karl said, "What's an almost?"

Knocky shrugged again, said, " I musta' gone under the Boardwalk with twenty chicks this summer, most were cock teasers. We'd neck away, they'd get me all hot and bothered, then, at the last minute, they'd give me that 'No, no, I've never done it before,' routine. You know how girls are."

"Actually, I don't know how girls are," Karl confessed." How are they, Ratcho?"

Positive vibes here; Knocky was back with more spring and zip in his gait. Karl was breaking out of his shell of grief, coming out with funny lines again. We were heading through Rubenville, slummy tenements, theoretically dangerous territory, but folks around here never messed with us, they had seen us passing through since we were tykes, At Ruben's bar, Marshall and Noble, "Stagger Lee ' was playing on the jukebox, hep cats were grooving outside to the beat. Knocky gave my shoulder a light punch, and said, "How about yourself, Doc Burris? Playing your cards close to your chest? So far you aint said jack-two about nothing."

"What's to say? You heard of the 'Lost Weekend?' This was the 'Lost Summer.' Drearyville. I learned how to make cole slaw."

"That sure aint the way I heard it," Knocky scoffed. "From what I heard you banged my cousin Rita. Down by the Riverside."

"You sure didn't hear that from me," I said, defensively.

" Ah, you're such a fucking gentleman, Paulie. Rita told me. She said she likes you a lot but you stiffed her on the malted milk shake you promised her, at Gansky's. You welshed on your promise. "

Not an accurate description, not the way it was, but if you have to give explanations, explanations don't help. Instead of trying, I said," I hope you don't mind too much, man."

Alexi sniffed." Ech, it aint like you were exactly the first."

"Woha," Karl, said, and whistled. "This is sensational news. Attention, Mister and Mrs. America, and all the ships at sea! This just in! Bhudda-Bhudda Little Doc Burris got laid, and doesn't even spill the beans to his best friend. How come, you bastard?"

What, to answer? How did I get laid when we were standing up? That I had no bragging rights? A wall-job up the alley with Rita was not exactly a weekend in Palm Springs with Hedy Lamar. But why knock Knocky's family when their neighbors on Randolph Street already handled that assignment with gusto. I said, " Rita is a very sweet girl. I didn't want to compromise her reputation."

Both of them started throwing punches at me for that comeback. We were acting goofy, giddy, from the camaraderie; the gang is reunited, the Dalton Brothers Ride Again. Then, big surprise, we reached Callowhill Street, Knocky generally tries to cut over to Ninth about now, to avoid chance meetings with his father staggering out of a saloon. Today he straightened his shoulders, determined to face down that threat. We continued up Eighth Street into the Tenderloin. The Winos and Hobos were out in full force this afternoon, arguing, mumbling to themselves, According to Dad many of these derelicts were once solid citizens, for reasons X they slid down the tube. The merchandise on sale in the hockshops matched the shabby figures on the sidewalks, Second and third hand guitars dangled like broken dreams in the pawnshop windows. The red velvet cases of dully glinting hocked engagement and wedding rings were chintzy cemeteries of crushed hopes. I was keeping my hand in my pocket, protecting our cash, though skid row is weirdly safe. These drunks and vagrants torture, torment, and bully each other, hardly ever mess with civilians drifting through. Today the bums were calling to us, "Hi, Billy. Hi, Jimmy. Could you sport an old cowhand to a little taste?"

Knocky was wearing the resolute expression of a Captain Hornblower at the forepeak of his frigate, as if daring his father to make an appearance. Karl noted that, nodded to me, acknowledging that this was no simple stroll for Alexi. Past the used bookstore was the geeky shop selling the plastic artificial limbs and yellow surgical girdles, next came the Gypsy Fortune teller den with sheets hanging in the windows. Three swarthy temptresses were sitting on soda crates out front; one of the Gypsy sirens blew a sarcastic kiss to Alexi. He ignored her. Karl responded for him, blowing a smooch to the Gypsy, she waved him off, assuring him that he didn't count.

An emotional hurdles test or obstacle course, when we crossed Arch Street Knocky let out his whoosh of relief. No more tap rooms, hockshops, missions, or flop houses. He had made it through this minefield unscathed. We turned onto Market Street, and were passing Strawbridge's when Karl said to me, "Y'know, Paulie, why does it have to be Wanamaker's? We could shop a lot cheaper down on South Street. And cheaper still if we head back to Marshall Street, "

"I used the same argument on my old man ten days ago but he shot me down, said he wants me looking spiffy when I enter Central, and he will be checking the labels on all garments because he wants you looking sharp and presentable for your teachers at Roman on Monday. Otherwise, he'll get a call from the Archbishop."

"Okay, " Karl said, " I made the offer because even when I get spruced up I look round rather than sharp. I'm no Beau Brummel, look more like Sydney Greenstreet. "

"Try slimming down a bit, " I suggested, " and you can shoot for the Peter Lorre roles. 'Rick! Rick! I need those papers!' "

Alexi was suddenly looking glum, concerned. Out of nowhere, his head was twisting around loosely on his neck; he seemed to be blinking away tears. What the hell was his problem? I thought he was fine after making it through that gantlet of winos on skid row. Or maybe he had spotted his father in one of those tap rooms?

"Ho! Whatsa' matter, man? " Karl asked.

Knocky said, "Ah, I had an argument about you guys this morning, Argument with my family. It's left me sick to the stomach."

For certain matters I prefer the philosophy of the old country song, 'I wonder, I wonder, I wonder, but really don't want to know.' I said, " I rarely argue on Saturday mornings. I reserve that time for meditation."

On a need to know basis, do we need to know the details?" Karl asked.

"Ech," Knocky grunted. "My Aunt Svetla was over the house. Had a bad hangover from a late date, a small bruise under her eye; some sonofabitch hit her. She was really tanked; my Mom was serving her lots of hot, black coffee. Then my Uncle Ivan showed up with his Wanda. He wasn't totally sloshed but he wasn't too steady either. I told them how I was heading downtown with you guys today to buy clothes for Karl, how great it was, what with the rotten shit that happened to Dmitri, how neat it was, what Doc Burris was doing. I hate to tell you this, Paulie, but Svetla started bad-mouthing your father, really pissing me off. I told her to shut her trap, I didn't want to hear that shit. Ivan ordered me to apologize, almost slugged me one, the first time my Uncle ever threatened to bop me one."

"The Bells of Saint Mary were not ringing in la casa Ratchinov, "Karl said.

I glanced up at the PSFS skyscraper, wondered what goods Trixie Malloy might have on my Pop. Physicians get accused of supplying drugs to addicts, doing illegal abortions, ordering unnecessary operations, over-charging, fondling their female patients, but most folks around Girard Avenue believed that Doctor Dan walked on water. There were also dissenters, detractors, envious of his Gelt, gossiping about his gambling, his overly active social life, but that was a miniscule minority.

"If it aint revealing family or state secrets, what specific gripes did your Aunt Svetla have?" I asked Alexi.

"Ah, it was so much crap. She was saying your father's no saint. She has it from other broads at the Troc that your father's in tight with the South Philly Bambinos, their favorite Jew, their go-to guy, the trusty sawbones when hoods need patching up, and can't go to a hospital or public clinic. "

I kept a straight face while wincing inwardly. This we had already surmised but filed the insight away as toxic, incriminating, and classified.

Knocky said, "I held my hands over my ears, told Svetla I didn't want to hear any more of these lies but she continued shooting her mouth off. Ivan swings around, you know how drunks are, first they say one thing, then the complete opposite. Ivan got angry at her, threatened to smack her, too, Ivan saying it was not too smart to talk about South Philly bosses, that could get her big ass in big trouble. Ivan said that you're old man plays both sides of the street, does cover-up jobs for the cops, too, and he acts too high and mighty, but it was not wise to mess with your father precisely because he is the Mob's favorite Jew, so Svetla better shut the fuck up because with her big mouth she could get our whole family in trouble. You know how it is when drunks argue: they jump around, from one minute to the next they switch sides."

"Sounds like a heart-warming scene of family bliss, "Karl said. "Blondie and Dagwood enjoying their Saturday morning jelly donuts and Postum."

Their favorite Jew, was this an honor? Sounded medieval, when the King had his chosen Jews under his special protection; those were the ones the King borrowed money from. Alexi had given me lots to digest, though nothing that I did not already know: Sara's hints, pats on the back the night Spinelli was shot, the way 'Big Sal' and Sam Sacco greeted Dad at the Dell, put them all altogether, they did not spell 'mother.' I wondered if John the Wizard were aware of what Dad said about him and his black hearse. The one truly positive note I heard here, Knocky defended us, even at the risk of getting slugged by his Uncle Ivan. The girls, the girls, they are lovely and sweet, but they come and they go, your buddies are your buddies forever.

No need to thank Knocky for standing up for us, with friends no thanks is required. We were passing by the Reading Terminal; Karl said to Knocky, "Apart from those deplorable incidents, Mrs. Lincoln, you're looking okay Ratcho-man, picked up a cocky stride down the shore. You used to flop around like a Raggedy Ann Doll, now you're strutting like a bantam rooster; that from all those sessions under the Boardwalk? "

"It's a front." Knocky said. "Yeah, I'm all jazzed up but underneath it all I'm scared shitless thinking of school on Monday. At Kearny I got by, they gave me B's just for not picking cozies out of my nose and flicking them at the teachers, but I don't know if I can hack it at Central."

"Well, my wayward son," Karl intoned, sounding like an orotund bishop, " it would behoove you from time to time to occasionally crack open a book. Otherwise, how will you be able to read your rave reviews on the sports pages?"

"Ah, I read," Knocky huffed. "It's just when it comes to homework, my mind wanders. Maybe you can help me, Paulie. To get some discipline."

"Discipline?" Karl scoffed." Asking Paulie to help you on the discipline front is like asking Chick Gallagher for a cup of the warm milk of human kindness."

Noon chimes were ringing in City Hall. We crossed Market at Thirteenth Street, and surveyed the stock in Wanamaker's windows, were appalled by the new-fangled concoctions in pink and purple tints. By our lights dress shirts were supposed to be white, for fancy occasions, white on white; these new color schemes, pink, purple, yellow, looked Tooty-Fruity to us. Karl's eyes were glazing at the price tags, he again suggested South Street, or returning to Marshall. While we were debating economics three distinguished ladies were staring at us, or, more specifically, at Alexi. The women were by the window displaying the fall sale on furs, elegant aristocratic matrons, the kind seen in art galleries, the lobby of the Academy of Music, the flower shows, coming out of the bridal showers in the Bellevue-Stratford. Behind cupped hands, they were discussing Alexi.

Nothing unusual about this, on the way down here the stout colored woman at Sixth and Buttonwood winked at him, the hawk nosed Gypsy Fortune teller had blown him a kiss on Eighth Street. Knocky glides through gantlets of admirers, like the troops ogle his Momma.

Out of nowhere, the slimmest of the demure ladies, she must have been forty, with still a good figure, but silvery hair, suddenly rushed over and grabbed Alexi around the head. She planted a hard kiss on his mouth, and then shoved him away, spluttering, "I'm sorry, I'm sorry."

The woman hurried back to her shocked friends, the three of them scurried off toward City Hall, ignoring the swerving traffic and red lights. They were laughing, three mature women giggling like naughty juvenile delinquents who had just pulled off a nifty prank. Shoppers coming out of Wanamaker's were gaping; nobody in Philadelphia had ever seen anything quite this shocking before.

Knocky was shaking his skull as if he had been conked up an alley. I crossed my arms over my chest and formulated my headline:

DOWAGER ACCOSTS HAPLESS PRINCE CHARMING

Karl said, "Why worry about Central and studying, Ratchinovsky, Your bright future is already cut out for you. You can always end up as a high-priced gigolo.

CHAPTER SIX

All-Boys Central High perched on a grassy hill in leafy West Oak lane, sixty blocks north of City Hall. Smart girls attended our Sister School, Girl's High, still downtown at Seventeenth and Spring Garden. The location struck me as peculiar. Why should Central High be miles north of North-East High? Something was askew in our city. Central had an open enrollment policy, meaning closed enrollment in practice. This was a magnet school syphoning off the male 'brains' from the entire city. Many of the chosen few endured long subway and trolley rides to reach this grail. Central granted a 'Bachelor of Arts' degree rather than a mere 'diploma.' A few brains might remain in provincial lock-ups like Olney or West Philly High, but gathered here were the little Lord Fauntleroys who won the gold stars for the cleanest fingernails in Kindergarten, the teacher's pets, prissy finks elected class president, whiz kids who finished the math problems first, sycophants, apple polishers, ass kissers, brown nosers, and also a goodly contingent of regular guys who just happened to be damn smart.

In incubation were the lads pre-destined to be employers, lawyers, C.P.A's, cardiologists, dentists, city councilmen, and Liberal Judges in their larval state. The renowned Faculty included dedicated pedagogues, excellent teachers, also four blithering fools, three bumbling Fuddy-duddies, and two doddering bats in the belfry candidates for the funny farm.

Colored at Central were the groomed and manicured children of civil servants, preachers, teachers, and funeral home operators. They carried expensive brief cases and tended to have better manners, be more polite, and dress better than us Whiteys. You could almost stamp them Kosher.

Our Gentiles came from genteel, pedigreed families without the bread to send them to proper private schools like Friend's Select, the George School, or the Episcopal Academy. Christians wandered lonely around deserted halls on Yom Kippur. I'm not sure what exact percent of the student body were Jews but surveying the faces in the assembly hall one might ask why the school song was 'The Crimson and the Gold: ' lets others sing of college days their Alma Mater true.' When our anthem could just as easily have been ' Hatikvah' or 'Hava Nagila.'

Central monopolized the Mayoral Scholarships. Our chess, science, and debating teams reigned supreme. The Ivy League courted our top graduates. Central was the elite public high school, often compared to Boston Latin Grammar, Bronx School of Science, and New Trier Township outside Chicago. Our professors took care to remind us that it was a privilege to attend Central. There was no need for that. We were well aware of our elevated status.

Neither Knocky nor I belonged at Central. This soon became apparent. Teachers shuddered when they returned his exams to him; instead of a failing 'F' they gave him 'K's, and Z's. Me, from the get-go I was in trouble in this Citadel of Sobriety. The teachers classified me as a criminally inclined ringer, and in less than a month I established my rep as the Class Wisenheimer. I regarded my fellow students as squares: they regarded me as the Repulsive Beast from the Outer Marshes.

Doctor Farber was the Vice-Principal in charge of Discipline. I was making frequent visits to his office, usually for my sarcastic ripostes, but had avoided major clashes until the try-outs for the freshman basketball team. Sixty two candidates in the gym, we had five minutes on the floor to strut our stuff. Absurdly enough, there were doubts about Knocky making the cut. Articles had appeared in the Daily News and Evening Bulletin about Alexi Ratchinov, a prodigy already getting his minutes off the bench on a semi-pro team, and destined for stardom in the Public League. In the Inquirer sports pages the columnist gushed that this kid was something else, a razzle-dazzle ball-handler who could be a starter on the college level.

Mister Schneyer (so called as to avoid lawsuits by his descendants), coached the freshman team, also coached of the Varsity Football team. Schneyer preferred to reserve slots on the basketball team for his future rugged football players. Schneyer was a hot- tempered bantam rooster, much given to huffing; he had huffed that he alone, and not any damn newspapers, would pick and choose who would be on his teams. There was certainly no spot for anybody who played outside ball, and we all knew who that meant. At Central they taught us to say 'whom' but I am still from Sixth and Girard.

Alexi was nervous when he first went out there, missed his first two shots, then he clicked into his groove, began slipping bounce passes through the opened legs of befuddled defenders, snatching rebounds from lunks a foot taller, dribbling circles around the bug-eyed stiffs trying to guard him. He nailed two hook shots and was zipping around at the top of his form, a Nijinsky sharing center stage with a pack of spastic slew foots.

No Huzzahs! No Oles! Even after that superlative showing Coach Schneyer pulled a theatrical number on Alexi. He gave the whole batch a dismissive wave; they could all proceed to the showers. Onlookers were wincing in amazement. Knocky was slinking off with drooping shoulders, crushed, unable to look our way. At the last second, as if it were an afterthought, a kind change of heart, Schneyer motioned to him to stick around for a while, kid, maybe for another look-see.

Disillusioning to observe so-called adults playing shitty little mind games with adolescents. Knocky gave me the thumbs up sign as I trotted out with the next batch. Of course he'd never say it but Dad would be disappointed if I failed to make the cut. He starred for Central back in the hoary days of the two-handed set shot, back when basketball was a Jewish game, the guards bossy little field generals directing traffic, a center big at six feet. Dad had been a towering center, the rugged rebounder.

Shirts on versus shirts off, a minute into the scrimmage I noted that Schneyer and his assistant coaches were paying no attention to our efforts. We were clowns, playing our hearts out, while they were chatting among themselves, glancing at crap on their tote boards. As far as they were concerned we could have been cornholing the Queen of Rumania out here. I was grabbing rebounds, blocked two shots, threw a long pass for an assist, made a steal Speedy Gonzalez would have been proud of; from the field I was two for three with left hand stabs.

Not exactly Joe Fulks on a hot night, nor would it get me a starting spot on the SPHAS, but this was a respectable showing. When Schneyer blew his whistle Knocky gave me the nod, assuring me that I would be told to hang around for another screening. Coach Schneyer pointed at two lunks from the football squad, big beefy weiners who couldn't pop a tennis ball into a bushel basket. These two bozos should stick around; the rest of us can hit the showers. Knocky was not the only spectator shaking his head at the gross unfairness.

MASSIVE DEMONSTRATIONS PROTEST RIGGED TRY-OUTS

Today a Star would not be born. I headed toward the exit, merely scrunched my lips, to hide any disappointment, anger, contempt I might be feeling. Apparently I failed in that attempt. As I passed the coaching staff, Schneyer snarled," Wipe that expression off your face, Burris."

"Which expression is that, sir? I thought I was hitting you with a blank."

" Just wipe that snotty sneer off your face, and don't you dare to ever look at me that way again," Schneyer huffed.

"Jawohl! Ubergrupenfuhrer!"

Though my Deutsch is lousy, I answered in German; a great language for growling, My German instructor, after hearing me read one paragraph of Goethe with my Marshall Street accent was ready to punch my ticket for the next boxcar to Poland. Schneyer's eyes were ablaze; think Lon Chaney's in 'The Wolfman' when there's a full Moon. Schneyer groaned, "Was that German, Burris?"

This schmuck doesn't go to war movies? The first words we learned in German were 'Mach Schnell, Schwein!' That was for when they march the prisoners off.

I said." Just the German equivalent of 'yes, boss, sir. "

"All right, Burris. To the office. Straight to the office. I've put up with all I can. I've just about had it with you."

"Could I please shower and dress first, sir? I don't want the old biddy secretaries in the office to get overly excited at the sight of me in my gym shorts."

A Totalitarian cracking up is not a pretty spectacle to behold. His face dissolved into a minor maelstrom of tics and twitches, the man going ape over a little backtalk. There was oohing from onlookers, consternation in the gym as he crouched to lunge at me. I see things in terms of movie scenes: Schneyer looked like a Himmler being informed by the Swiss Red Cross that he must send Matzohs to Buchenwald for the Passover services. If his two assistants had not grabbed his shoulders, intervened, teacher would have slugged me one.

Schneyer and his assistants rousted me over to the office as if they intended to dunk me into a solitary confinement cell in Sing-Sing. Schneyer assured me that I was a disgrace to the hallowed traditions of Central. When they shoved me into the Vice-Principal's office. Doctor Farber looked up and said, "You, again?"

Over dinner that evening Dad kicked off our confrontation with his bleak silence treatment. He'd been grouchy lately, anyway: Mrs. Maxine Barufkin had broken off their relationship; him bringing Karl aboard the ship had been about the last straw for the zaftig Mrs. Barufkin. Even long-suffering Mrs. Fiore was kicking at the traces.

Karl was looking contrite, slouching low in his chair, wearing a wary expression, I know not why, I was the felon in Dutch, In the kitchen Miss Pearl had her ears cocked for the scheduled fireworks, she is always attuned to the clues. Dad was concentrating on spreading the chopped liver and minced scallions uniformly over the saltines. He is a meticulous spreader; each dabbed cracker must receive exactly the same size shmear.

It was not until the split pea soup was served that he turned to me and said, "Suspended from Central? Not to be readmitted until I come in to vouch for a total modification in your behavior? Do you realize how embarrassing this was for me?"

A series of rhetorical questions loaded with dropped axioms.

"I'm trying to measure it but probably can't grasp the full dimensions, sir."

"Don't cap this off by wising off at me, wise guy. I was obliged to get on the phone, whine and wheedle. The truth is, I do have patients coming in every hour of the day for the entire week, not a minute free till next Thursday, but do you think I enjoyed pleading, beating my breast, making other calls to get you re-instated. Doctor Farber said that not in his twenty years at Central had he ever heard a student dare tell a teacher to 'go fuck himself.'"

"Sir, that part of it is a total lie. A fabrication. When Schneyer exaggerated the extent of my misbehavior in the gym, I told him to 'screw off.' "

"Nevertheless, that's not the kind of language Doctor Farber is accustomed to hearing at Central," Dad said.

"Tell him to spend his Sabbatical at Franklin. He'll hear lots worse than that, "

Karl almost chuckled. At Ben Franklin High *mother* was usually only half a word. Karl saw Dad stiffen; decided it was unwise to laugh.

"And you're still not repentant," Dad said. " I had to touch levers I hate to use to get your punishment reduced to after-school detentions for the next two months, but you come off as the offended party. You did not make the cut? So what? Fifty other boys did not make the cut, none of them mouthed off like you did."

"Sir, the whole drill was an unfair, rigged, locked-in snow job. Why bother to have try-outs if they already know who's anointed? It was phony theatre, a put-on, unfair from the starting gate."

Dad opened his palms and asked, "Whoever said life is fair? Was it fair for Dmitri to be shot by lice trying to make off with a lousy fifty bucks? Get used to dealing with unfairness, entering situations where the fix is in and the winner pre-selected. Nature is not fair. Certain children are born beautiful, others, deformed hunchbacks with harelips. Society is not fair. Where is the justice in one infant being born in a luxurious mansion in Chestnut hill, another into a cramped Father, Son, and Holy Ghost rattrap down on Oriana Street? The unfairness starts before I ever slap the baby's ass, and hear their first wails."

Dad noted that Miss Pearl was listening, he paused, forcing her pretend she had tasks to perform, go to the pantry, then he said, "What bothers me most is not the vulgarity or the grossness of what you did. What annoys me is the stupidity. With nothing to gain, you displayed impotent rage. Not too clever of you. I want you to be smart, kid; you, too, Karl. No theatrics. No blow-ups. Pick how and when to vent your anger. Only morons reveal what they are truly thinking and feeling. You only do what you can get away with. And your main duty is to not get caught at it. "

Not exactly Polonius advising: 'To thine own self be true.' Pop had given me much to think about while I sat stewing every afternoon in the detention class. An hour of confinement after school does not constitute a sentence to twenty years of hard labor on Devil's Island, to me the injustice was of the same magnitude. Then, the Law of Unintended Consequences kicked in. I'm an egomaniac imagining myself to be a whiz that never needs to study; this incarceration guaranteed that I devote at least one hour a day to homework; Schneyer and Doctor Farber had done me a favor. It would gall the bastards to know that.

Returning home, instead of the subway, I usually took the 65 at the Olney depot. The trolley trips were slow, endless, like draggy novels where you want to scan ahead to see if there are worthwhile action scenes or sexy parts later, but I killed the time by analyzing Philly's socio-geological strata. Every ten stops the urban texture changed tones like the concentric rings in the trunks of ancient trees. Hidden behind prosaic facades were ethnic enclaves and tight-knit duchies. First the 65 clanged down Old York Road, through sedate Logan, white semi-detached houses with small lawns, white porches, white occupants, generally Jews. By Allegheny Avenue the houses were brownish and shingled with gray stone porches, occupants still white, no more Jews, here dwelled the Krauts with names like Gerhardt und Wrangel, and Lace Curtain Irish Mcguillicuddies. The 65 turned onto deadly dull Germantown Avenue, featuring boring businesses, plumbing supplies, linoleum outlets, the kind of commercial strip that inspires despair, thoughts of suicide. After Lehigh Avenue we were back on my turf, redbrick row houses, sharpies goofing off in front of corner candy stores, kids playing stickball on empty lots, frowsy housewives in their pink bras gazing down at the soporific panorama from second story windows. Canvasses Hopper forgot to paint.

On unlucky days I was hit by the plague at the change of shifts, again heard Dad asking, 'Whoever said life is fair?' On unlucky days the female workers from the Phillies Cigar Factory piled onto the 65 at the Diamond Street stop. Crowding aboard they brought a rank stench with them, worse than the stink of ashy tobacco, more the fumes of a sick animal's manure. It was bad enough that the poor women had to endure the foulness flowing from their own polluted flesh, after a day of work they had to put up with the cruel abuse of the passengers groaning 'Phew, Uich!' and wrinkling their noses at them. Some ladies responded by sticking their tongues out, and giving their tormentors the 'up yours' sign; most sat there curdling silently in their shame. When I hear the opening strains of Carmen I snap off the radio.

Last time I had the misfortune to arrive for the shift change I had a count your blessings moment, measuring how lucky I was, far removed from these hapless drudges in their smelly blue uniforms that made them look like disposable drones. I attend a top school, have a first rate Dad, a doting cook catering to my every whim. I had a new brother. We're not supposed to have such thoughts but Dim's getting shot was a lucky stroke for Karl. He went from grubby cubicles behind a gas station to our whole guest suite, all to himself, and from slaving summers pumping gas and fixing motors to having a generous guardian giving him the same allowance I get. Dad was even saying that if Karlie does well at Roman he will go to the university of his choice, why not Notre Dame?

Only reason I remember this moment so clearly, that night our telephone began ringing at two in the morning; first, the office telephone. Out in the void thrive inconsiderate clods with the brass balls to call at impossible hours to say, "My husband is bleeding, Doctor. My nephew has overdosed. My Bubba is dying. " Call at this time of night are Beethoven's four gloomy chords of destiny, never jolly news.

After minutes of ringing in the office the annoying tingalinging came from our private phone in the parlor. An idiot out there was maddeningly persistent. I wondered who dared? That might possibly be one of my aunts, or relatives, one of Dad's lady friends. I heard no stirring. Dad was certainly making no effort to answer.

The light clicked on in Wronsky's room. Karl was standing in the hallway, in his pajamas. He was rubbing his eyes, mumbled, "I'll get it."

"Don't bother, man. Sonsabitches, it could even be a wrong number at this hour."

"Nah, I'll get it, "Karl insisted, hurried downstairs to the parlor.

A minute later he was back, wheezing at the exertion of climbing three flights so quickly. He gasped, "It's Knocky. Says it's real important, he needs to talk to you, urgently, but it's your father he really needs to talk to."

"Oh, crap," I moaned, "what a goddam nerve." But I rose and headed downstairs. As I passed the master bedroom the master was snapping on his night lamp. I heard noises resembling the rumblings of a bear in his cave.

Picking up the phone in the parlor, I snapped, "What the hell you doing to me, man, calling at this hour? My old man is pissed as hell. He's coming down the stairs."

"Paulie, I'm in a bind, "Knocky moaned. "My Aunt Svetla is all over us, bugging me no end, she's downtown with one of her girlfriends from the Troc. Her friend was with a nurse, they were doing things to get rid of a baby, that got messed up, the nurse doing it just left in a panic, flat ran out on them, her friend is bleeding, out of control. Svetla says she is passing out, sinking into shock. I should please call your father, Doctor Dan could handle this."

"What the fuck, " I groaned. "Why don't they go to a hospital? Why don't they call an ambulance? Why the fuck do they hit on us?"

"I don't know, man, " Knocky said in a pleading tone. "Only thing I know is Svetla was giving us these frantic calls begging me to get to your father, I didn't want to, but my Mom is here, screaming at me to do it. I'm sorry to bug you, man."

Karl was shaking his head in disgust. Dad loomed in his rumpled gray pajamas; he was offering a fine imitation of a Kodiak bear emerging from hibernation.

"What?" Pop said. A hostile 'what?'

"Knocky. He's sorry for calling at this hour but he's pleading with me, crap about his Aunt Svetla needing to talk to you, an emergency, a woman bleeding to death."

"Trixie Malloy? " Dad said, and he took the receiver from my hand, held it to his ear. I found it odd that my staid old man knew from bump and grind dancers at the Troc. The ferocious aspect vanished from his face. He seemed almost amused.

"Calm down, Alexi, " Dad said in a gentle tone. "Calm down. Give me the address and telephone number, then have your mother call your Aunt Svetla, tell her I'll be there as soon as I can make it. "

He was so damn calm, jotting down he details on his note pad. I was jangled, unstring, Karl looked nervous enough to dance a Ukrainian jig. Dad was actually going to fly the mission at this time of night. I was inclined to shout, 'Why don't you call Svetla and tell the treacherous, two-faced twat to fuck off?'

"Okay, I've got the address," Dad said to the phone. "Now go to bed, Alexi, you have school tomorrow."

After Dad hung up I said, " I'll go out, open the back yard door, so you can pull the car out, sir. "

"Skip it, I'll grab a cab, you two get back to bed, you have school tomorrow."

"I'm sorry, sir. I didn't want to bother you but Knocky was frantic. He said they were driving him nuts, trying to get at you through me."

Dad shrugged, and said, "Yes, and, it seems that their tactics worked."

Minutes later we heard Dad leaving the house. Upstairs, I said to Karl, " I have finally found out what the word '*indignation*' means."

"What's your big discovery?" Karl asked.

"It means that so far in this life I've known what it is to be pissed off, teed off, angry, enraged, and infuriated, this is the first time I've experienced old-fashioned indignation. Buddies have the right to ask for favors but by what right does Svetla get to pull my string, take advantage of my friendship with Alexi to harass my old man at this hour of the night, and for something as sickening as a botched abortion? That's after she even bad-mouthed my Dad, the drunken session Knocky described for us on Market Street. How can the hypocritical bitch dare to call us in a crises?"

"I don't know what the rules are," Karl said. "Maybe you have the right to do everything you can get away with. What is the guideline? Just don't get caught, "

Alexi was apologetic the following day, at lunch, He touched my shoulder and said, "They forced me, Paulie I didn't want to do it, call you that late, but Svetla was shrieking at me on the phone, my Mom shouting at me, too, between the two of them they had me up the wall, man. "

"That's okay. Forget it. Did you hear anything about the woman being okay?"

"Yeah," Knocky said. " Svetla called, said your Dad's a wonderful Doctor, saved her life, if he hadn't arrived just in time her friend woulda' died. Did your father say anything to you this morning, give you a hard time?"

"He was cool. Over breakfast he said it's just part of a physician's routine."

I did not add that apart from his bleariness, and the crow's feet under his eyes, Dad had a wicked twinkle in his eyes, leading me to suspect he enjoyed making the acquaintance of Trixie Malloy, even in such gory circumstances. The man lectures me on Hegel, Schlegel, Nietzsche, Kant, and Schopenhauer, but, what can I say, he has his Dionysian Don Juanish streak, the man does love the ladies.

In the recondite way that grapevines leak, the bloody mess on Lombard Street was soon mouthed about in the public domain. A sharpy from Dave's poolroom was hustling in center city Allinger's, scored big, and celebrated afterwards at Arthur's SSteak House on Juniper Street. Who does he spot acting lovey-dovey in a back booth? That was none other than Doctor Dan holding hands with Trixie Malloy.

Word of this dalliance reached Marshall Street. Ladies, yentas, and gossips were, ostensibly, scandalized. Boys, men, and the swingers on Girard Avenue understood this perfectly; his dating the voluptuous Svetla enhanced Big Doc's aura. Local cruds and creeps touched my shoulder, congratulating me on the good times my Old Man was having, as if I were deriving tangible benefits.

Quite the contrary, I had been the pining Werther, denuding the Demetrescu sisters in lurid phantasies, who scores with one, my rascally old man. What was my lot? Rita on garbage can up the alley. Snoopers asked me if they were really having an affair, what did I know? Only that for several weeks Dad skipped the 'Roll out the Barrel 'jamborees at the Broadwood. Sunday happened to be the one night that Trixie had off from her labors at the Troc.

 I don't know enough Freud to speak Freudian but this situation struck me as Greek Mythology Lite. Dad was more popular than ever. Our neighborhood loves rakish rogues; if Dillinger hid out in our ward he'd have never been caught. Slick Willy Sutton was a folk hero in our neck of the woods, Dad had cultivated a winning image: the Good Samaritan Doctor who occasionally sleeps with the native wenches.

Meanwhile I'm a downtown wise guy commuting fifty blocks north to mingle with the Upper Crust and upwardly mobile eggheads. Professional writers would skip over this period, spin the hourglass, and say, 'One year later.' but few of us are granted the boon to breeze through a well-edited text. I am sentenced to draggy rides on slow-ass trolleys; the subway conveys me to a cleaner, richer country where the inhabitants appear to be milder, kinder, and more civilized, but can also be smug, two-faced insidious bastards.

I was a stranger in a strange land. 'Alienation' was not yet in my vocabulary so I was merely a fish out of water in the stultifying environment of pompous faculty and holier-than-thou students. Still, by the second semester at Central Knocky and I had found a few kindred souls, jocks and rebels we could hang out with. We formed our band of outcasts, undesirables, roughnecks, and renegades. By subscription only our clique included Jack Kraft, the baseball player, Seymour the Simian- an uncanny terrifying resemblance to King Kong but essentially a vegetarian pacifist; Donny Steinberg, star football player yet incredibly shy for a powerful bull, and Howie Toll, sort of a non-descript ringer, no noteworthy attributes.

For the goody-goody boys on campus we were the equivalent of scroungy low-class Townies versus their stance as the haughty Gownies. These pipsqueaks were our age but already making Joe college noises, our noises were unprintable. Lunchtime our pack gathered on the South Lawn to engage in raunchy ranking contests, the goal to see who could tell the scummiest joke, whip off the slimiest riff on disgusting subjects, like the most nauseating way to rise in the morning, Our obscene performances attracted eager audiences. The 'brains' gathered around us to roar at our salacious sallies and subsequently sneer at our antics. The faculty knew about our scandalous shenanigans; teachers refused to believe that I could possibly be the offspring of the distinguished physician who had made generous donations to the library and had served in key positions in the Alumni Association.

As spring arrived our daily shows evolved into stylized rituals, starting off with obscene insults, explosions of impure creation. We were all targets: Kraft would rank Donny Steinberg saying, 'I saw you leaving the Esquire movie Friday night with that fat chick: a figure like the north side of a south bound bus, great set of teeth-upper, lower, and mezzanine. She had everything a boy could want: mustache, muscles, and hair on her chest.' Howie Toll would rank Seymour the Simian with: 'You've got the complexion of a day old pizza with extra soggy mushrooms and pimentos.' When the insults became unbearable verbal abuse was suspended, it became a free-for-all wrestling match, different victim every session. At no pre-arranged signal we jumped and mauled whoever had dared to dress decently that day, drag him all over the grass.

This was our escape from der Dativ und dem Genetiv, isosceles triangles, and binomial equations. We were young apes talking wild shit. What were we rebelling against: Conformity, Motherpie and Applehood. Mothers became a hot topic; we did vile work on mothers. I'd say to Howie Toll, "I hear you mother got a sign over her crotch: The Tunnel of Love. Discounts for the disabled " Toll came back with " I hear the Eighty-Second Airborne plans to rent your mother's box for it's next maneuvers.'

What is the speed limit on Route Sixty-Nine?' Lickety-split, of course. As our shows grew lewder our crowds grew larger. Our serious, sober classmates cackled at our performances, then put us down as unspeakable retards. Daily we arrived with fresh vintage material, corny vaudeville and burlesque routines. The vileness and the wrestling matches were the highpoint of our day, our rejection of Apple-Mother and Pie-Hood, systems, rules, regulations, you name it, we hate it.

All in good clean dirty fun until the afternoon Sylvan Gans approached our carnival act. I don't know how they let this oaf into Central. I mean, I don't know how they let me in, but Gans was an obtrusive encumbrance taking up unwarranted space, a slow-witted pimple on the ass of progress, a solid C minus student. It was May now; so far we had managed to be here since September without once ever acknowledging each other's existence, nary a nod.

Fifty spectators were chortling at our impromptu production; Gans infiltrated our ranks, was hovering where he should not be lingering. This is not done: a high school clique is harder to penetrate than the most exclusive Old Boys Club in London. Today Knocky was the designated victim. We were riding Alexi. Usually he is off-bounds, not a target, exempt because he's not that fast between the ears but occasionally, to spread the venom around equitably, even Alexi was submerged in our acid baths; the theme this afternoon was how dense Knocky is.

Kraft, Steinberg, Seymour the Simian got their cruel shots in at Alexi; Gans had the audacity to make an unsolicited, unscintillating contribution to our weenie roast: He said," Ratchinov. You're so dumb you think Manual Labor is a Mexican."

I mean, after all, are we back in the sandbox? That was so weak, pathetic. Boo. Stop the music. Our pack turned slowly to examine Gans, our blank expressions might be interpreted to read as: who rattled your cage, birdbrain? When did you become our kind, numbnuts? When did you become one of us, creep? The only way Sylvan could cover his discomfiture was to glower at me, and ask, " Got a problem, Burris?"

Here we go again: Up went our fists; we were swinging away, the shouts loud but distant in my ears. Trapped by the obligations of the gunslinger, and the code of the schoolyard; I wanted nothing to do with Gans but periodically must duke it out with this wart-head. I wondered if every proper adolescence was assigned a Gans, but Sylvan made for a piss poor Bête Noir. We were evenly matched; he was throwing wild barn-door haymakers, me clipping him with deft right jabs. I felt embarrassed; Fighting was not done here. Central was Highbrow, Talmudic. Central valued the sharp verbal jab, the thrust and parry of nimble intellects; the knockout blows of crushing arguments. Brawls and fisticuffs were for the crass provincial institutions, the Igors at Frankford High, the Bookers at Ben Franklin, the lesser breeds in the industrial league, Physical Violence was déclassé, not Central at all.

No merit badges for taking on a lug bigger than myself, I was looked upon with scorn by this crowd. Most of these guys came from the 'nice' neighborhoods, East Oak Lane, Oxford Circle, many had Dads who ran businesses downtown, knew what life was all about, what it was to deal with workers who showed up drunk or never showed up at all, Dads who had done their best to provide them with a privileged and sheltered existence. Many of these uptown twits had never been slapped as a child, or ever been in a fistfight, never taken a hard punch in the mouth, rolled around on the ground to see if they had the guts to get back up. The All-A's boys and honor roll brains watching this bout forgive the rowdy jocks in our pack, not much was expected of them, their contempt was reserved for me. To them I was a blatant jackass, a traitor to the cerebral community.

In deplorable taste, this entire matter, and messy, my nose was bleeding, once again I had wreaked havoc with Sylvan's acne, punches were flying, you don't feel the pain till afterwards. I suppose that for natural fighters combat is as real as scratching your nose and wiping your behind but I'm no fighter. I was dancing in a nightmarish charade with no sense of reality, Gans trying to use his weight and bulk to throw me to the ground, turn this into a wrestling match. Weirdly, in a fierce fight, the struggle to survive, precisely when you are most agonizingly alive, this ultimate reality feels filmy, tenuous, off the clock, unreal.

CHAPTER SEVEN

Shredding carrots in the deli I was wondering if I really had those sociological thoughts during the fisticuffs with Gans. What I clearly remember from the fight is how the school nurse ratted me out afterwards when I went to the infirmary. First she attended to Gans, and let him go. Then she applied the Mercurochrome to my cuts and insisted on escorting me to the Vice-Principal's office. Doctor Farber looked up, noted my swollen nose and torn shirt; I was expecting his usual 'You, again?' Instead he said, "Extending your range of activities, Burris? No more just an annoying pest, you're working on becoming a hoodlum?"

Shredding the carrots for the coleslaw it feels as if I'd never been away; I'm condemned to shred carrots for all eternity, secula seculorum. Time is mysterious. Freshman year seemed endless, then over in a flash.

Wronsky was shredding the lettuce. At stern Roman Catholic high this June Karl had the second highest average in the freshman class. One Chinese immigrant kid beat him out for first; you can expect that kind of obstreperous behavior from the Chinese. Knocky, at Central, copped an A in gym and D's and F's in all other subjects, meaning Kaputsky. he will not be returning in September; he has been transferred, one might say, relegated, to Ben Franklin.

Dad accords us equal treatment under the law: translation, Karl gets to build character and work in the deli this summer. So far, two of my other Aunts have clutched Karl to their pendulous bosoms; my invitations to dinner he is invited along, they adore how Karl scarfs down their starchy latkes and praises their divine cutlets. One glaring exception, Aunt Ros; for every ointment fate provides a fly. Ros initially made gastro-intestinal gurgles when Dad became Karl's guardian, calling up her sisters to ask why Dan was bringing a Goy into his home? Why not a nice Jewish Boichick? They told her to shut up, mind her own business. Now she's in a campaign to prevent Dad from legally adopting Karl. He is only contemplating the concept but Ros is nightly on the horn, bitching to her sisters that Dan is growing dotty, the old coot might change his will; if Dan formally adopts this Schaigitz the Cossack might be entitled to half of Paulie's rightful inheritance. For Leonora's sake, for the sake of their dead sister, they must all unite to protect Paulie's rights; they must demand a sit-down conference with Dan.

I hate talk about wills, properties, and testaments. Fortunately, Sara told her that was a catastrophic idea; Dan was quite capable of telling them all to stick it where the sun don't shine, but Ros continues to buzz around, already shopping for a caskets for Pop when the old buck is still full of beans, back to cutting a rug at the Broadwood, spinning and twirling his Evas and Idahs to 'Night Train.'

Moe came over and told Karlie to go wait on trade, prepare a hoagie for the Porto Rican who just came in. After Karl went behind the counter Moe murmured to me, "That kid has got the knack."

"Which knack is that, Unc?"

"The people knack. You got it, or you don't. Karl doesn't try to lick in with nobody but he knows put people at their ease., how to win them over."

Karl was chatting away in Spanish with the Porto Rican as he made the hoagie. He has a facility for languages, already spoke Russian and Ukrainian, now he was picking up Español, and he can toss around phrases in Serbian, Kalmuck, and Polish. Karl picks up things fast, the way Alexi can spot a flashy move on court and seamlessly incorporate it into his game.

"How about me, Unc? Do I have the knack?"

"You, Paulie? You kidding? I love you to death, but you're an abrasive Kid, You'd best find a profession in this life that doesn't involve much contact with the public. Like maybe you could man a solitary weather outpost up in Northern Alaska."

I gave him a hurt look. Moe playfully punched my arm, and said, "C'mon, I'm only busting your chops. I like your sarcasm. How's your other big buddy doing? Alexi?"

"Knocky's down the shore again this summer. Busboying. Mostly playing basketball. And, probably getting laid, the lucky bastard."

"Hey, watch your language, Nefel,' Moe said, and then he shook his head and his expression became serious. He was debating whether to tell me something or not. Crouching, he used a confidential tone, saying, "Y'know, the other night, I went down to South Philly to see your Aunt and Uncle, Sara wasn't feeling too well so I went alone. We finished supper early, I took the 47 trolley to return home, but then figured what the hell, I had extra time on my hands, free time, so I hopped off at Locust Street, wandered around downtown for a while. And, I don't usually do things like this, but, what the hell, why not, you only live once, I dipped into a strip joint on Juniper Street, and guess who I saw in there."

"Rita Hayworth? Blaze Starr?"

Moe frowned at the wisecracking, then said, "No. Alexi's mother."

"Mrs. Ratchinov? No kidding."

"Yeah, Sonya, herself. She used to be a regular customer in here until she got into an argument with Sara about her unpaid bills. But there was Sonya, doing double duty, hatcheck girl and barmaid. She don't clip nails no more, Then, guess who I spot up on the stage. Shaking her bottom to the music of 'Love for Sale.'"

"Cyd Charrise? Hedy Lamarr?"

"No, smart-ass, none other than Alexi's Aunt Svetla, Trixie Malloy. Sonya told me that Svetla quit her job at the Troc, hinted they really fired her because she was getting too chubby for the chorus line. Maybe so, but with the extra pounds she was just the way I like it, looking tasty in the spotlight in just a G-string and two pasties. "

I blotted away that vision. Some images are unbearable.

Moe's tone became conspiratorial as he said, "But let me tell you something: while I had my drinks I watched those two broads operate. Sure, there was a manager strutting around, making big boss noises but, oof, those two broads were really running that joint, they run that club like they own it. "

From behind the smoked fish counter Aunt Sara was making dubious faces at us. Whenever she sees Moe and me conversing in low tones she wants to know what's going on. Moe nudged me with his elbow and whispered in a cunning tone, "So, give me the low-down, is it true?"

"What, true?"

"You know, a couple of months, the rumors insinuating that your Dad did the lady a personal favor in the middle of the night, a salvage job on a friend of hers, and, as a reward, your Dad got to Shtip Trixie Malloy."

Shrugging, I said, "Dad rarely discusses his social life with me. He is a reticent man. When he meets strangers he rarely tells them that he is a physician; they'll start talking about their gall bladders and kidney stones. People think that doctors, even on a beach, are available for free consultations."

"Well, that was evasive enough," Moe said. "So what you're saying is that you don't know, and, if you did, you aint telling."

Exactly. So far Dad had never given me that man-to-man talk on the birds and the bees. In his own way he was a prude. According to him, when he goes to Cape May it is strictly for the fishing. If a woman accompanies it is because her house is being repaired, or painted. He is doing her a favor, so she can escape all the paint fumes. He explains that she sleeps in the guest bedroom.

So that's where they do it, eh?

"Yeah, " Moe said," I guess you're right to answer that way, Paulie. Defend your Pop. I was on kind of a fishing trip on that one." Moe glanced up at the clock. It was 3:15, we are supposed to work till 5:00, but he said, " Alright, that's enough. You two can get the hell out of here. Go play ball. Enjoy your childhood."

ENJOY YOUR CHILDHOOD

Sounds like a Federal Injunction. Not enjoying it is un-American, but an unhappy childhood can be a gold mine, a perpetual source of inspiration.

"Thanks, Unc."

I signaled to Karl that we had made bail, could take off, scot-free. He tossed a salute to Uncle Moe and gladly whipped off his white apron. On our way out Sara gave him a quick hug. Karl wins people over. His tactics, he behaves like a low-keyed second cousin, asks for absolutely nothing, so people give him things.

Outside the blistering heat on Marshall Street scorched us. It was only late June but already steaming like deep August, moisture glistening on the grapes in the pushcarts. Rotating fans were turning in the stores and delis; most of them still did not have this newfangled technology called air-conditioning,

Karl said, "Moe and Sara are good folks."

"They're okay," I agreed. I found it hilarious that my runty Uncle Moe would sneak into strip joints when he finally had a free moment. Does everybody have a secret life? It must have been a thrilling moment for Moe, the distant drums beating in the jungle. What I hear when I slink off to the waterfront.

"Dave's," I suggested. "Some One Ball. To escape this heat?"

"I'd rather get my running in," Karl said," If you don't mind?"

I shrugged in agreement, though I did mind, then cancelled that thought as I saw Karl straining to sneak a peek at Bloom's Sweet Shoppe. The window was festive with sculpted chocolate grenadiers, frosted cookies, little Black Sambo orange and lemon dolls, striped candy canes, and red valentine shaped gift boxes. Karl did not see what he hoped to see in Bloom's. Cherchez la Femme, in this case the lady is Skinny Judy Bloom. Believe it or not, Mister Ripley, for the first time in his rotund life a girl had looked cross-eyed at him. Her fluttering lashes blitzed Karl like twin thunderbolts. Where do girls, even undernourished skinny ones, get this power? Sassy, viper–tongued Judy Bloom had triggered a major metamorphosis.

We cut through the back alley feeding into Sixth Street. Mom passed through this alley before getting run over. We came out at the spot where the red car swerved, the cops jumped out, eager to bash us, only last summer but seeming a century ago. Though I feared that Dad might spot us, getting off work early, we crossed the street, entered my house, stealthily. Dad's waiting room was packed, seven patients in there. Stubborn Dad was slaving away even when his own health advisors were urging him to retire already; what did he want to do, drop dead in his office and leave Paulie a millionaire? A wastrel like Paulie would only fritter it all away.

Miss Pearl was vacuuming in the parlor. I brought a finger to my lips, soliciting silence. She gave me a wink. Does Dad suspect how much his staff undercuts his authority? Upstairs Karl and I quickly changed into Levis and sneakers. When we snuck back down Miss Pearl gave us another wink of complicity.

This daily running regime began weeks back when for the first time Karl said no to Miss Pearl's after-school snacks. It had been his gluttonous custom to devour immense tuna fish sandwiches only hours before the heaping suppers she prepares. The world changed, Wronsky said, "Nyet." Who provoked this upheaval? None other than Judy Bloom, a freshman, or should we say fresh woman at Girl's High. She still wears thick goggles, only recently did she shed the fangy braces that made her an atrocious candidate for Bride Of Frankenstein. Up until this year her bosom might be described as two raisons on a breadboard, she now has an incipient décolletage with mild bumps in her blouse. Yet one cross-eyed glance from Judy was enough to make Karl eschew his after-school sandwiches, skip his midnight snacks, and run every afternoon. He has finally fessed up. They make goo-goo eyes at each other every time Judy flounces into the deli,

Trotting down Sixth Street we passed the Poplar Theatre where two Russian war films were playing, Mucho action in these Russian war flics, great tank battles. In solidarity I pace Karl in these mini-Marathons, my unlikely brother- the Cossack. After cutting through the Kearny schoolyard we turned onto Seventh Street, and jogged by the house with the plaque that says Poe wrote 'The Raven' here. Did he, now? Baltimore and New York have houses claiming The Raven' was concocted in their confines. Could it be different drafts? Or was that spectral bird trailing after Poe? Haunting him?

Karl was already huffing when we reached Spring Garden Street and turned right to aim toward Broad. He was puffing away, but ex-porker Wronsky was making progress, not yet about to give Charles Atlas much competition but In just a month he had lost twenty pounds, and no longer had the puffy tits of a twelve-year-old girl. You could see the first faint lines of definition in his abdomen,

Hep cats were grooving in the Blue Room Bar at Franklin Street, 'Sixty Minute Man' was blaring on the jukebox. Every time I trot down this sway I'm hit by the misnomers: Philadelphia; City of Brotherly Love, Oh, really? Try entering the wrong Diner, brother. And, this street? What's Springy or Gardeny about dull, inchoate gas stations, no panache whatsoever, the scraggly empty lot at Eighth Street, the tire retreading joint? Across is the Army-Navy surplus store, the Brooks Brothers for the nattier local truck drivers. Spring Garden is where the hard ass workers on the loading platforms clutch their balls to greet the snootier secretaries sacheting by.

Reading Railroad Tracks cross overhead at Ninth, we welcomed the shade of the stone bridge, but not the ammonia smell of nitrates and stale urine. Why do ambulatory pissers invariably use these tunnels, these dim shadows to relieve themselves? Is that related to the links between dogs and fireplugs? Logically, dogs can pee anywhere they want to but dogs seem to prefer fireplugs.

The Sun slashed at us again, as we reached Tenth Street. I said, " Ever onward, ever upward, how about all the way to the Art Museum today?"

"No, "Karl wheezed. " Just to Broad Street, man. Then we'll walk back."

"All the way to the Museum, jellyroll. We are whipping you into shape, getting you dapper for your hot-to -trot romance with Boney Maroney Bloomy."

"I'll try, "Karl groaned, "but I'm feeling pains and cramps in my side."

"Proper punishment for your long career of pigging out, humpty-dumpty."

We jogged past the Diner at Ridge Avenue. Not advisable for stray wayfarers to wander into this spot. The pack in the back booths gives strangers the Dan Duryea Evil Eye. Chance glancing their way, they will hit you with," What the fuck you looking at, asshole?" "Nothing," is not the right answer. Their next line will be to coo, "So we are nothing, eh?" There is no way to win in this exchange of pleasantries.

Beyond Ridge was the big textile plant with endless galleries of spindles and looms. Pull that barge and tote that bale, all employment may be honorable but I'd rather slit my throat than spend the rest of my life in a soul-killing dump like this. At Thirteen Street was Stoddard Junior High, mostly Negroes from the Housing Project. Adjacent was The Thaddeus Stevens School of Practice, public, but special, for the gifted, or the ungifted whose parents have pull or dinero. Stevens was unzoned, like

Central, but on the elementary level. The Colored kids were better dressed and more refined than us Whiteys. They carried brief cases. Many of the Colored arrived in taxis. Rain, sleet, or snow, I had to walk all the goddam way here from Sixth and Poplar. Pop began his character building campaign for my hide when I was in the second grade.

Karl sank to his knees, and groaned, "Time out." when we reached Broad Street. Crouching there, he looked like the Indians running out of gas, and collapsing, when they could not catch up with speedy Henry Fonda in 'Drums Along the Mohawk.'

One block up Broad, at the corner of Green, was Franklin High. The gray stone fortress housed Central before Central moved uptown. Franklin's student body was ninety-five percent Black. Dad said this was a northern variation on the quaint Dixie custom of donating used textbooks to the Colored schools after the White students were through with them. A few Hebes from Marshall Street, good athletes, attended Franklin: Herb Fisher on the baseball and football team, Lefty Goldfarb on the basketball team. Charlie Carr, a Whitey from Oriana Street around our way was on the fencing team. The gang from Go-d's bar kidded Carr a lot, saying," What fencing? Get outa' here, Franklin only has a switchblade team."

Up at Central we also made jokes about Franklin: in gym class you learned how to be a second story man; in English you practiced how to fill out your welfare application; in the advanced math class you learned how to run a numbers operation. Meet a white guy in the hallway, the password is 'Doctor Livingstone, I presume.' Franklin is the preferred prep school for Eastern State Penitentiary, conveniently located just a few blocks away.' I had laughed at those jokes even though a woman of color that had to be the sweetest person on this planet was raising me.

Karl read my mind. After finally controlling his wheezing, he pointed his chin at Franklin, and said, "Where Knocky will be going in September."

"Right. I spoke to Miss Pearl about that. She muttered ' Oh-my, poor Alexi, but then said she has a couple of nephews still in Franklin; she will ask them to do their best to protect the guy."

"That should help," Karl said. He gazed down Broad Street, at the Statue of William Penn over City Hall, and the massive white building of the Philadelphia Inquirer, then asked me, " You still planning on becoming a reporter, Burris?"

"Mulling it over. Reporters scribble about what other people are doing. There's a huge difference between being the player out on the court and the columnist writing snide remarks about him. Maybe I'd like to be one of the doers, the guy written about, and have a gig with a little pizzazz to it."

"Those are hard to come by, "Karl said. "If you've seen the ads in the Inquirer what they're mostly looking for are accountants, druggists, and stock boys. How thrilling. But, we all have to become something. *Some Thing.* While the only thing I'd like to be so far is Dictator. That would be a fun job. Not President. Cheese, to become President you must shake the hands of a million fools, kiss asses all over the map, beg congress to pass your laws but if you're Dictator you can give the order: 'Clean up the park over there, or your empty heads will roll at dawn.'"

Rush hour traffic was stalling on Broad Street; frazzled drivers honking their horns, shaking angry fists at each other. I said, " I could buy into Dictator, too. That may be the secret of the Universe; fifty million tools slaving away as flunkies in dull jobs while dreaming of being Der Fuhrer. And that's enough B.S. and philosophizing for one pit stop, fatrat. Think you can make it all the way to the art museum?"

Rising, heavily, Karl muttered, "I'll chance it with one eye."

Not exactly a Phoenix rising from the ashes but he'll give it the old college try. Folks can be nasty in this town. Karl retains rolls of residual blubber; pedestrians snickered at his jiggling as we jogged across Broad Street. The sight of a kid making dedicated efforts to streamline himself should garner applause, not scornful yucks, but this is a nasty town. Around my way we are pigeonholed early. I'd already been assigned my tag, niche, notch, goof-off with the 'Preacher's Son's Syndrome.' Make a move to change, the hounds howl in the kennel, we receive awful ribbings,

Past Broad the sidewalks are wider on Spring Garden, there were even honest-to-goodness trees. To our left was the U.S. Mint. This was supposed to be cushy employment, on Uncle Sammy's tit, but we were always reading about workers getting scalded and maimed in this Mint. There may be a primeval curse on money?

Across the way was Girl's High. Karl surely is thinking about his Judy. Does he fantasize about his slim princess, Bloomy peeling off her prim blouses to reveal her pink training bra, Teachers want us to concentrate on Isosceles Triangles; my brain is tormented by curves, it's a fetid swamp with satin covered curves blocking the horizon. When I'm not digging in at the plate, bottom of the ninth in the World Series, two outs, two strikes against me, I'm undressing the budding damsels of Marshall Street: Ana Schiff is stretching to pull down a gown from the rack, Bunny Green is bending over by the potato bin in her gossamer violet skirt.

ENJOY YOUR CHILDHOOD

I would certainly be enjoying my childhood more if the young ladies I was *seeing* would let me see more of themselves, and provide greater access to their charms. But I suppose I'm a typical American teen-ager, meaning mucho frustration and spurts of joy orchestrated by Madam Palm.

Overhead, the Blimp is cruising, advertising tires. A Piper Cub is flitting over the Schuykill River, with a trailer advertising Wings Cigarettes. Karl is getting red in the face, may poop out on us at any moment. I suppose we look like two carefree kids off on a lark but shadows hover over the House of Burris, Mister Anthony. Another gang war has erupted in South Philly, a war over the control of the taxi driver's union. Mangled Goombahs are found in the bushes around the Navy Yard, in car trunks, swamps around the refineries, planted in the Jersey bogs. We hear the creaking rear yard door open at two in the morning, or cars arriving to pick Dad up. I prefer to adopt the attitude of an ostrich. Like Scarlet O'Hara says, 'I will think about it tomorrow.' Karl also pretends not to hear Dad's creeping out of the house at ungodly hours. He is a loyal son, a full-fledged member of our clan..'

Veering off Spring Garden, we jogged up the Franklin Parkway, the clean lungs of ou city, the formal vistas of cultured Philadelphia on the glossy post cards. Dad says this leafy Parkway is part of the escape route enabling plutocrats and coupon clippers from the Main Line to zip through Fairmount Park down to their offices on Walnut Street and shoot back home in the evening without ever sniffing the crappy slums where us underlings rut.

Karl grunted in grateful relief as, approaching the majestic art museum, I slowed to a reverential pace. Culturelandia. Below, by the banks of the Schuykill, nestles our aquarium. Eastern State Penitentiary is juxtaposed kitty-corner to the museum. This pen was once regarded as the most progressive jail in the world; hundreds of copycat calabooses were built using its design. The penal system was so advanced here they even flushed the toilets in the cells twice a week. Pardon me, Lord, and you Muses, too. I've always seen Eastern Pen and the Art Museum as gargoyle twins. My aunts dragged me into this this Pharaonic Tomb because Art is good for you like, spinach and castor oil, but *Culture* to me felt like an invisible strait-jacket, an instrument of force, obligation, confinement, asphyxiation, sterility. When my aunts took me to the zoo, you never saw real animal, only imprisoned creatures, the apes and elephants were locked in cages, denatured; the Aquarium, fish were trapped in tanks, the State Pen convicts were locked in cells, dehumanized, and in this Mausoleum of an Art Museum the paintings side by side were exiled, imprisoned, ripped out of context, great masterpiece reduced to competing brands in a glorified supermarket: Monet's mustard versus Cezanne's pickles and El Greco's asparagus. When I explained my theory to the psychologist Dad sent me to, Doctor Schwartz said I was in lots of trouble.

Karl and I reached the Museum steps, water gushing in fountains adorned with the Greek mythological figures, Griffins. Dolphins, whatever these rusting green gargoyles were called. I had pushed Karl too hard. He was close to passing out from heat stroke. He flopped down on the rim of the fountain.

Almost twilight time, still a scorcher of an afternoon, I signaled to Karl that I was about to do a strip tease. A bunch of girls descending the steps giggled as I removed my sneakers, climbed out of my Levis, peeled down to my BVD's, and sprawled out in the bubbling fountain. In spite of the ferocious heat the swirling waters were cool. After grimaces of disbelief Karl shrugged, then boldly did the same. The girls were laughing their cute keisters off but other priggish art lovers departing this morgue of a museum awarded us dropped-jaws horrified glances. They were more shocked than Claude Raines in 'Casablanca.'

What's the big deal? We're refreshing ourselves on a steaming afternoon. In our jockey shorts, gapers could not see any more than you'd see on a beach unless they had a morbid, prurient, and deviant interest in seeing more, but several starched-ass guardians of propriety were wobbling outraged jaws at us. If there were a guillotine nearby they would want our heads severed.

I sloshed around in the foaming waters shooting out of the Griffin's beak, reached over, brought my mashed deck of Luckies out of my Levis, lit up. Karl rarely smokes but he accepted a cig. The sight of two delinquents smoking in the pool increased the firepower of the glares beaming in our direction. These tourists looked like Schneyer, eyes aflame, cracking up in the gym,

Hey, you jerk-offs, don't you know that the best part of a workout is the cigarette afterwards? Above us, apprentice artists in paint-stained smocks had their easels set up, were daubing away at the consecrated profile of our Philly skyline: the Logan Library, the Cathedral, the gray downtown office buildings acquiring a lemony tint while rush hour traffic streamed up the Parkway. One of those moments when nothing monumental is happening, you sense you will remember it forever.

"So when are you asking Judy out on your first official date?" I asked Karl.

"I already did. Sunday she'll pack a picnic basket, we'll stroll in Fairmount Park."

"Oof. I smell fire and passion in the forest primeval. "

"It can't be like that, Paulie. I'm scared to even take her hand."

"Play it cool, lad, the reluctant dragon. It's much better, sexier, if you play the shy gunslinger role, force the little lady to make the first move, she lunges at you."

"You're the big expert on the subject?"

"Only in comparison to you, King Farouk," I said, and we both laughed.

Our laughter faded when we saw that outraged art lovers had detained a passing red car: they were haranguing the cops while pointing at us, calling the attention of the Law to our barbarian desecration of a public treasure. Irate citizens were demanding decisive actions. Karl summed up the situation by saying, "Oh, shit."

I thought about scrambling back into my togs, already too late for that, the cops were out of the squad car, coming our way, shaking their heads as if asking the Lord 'what the hell is this world coming to?'

With cool daddy Gallagher as my role model, Gall always says to cops, "So what can I do for you, officer?" I was thinking of hard-nosing this confrontation, and lighting up another smoke. Karl saw me reach for the Luckies, whispered a desperate plea to me, "Knock it off, Burris, sometimes you aint as funny as you think you are."

I prefer not invoking influential connections but at the Buttonwood Street station where the desk sergeant was theatrically threatening to throw the book at us for malingering, loitering, indecent exposure, sundry other malfeasances and misdemeanors I mentioned to the cops who my father was; they told us to get the hell out of there, to go home and play with rubber ducks in our bath tub.

Our last and memorable dip into the Art Museum pool. During the rest of the summer we alternated routines, basketball one day, next afternoon, jogging: out to Shibe Park to grab a seat in the bleachers, or we explored areas we had never traversed before, leading to hairy situations in certain neighborhoods, toughies cracking their knuckles and asking, " So what are you doing around here, Yussel?" Witty responses were not advisable.

 Though not sure if I still wanted to be a journalist I was keeping scrapbooks of of local stories: a shooting in the Third and Brown poolroom. A brawl in the back room poker game at Dave's, knives came out. Izzy Dubinsky was murdered in his butter and egg store at Second and Fairmount. Hawaiian Jack lost a foot when a forklift prong on the brewery platform sideswiped him. Two core makers were scalded in the Fifth and Noble bronze foundry. Seven Franklin Square Winos died from a bad batch of rotgut cooked with Sterno. There was a riot over which race controlled the basketball court at the Fourth and Green Quaker Guild. This did not make the papers, she was still a minor; Cousin Rita was sent to a reformatory for lifting the wallet of a traveling salesman after slipping him knockout drops in a seedy no-tell motel. Otherwise, a somnolent summer. We were waiting for Knocky to return to town; for kids in school the New Year really begins in September.

Labor Day we were playing basketball, the garishly bright green door opened on Randolph Street. Heads whipped around to see what tight, outlandish outfit Mrs.

Ratchinov might be sporting this afternoon, but it was Alexi stepping out, and causing a stir. We immediately saw that Knocky must have had a tremendous season down the shore. He had filled out, his shoulders were broader, he had shot up inches. Slouching into the yard, he was greeted by sarcastic well-wishers slapping his palm. The gang started ribbing him about next week, telling him he he'd better learn to do the Hucklebuck and pull an Al Jolson, smear on a black face or he 'd never make it to Thanksgiving at Franklin. Knocky was grinning, seemed to be taking the kidding well, but the guy was faking his moves. His eyes were glossy, opaque; He was in trouble,. and immediately confirmed my suspicions, giving me the same quick desperate signal Karl gave me back in Slovak Hall, a telegram that he needed consultations. Postponed, as Mrs. Ratchinov opened the door right then, waved for him to return home, for supper.

The following morning we shot downtown for the fall shopping, same deal as last year, Dad matching what Karl and I saved of our wages. Our trio had burgeoned into a quartet. Sassy Judy was tagging along. She had spunkily informed us that, whether we liked it or not, she had joined our team, will be the distaff D'Artagnan to our Three Musketeers; also our fashion consultant, since we had terrible taste in clothes. Only the Lord knows what happened at that picnic in the Fairmount Park, magical hanky-panky in those woods. This pair had been inseparable all summer, and good for each other, Karl slimming down, Bloomy filling out, packing her jeans more tightly. Yet Judy still retained traces of the tomboy; if this couple were ever mugged Bloomy would be the first to put up her mitts, take on all assailants. Staring at Bloomy, Knocky was scratching his chin, not too sure he wanted a girl as a buddy as yet. Girls are strange. Girls are aliens. You can never tell what they are thinking.

On Spring Garden the gas station was tilting as if it had been abandoned ten, and not one year ago. Fresh Graffiti with valentines proclaimed ' 'Buz loves Fannybaby Coleman.' Darmopray, our family lawyer, had been unable to find any commercial takers, and sold this property to the Development Authority for a measly seven grand. City Hall plans to gentrify our blight, eventually market this run down area as 'SOCIETY HILL NORTH, ' provoking chuckles and chortles from us aborigines.

Wronsky never looks at the station. His gaze is firmly to the west. One block further down, at Sixth and Buttonwood, the three stout black ladies are still passing around the mason jar of moonshine circulating since last September, trapped in time, like the foot scrappers and kerosene drums. The sight of the brown paper bag inspired Karl to ask Alexi, " So how did the scoring go this summer, Ace?"

"Basketball-wise, " Knocky said, "I averaged eighteen point five average, coming off the bench as the sixth man. If that's what you're talking about."

"More or less, "Karl said. "How about other than the lay-ups and hook shots?"

Knocky began counting on his fingers, reached ten, and fluttered his fingers to indicate that he did not have enough of them to do justice to his stats.

Judy snapped, " If you slobs are talking about what I think you're talking about, you should wash your dirty mouths with soap and water."

"Hey," Knocky said, "these are my buddies. Every year I give the report. This season I scored four touchdowns and was shot down on the one-yard line maybe twenty times. Actually, inches away."

"Four touchdowns? " Karl grunted in envy, or admiration.

"Yeap, plus extra points," Knocky said." No more quickie wham-bams under the boardwalk. Twice on sofas, twice on authentic beds."

"Goddam it, "Judy grumbled. "Why can't you dirty-mouthed hyenas just do your shit, and keep it to yourself? Why do you have to brag about it to everybody?"

"Hey, baby, bragging about it is half the fun," Knocky explained. " If you can't give your buddies the play by play it might not even count."

"Ah, you're all a pack of foul-mouthed baboons and bastards," Judy assured us.

"Sure we are, " Knocky agreed. " That's why you love us. So, how's about yourself, Bloomy? You giving Karlie any on the sly? Letting him cross over Jordan?"

"Nah, " Wronsky sighed, morosely. "She says she aint giving me none till I get circumcised first. She wants to turn me into a Hebe."

"Hey, what you want to do that to the poor guy for?" Knocky protested. "I've seen Karlie in locker rooms, he slings a salami that should make you happy. Why do you want to cut down on your future joystick? Or does it have to be stamped kosher before he can stick it into you?"

"None of you're your rotten business," Judy snapped. " What Karl and I do when we're all alone is nobody's business but out own."

Just to be obnoxious I sang, "Nothing could be finah, than to be in her vah-gina, in the morning...."

"Uch," Judy groaned, "you're even worse than these two, Paul. You come from a fine family. You're supposed to be smart, and well-bred, but you've the dirtiest mind and scummiest tongue in the neighborhood."

I sang," Listen to the Mocking Bird, pecking on a Frozen Turd,"

"Speaking of well-bred, " Knocky said, "Youse guys heard that my Cousin Rita got sent up the river? Shipped to that stone home for bad girls?"

"Yes, " I said, and began to sing, " The object of my Affection, is in the House of Correction, she's serving ninety days."

After shuddering, Judy said, " You see, you're a pack of fucking no good rats. I don't know why I bother to associate with shitheads like you."

What she said, though it was easy to see that Bloomy was getting a large charge out of hanging out with the troops, and talking dirty. Judy has become The Defiant One. Her folks did not approve of Karl. 'What do you mean? A Schaigitz, noch?' Her best girlfriends are now ex-girlfriends. The Capulets and the Montagues, doesn't anybody read the Bard anymore? Parental opposition fuel is a potent aphrodisiac.

Knocky was rubbernecking, back on Daddy alert, hoping to not see his father crawl out of one of these bars. We had reached the Tenderloin; skid row bums were calling out to Judy, " Hey, honey-bunny, can you spare two bits for a taste for an old sailor, Sweety? Blow me a kiss, little darlin'. For a nickel they let me suck on the bar rag. Don't be a Meany; slip me two bits for a little Sneaky Pete, honey. "

Kids are aliens on skid row, peewees from a Tom Sawyer or Andy Hardy film inexplicably wandering into a movie about the Depression. This festering squalor is also targeted to be cleaned up, the process already starting, several saloons and hock shops shut down, the store with the freaky medical supplies was still operating but the Gypsy Fortune Teller joint was gone. Where will these hobos, winos, bums, and beggars go? The windows of the Gypsy joint were smeared over with soap. No more would the swarthy hawk–nosed sirens blow evil smooches at Knocky.

He let out a sigh of "woof" as we reached Arch Street. I thought it was a sigh of relief at having not spotted his father coming out of a taproom, I was wrong. He had switched modes. Two minutes ago he was snappy, bouncing, jocular, giving Bloomy a hard time of it, now his eyes were bleak with panic. His head twisting on his neck, It seemed a replay our excursion last fall, after his argument with his Aunt Svetla. We could put this on the calendar as an annual event, like the last concert at the Dell.

We fell paces behind the lovebirds, and I murmured to Knocky, "You okay, man?"

A stupid thing to ask; in every dumb-ass movie the hero's sidekick is hit by a car, blown off a roof, blasted by a rocket, a moron runs up and says, "Are you okay?"

"Yeah, I'm alright. " Knocky wheezed.

Yesterday, when the troops were kidding him about Franklin, his eyes were glossy smokescreens. I was now seeing naked grief on the hot griddle, not a kid who just spent two jolly months down the seashore.

"You sure don't look alright, buddy."

"Ah, shit, he groaned, "I've bad stuff on my mind, shit I can't talk about."

"Worried about Franklin?" I asked.

"Screw high school. I may just drop out, take off. It's my Mom driving me pure fucking nuts. She has a new boyfriend. Roy. Roy Bauer, a big bruiser. He's the bouncer in the exotic club she's working in."

'Exotic?' Knocky had added a new word to his vocabulary."

"He's giving you a hard time?"

"The fucker's a gorilla with an ugly temper, ex-con, served hard time in Jersey, and he's real strong, brags that he was arm wrestling champion in the pen. He likes to give me hard handshakes where he almost snaps my wrists. Mom says that underneath it all he's a softy, a pooty-cat, she can handle him, but the bastard has brought tears to my eyes with his grip. Then he says ' I'm just trying to toughen you up kid, smile, unless you want to run and squeal to your Momma."

"Sounds like a real winner," I said.

"Yeah," Knocky agreed. "Real winner. My Mom's been seeing him all summer. Now she's talking about Roy moving in with us, shacking up in our house. It's driving me up the wall. I'll go bats, I don't know what I'm gonna' do if that miserable prick crashes in on us."

"I don't know what to tell you, man."

"I'm thinking about taking off, Paulie. Sticking my thumb out, leaving this town, hitting route Sixty-Six, heading for parts unknown."

"Maybe you could move in with your Aunt Svetla or Uncle Ivan," I suggested.

"They aint no better than Bauer, and might be in cahoots with him. Ivan's now working three nights a week as MC at the club. I heard them talking wild shit about the rich suckers, fatcats, and patsies coming into the Club Cosmo, how easy it would be to take them for a ride. I don't know what kind of crazy shit they're up to, it scares me, I don't want any fucking part of it."

What to say to a guy with Big League Troubles? Mine were miniscule: the world will little note nor long remember that my classmates at Central detest me, and the teachers are not my big fans. The medical calls Dad was making after midnight wlll only be a problem if he gets caught. I was licensed to be an advisor nor did I have much of a track record as a sage counselor.

Talking to himself, Knocky said, "Maybe it would be best for everybody concerned if I just take the fuck off, vanish, clear out. "

Ahead of us, Karl and Bloomy, arms wrapped around each other's waists, were star-crossed lovers nuzzling away in broad daylight on a public thoroughfare. Knocky sniffed at their cuddly spectacle. These two seemed to be sampling bites of a Happy Childhood. According to my crystal ball, this would not be a long running show.

CHAPTER EIGHT

A week later we had our first sighting of Roy Bauer. He came out of the house on Randolph with Mrs. Ratchinov, was not quite as tall as Sonya, an inch shorter, but a powerful bull, built like a recently retired fullback, with ugly tattoos on his arms, snake motifs, besides the freaky high-heeled snakeskin boots he was wearing. Taking Mrs. Ratchinov's arm, he sneered in our direction before heading toward

Girard with her, with a weird touch to his highly- mannered arrogant strut; Bauer seemed to glide, Maybe it was those tattoos or the snakeskin boots bringing this to mind but Roy Bauer sidled along as if a venomous snake had been half-bifurcated and was now slinking around on two legs.

The guys in the schoolyard were shaking their heads at the sight of this twosome. Nobody said it aloud but the general consensus was that Mrs. Ratchinov could really pick them; her new boyfriend was a doozy.

Meanwhile, classes had started, we were seeing less of Knocky as he was at Ben Franklin, which meant weekly fire drills due to bored inmates dropping lit matches into waste cans in order to escape class early, and called-in arson threats triggering mass evacuations with thousands of lads filing merrily out to Broad Street. It was not wise to raise your hand to give correct answers in class. Sullen cold cockers, quick-punch artists, and mean-ass rumblers abounded; punch-outs in the halls, scuffles in the cafeteria, dust-ups in the streets, were daily occurrences. At Central we dreamed of becoming neurosurgeons, Deans, Chief executives, Pillars of Society. Franklin, they were talking Kid Gavilan, Jersey Joe Walcott, Sugar Ray.

Theoretically, a pretty boy like Alexi should be suffering through nightmarish times in these confines, it did not work out that way at all. For reasons and chemistry beyond my powers of analysis, he became wildly popular at Franklin, picking up a new nickname: 'Lefty-Two.' Eugene Goldfarb was Lefty-One. Mystifyingly, Lefty-Two was one of those rare white dudes who rates as a smash hit with the Colored. There were resentful Bruisers stalking around those halls who'd just as soon bash you in the nose as say 'Good morning,' nobody took a swing at Lefty-Two.

Karl, always the astute observer, said that it was as if an unseen hand had flipped the hourglass in Knocky's life, turned everything around. Before, school had been the torment, now school was his safe refuge; his home was the place of torture.

Verification of that claim came when Central faced Franklin in their gym. Karl cut his last class at Roman; Judy cut her class at Girl's High, the first time either of them ever cut a class in their upright lives. They had every right to be nervous when we entered the packed gym. The girls here were from William Penn High, Franklin's sister school, they were giving us meaner glares than the boys, one might say the

ambience was hostile, and we were in a miniscule minority. Taking our seats, near
an exit, I examined the stacked house. Only thirty or so supporters had come down
from West Oak Lane to root for our team. The uptown boys were sensibly leery
about slumming, reasonably so. Even when Central won the game we usually lost
the brawls in the streets afterwards. In my florid imagination I was wondering what
the reception might be if the champions of the Ku Klux Klan League flew over to
Ethiopia to take on the Addis Ababa All Stars.

The menacing stares asking us 'what the hell are you doing here?' subsided as,
spotting us in the stands, two kids we knew from the Kearny Schoolyard, large Leroy
Lincoln, the football player, and enormous Boony Washington, waved to us. Big
Boony was Miss Pearl's nephew. Then, both teams came trotting out of the locker
room, Knocky waved our way, stamping us as legit for this crowd. Ominous glares
were redirected back to the uptown chumps who had dared to venture into these
thickets wearing Central's Crimson and Gold Sweaters. In the local parlance these
turkeys were cruising for a bruising.

Fortunately, our cheerleaders had not traveled down here for this game. Since
we had an all-boys school our cheerleaders took awful razzings. When we played
Olney High, at half- time their fans hooted and snickered at the feeble efforts of our
Rah-Rah-Rah Milquetoasts. Olney retaliated by sending over their leggy beauties to
wag their tart tails at us and chant: 'I used to go to Olney High but I was quite
contrary. Now I go to Central High. Whoops! I'm a fairy!'

The teams were warming up, dribbling around, tossing up long set shots. Knocky
was putting on a show, coolly popping in one ball after another. Judy asked me, "If
Alexi is such a hot shot, how come he isn't in the starting line-up?"

"Internal politics, my dear. He just transferred in from another school, and he's
only a sophomore, maybe still a freshman because of his grades, and they've got five
Colored guys in the starting line-up, all seniors. So even though he might be their
best threat as a scorer Knocky comes in as their first sub."

"Besides which, Karl said, " in many cases, the Sixth Man, the Flash coming off the
bench, is the key player, the sparkplug who has to shore up a faltering defense,
galvanize a drooping offense, or stop whoever's hot on the opposing team."

"Ah, you two are such big experts on every subject, "Judy scoffed.

"I'm gad you recognize that, my dear," I said.

I'd recently seen 'Gone With the Wind' again, picked up the irritating tic of calling all girls 'My Dear.' It bothered even me but I could not shuck the tic. Meanwhile, a whoop went up as the game began; Howie Landau, Central's All City star guard, grabbed the opening toss-up. Landau stylishly loped down court for an easy lay-up. As punishment for his leisurely lope, Franklin's Roy Witherspoon clobbered Landau. The hard foul sending Howie sprawling amidst the gaggle of photographers clicking their bulbs. The highly partisan crowd cackled and laughed, vociferously enjoying Landau's tumble. One might suspect this game could get out of hand

Howie was heading to the foul line. Judy asked. "How come Knocky doesn't look up in our direction? He gave us one perfunctory wave, then totally ignores us."

"He's an athlete with a pro attitude," Karl explained. "Pros don't get loosey-goosey and kowtow to their fans in the stands. When they're on the bench their principal duty is to concentrate with a hard, steely gaze, be fixed on the game."

"Ach, Judy sniffed. I think Alexi is a prize poodle show-offy hotdog, but you two, no matter what, you'll defend him."

"That's what buddies do," Karl informed her. "We will piss on and knock all others, not one word will we hear against a buddy."

 I was watching the action on the court; Bloomy was staring bug-eyed at the way the big Black girls from William Penn High were maliciously flirting with Alexi, gleefully blowing him torrid smooches, licking lascivious tongues at him. They were exaggerating, just to be outrageous, only funning here. Knocky did his best to ignore this tomfoolery, he had his pro blinders firmly in place, but several of his fellow bench-warmers were nudging him with their elbows, urging him to respond to the provocative sighs of his fan club.

Big Boony waved at us again. Miss Pearl's nephew, Dad had seen him in the office last week. Boony is over six-three and weighs close to three hundred pounds. He has diabetes and terribly high blood pressure, is ticketed to die young. Dad says he will do all he can but there's little he can do for him. Mrs. Jordan does not like it when

Dad sees Miss Pearl's relatives, and other Colored patients, for free. Ech, I'm here to watch a basketball game; let us skip further extraneous social commentary.

Seven minutes into the game, my uptown Hebes-Freidman, Fell, Landau, et al, were ahead by one point, in spite of being pushed and knocked around by Chaney, Witherspoon, Wiggenbottom, the taller, stronger warriors of Franklin. The physical beating was taking its toll; you could tell this lead would not last long. A shout went up from the Franklin cheering section, meaning ninety-five per cent of this gym; the stands were calling for Lefty, Lefty-Two to be sent in. Franklin fans began stamping their feet and clapping hands in unison. The girls from William Penn were moaning and cooing, "Lefty, Lefty-baby," as if creaming in their jeans. If you've ever heard them moaning for you this way it hardly matters what happens during the rest of your rotten life. 'No, No, they can't take that away from me.'

The Franklin coach gave Alexi the nod, whistling and whooping erupted in the gym as Knocky scooted over to the scorer's table. Two William Penn girls stretched out flat in the aisle, quivering their hips, raising their skirts above the knees, and simulating volcanic orgasms. They were funning but Judy rolled her eyes and shook her head in disbelief. The roaring grew louder and wilder as Wiggenbottom took a seat and Lefty-Two hopped onto the court with the Central team nodding to him. Except for Algebra, English, and French, Knocky could have been one of them. Displaying real sportsmanship, two of the Central starters, Fell and Landau, touched Knocky's shoulder. Coach Schneyer thrashed in disgust; he considered this consorting with the enemy to be an act of betrayal.

A mini-drama was unfolding here; it's been done before, the hide-bound stuffy coach versus the cocky kid script. Schneyer's face twisted in misery as Knocky began offering an advanced clinic in the art of basketball. He became the unrepentant gunner and popped in four long left-hand stabs, pure net. Schneyer assigned Landau to guard him, Howie did an effective job of shutting down his scoring, forcing Knocky to shift modes, display his versatility. He began stealing the in-bounds passes, controlling the pace, drawing the double team till he found the open man, feeding his forwards pinpoint passes and bloopers for Alley Oops. He was doing what the stats can hardly describe, elevating his teammates to a higher level.

With six minutes left on the clock for the first half the score was 37-35, in Central's favor, but the box score never tells the whole story. It is never just about the game. Points were being tallied on more significant scoreboards. This was the Revolt of the Masses, Blacks against Whites, the dreary downtown slums versus leafy uptown opulence. Knocky was the Prole showing the Plutocrats what they had missed out on. On another level this was a battle between the fledgling high fliers who will one day be taking elevators up to the executive suites against the guys who did not have much waiting for them out there.

It became nastier as Franklin took the lead, 43-42. Coach Schneyer bustled over to the scorer's table to invoke the rules, complaining to the refs that Ratchinov had flunked out of Central meaning that, technically, he was still a freshman. Also, he was a transfer, according to Public League rules, transfers were supposed to sit out one year of eligibility.

Fans in the stands hooted and whistled while Schneyer argued with the refs and Franklin coaches. The referees said he should have registered his objections before the game began, and Schneyer was hit by howls of derision as he blustered that the game could continue but he fully intended to lodge an official protest in downtown headquarters.

Five minutes left in the half, I was watching with conflicting loyalties. I should be rooting for Central but this was my pal in the firing line, ticketed for greatness, or tragedy, maybe both. He wowed the crowd today with no-look passes, dribbling behind his back, a dispsy-doodle reverse lay-up in heavy traffic that defied gravity, hovered on the rim, improbably rolled in to proclaim that this kid was favored by the Gods. All this was accomplished against an already famous and formidable opponent: ten colleges and universities were chasing after Howie Landau, offering scholarships.

Or did the Gods favor Alexi? He was having a terrible time of it at home. Sonya was not pulling tricks anymore: that was the good news: she was shacking up with Roy, the bad news. Bauer entered Dave's poolroom with his sinister yard-bird gait and cowboy boots, advertising that he is a mean-ass mother, nobody you want to fuck with. He compounded that impression with his geeky laugh and the demonic snake tattoos on his forearms. In just a few months Roy had managed to make himself detested, and had acquired a bad rep; nobody in Dave's cared to shoot pool with him anymore. He intimidated people and was a bad loser; rather than pay off his gambling debts he invited winners to step outside. So far nobody had taken Bauer up on that.

Two stars were dueling in an exciting match, Landau and Knocky in a brilliant mano a mano; Me, instead of concentrating on the game at hand I'm worrying about domestic squabbles, Orphan's Court kind of crap.

The tide definitively turned. Just as the buzzer sounded Chaney tossed in a nifty hook shot to leave the score at 48-43, incredible totals for a high school game at half time. This should have made the home court rooters happy but Karl looked at me. He also smelled trouble brewing, more than brewing, about to boil over. From previous altercations at the Quaker Guild and Fairmount Avenue Police Gym we could gauge when over-excited fans feel the urge to express themselves, join the action, take a few swings at the visitors for the sheer joy of messing around.

Judy rose, saying, " I think I'm going to visit the little girls room."

Karl touched her wrist and said, "That would not be a good idea right now."

Judy was about to object, plead her case, we received instant confirmation of Karl's views: shouts from the hallway, anguished groans, gleeful yells, the plopping sounds of soft bodies bouncing off metal lockers, teachers blowing whistles. One might surmise that the Central turkeys, flaunting their crimson and gold sweaters, had made the mistake of heading for the boys room, and they were being waylaid at the pass, meeting opposition out there.

It was advisable to not investigate the causes of this ruckus, stay put, this rude commotion was not our concern; we wore 'hear no evil, see no evil' expressions. Until we saw the fearsome contingent of Franklin students plus robust specimens from their William Penn Ladies Auxiliary charging toward us. Apparently they had forgotten that Lefty-Two gave us his blessing. We groaned a "Woha," and scrambled higher in the stands. I conk out at times like this, lose all sense of reality in these moments that feel like an impossible nightmare, yet also a Saturday matinee, the merry cartoons where three timid white mice are chased by fierce black cats.

THREE FANS SLAIN IN BROAD STREET MASSACRE . That could be the last headline to ever flash through my mind. In the cartoons the savior for the mice is usually a bristling bulldog rearing to scare off the alley cats. In our case the deus ex machina turned out to be Leroy Lincoln and Boony Washington, both size extra large, cutting off our prospective assailants, Boony roaring, "Hey, you fucking assholes, leave these people alone. They're from around my way. They're okay. Touch them and I'll break your fucking heads, they're okay."

His stamp of approval would hardly of helped except for his size. Dad said Boony is scheduled to die young, none of our would be attackers were venturing to check out the status of his health as Boony threw haymakers that scattered the vanguard. Leroy put his football blocking skills to use, lowering his shoulder to crash through the line opening, a path for us, knocking over a pack of assailants that went down like bowling pins. Then Big Leroy swept Judy into his arms to protect her while we rushed out to the hall. Damn if Leroy did not look like a gallant Rhett Butler in the scene where he carries Scarlet up the staircase.

Fire alarms were ringing, the hallways were filled with smoke, from matches dropped into the waste cans again. Mixing with the sounds of kicks and punches landing on flesh, we heard the shrill whistles of the teachers and snarling police sirens, the honking of the traffic stalled on Broad Street.

Leroy put Judy down as we slipped out a side exit. Ten different versions of the cartoons where the black cats chase after the fleeing white mice were unfolding, the Franklin avengers were concentrating their efforts on the uptown boys sappy enough to wear their Crimson and Gold Central sweaters into this precinct, trying to run them down before they reached the subway stop at Spring Garden.

We hurried across Broad and Boony said, "C'mon, I'll walk you guys a few blocks. Some of these fucking Niggers might still want to come after your Asses."

It jars me when Blacks as black as Boony say 'Nigger.' Jews don't go around calling each other Kikes and Mockeys. I said nothing. I am rarely brought in as a consultant on matters of verbal etiquette.

Karl wheezed, "Jesus, thanks a lot, you guys . It was getting pretty hairy in there."

By the Diner at Ridge Avenue we heard the sirens of police cars still arriving. Judy was laughing, I asked, "What the hell you giggling at, dum-dum?"

"Wow, that was really exciting," Judy said. "Really lots of fun."

Ut-oh. Aside from being Karlie's sweety, this Bloomy is truly nuts.

Leroy grumbled, " I can't figure it out. We're winning the damn game, every-thing fine and dandy, we're ahead, then there's shit like this. Why can't everything just be fucking nice and okay?"

Great question. Could we blame the Founding Fathers?

"Knocky played a great game, didn't he? "Karl said.

Boony winced and asked," Knocky-who?"

"At Franklin they call him Lefty," I corrected Wronsky. "Lefty-Two."

"Yeah, Lefty, " Boony said. "When he came in September there were fuckers around school hot to waste Lefty, I told them Niggers if they wanted to get at Alexi they had to come through me first. Now everybody likes Lefty except some of the teachers. I've heard teachers say Lefty is more Nigger than all us Spades,"

"That to be interpreted as a compliment?" Karl asked.

The question puzzled Boony and Leroy so I diplomatically changed the subject, said to Boony, "I'm gonna' have to tell my father to raise Miss Pearl's salary, in compensation for all the medical bills we saved on. Really, thanks a lot for stepping in, you guys."

"What the fuck?" Boony said. My aunt really loves your father, likes working for him. She says Doctor Dan aint like all the others."

I did not ask Boony who the *'others'* might be. We could guess that one. Meanwhile we had reached the bridge at Ninth Street, the pissy arches under the railroad tracks. I looked back over my shoulder; saw that we had no pursuers though police cars were still racing toward Franklin. Speaking of race, I never once heard anybody in our neighborhood employ the word. Racism, or racist was not in our vocabulary. Ours racism came to us so naturally we were like fish that probably have no need for a word like water.

Leroy and Boony were all jazzed up from performing their good deed for the day; they were strutting along with us in practically a New Orleans style cakewalk.

As we passed the empty lot at Eighth, Boony said, "Yeah, looks like nobody's trailing after our hides so I'll be cutting off here. I live up this way by Brown Street. You three should be okay now, Shit, we were winning the goddam game, and now it could go down in the loss column. A fucking forfeit."

Karl and I shook hands with Leroy and Boony. Judy stretched up to give them kisses on the cheek. Funny, the ground did not tremble nor did distant volcanoes erupt but that was the first time I'd ever seen a white chick kiss a colored guy, even on the cheek. Bloomy is kind of advanced for a sophomore.

The Evening Bulletin sports pages offered the score as 48-43, and noted that the game had been suspended at half time due to a fire in the cafeteria. The article also mentioned that there had been incidents during the evacuation. The Inquirer and Daily News noted unruly behavior, scuffles in the hallways, but failed to detail that the game had been aborted. I had suspected that newspapers were manipulative sources of information; this coverage of events confirmed my darkest suspicions.

Ratchinov was worried about his stats. In baseball .300 is the magic number, the benchmark for Stars. There is a vast chasm between .299 and .300, maybe only one stinking Texas leaguer of a difference but not the same thing. For basketball, glory is invested in the number Twenty. Knocky scored twelve points in that abbreviated game, was bugged by the notion that the twelve would be unfairly slipped into his totals as a full game, dropping his season average to below Twenty. He was fixated on that Twenty. I had to do the math calculations for him, explain that he'd have to average 22 a game for the next four games in order to return to the pantheon.

His other pressing concern was that the upcoming match with Overbrook might be cancelled. Overbrook was the team to beat to reach the finals, but there had been a contentious Assembly Hall at Franklin where the Principal warned the student body that if there were any more incidents in the hallways the entire rest of the season might be cancelled.

Adults sniff at our infantile concerns, but we live or die by our stats. The evening before the Overbrook game Karl and I were in Dave's. Dad lets us shoot pool if we first put in two hours of studying, and tell him where we are going. What he will not tolerate is lies. For my stats, this night was an historic occasion, the first time I ever ran a full rack. I was playing against Burdumi; he was not better with a cue stick than he was at basketball, a five-buck bet. When my fifteenth ball dropped into the side pocket after a fancy bank shot the kibitzing spectators whooped and said that Little Doc was ready to head downtown to Allinger's and take on Willy Mosconi.

Knocky came slouching into the poolroom, strangely off, like a clown collapsing out of those miniature cars in the circus. Karl waved for him to come over, join the celebration; Knocky waved us off, staggered directly toward the bathroom in the rear. He was hunched over in pain, like a guy in dire need to take a piss but holding it in. Karl said, "Shit, something's wrong. Knocky looks like he's hurt bad."

Burdumi said, "c'mon. Burris. Another go-around. Double or nothing."

"He looks like he was jumped out on the streets, banged around pretty badly," Karl said, then hurried towards the smelly John in the rear.

"Just pay the goddam time, forget the damn bet, " I said to Burdumi, and followed Wronsky down the aisle. No doubts bastards around the table would accuse me of chickening out on demanding my dough from Burdumi.

In the toilet Alexi was slumped against the wall. His face was damp, glistening from water he splashed on it; the water could not hide swelling, bruises and gashes. Blood splotched his scalp. Karl was saying, "Woof, were you hit by a truck, man?"

"Nah, nah," Knocky mumbled," I'm okay, I'm alright."

That is said in practically every stupid movie.

"What the hell happened to you?" Karl asked Alexi.

"Ah, I was coming out of this candy store over by Fourth and George, five Porto Ricans jumped me, came charging out of the alley."

From his halting delivery, that did not sound too convincing. So far, around our way, nobody ever heard of Porto Ricans jumping anybody. Karl caught that weak tone, too, and snapped, "What the fuck you lying for, man? Tell us what the hell went down. You're covering up for somebody."

"C'mon," I said, "If my father is still at home I'll have him fix you up. Otherwise, we'll walk you over to the emergency ward at the Northern Liberties."

Knocky spit blood out of his mouth and protested, "Nah, I can't bother your old man, I've bugged him enough already, I'll go to the emergency at the Saint Joe's."

"Shut the fuck up, dumb ass," Karl ordered Knocky, putting his arm around his shoulder to steady him. I joined in the effort; between the two of us we walked Alexi out of the pool hall. His legs and knees were rubbery, like dissolving easy putty; he would have hit the deck unless we held him up.

A freezing night; Alexi was wearing no jacket, only a flannel shirt. As we crossed Girard, Karl said, "You've been worked over. Was it your Momma's boyfriend?"

Knocky tossed his head, not caring to answer, fighting off zephyrs and swirling stars. I said, "Spill it, man. What the shit is going down?"

"Ach," Alexi groaned," she was home tonight, said she wasn't feeling well. Roy was pissed because he had to go in to work. They got into an argument; I don't know what the fuck about. Bauer slapped her. I flipped out when he did that and threw the radio at him. Threw it at his head but it only hit his shoulder. Roy came tearing into me, pounding me with lefts and rights, my Mom began screaming like crazy, and she hit Bauer with a flower vase. Then it really got weird. Roy turns around and gives her this weirdo laugh. They start making up and tell me I should mind my own business; I shouldn't get into the middle of their personal fights, that's their stuff. I was all woozy and ready to pass out but I had to get the fuck out of that nuthouse."

Karl sang, "There'll be Blue birds over, the white cliffs of Dover, one day, just you wait and see, love and laughter, peace forever after, one day, just you wait and see."

"You do better with the 'Bells of Saint Mary,'" I told Wronsky.

"Screw it all," Knocky groaned. The Balls of Saint Mary."

In another minute we would have missed him. Dad was just coming out of the parlor with Mrs. Minnie Gottbaum, one of his new girlfriends, as we entered the vestibule. She was in a scarlet wool suit and stylish mink coat; they were leaving for dinner. The smile vanished from Dad's face as he saw that we were holding up a drooping Alexi. Mrs. Gottbaum exclaimed, "Oh, my God, what happened to this boy?"

Knocky looked up and mumbled, "Sorry to bother you again, Doc. I told these guys to take me over to Saint Joe's but they dragged me in here. Sorry."

Pop has a knack for acting calmly when everybody else is excited. He said. "Minnie, dear, please wait in the living room, fix yourself another drink while I attend to Alexi here. He looks like he needs a simonize and lube job."

"Your nurse is gone for the day, "Mrs. Gottbaum said. "You're sure you don't need my help, Dan? I can help you scrub the boy up?"

Mucho noblesse obliges here, or is she stooping to conquer? Along Marshall Street it is known that Mrs. Gottbaum is a prominent socialite widow with extensive holdings in Sun Oil and Eastern Air Lines. Even Aunt Sara conceded that she was not after dad for his money.

"No, I'll handle this. Fix yourself another drink, dear. This might take a while."

Mrs. Gottbaum touched Dad's cheek., possessively, before gliding back past the potted plants toward the parlor. A stacked brunette, cross between Mrs. Barufkin and Mrs. Fiore; Dad was hardly faithful to a woman; more faithful to a type. Come to think of it, Mrs. Gottbaum resembled what Leonora might look like by now.

Examining Knocky's face, Dad asked him, "How's the other guy look?"

"He's bleeding, too. I caught him with a few shots."

"Glad to hear that. C'mon, let's patch up your movie star profile, Alexi. Unless you intend to do the Boris Karloff roles."

Karl entered the office with us, the medical area of this house was virtually Terra Incognita Ultima Thule for me, I rarely came in here. Nothing had changed. Adverse to most innovations, Dad still had his antiquated scale with the metal doojiggers on the balancing rod. Mrs. Jordan was always urging him to renovate and modernize his facilities. She especially complained about the fading yellow anatomical charts on the walls, one for arteries and veins, one with the muscles and ligaments, another for the skeleton and the bones. Dads said why bother to change them when human anatomy had not changed much in the last five thousand years.

"I'm sorry about imposing on you Doc," Knocky muttered as Dad eased him onto an examination table. "Coming in here messed up when you're all ready to go out."

"People don't drop in to see me when they're feeling top the morning, Alexi."

The walls were covered with photos of Dad at political conventions, dinner with the Mayor, dinner with a Senator, Degrees from the University of Pennsylvania,

Magna and Suma. Board Licenses, Certificates of Merit, and photos of Sporty Dan Burris holding up a prize sailfish in Cape May. On the far wall was a larger version of the portrait of Leonora that I had in the mother of pearl frame upstairs.

Dad donned his white smock and snapped on rubber gloves. The man has such an old fashioned way of working. He brought out his rubber hammer, checked on Knocky's reflexes, then began tapping the hammer on his back, chest, and ribs, searching for fractures. Satisfied that nothing was broken, Dad began cleaning up the more blatant cuts and gashes with alcohol. Knocky was squirming and twitching like a fish trying to avoid having his head cut off, his head flopping from side to side.

After kneading the scalp, Dad said, "You'll be needing stitches for this hole in your head, Alexi. First you get two shots, an anti-biotic, and an anti-inflammatory. These will hurt you more than they do me. I will allow you one small scream."

Wronsky and I winced as the injections were applied. We were also wincing at Dad's dry attempts at levity. Whatever merits Mrs. Gottbaum saw in this man, it could not be his rip-roaring sense of humor that mesmerized her.

Knocky was doing the John Wayne routine, 'just yank out the arrow and let me get back to the fight,' he emitted only a low moan for the needles. Dad said, "Good soldier. And now would you care to talk about it, Alexi?"

"Talk about what? " Knocky said, playing it dumb.

"Well, was this a street rumble, gang warfare, or did you attempt to force your attentions on a young lady conversant with judo?"

"It's sort of embarrassing," Knocky said.

"I'll bet," Dad said. " But, if this, by chance, happened at home, you're a minor. By law I am obliged to report suspected cases of domestic abuse to the authorities."

Karl and I glanced at each other. We were sharing the same thought.

Alexi said, "It's over, "I'd rather not talk about it."

"Bullshit," Karl snapped. "If you aint gonna' tell him, I'll tell Doc. You didn't get any spanking, Knocky. That bastard whacked you around. You're a bloody mess."

Dad applied his surgical scissors and began snipping away the hair over the gash in Knocky's scalp. It puzzles me how his powerful hands become tippy-toe-through-the-tulips delicate when he performs these procedures. He resembles a nature lover merrily snipping away the weeds in his garden.

Alexi said, "We have this boarder at our house. He lives on the second floor back. My Mom got in an argument with him. I opened my mouth when I shouldn't have."

"A boarder eh?" Dad said. "Do his leasing arrangements include the right to bounce you off the furniture?"

Knocky shrugged, and mumbled, "Well, Roy Bauer is also the bouncer at the night club where my Mom hatchecks, they're kind of engaged to be married."

Nightclub? Knocky doesn't know a euphemism from his Bubba's bloomers but tonight he was tossing around the euphemisms.

"Kind of engaged to be married," Dad repeated. "Yes, I'm familiar with that area."

Knocky shuddered, verged on passing out, but straightened up as Dad brought out the surgical thread and curved needle, began sewing the stitches into the raw scalp. Karl and I were writhing sedately in our chairs. Each dip of that needle was a deep dig into our own hides, Karl reacting the same as me, the Curse of the Corsican Brothers was in full force, while Knocky was gutting it out, not a groan out of this plucky lad, John Wayning it all the way. 'Yank out the arrow, Clem.'

Too painful for me to watch, I looked elsewhere, spotted an object I had never noticed before in this office, a glass bowl on the shelf behind the desk. Unless I was mistaken the contents of the bowl were cartridges and spent bullets. Was that Dad's secret temple of vanity, a mystical chalice of misdeeds past? Could one of those bullets have been extracted from the hide of one Joseph Spinelli? Karl was also staring at the bowl. I suspected we might again be sharing the same thought.

Doing the last stitch on Knocky's scalp, Dad said, "Roy Bauer, eh?"

Knocky said, "From Jersey but he tries to come off as a rootin-tootin Tex Ritter."

Dad gave his shoulder a gruff, paternal punch and said," That's it, I'm impressed, you've been a good soldier. You okay, or do I bring out the smelling salts?"

"I'm okay, " Knocky wheezed, not too convincingly. Then he shook himself like a shaggy dog escaping from the scrub brush and wash pail.

Snapping off his rubber gloves, Dad said, "What you need now is rest. Sack out. In fact, you will spend the night here, up in the guest suite with Karl. Call your Mom and tell her you need further medical attention. As a precautionary measure I'd like to see some x-rays of your thick, empty skull."

"She'll be pissed, sir. Even pissed that I came to you."

"Don't sweat it," Dad said. "I'll call her, and tell her to cool it. Often, in these violent domestic episodes and loving family tiffs the bouts can go into extra innings."

Karl frowned, also puzzled by the way Dad was mangling his mixed metaphors.

"I have one question for you, Doc," Knocky said.

"Shoot."

"Tomorrow we have a decisive game against Overbrook. I can play, can't I?"

"You nuts, son? In the shape you're in?"

"Maybe a little nuts," Knocky conceded. "But it's a key game, could easily decide who clinches the championship. I can't let the team down."

"Of course not," Dad said. "And, what does it matter if you get banged around, knocked down, stepped on, and all my beautiful stitches snap open. Who cares if there's permanent damage to your health? We must never let the team down."

"You're saying I can't play, eh?"

"We're finally communicating," Dad said. "Good. Now you three boys go to the parlor and say goodnight to Mrs. Gottbaum, tell her I'll be with her shortly."

"I don't know how to thank you, Doc," Knocky mumbled.

"First by getting the hell out of here. Scoot. Scat," Dad said, and then repeated," Roy Bauer, eh?"

"Yes, sir. From Jersey. "

Leaving the office I saw Dad scribbling the name down on his prescription pad. As with most doctors, his scribbles can pass for Etruscan hieroglyphics. I'm always connecting items that don't necessarily link up but the way he wrote that name down reminded me of Gall moving his finger in Go-d's bar.

CHAPTER NINE

The X-rays proved negative but Dad called Franklin in the morning and informed the office that student Alexi Ratchinov would be taking the day off, sick. Over breakfast Knocky swore to Dad that he would head back upstairs, clock in more rest and recuperation. That did not happen. When Karl and I returned from school that afternoon Miss Pearl told us that around Noon Alexi gave her a wink, snuck out of the house, wearing one of my heavy winter jackets.

Dad was teed. He does not like to be deceived, said he might wash his hands of the whole matter, have nothing more to do with Alexi. I could understand his sentiments; you do your best but some dummies are too stupid to handle help.

That evening snow flurries were whipping around, it was too nasty to walk even the half block up to the poolroom. Karl and I played chess in our game room while listening to records, the Harry James and Benny Goodman jazz concert with the great riff on 'American Patrol. Dad was in his second floor library with Mrs. Fiore, listening to his vintage Lily Pons and Caruso records. I don't know who called whom first but prima facie, she was restored to the roster. They had reservations for dinner in South Philly. Last night, Mrs. Gottbaum, tonight, Carla; how does the man get away with it? Maybe he believes there is safety in numbers?

Near eight the doorbell began to ring. Miss Pearl had gone home. Nurse Jordan had already closed the office. Often Dad sees patients past eight; tonight he had cleared space for an Italian Dinner at Victor's where you can call in advance and request the opera of your choice along with a personal menu.

The buzzer continued buzzing. Karl and I snorted. It's a real pain in the kazoo to live in a house with a doctor's gold plate outside; the plaque is a neon sign blinking HASSLE ME. Not a week goes by without strangers pressing the doorbell after midnight; victims of muggings or kitchen tussles bleed on our steps.

Tipping my King over, as usual I was losing, I said, "I'll get it. And tell whoever's out there to go the hell to Saint Joe's or the emergency ward on Seventh Street."

Rising, Karl said, "I'll go down with you. We might as well eat now. Miss Pearl left tasty-looking hoagie sandwiches and potato salad for supper."

As we descended the stairs, Dad winked at us from the music room. When his lady friends visit he leaves the door open to certify that no kitschy-cooing is taking place. He should not bother. We trust him, to a degree.

The buzzing grew shriller. Usually, ringing this frantic and persistent meant a father from one of these houses without a telephone to blurt out that his wife had just broken water. I opened the frosted inner door of the vestibule; tonight it was Knocky on the steps with wild flurries swirling behind him. He was wearing his woolen rag picker's raggedy-ass overcoat making him look like a drab Muzhik climbing out of the rubble of Leningrad. Over his arm he was carrying the winter jacket I had not authorized him to borrow. Opening the door I saw bloodstains on my jacket, blood smears under his nostrils, pinpoints of blood from ruptured stitches mixing with the glistening snowflakes in his scalp.

"Jesus," Karl groaned as Knocky staggered into the vestibule." What the Sam Hell happened now? You looked like the Abominable Snowman standing out there."

Cheeks red and raw, eyes wild, dried tears under them, Alexi had been slapped around again. From the swelling, tomorrow he would have a great shiner.

"Try not to bleed on the potted plants," I said. Karl steadied Knocky while I dipped into the waiting room, brought out a chair for the walking wounded. He was in worse shape than when he staggered into Dave's last night.

"My old man is pissed off about you disobeying orders," I said, helping Knocky to sink into the chair "Before I call my him again tell me what the shit is going on."

Tossing his head, Knocky said, "Ah, I'm all fucked up. After the game I went home to see if the coast was clear. My Mom was out, Roy was there."

"You went to the game?" Karl moaned in disbelief. "You played?"

"Yeah," Knocky mumbled. "That's a different story. The thing is, I was still in my basketball uniform when I came home. The coach had called a taxi for me, even paid for the taxi. Bauer started to snicker at me, asked how come the poor, hopeless baby could play ball when I'm supposed to be all beaten up and battered, poor baby. He called me a treacherous fink gutless rat for squealing on him, and purposely trying to get his probation revoked, to have him sent back to the clink."

Karl said. " Hey, that would be a good idea."

"Yeah," Knocky agreed. "But I took all his crap, didn't say a word back. Then he called me a phony two-faced shit acting up to spoil my Mom's happiness, trying to break things up between them because deep down I am jealous, down deep I am a sick fuck who wants to fuck my Momma myself."

"Woof, " Karl groaned. "What a sweetheart. And a Freudian psychologist, too?"

"I couldn't take that," Knocky said. "I swung at him; that was all the excuse he needed to tear into me with rights and lefts, finish it with a head butt. Then he swore that if I squeal on him again he will snap my spine."

Knocky brought out a handkerchief; his nose had started to bleed again. I was about to hurry upstairs, ask Dad to come down. No need to, the Arabesque door opened. Dad was in his blue cashmere overcoat, Mrs. Fiore in a silver fox shorty as elegant as Mrs. Gottbaum's mink last night. Looming above, Dad spotted Knocky and bristled like a Boris Godunov about to order heads lopped off, but as he descended the staircase, saw Knocky pressing the bloody rag to his nose, his expression softened. All he said was, "You're beginning to make a habit of this, Alexi."

"I'm sorry, Doc," Knocky mumbled, The handkerchief muffled his apologies. Dad's eyes rose to the heavens as Knocky dropped my blood- stained jacket to the floor, slipped out of his scraggly overcoat to reveal that he was still in his basketball uniform. Mrs. Fiore joined Dad in arching her lashes. Dad opened his mouth to offer her profound apologies, suggest she have another drink. Pushing him toward the office door, Carla said, "Forget it, Doctor Christian, you've an urgent case to mend here. The Rigoletto can wait. But I'd also like the chance to dig my nails into this boy for delaying our dinner plans."

Knocky was gulping; he was not sure whether she was kidding or serious.

Off went Dad's cashmere overcoat. On went the white smock and rubber gloves. Next, the deep injections and out came the stitching needles again. With minor modifications in the text and cast this seemed like a sequel to last night's drill, or maybe last night was a rehearsal for tonight's performance. Mrs. Fiore was not a woman to remain upstairs with a drink and Verdi while her date was tending to business. A take-charge type with her First Aid Red Cross badges, she slipped on rubber gloves, started helping Dad, dabbing cotton balls into alcohol, cleaning up Knocky's more overt bruises. I had a vision of her having done this before. She was classy lady but had a touch of the rough and tumble 'I've seen it all' mob moll.

"Against my explicit orders, Alexi, you went and played ball?" Dad said.

"It wasn't quite like that, sir. I went to school, the coach saw the patches by my ear, but he let me suit up to sit on the bench, to give moral support to the team."

"Then, you didn't play?" Dad insisted. "You rooted rah-rah-rah, that's all."

"Well, yes and no, sir."

"What the hell does that mean?" Dad snapped,

"Well, sir, the coach definitely didn't intend to send me into the game, but with four minutes to play Overbrook was leading by five points, sixty-one to fifty-six, I was pleading with him to send me in because all our guys were cold, nothing was dropping for them, while the crowd was chanting, 'Lefty! Lefty!' but he said no way."

"Hey, this is really dramatic," Karl whispered.

Dad glared at Karl to silence him, then said, " Cut out the B.S. please. Alexi. Were you actually allowed to play? In the rotten condition you're in?"

"Well, the coach said, 'Can you give me two minutes, boy?' And I said, 'you got them, coach.' And I went out there, and shot two fast buckets, the crowd was going ape. Seconds left, just as the buzzer sounded, I threw up a Hail Mary shot. It was right in there, but rolled around the rim twice, and fell out, so we lost by one point."

"Ach, you blew your chance to become a legend," I said to Knocky.

"That's enough out of you, " Dad told me. To Knocky he said, " I'll be talking to my lawyers tomorrow about our suing the coach, the school, and the Board of Education for endangering the health and welfare of a minor."

"Please don't, Doc." Knocky pleaded." The coach is a great guy, he even sent me home in a taxi, paid for the cab. I'm really sorry that I have to bother you so much but I couldn't take it if anything bad happened to the coach."

"Very noble of you, "Dad said. " And maybe I'm the one who should be sorry. This is a matter I should have handled instantly, Alexi. I let it slide this morning,"

Mrs. Fiore had finished swabbing the clots. She pinched Knocky's cheek, not too gently, and said, "You're a real sweety-pie. Dan told me about you, said you were gorgeous, but not the brightest bulb on the Christmas tree."

"Hey, why get down on a guy when he's down? " I said in Knocky's defense.

"Another country heard from," Dad said with a snort. "You have my permission to remain silent until further notice. " Then Dad held up his surgical thread and curved stitching needle, while asking Knocky, "So what do you have planned on your busy schedule for tomorrow, Alexi? A double-header?"

"Nothing, sir. I'll do whatever you say."

"Fine, the first order of business, please try not to moan too loudly," Dad said and began to stitch up the slash on Knocky's shoulder. None of that 'yank out the arrow' Sergeant Stryker crap tonight, Knocky was trembling with every knit and pearl as Dad worked on the gashes on his back and neck. Mrs. Fiore was delicate enough to see that Knocky was embarrassed by her seeing his suffering, She went to Nurse Jordan's desk in the outer office to phone Victor's, and explain that they would be late for their reservations.

Dad said to Knocky, "So, after you failed to become a legend, you went home, and I surmise that you antagonized the same individual?"

"Not quite, sir. I tried to play it cool, but my Mom was not there, and he did his best to provoke me. Finally he said horrible stuff that I just could not swallow. So I swung at him, and he tore into me, and banged me around."

"Care to tell us what was so terrible?" Dad asked.

With his chin Knocky pointed at Mrs. Fiore, sitting maybe within earshot. He whispered, "I can't repeat it, Doc. Not with a lady around. "

"Good enough, "Dad said. "And, that was the extent of it?"

Gulping first, looking sheepishly at Karl and me, Knocky said, "There was more. I didn't want to touch this but Bauer knocked you, sir. Said stuff about you being no plaster saint, stuff about you and my Aunt Svetla."

Karl and I glanced at each other. Alexi had not mentioned that detail in his initial recapitulation of the catastrophe.

Shrugging, Dad said, "Shows that the man is up on his local gossip." Dad brought out his rubber hammer for the tapping routine, and said, "So far, nothing is perceptibly broken, I don't think we'll need more X-rays, but you'll again spend the night here. Go upstairs, and rest. No need to hit the sack immediately, but get some rest."

"Maybe he aint et yet," I suggested to my father.

Wincing, Dad said," Oof, you are a disgrace to Central, my son. Go feed him then."

Knocky mumbled, "I'm truly sorry about disturbing you so much, sir. "

"Prove it, " Dad said, snapping off his rubber gloves and ordering us to vamoose with a dismissive toss of the chin. Mrs. Fiore returned, and gave Alexi an affectionate shove as we left the office. She'd make a great stepmom; she combines a cool and zesty mix of tenderness and vinegary ornery toughness.

Karl set the table in the parlor; we split up the bowl of potato salad and tore off chunks of our hoagies so Alexi could eat. I heard Dad dialing in the outer office. I'd never done this before. Bringing a cautionary finger to my lips, I picked up the extension to eavesdrop. Karl and Knocky scowled, warning me that this was a no-no.

Dad was talking to Dave from the poolroom, asking the manager to put Billy Schmitz on the line. I heard the clicking of billiards balls, the din of the TV in the background. I'd no idea that my righteous old man knew a lowlife like Billy.

Schmitz answered the phone saying," I'm here for you, Doc."

"We need a small favor, William."

"Shoot, Doc. Anything you say."

"I know it's snowing, nasty out, but I've a badly banged up kid here. If I call the authorities they'll send four social workers, three investigators, and two supervisors to hop around with their fingers up theirs Asses before anything gets resolved. I need you to drop by the Ratchinov house on Randolph, like, at once, and pick up Alexi's things. Tell them to hand over his clothes, textbooks, and toilet articles. Give them to you; you bring them straight here tonight."

"Gotcha, Doc. But you say *them*. Who is the *'them'* I gotta' deal with?"

"Sonya will be with one Roy Bauer, a thug that I understand recently joined our local collection of thugs. I believe he's the bozo who smacked Alexi around."

"I've seen the fucker coming into Dave's. Pushes people around, doesn't dare look my way at all, but I'd love to lam into the prick just on general principles,"

"No, William, no. Maybe that can come later but the object tonight is not violence. I want you to fly the mission and bring back the goods."

"What happens if they balk and give me back-lip? How persuasive can I get with them, Doc?"

"Avoid rough stuff tonight. Suggest to them that if they don't want to deal with a nice, sweet guy like you they can choose from A or B on the menu. A is a patrol car arriving from the Buttonwood Street Station to pick up Bauer for abuse of a minor and parole violations. B is more serious. Individuals will drop by to talk to Roy. I'd call on them tonight but they tend to go overboard when I ask for small favors."

"Gotcha, Doc. Nobody likes Bauer. And now that I hear he slapped Knocky around I'm really anxious to lay into him. I'm shooting pool with Hawaiian Jack, here. He's a peg leg now but maybe Jack could tag along with me for emphasis. Jack always likes a little action."

"If you want Jack along for back-up, fine, but I need you to finesse this, William. No action or rough stuff, tonight. Who knows what the future holds? Tonight you're to get the boy's things from the house, and bring them here. Is that clear, William?"

"We hear you, Doc. I will wrap this up fast."

I waited till Dad clicked off before putting down the receiver. Karl and Alexi stared at me, awaiting my report. The voice had been unrecognizable. I was accustomed to Dad sounding like the cryptic football coach, the genial small town physician on the family-oriented radio show; the man on that call sounded like Edgar G. Robinson ordering the rub-out of a rival rum-runner.

Knocky moved in upstairs, and that was that. No papers, nothing written down, this arrangement was de facto, informal, probably illegal. Miss Pearl can be testy at times but when it comes to kids she believes in the more the merrier. Besides that, since she had another mouth to feed, another batch of clothes to launder, Dad increased her weekly wages by ten dollars. Nurse Jordan muttered objections. After Dad snarled at her for broaching the subject she mentioned Alexi no more. Saturday morning, when Dad gave Karl and me our weekly allowance he casually passed a ten spot to Alexi. Knocky protested, Dad thrust the ten into his shirt pocket, his reticent style of establishing that Alexi would be treated as one more son cluttering up the House Of Burris.

In the stalls along Marshall they clucked about how Billy Schmitz and Hawaiian Jack dropped by the Ratchinov house, left with a duffle bag containing Alexi's gear.

Roy Bauer, supposed to be such a Holy Terror, did not say Jack Shit. In the Girard Avenue restaurants observers with a literary bent said that Doctor Dan was a character out of Saroyan or Thornton Wilder, and seemed to be setting up his own replica of 'Boy's Town.' In my own family, running a poll, Moe and Sara thoroughly approved; Aunts Ethel and Fanny, plus their spouses were dubious but neutral; Aunt Rosalyn was consistently outraged. But then, Ros is the relative nobody pays any attention to.

Dad had all the prestige and admiration a man would ever need. His reputation soared after articles appeared two weeks later, describing the brutal beating of the bouncer at the Cosmo Club. Nobody was talking about heart-warming sentimental Saroyan or Thornton Wilde now. Anything literary coming to mind it was 'I, the Jury,' Mike Hammer. Mickey Spillane. Bauer already had his terrible rap for welching on bets and his bullying tactics in the poolroom, so local readers chuckled at the accounts of rowdy irate patrons, expelled earlier from the Cosmo Club, waited for Roy after closing time in the Locust Street parking lot to administer savage gangland style retaliation. The bouncer suffered severs facial damage, lost teeth, and his right arm was broken. He was no longer in critical care but was still convalescing in the intensive care unit at Temple University Hospital.

Nobody along Marshall Street bought that baloney about rowdy patrons. Commentators contended that it was Billy Schmitz and Hawaiian Jack in the parking lot; other experts claimed that this was a classic South Philly style working over. When a debate like this rages the mere facts soon hardly matter. Whether it was mob muscle or two of our own up-and-coming gorillas, it became firmly fixed in local lore that Big Doc had pulled levers of power, and still had access to those levers.

Given the geography, propinquity, and the irregular circumstances our trio now had to avoid Ludlow schoolyard. For the next few months we played our basketball at the Christ Church gym down by Second and Arch, and the Stoddert Junior High gym at Thirteenth and Green. Only once did we run into Mrs. Ratchinov, and her 'boarder.' We were coming out of the Ambassador Dairy Restaurant, Seventh and Girard, Sunday night, bars and strip clubs closed due to the Blue Laws, up the street, leaving the Astor Movie, come Sonya and Roy, the lovebirds arm in arm. I'd seen Bauer around before this; he was no longer wearing that dirty gray plaster cast on his forearm. We paused, twenty yards apart, a tremendously awkward moment, Knocky staring at his Mom; she was looking back at him, separated by an invisible, painful gorge. Mrs. Ratchinov had gone down a great deal in my estimation: I did not mind her being depraved and sexy, in fact, I thought that was pretty nifty, but it was going too far to be 'a bad mother.' From the way she was trembling I expected that at any moment she would rush at Alexi, opened-armed, like the peasant women do in the Russian war flics, Momma racing through the swaying wheat fields when she spots her wounded son returning from the front. Karl afterwards said he had been expecting a similar reaction but that never happened. She offered resistance but Bauer wrapped his arm around her waist, hustled her across Girard toward the Capitol restaurant.

Our next sighting of Bauer came two weeks later. Our quartet was in Dave's; Karl was teaching Judy how to shoot pool. Bloomy is a breakthrough pioneering type: first White girl I ever saw kiss a Colored guy, first chick ever to shoot pool in Dave's. There was no sign on the door but till now the only females entering this joint were Jiggs and Maggy wives bursting in to drag hubby home by the ear. Judy was here to shoot pool, which the shaggy clientele found to be amusing; she was by no means as yet curvaceous, only tentatively filling out, but when she stretched across the green felt for a shot spectators at adjacent tables gave her the same hawk-eyed squints they awarded Mrs. Ratchinov for entering a taxi.

There was a split in time, a dip in the racket, when Roy Bauer entered. A lull. You might have thought a storm trooper barged into a synagogue flaunting a Swastika on his armband. We were instantly in a fishbowl, periscopes shot up, every sharpy in this joint was wired into complications and complexities of this arrival.

Seeing this creature was like spotting a black roach crawling across your creamy white wedding cake. The hoods in the center city parking lot had done a flawed job of putting Roy out of commission. If I had the balls I would ask Dad for a sequel.

Strutting along in his freaky silver-studded snaky cowboy boots, Roy still had the audacity to project a malevolent aura though everybody knew he had chickened out when confronted by our local muscle, then had the crap beaten out of him down by the strip club. Billy Schmitz and Hawaiian Tom spotted Bauer and stirred like lions observing a plump antelope entering their glade. They looked at me, I signaled them to cool it when I saw that Bauer was not going to approach us, he was heading for the poker in the back room. They relaxed and the door closed behind Bauer, the din and buzzing returned to normal levels, newsy bodies were still staring our way.

Judy was about to say something sarcastic; Karl motioned her to can it for once. Knocky had been with us since January, so far we had never once discussed his offbeat situation. After tossing his head, Knocky chalked up, glanced at the poker room door, and said to us, "Yesterday I saw my Mom over at Svetla's place."

"Doc knows about that?" I asked him.

"Yeah, the only direct order your Dad has given me, I can see her but I need to tell him first, and, if I see her, it has to be a place where Bauer aint around."

"A shame the hoods in the parking lot didn't finish that job," Karl said.

"A crying shame." Knocky agreed. "Make my life simpler."

What could that conversation in Svetla's house been about? Mrs. Ratchinov had always been so sickeningly icky-gooey lovey-dovey with Alexi, how could she let him drift off into exile in a neighbor's house? What does Knocky feel when he sees a bastard like Bauer grab his Momma around the waist, hustle her off.

Later we drifted over to Gansky's for the Texas Tommies and malted milks. Then we walked Judy home to the Sweet Shoppe on Marshall Street. Knocky and I hung back to let Karl and Judy get in their last minute smooching in the darkened doorways. Bloomy was all over the guy, she is brasher, more forward than Wronsky.

"Bauer's recovered," I said. "The cast is off, he's not gimping anymore."

"Yeah," Knocky agreed. "Back at work and Mom says he's mostly forgiven me."

"He-what? Forgiven you? What the hell does that mean?"

"Mom says guys who've been in the slammer a long time come out with their heads all fucked up. Cons don't think like we do, so we gotta' give them leeway."

"I believe that I will never understand women," I said. "And I'm starting off my career of confusion by not understanding girls."

"Me, neither," Knocky said. "But the next time I'm supposed to see Mom is in church on Sunday. Doc has already Okayed it. The other, I don't know about. My Mom asked me if I could find it in my heart to pray for the soul of Roy Bauer."

June, we returned to Ludlow, Knocky had it from his Aunt Svetla that his Mom and Bauer were on vacation over in Jersey, Wildwood, so the coast was clear for us. Entering the yard it was the Return of us Natives, handshakes, slapping of palms, wisecracks like, "Ah. You made bail, eh?" Our pack in this yard was not noted for its delicacy but, to my surprise, nobody mentioned the real causes for our prolonged absence. The entire neighborhood knew where Knocky lived now, and why.

Karl was teaching Judy basketball, she was shaping up as a regular jock, matching up against the boys. Several holdouts objected to paying with a chick, other guys enjoyed how her apples jiggled in her polo shirt while she dribbled around. Rebounding, forget it, but it turned out that she had a good eye; in spite of those goofy goggles she needed for reading, she could pop in set shots from half court To tease her, Burdumi said, " You know, Bloomy, I don't know who's side you're on. We usually play shirts on against shirts off."

Accepting the challenge, Judy said, "I'm game if you're game." She moved as if to peel off her polo shirt, provoking a whoop from the assembled scrounges. Then she said, "Why not pants on against pants off. Show me what you got, big boy. " With that she lowered the side zipper of her skirt, showing off a patch of pink panty.

That earned her more hearty whoops; we all broke out laughing. A mild afternoon, skies a pastel blue, why could it not be like this always, kids yucking it up in the schoolyard? Sure, we each had problems but this might be a tiny slice of a Golden Age. Most people do not know they are living through a glorious period until afterwards, when the historians tag it as a Golden Age. For our trio of Mosqueteers this was our Pony League Golden Age. Introduced by my Central high Rat pack I had begun dting uptown family girls; in his guise as Lefty-Two, Knocky was making out like a bandit with the dusky ladies of William Penn High, he said they were showing him dance steps, the mashed potatoes and bugaloo, they were showing him lots more than that; Karl and Bloomy were conducting their torrid romance, every afternoon he walked up from Roman at Broad and Vine to pick her up at Girl's High, they nuzzled and necked all the way back to Marshall Street. For this pair prosaic industrial Spring Garden Street could be a tres Jolie Rue de la Paix and cruddy Center City Philly was Paris in the Spring.

Then I saw Sylvan Gans entering the schoolyard by the far gate. 'Hey, what the shit was this slob-ass bastard doing invading my Golden Age?' Back to Earth. Well, Thank you, Lord, for that brief tour of Felicity Acres, but why did you have to bring me back to crappy old Earth?

That evening Mrs. Minnie Gottbaum took us to dinner at Schoyer's Restaurant on Arch Street; she was just back from Florida, apparently wanted to make a big splash to celebrate a triumphal return. Dad had more or less narrowed down the field, he was again seeing Mrs. Fiore, but Mrs. Maxine Barufkin had called him, indicating a desire to resume their relationship.

Fidgeting with his necktie, Knocky took in the plush establishment, the polished wine goblets, silver tureens for the soup, pompous waiters tramping around like Prussian Field Marshalls. Schoyer's was by far the plushest feeding lot he had ever seen. In comparison the Capitol up on Girard was a Texas League roadside hash house; Himmelstein's might be AAA, Schoyer's was the Major Leagues. Dad signaled Knocky to stop fidgeting. Lately Dad's been acting more like a full-fledged father, correcting his manners, and forcing Knocky to study more.

"You boys look so beautiful in your suits," Mrs. Gottbaum gushed. "I've brought along my camera to take pictures of the occasion."

An expedition to Wanamaker's brought Knocky's wardrobe up to scratch. Dad also insists that Alexi wear shoes nowadays, sneakers only for athletic occasions.

"Maybe you should leave me out of the picture?" Karl suggested. "I am not too photogenic. My friend, Judy, took snapshots of me up at the zoo, by the gorilla cage. The gorilla beat me out for leading man."

"You're attractive enough in your own special way," Mrs. Gottbaum assured Karl.

"Judy thinks he's Robert Taylor," Knocky said. "She truly needs those specs."

Dad motioned to Alexi to knock that off, then summoned the waiter to use Mrs. Gottbaum's Kodak. We squished together in the booth; Mrs. Gottbaum draped her arms possessively over Karl's and Alexi's shoulders. The lady was working hard to make a favorable impression, coming on too bubbly and effervescent. So far she had not dared to latch onto me. Like the Quakers say: 'do not thou me until I thee thee.'

"Smile for the birdy," the waiter chirped.

Isn't it time these clowns got some new lines? Next he will ask us to 'Cheese.'

The waiter snapped us 'en famille,' then the lady squirmed over my lap to be at Dad's side for a classic HIM and HER photo. Frankly, her bottom felt quite appealing as she slid over me to get at my father; we are supposed to cancel such thoughts.

Dad ordered ginger ales for us kiddies, Manhattans for the adults, a Chardonnay Blanc for the shrimp cocktails, a Bordeaux sec for the main course. He studies texts, catalogues, knows his wines, rarely makes a fuss about the grapes, his shows and pedantry are reserved for music. Knocky and Karl were gaping at the prices, and mumbling about ordering the meatloaf. Mrs. Gottbaum waved them off, ordered the porterhouse for all around. Winking, Dad told the waiter not to remove the goblets from the places of the three youngsters. He lets us have one Copa; he is training us to handle our alcohol intake.

Will it always be like this, Pierre: tinkling spoons, the shrimp, the porterhouse, a Kitschy violin, the cultivated buzz of refined people marinating in their privileges? Was I living through a Golden Age while failing to fully appreciate my good fortune? At adjacent tables were the familiar faces from the Dell and the lobby of the Academy of Music. The only new face here belonged to Alexi. He motioned to Dad, seeking permission to loosen his tie knot a bit. Dad signaled a negative. Mrs. Gottbaum overrode his veto. With pincering fingers she suggested he could loosen it a little. Scoring points, the lady. Three grown sons, she knows how to coddle cubs.

Wronsky took advantage of the permit granted Alexi to loosen his own tie. In his charcoal gray suit and sincere tie Karl looks like an incipient funeral parlor director, the solicitous kind offering deep discounts for double burials. In his azure blue suit Knocky could be a junior master of ceremonies, or the next flashy John the Wizard.

Over the shrimp cocktails Mrs. Gottbaum insisted on chatting about the subject of least interest to kids, our education. We made the polite and perfunctory noises appropriate to our age, and then the conversation went split-level: adults talking stock market, adolescents talking about the Phillies. Dad was advising Mrs. Gottbaum to get rid of her railroad stocks, dump the Reading and the Pennsy, stay away from the airlines. Historically, they've lost more money than they ever made.

The pumpernickel and the rye bread were crunchy, the pickled green tomatoes tart, the chilled Chardonnay exquisite, everything about this excellent meal was hunky-dory until Mrs. Gottbaum, out of left field, asked us, "How would you three boys like to live in Florida?"

What say? Why not the backside of the Moon? Why not Mars? Florida? Where did she pull that one from? In strictly physical terms none of us were gaping slack-jawed at her but, mentally, four males were erecting instant barricades. Dad signaled to me that my judicious silence would be his preferred response.

"Miami Beach, to be exact," Mrs. Gottbaum, explained. "I've a lovely home right on the beach, three empty bed rooms. You boys could swim every day, enjoy our fishing boat, wouldn't have to put up with these miserable Philadelphia winters anymore. And, there's a highly rated private school nearby; that would be my treat."

Dad was indicating he wished no precipitous noises from our peanut gallery.

"Here's the lowdown on this deal," Mrs. Gottbaum continued. "I'm trying to seduce your father. I proposed matrimony to the man. Dan still has his lingering doubts. I'm trying to persuade him to retire, move down to Florida with me, where he can still have a small practice if he needs that, but Dan can have a warm and wonderful life down there. And, so can you boys. One of his objections was that you three wouldn't want to go along with my schemes. I think you'd love Miami, the weather, the girls are so pretty. It is so much livelier than stuffy old Philadelphia. Besides, I've told the man, in just a few years you boys will all be out of the house, you'll all be in college."

Dad was being bushwhacked here. He had the right to be wearing the startled grin of a dolphin harpooned in mid-somersault, but wore his poker face, shrouded eyes gazing at distant horizons. We were all running our calculators, Dad worried about his freedom, Mrs. Fiore, his high-stakes poker, his stray Yettas from the Broadwood dances; Karl was in a panic, what about his Bloomy? Knocky was scared, his staying with us was totally off the books, shrewd hustlers like Sonya, Trixie, and Ivan could accuse Dad of a kidnapping if he transported him to Florida, could sue Dad, try to shake him down. Me? As much as I hate Philly, I love it. I'm an urban beast, crap on Miami and all suburbs, I'm camping out in cities with less than two million inhabitants. I need the beat of the streets, the wising off on the corner. What Miami? I'm not Cuban.

Noting our hesitation, Mrs. Gottbaum said, "Nothing as yet is engraved in stone. I'm just throwing this idea out so you boys can kick it around among yourselves. Your summer vacations start soon. I've already invited your Dad down to visit me. Now I'm inviting you three boys to come down and see what would be your rooms, the beach, our pool, the boat, this could be a glorious fun-filled vacation for you."

The sommelier had already uncorked the Bordeaux. Karl's jaw moved, he was about to voice objections, Dad telegraphed him to make with the mouth shut. We were spared the need to immediately respond, another waiter was arriving with the cart, the sizzling porterhouse, we could all ooh with anticipation.

The lady was a Lilith seeking to infiltrate our Oasis of Tranquility and Bastion of Manhood operating on Sixth Street. We all have our agendas and vested interests but who invited her? She was cute, reasonable, 'nice'; I see here as a Soviet Commissar laying out the strictures of her next Five Year plan. What might be a suitable headline for this story of a well-intentioned and determined woman glibly intruding her geriatric cravings into our mucho macho existence?

AMBITIOUS SQUAW THREATENS HAPPY HUNTING LODGE

During the remainder of the meal Mrs. Gottbaum continued singing the praises of Florida, extolling the merits of Miami, and the logic of her proposed arrangements while wearing the expression of a perplexed saleswoman refusing to believe the customers would not snatch up the grand bargain she was offering. Still, decorum prevailed. The uncomfortable moment finally came when Mrs. Gottbaum signaled to the waiter for the bill. Dad had skipped the cherry cheesecake for dessert; he had gone to the Men's room to wash his hands, now he was back. Mrs. Gottbaum was not pleased to hear the waiter telling her that the bill had already been taken care of.

CHAPTER TEN

We never reached Florida that summer. Neither did Dad. Shortly after that unfortunate incident at Schoyer's we had another invitation for dinner, this time from Mrs Barufkin. I'm not party to the behind-the-scenes-particulars, who called whom first to ask for forgiveness, beg for another chance, but after that overly forthright production number Dad cut Minnie Gottbaum from his roster, reinstated Maxine into his line-up. I'm ill equipped to decipher the erratic behavior of adults. Once, I was downtown on a Sunday night, snuck into the Broadwood to eavesdrop from behind the curtains on the antics of the fox trotters in those Golden Age Dances. From the way those flighty widows, matrons, and divorcees, were carrying on with the creaky codgers cavorting in there, changing partners and playing switchies, these affairs resembled highly traumatic Junior Proms.

June 25,the date sticks in my mind, horrible news on the radio, fighting erupting in Asia; the North Korean Communists had invaded the South; President Truman was considering sending in American troops. I remembered December 8, 1941, after the Japanese attacked Pearl Harbor, two buddies and me played hooky from Stevens Elementary, we shot downtown to the recruiting station at Thirteenth and Chestnut to behold a beautiful sight, the long lines of patriotic volunteers stretching around the block; Men, Women, Whites, Blacks, young toughies, old futzes. For Korea there were no lines. Nobody gave a damn about Korea. The word you heard on Marshall street was let them all kill each other, and we will congratulate the winners was.

Korea was distant on this sunny evening in June. Dad was strolling hand in hand with his Maxine; she lost weight since we last saw her, was a lovely pixey tonight in her yellow frock, Claudette Colbertish rather than Ruth Romanesque. In the cocktails at home before embarking on this expedition these two had bandied around the number Two. *Two'* had taken on a great significance. Who flinched first? I suspect that Dad had called his old flame and said, "In two more years the boys will be out of the house, darling." She was here, inviting us; the old buzzard seems to have negotiated another two-year lease on his bachelorhood.

Trailing behind, our trio was in Polo shirts, as was Judy. Karl had managed to get Bloomy included into the invite; Karl and Judy lolling along, hand in hand, Alexi and I were bringing up the rear on this caravan. As we passed the Kearny yard Knocky refrained from the noise he usually makes to commemorate the years he spent in this institution, he said, "You talked to Doc about it? You sounded him out, Paulie?"

"Forget about it, man. This summer you will be building character."

"But, you told him my Uncle Ivan won't be down the shore this summer, he is emceeing full time at the Strip Club. Ivan said he could still get me the same deal at the hotel, four hours of work, room and board practically peanuts, Even better, Ivan said they could promote me to part time waiter instead of busboy, I'd be getting tips, because the old ladies like to tousle my hair."

Knocky was thinking about his hotshot basketball league, his chicks on, and under, the Boardwalk, Paradise Lost, but not thinking too clearly. My father was a hero, not a plaster saint. When I mentioned to him that Knocky was asking about contacts involving his Uncle Ivan again, Dad said, "Alexi is free to return to his family any time he wants to. I certainly won't hold the boy prisoner."

"Buddy" I said, " it would not be too wise of you to bug Big Doc right now. The man has heavy loads on his mind."

"He doesn't come off that way. Doc always seems to have everything under control, " Alexi said. "Calm, self-assured."

"Sure, he doesn't burden us with his troubles, but he has a tax audit pending, he's getting anonymous calls from female voices, threatening him. He's caught flack from welfare agencies about you.; they're letting matters slide but that could change the minute some bureaucrat gets a bug up his ass."

"Sorry, Alexi said. "I didn't know that."

"Right," I said. " So cool it, muchacho. "

I had not mentioned to Alexi the other bad stuff; Dad was thinking of firing Mrs. Jordan, vacillating. He said that firing a long-term employee was a wrenching experience, like getting an abscessed tooth pulled or moving to another home. "

When we reached the Oyster House, corner of Randolph and Green, both Dad and I frowned at the signs in the windows. For SALE or RENT. One of our favorite family restaurants, the Oyster House had been here forever; always closed in the summers when you can't eat shellfish, but the smaller sign in the window said it was closing permanently last week of business. The bell tinkled overhead as we entered; nothing seemed to have changed, an understated fish shack décor with white stone tables. Behind the bar were photos of trophy swordfishes and marlins.

Dad, a steady patron since the Pleistocene, received his regular hearty welcome. Waitresses were the wives of local cops, firemen, he had delivered their babies; there were women in here who could reminisce about when he arrived with Leonora and toddler me, my wicker carriage was left outside, back then you could do that, nowadays it would be gone in a jiffy.

Mister Donovan, the proprietor, joined us as we took our seats. After the introduction to Maxine Dad asked him, "Why you running out on us, Mike? I thought you were the last of the stubborn holdouts. But, you made too much money?"

"Money?" Donovan said. Oh, sure, I remember money. I just haven't seen much of it lately, and figure it's best to get out while the getting's good. "

"Your place has always been crowded," Dad said.

"You've a fine memory, Dan, but business is not what it was. I still have the lunch trade, teachers coming up from Paxton and executives from nearby factories, the SKF plant, but this place is deader than the morgue at night; there are fewer adventurers who care to venture out on these dark streets."

Customers were approaching the cash register. Saying," Excuse me," Donovan rose. Our traditional waitress, Mrs. Carey, leaned over to give Pop a kiss on the cheek. He introduced her to Mrs. Barufkin. Mrs. Carey nodded, amiably, while her eyes were asking what had ever happened to Mrs. Fiore, his usual companion here?

"Ginger ales on the rocks for the junior brigade, "Dad said, " Manhattans on the rocks for us, you can skip the menus, Helen; we'll have the usual all around,"

Tears welled in Mrs. Carey's eyes. Dad said, "What's the matter, Helen?"

"Why did you have to say 'the usual, Big Doc? It just drives home the fact that we're shutting down after all these years. I can hardly believe it, still. "

"Take it easy, dear, " Dad told her, "you'll be alright."

After Helen brought our ginger ales and Manhattans Dad took a sip, began lecturing us on urban decay: our neighborhood was close to reaching the tip-over point; factory jobs moving elsewhere, local movie houses shutting down, once they shut down streets became darker, the corner ice cream parlors shut down. The Jews and Irish and Poles were moving uptown; the people replacing them had lower incomes, with less money around more businesses close. A vicious downward spiral, so far everything the bumbling city had tried to do only made things worse, building housing projects that only spurred the flight to the suburbs.

"You're thinking of moving out even sooner then, Dan?" Mrs. Barufkin said, prompting Dad, and trying to nail down commitments.

"Two years, dear," he assured her. "I'd say another two years here, maximum."

The significant 'Two.' Funny how we get hung up on numbers, like Knocky and his obsession with his twenty. The closing of the Oyster House was giving me a queasy case of the heebie-jeebies. Was it a dark omen, a harbinger of bad times to come? Linked in my mind to Korea. Jeez, another war? After V-J day, World War Two ended, there was dancing in the streets, all the talk was about bringing the boys home. This Korea threat was like Monster movies where you think the Monster is finally dead, a Crucifix nailed in his heart, you believe the movie is over, but no, the Monster leaps up for another gory, protracted battle.

A bottle of white wine arrived, courtesy of Mister Donovan. We oohed and ahhed as Mrs. Carey approached with the cart bearing *The Usual*. The Usual seemed superlatively more abundant than ever tonight, sizzling trays of breaded crabs, clams, oysters, shrimp, and mackerel, lobster tails, plus tons of hash fries. Donovan was shedding inventory in our favor. I dumped hot sauce and spicy horseradish on my oysters while noting that Judy had sighed with fictitious enthusiasm, this meal was shaping up as an ordeal for the girl. In her cloistered life she had never confronted this boneless Traif, forbidden delicacies that only the Goys ate. Her eyes were glistening with panic; Karl was signaling to her, "Try it, you'll like it, it won't kill you." Knocky whispered to Karl, "Tell Bloomy oysters are healthy and good for you; shell fish stiffen the back bone, maybe the forebone."

Dad motioned to Alexi to knock it off. Mrs. Barufkin saw how Judy was staring at her plate, like an ingénue explorer invited by the Bedouins to try specialty of the tribal chef, the braised sheep's eyeball. Maxine said, "It's not too late for us to order a steak for you, Judy. Dan told me they do a nice rib eye for people adverse to fish."

"No, I'm fine, ma'am, " Judy assured her. "It's just this is a new world for me."

"Yeah, "Knocky scoffed, " in Bloomy's old world there's only lox and gefilte fish."

Dad again motioned to Alexi to cool it, and then our table conversation went two tracks. In the kiddy department we were talking about the A's, Connie Mack was so cheap he was fielding a shortstop wearing eyeglasses. Eddie Joost could hit the ball hard when he saw it but he rarely saw it. Dad, meanwhile was offering Mrs. Barufkin financial advice, recommending changes in her stock portfolio; dump the Reading and Pennsy Railroads, avoid the airlines, they fly high, then crash.

At least Dad is consistent in his advice. I'd never seen a French farce on stage but during these invites I felt like Karl, Alexi, and I were in a farce, obliged to sit here, straight men wearing blank faces, while Dad uses his polished dialogues and well-rehearsed scripts on a series of revolving leading ladies. Karl and Alexi flow along with his act. I suspect that these two worship this big old bear more than I do.

On the radio, near the cash register, tuned low, they were talking about Korea. Why, Lord, must there always be something wrong? Is that the definition of Life: an experience with flaws, defects, tribulations, and pitfalls? It was certainly the prime ingredient for a story; if nothing's wrong, you have no story. Mister Donovan was answering the phone. He winced, then glanced in our direction, and twisted his chin. Well, that was fast. I asked for it. Do not think negative thoughts. Do not say the name of creatures that must remain nameless. Do not tamper with sealed vaults.

Donovan whispered to Mrs. Carey, she responded with an exasperated frown, came toward out table swaying her chin from side to side. We were not about to hear her sing ' The Blue Bird of Happiness.'

"Sorry, Big Doc, " Mrs. Carey said. "The Boss says you have a call, sounds urgent."

"Thank you, Helen."

Rising, Dad looked up to the heavens. He constantly glances upwards when he is supposed to be Mister Dyed-in-the-Wool Agnostic. " Sorry, Maxine," he said. "I'll be right back, these urgent calls are getting to be like the tiger at Kafka's Mass."

Mrs. Barufkin showed she was a good soldier, seasoned vet; she had been out with Dad before when he received these emergency calls. Instead of answering with words she pointed to the phone, ordering him to do his duty.

"It must be horrible to be a doctor," Judy said as Dad went to the bar. "They never leave you alone, you can't even go out for a dinner in peace."

Donovan apologized to Dad as he handed him the phone. These two had been pals and poker partners, matching wits since Coolidge was President. It seemed incredible to me that our traditional Oyster House was closing but they just closed the Poplar Theatre on Sixth, there were empty houses on George Street, boarded up, no buyers, no renters. Our neighborhood was just starting to slide downhill.

Dad scowled at whatever he was being told on the phone. His frown took in the heavens, he believes that his donations rate him special dispensations. After hanging up he chatted with Donovan. They were agreeing that existence could be frustrating.

Returning to our table, Dad plunked down into his chair so hard he reminded me of Dmitri making our booth tremble the night he burst into the Diner. For a hulking bull Dad is usually lighter on his feet but we saw that he was harried, frazzled, left distraught by that phone call.

"And?" Mrs. Barufkin said. " The bad news, if you will?"

"Sorry, dear," He said to Maxine. "A dire emergency down in, over by, West Philly. An ambulance will be arriving to pick me up in five, ten, minutes."

Knocky did not catch that slip of the tongue. Karl did. 'Down in?' From where we were sitting, geographically, vector-wise, you wouldn't say ' down in West Philly.'

"No rest for the weary, Dan? " Mrs. Barufkin said. " They couldn't find anybody else to handle this? You're all there is?"

Instead of answering, Dad tugged at his collar I'd never seen him this agitated. His modus operandi was to roll out the equanimity precisely when everybody else was in a tizzy. He turned to us and said, "Okay, troops, orders of the night, you will finish your meals in peace, have your dessert, a coffee, then you, Paulie, will take a taxi with Mrs. Barufkin, you don't leave her until she is safely inside her door. Alexi, and Karl, you will escort Judy home, same instructions, you don't leave her until she is safely inside her door. I suspect I'll be home pretty late."

I snapped him a mock salute and said, "Orders are orders, sir."

Dad was about to take one more munch on his lobster, changed his mind, pushed the plate aside, brought out his wallet. He peeled off a twenty-dollar bill, two Franklins, and said, "Paul, the twenty covers cab fares, these other two bills take care of the check."

Dad was usually not this overt with money; his method was to excuse himself toward the end of a meal, bills mysteriously vanished.

"Hey! "Mrs. Barufkin protested, "This invitation was on me, Dan."

He touched her wrist and said, "This dinner has been marred by untoward events. Save your invitation for a more festive occasion, dear."

Examining the two-hundred bucks, I said, " This is way over what the tab will be, sir. I'd say close to double."

"I know," Dad said. "Tell Donovan the change is the tip for Mrs. Carey." Then he lit up a smoke. Mrs. Barufkin arched a lash, she was trying to get him to cut down, but also smart enough to sense that this was not a good moment to nag the man.

There were still industrial quantities of food on the table; we went back to our nibbling. Essentially, the dinner had been ruined. After a lull in the conversation Judy took up the slack, started telling us about the scandals at Girl's High: three girls had dropped out, due to being overdue. Everybody was shocked. This was unheard of at prestigious Girl's High, where the bright girls prepped for college. That sort of thing happened at Olney, Bartram, Germantown, and William Penn, not Girl's High.

Trying to be humorous because Bloomy was getting too ponderous, Karl plagiarized Dorothy Parker and wise-cracked, "I would not be surprised that if the whole senior prom were laid end to end...."

Mrs. Barufkin was waiting for the punch line, and she did not realize that that was the punch line. We all frowned as we heard honking outside. Dad rose, saying, "That's them, damn their hides."

Mrs. Barufkin kissed his cheek, and said, "You will be careful, dear."

Did she know things? Had Dad confided in her?

"I'll call you first thing tomorrow," Dad said.

There were more impatient honks, Judy gave Dad a kiss, and he wagged a finger at us boys, ordering us to handle the situation. At the door Mister Donovan shook his hand, Mrs. Carey gave him a kiss. I'd never before seen Daniel Burris in a funk, and sagging like this. He straightened his shoulders but It was not a convincing gesture, seemed more like he was giving himself an interior pep talk, on the lines of, ' You can do this, buddy. You can handle this.'

An ambulance arriving should arrive with screeching sirens, not dull honks. Snoopy me, I had no call to investigate but slipped over to the curtained window with the maritime decorations, the coral and seashells, goldfish tanks. I pulled the curtain two inches aside. No sirree bob. No white ambulance out there with the Red Cross markings. Dad was entering a black Cadillac. I could not swear to this in court but it seemed to be the same Caddy that dropped Dad off two summers ago.

Next morning there were articles about a confusing shooting in South Philly. Neighbors heard gunfire lasting over a minute coming from the Naples Private Social Club, down the block from Palumbo's. Eyewitnesses said that they believed it was Salvatore 'Big Sal' Bonafaccio entering the back room club, prior to the pistol shots. When the police finally arrived they found pocked walls, and overturned tables, no bodies or blood stains. Staff was mopping up the floors. No neighbor or eyewitness wished to furnish his or her name for attribution.

Dad did not return till eleven in the morning where he faced an ugly scene; a waiting room crowded with miffed patients: He'd never been known to stand up his appointments. Aggravated Mrs. Jordan dared to raise her voice at him, complaining that he had failed to call his service to provide his whereabouts; she had had to put up with all the abuse from the angry patients in the waiting room.

Our private history, otherwise that dinner at the Oyster House marked the beginning of one miserable, rotten summer in American History. We read about nothing but bloody defeats and chaotic retreats. The North Koreans were kicking the butts of our undertrained, poorly equipped, demoralized troops. This was hard for us to swallow when we had been brought up on Gung-ho war flics like 'Back to Bataan' and 'Guadalcanal Diary' where we were virtually invincible. Sure, we lost guys, took casualties, but we always triumphed in the end. Who could beat those gallant squads assembled like an All-American Noah's Ark: the Jew from Brooklyn, the Texas cowboy, the hot-blooded Italian from San Francisco, the Cool Apache, the sensitive intellectual supplying the philosophical insights in the voice-over. This summer American forces were driven back to a precarious foothold on the southern tip of the Korean peninsula, the catastrophe was shaping up as another Dunkirk, pessimists were saying that Japanese junks might be needed to evacuate our scant survivors from the bloody beaches of the Pusan perimeter.

On our Home Front the standing joke along Marshall was that if Doc Burris kept on adopting stray waifs Moe and Sara might have to open a branch annex to their deli. Alexi was receiving equal treatment, meaning toiling alongside Karl and me in the sawdust and pickle brine. Stacking cans on grocery shelves was surely a come-down from starring in the summer league and picking up loose ladies on the Boardwalk but Knocky never complained. Maybe because he was enormously pop-ular on Marshall,. Shopkeepers minding the stalls, aware of his athletic prowess, glad-handed him, and treated him as if he were a hot prospect, he could have been a rookie toreador touring his humble barrio in Sevilla where everybody is predicting a grand future for this prodigy.

Ladies, the situation was more complicated. Everybody knew who and what Sonya was: he inherited a tad of her racy reputation. The Mothers of Marshall Street certainly did not want their daughters associating with this footloose rogue and they repeated the dark rumors about his fan club at William Penn High, forbade all contact with him. That did not prevent the Myrnas and Elaines in the Mom and Pop stores from fluttering their lashes and flirting outrageously with the notorious Alexi Ratchinov.

The frieze in the third week of August when Roy Bauer popped into Moe's deli: a grocery order had come in, sixty cases of canned goods, Knocky and I were perched on the ladders, Karl was passing the cans of chile con carne and sauerkraut up to us. Bauer slouched into the deli, silver studs clicking on his snakeskin boots; the sinister gunslinger slinks into the Last Chance Saloon. Moe and Aunt Sara gaped at him. They had never seen Bauer before but instantly knew who this smirking thug was. Moe was about to intervene, I signaled him to hold off. Bauer sneered up at us, as if amused to find people actually working. He said to Alexi, "Your Momma wants you to call her tonight. She'll be home."

As far as I knew these were the first words between these two since Bauer smacked Knocky around last winter. Alexi nodded; Bauer saw that his Adam's apple had quivered in a definite gulp. Bauer gave us one more contemptuous once-over, sniffed at Karl, included Moe and Sara in the sniff.

The buzzard knew how to make an impact impression. His entire number, the entrance and the exit, lasted, at the outermost, ten seconds, but it was enough to shatter a tranquil afternoon. You are enjoying a picnic on a balmy day in the park; a diseased hyena casually strolls by.

Moe was pale; he motioned for us to climb down from the ladders. When I reached ground level Moe whispered to me," That him?"

What was the big secret around here? In a normal tone, I said," Yes, him."

Aunt Sara groaned," Just from looking at that grubyahn he should be arrested. "

"Why arrested?" Karl asked. "Executed."

Knocky said nothing. His worried expression said it all. Uncle Moe surveyed the deli. Besides us three he had two Porto Ricans, Paco and Pepe, working full time now. Thirty or so cases of canned goods remained to be put up. Moe was still unnerved by that entrance. Running into Bauer for the first time was like entering an elevator where the departing passenger had deposited his gasses. Moe received a nod of approval from Sara, and he said, "You three bums get out of here. I'll have Paco and Pepe finish putting up the grocery order. Go play ball."

"Thanks, Unc, " Karl said.

"That's to the school yard," Moe admonished us." No pool room."

"Sure, Unc, " Knocky said, and he tapped Moe on the shoulder in gratitude. We whipped off our white aprons and as we headed out Sara detained Alexi, slipped him five bucks. Back in June Sara emitted negative noises of resistance about having

Knocky board our ship, now she was totally Ga-Ga about her new nephew, she slips him more spare fivers than I get.

A Woody Herman record blasted from the Jazz Shop loudspeaker while we head up Marshall. From the pushy crowds swarming around the stalls you'd never know there's a war on. Next year, if I can get Dad's permission, at seventeen, I enlist. Meanwhile, with Knocky slouching the along, the fruit peddlers put up their fists, as if to shadow box with him, and others simulated the act of tossing up a basketball. For so young a kid he gets the five star celebrity treatment.

We reached Bloom's Sweet Shoppe, Karl said, "Let's see if Judy can come out."

"Cheese, "Knocky grumbled, " why don't you marry Bloomy already?"

"She's sure willing, "Karl said. " Soon as I get circumcised."

"How come she knows you aint circumcised?" Knocky asked "You been showing Judy your hardware, you evil devil, you?"

"That's none of your goddam business, "Karl snapped.

"Ah, that's true love," Knocky sighed "When a guy refuses to talk about it, that's is hearts and flowers, peachy-pie true love."

"Screw you, Ratchinov." Wronsky said.

"Speaking of screwing, there she is," Knocky said.

Dutiful daughter Judy was behind the candy counter in the store, learning the trade, dipping the raw apples into the deplorable sticky red goop used to make the candied apples. Karl caught her eye, also the flinty eyes of her watchful parents. This was another quaint cover that Norman Rockwell never painted: Playmate, come out and play with me, slide down my cellar door, climb up my apple tree, with two grimacing adult ogres lurking in the background.

Arms folded across our chests, we watched the Walky Talky pantomime of a Punch and Judy show, Bloomy asking permission to leave while Mister and Mrs. Bloom were glaring out at us as if we were three of Ali Baba's Forty Thieves arriving to abduct their precious princess. Ma and Pa Bloom were refusing permission. Voices were rising, the rebellious daughter was flinging off her goop-stained apron, apparently talking trash, Such wayward girls will invariably come to a bad end. Judy burst defiantly out of the Sweet Shoppe, moaning, "These people will never leave me alone, never get off me, never."

Usually 'these people' is a term reserved for minority groups we don't like. The first time I ever heard a girl use it on her parents. After a quick conference in front of the smoke shop selling the fancy pipes we decided to hit Kearny, avoid Ludlow, we'd seen enough of Bauer for one day. Up at Ludlow, there was always the chance of that green door opening, Sonya or Roy stepping out.

We picked our way down bustling Marshall. The situations were hardly similar, but I detected a weird linkage; we lived so close by it felt like the Cold War might feel in Berlin. East and West close by, only blocks away, but Ludlow has become the forbidden zone for us, we can't go up there.

Family? For no reason whatsoever I remembered the night in the Academy of Music when I spotted a gentleman in the lobby who looked more like my father than my father did. Philly is a great big village; you can't help but bump into people you don't want to see. The stranger turned out to be Dad's bother, Jonathan. Dad came out of the bathroom; the two supposedly mature adults stared at each other for several moments, then went their respective ways without a word. How can families twist themselves into such impossible knots and sickening stances?

Over dinner that evening Knocky hesitated before telling Pop about the need to call his mother. His game in the Kearny yard had been off this afternoon, he was not getting the roll on his lay-ups; missed mid-range jump shots that were normally duck soup for him. It does not take much to throw you off. Knocky was still spooked, freaked out, by that dick barging in with his arrogant sneer. Should I put him down for not being Alexi the Lion-Hearted? Nobody had ever knocked me around.

Dad made life simpler for Knocky by saying, "Uncle Moe phoned, told me that Roy Bauer entered the deli this afternoon with a message for you."

"Yes, sir," Alexi said. "To call my mother. That's all. "

Tapping the tips of his fingers together, looking like Ronald Coleman dissecting a conundrum, Dad said, "You've my okay to call her, but let me know if anything significant is discussed. I don't want to disturb your privacy but lately I've been receiving strange phone calls and unsettling vibrations, Alexi."

"Yes, sir. "

In spite of the crispy roast beef and home fries with gribenes Miss Pearl had served a pall was cast over this dinner. Bauer was nowhere in sight but the mere mention of his name produces visions of maggots crawling out of cadavers. I was hoping that Dad was thinking about calling Billy Schmitz and Hawaiian Jack again. Or, better yet, contact the muscle that did the job in the Locust Street parking lot.

After the fruit compost dessert Dad told Alexi he could use the phone in the second floor library. He waited until Knocky was upstairs, dialing, to ask us, "You were there when Bauer entered?"

"Yes, sir," Karl answered. "He said, call your mother, she'll be home tonight."

"Anything else?"

"Just that, sir," Karl said. " But he has such an obnoxious style, he made it sound like some kind of curse. He's a guy who can make you barf, sir. "

From the way Dad was peering at the extension in the parlor I knew he was tempted to pick up the receiver but he was not about to do that in front of us. We excused ourselves, headed upstairs. As we passed Knocky in the library he shook his head, opened a palm to the heavens. He was being harried and hassled in a one-way conversation, Sonya blasting him with a harangue.

Karl and I began a game of chess. Sonya had her son on the horn another fifteen minutes. Alexi came up to our third floor game room his tossing his head as if he had survived an artillery barrage. Karl was gearing up for a caustic remark, held back as Alexi groaned, "The fucking woman is driving me nuts."

Woof, that was a bit stronger than Bloomy calling her parents 'these people.'

"Your Mom giving you a hard time? Karl asked, one might say, ingenuously.

"She's batty, all over the map. I need to talk to Doc, Paulie. Tonight she hit me with really wild shit, serious shit that can spell bad troubles for Doc."

"Itemize that," Karl said. "Details, please."

Plunking down on the side sofa, Knocky groaned, "She's always been bugging me about moving back home, claiming she knows how to handle Roy now, has him under control, made him swear he'll never touch me again, but then she totally contradict herself and says that she's all that's preventing Bauer from going after Doc, getting vengeance for that beating he took downtown."

"Oh, shit." Karl muttered.

"Wait, it gets worse, " Knocky assured us. "She said that the only reason Roy aint pulled nothing yet is because Ivan ordered him to cool it. And, that's only because they got a big dough caper cooking. Ivan says that once they pull off the deal Roy can do anything he wants, he won't care as long as he gets his cut, and cuts out of town."

"She give you any idea of what the big dough deal was?" I asked Knocky.

"She wouldn't go into that but hit me with all this other insane shit. I'd better come home to her or even if Roy doesn't mug Doc up an alley she will do her own best to fuck Doc over. She's been digging around, compiled dope to prove that Doc's a two-bit fraud, supposed to be so goody-goody but involved in stuff up to his ears, in tight with the Bambinos. For starters, she said my Aunt Svetla would testify in court that Doc performs illegal abortions."

"What? " I groaned, but Karl laughed, and clucked," Sounds logical. No good deed goes unpunished."

"That's rank rumor and scuttlebutt," I said. "She got anything to nail him?"

"She says she's got loads of other bad shit. She's been talking to hookers in the know, and dancers from her strip club, and Mrs. Jordan."

"Mrs. Jordan!" I spluttered. That was the first time in my life I've ever spluttered. "How the hell did she ever hook up with our nurse?"

"Mom said that at first she despised Mrs. Jordan because whenever she called the office Mrs. Jordan would never put her calls through to Doc. But now, catch this, Mrs. Jordan called her, and since then they've become asshole buddy-buddy. Mrs. Jordan has told her crap about Doc doing stuff off the books, stuff after normal office hours."

Karl nodded. We both could imagine what kind of trips Mrs. Jordan might be mentioning; interrupted dinners at the Oyster House, and trips after midnight.

"I can't decide what to do, Paulie. "Knocky said. "I can't move back in with her while that creep is still around. Maybe I should just take off, leave town, head for the Coast. I can't let any bad shit happen to Doc on my account."

"The first thing you have to do is go downstairs and talk to Doc," Karl said.

Knocky returned from the library ten minutes later, He had made the offer to Doc to return to his home on Randolph Street. Dad told him there was no way that could happen, he should relax, matters would be handled on another level. Knocky then went to the room they shared, I heard him telling Karl that Doc laughed when he repeated his Mom's accusations. I stared at the fading portrait of Leonora in the Mother-of Pearl Frame. I had been awarded such a perfect Mom. She never chided me, nagged me, punished me; the only dirt she ever did me was die on me.

Sacking out, I was unable to sleep. Under our roof, Doc permits traitors in the House of Burris. Surely he would now fire Mrs. Jordan. She had already supplied him with excellent reasons: she was nasty to the Colored patients and Miss Pearl's relatives; he had caught her trying to charge poor patients even though she had been instructed to let the bills slide for the indigents who arrived with cards signed by the priests from Saint Pete's or the Rabbi at The Sixth and Green Synagogue. She bitched about her wages though he was paying her top dollar, more than nurses earned in the ritzy practices down by Rittenhouse Square. She wanted him to up his fees and claimed that when the riffraff don't pay enough that means they swill down a few more beers, money that should well be used to increase her salary. Quite an indictment, and maybe it was mostly Chicken-Schnabel Crap, but to cap it all off the goddam witch turns to be a Bernadette Arnold.

Early in the morning, while Dad was shaving, I entered his bathroom. He was wearing just his pajama bottoms, his gut was sagging, but he still had the massive trunk of a gray bear. Given his exacting tastes in classical music I'd always wondered why he had the revolting habit of leaving his bathroom radio tuned to the Mack Mclarty Irish show, the rowdy, clanging beer hall stuff like, 'Don't tread on the Tail of me Coat, hah-hah,' and 'It's the Same Old Sheleighly Mee Father Brought from Ireland.' Those were his morning picker-uppers.

No good morning, I directly asked him, "Decided anything on Mrs. Jordan yet?"

"You've never liked the woman, Paul."

"That has nothing to do with nothing, sir. Alexi's told you that's she's joined Sonya Ratchinov's coven, shooting her mouth off in ways that could hurt you. "

He paused in his scraping with his old-fashioned straight razor, said, "Eventually, in good time, I will deal with her, Paul. We don't want to be hasty about this."

What kind of scary mumbo-jumbo was that? What was this *In good time?* Did she have stuff on him? Was he afraid of her? Was she holding any trump cards?

"Dad, I think you should just flat-out fire the bitch, get rid of her."

"One thing at a time, Paul. We're coming down to the wire, and it makes more sense to let her go when I shut down my practice, which isn't far off now."

Maybe his judgment was impaired? The old boy was getting up there in years. For the first time in my life I questioned his common sense. I had always seen Dad as hopelessly stuffy but a rock solid fount of wisdom. Do men reach a stage where they are weary of being sharp, and decisive; they are inclined to let things slide, hoping that matters will somehow resolve themselves by inertia , entropy, and osmosis?

CHAPTER ELEVEN

Mrs. Jordan had a new boyfriend; obviously she had given up her pursuit of Dad a long ways back. Her Mister Braxton was a skinny Wasp turkey from the Main Line; he wore droopy bowties, and looked like a Fred Astaire who could not dance. They had met at a church social for Unitarians. Braxton dropped her off in the morning, and picked her up at closing time. From the way she looked at me and the way I looked at her she was aware that I was aware of her treachery. The sight of her sickened me, contributed to my gloom. All the news from Korea was rotten; older guys from our schoolyard had received their induction notices, Hess, Fischer, Burdumi, Baer, Greetings from the President of the United States, which of these chumps is cannon fodder, ticketed to die on foreign fields in a war nobody around here wanted. The front pages were relentlessly depressing, the dreary mists seeping through my home. From reading 'Berlin Diary ' this last week of August felt like what Poland must have felt like in August of 1939, the Nazi invasion imminent, the sheep appear to be grazing serenely while black birds are buzzing on the horizon, a shit storm is brewing.

I had premonitions it would hit my home. Nothing happened. I kept on waiting for the other shoe to drop. No other shoe. Till the Tuesday morning after Labor Day, We left the house to clock in at the deli just as the gray Lincoln paused across Sixth Mrs. Jordan being chauffeured by her Mister Braxton. The stiff sits in Dad's waiting room in the evening, sneering at the patients until his ladylove comes off her shift. We watched Mrs. Jordan give Braxton a birdlike peck on the cheek; I wondered if these two just spent a steamy night of passion together or if Beau Braxton picked up his honey-pie early. I was merely thinking this, Karl said, aloud, "Can you imagine those two in bed? Together? Grotesque images contaminate my skull."

Knocky merely made an ugly noise. With his lips, thankfully.

Ferocious traffic was roaring down Sixth at this early hour. After the Lincoln pulled away Mrs. Jordan was poised there in her white uniform, waiting for a break in the flow. How important was she as a snake in our garden? You never know when a bit player will get to play a major role in your life. It became an awkward moment as the red light flashed up on Girard Avenue, we could cross if we hurried, and our paths crossed in the middle of Sixth Street. Normally, nominally, we should say 'Good Morning, 'or at least nod. None of us were so inclined. We blotted her from sight. Mrs. Jordan responded with a malicious smile, and cheery "Good Morning, boys," sounding more like an ominous curse, like she might follow this up with cackling, the irrepressible giggling of the green Wicked Witch of the West.

Something was way off. She sounded triumphant, like she had just scored a coup.

"Up hers, "Karl muttered. I was still wondering what the hell her merriment was all about as we cut through the alley feeding into Marshall Street. Her smile had not been jovial; the tone was hostile. Dad was nuts to keep this woman around.

We came out of the alley by Feinberg's Smoke Shop, with the magazine and newspaper racks in front. Today, over a fuzzy photo, the tabloid headline screamed:

STRIPPERS NABBED IN MAIN LINE HEIST

What kind of crap was that? There's a war going on. Why waste space and energy on such Chicken Schnabel trivia? The headline reminded me of the hokey faked-up front pages you can have printed up on the Boardwalk.

VIRGINS FLEE AS JOE GREARY HITS TOWN

We strolled on by, then I blinked as I examined the photo closer, it took a while to sink in. At first I thought it was a trick of the eyes, this was impossible, but there it was. I felt as if a ten-ton pillow had smacked me; the photo was of cops holding the doors open for culprits to enter a paddy wagon. Those under arrest were Mrs. Sonya Ratchinov, Ivan Demetrescu, Svetla Demetrescu, aka Trixie Malloy, Roy Bauer, and the magician's assistant, Wanda Kurowski.

Knocky stared at the grainy photo, squinted in disbelief. It took him seconds to react, too. He trembled, clutched at his ribs, folded like cellophane struck by a match.

Karl snatched a tabloid off the racks, flipped to page three, and began reading aloud: "Last night, at One-Thirty AM, Philadelphia Police, alerted by their suburban counterparts, arrested five employees of the Cosmo Club, a notorious center city striptease joint, after a dramatic car chase originating at the palatial Bryan Mawr estate of the prominent banker and philanthropist, Mister John C, Connors, and concluding when their vehicle, a black hearse, was overtaken at City Line Avenue.

"Among the apprehended were Roy Bauer, released from prison last year after prior convictions for burglary and armed robbery in New Jersey; Ivan Demetrescu, M.C. at the Cosmo Club, current warrants out for his arrest in Atlantic City; his sister, Svetla Demetrescu, formerly a featured Chorine at the Troc, charges of prostitution dismissed; another Sister, Mrs. Sonya Ratchinov, no known criminal record; and, Wanda Kurowski, illegal alien, prior convictions for shoplifting and solicitation."

Yeah, I could see why Mrs. Jordan was ready to cackle this morning. Knocky was covering his face with his hands. He looked unsteady on his feet.

Karl continued reading aloud, "According to conflicting reports and declarations, after being heavily plied with spiked drinks the inebriated Connors invited the employees of the Cosmo Club to his luxurious residence with the three women promising to stage a private 'Exotic Show' for him. The entertainers then allegedly took advantage of their entrée, proceeding to drug Connors, and force him to open a safe hidden in his basement recreation area, from which they removed jewels and other valuables, including an unspecified amount of cash.

"Police were summoned when the estate gardener, Booker Beaumont, became suspicious of unusual activities at this late hour, peered through the French doors of the main salon, and observed that the employees of the Cosmo Club were apparently toasting their success with goblets of champagne while Connors was stretched unconscious on the dining room rug. With the suburban police in hot pursuit the accused were taken into custody after fleeing the mansion and reaching the outskirts of Philadelphia while possibly strewing their trail with items removed from the safe. The five fugitives are presently detained in the lock-up of Central Police Headquarters. Bail will be set or denied at a preliminary hearing to be presided over by Judge Stanley M. Greenberg at Ten AM this morning. "

I'd been anticipating bad stuff, this was not as momentous as a Nazi Blitzkrieg, but surely a heavy load, right out of left field. I grabbed a morning Inquirer off the rack, read the short article on the front page, turned to page seven where there was a longer column plus photos of the gamey five being hustled into the paddy wagon, Sonya, Svetla, and Wanda trying to hide their faces with their hands.

Inside the smoke shop, Mister Feinberg was rubbing the tips of his fingers together, meaning to convey 'Hey, buddy, this aint no free library.' Then he saw who we were, mostly fixing on Alexi Ratchinov, he gave us a strangely generous wave, indicating we could carry off Daily News and a Morning Inquirer for free today.

Dad hated the Daily News. He never explained why but he insisted on calling it the 'Daily Noose.' That was not that funny but I'd never been able to break the habit of calling it the *Daily Noose*.

Karl said, "Let's head straight home, Knocky. Talk to Doc. Show him the papers if he aint seen them yet. He hasn't seen them or he wouldn't have let us go in to work."

"Nah," Knocky said." I'm going in to work. Screw it. This aint got nothing to do with me. I'm gonna' fucking ignore it."

An admirable attitude but Marshall Street already had the word. Still early, shoppers sparse, none of the vendors playfully put up their fists, or simulated tossing up a basketball as we passed the stalls and pushcarts, but Alexi received more than his usual level of attention; acquaintances waved, men reached out to touch or tap his shoulder, give him the thumb's up sign. Inside the stores shopkeepers were doing double takes, then calling to their wives to come and see the Ratchinov kid passing. Once, in my silly imagination, I saw Alexi as the novice toreador basking in the adulation of his home turf in Sevilla. This morning, the only element lacking were the trumpets of La Virgin de la Macarena: eyes glazed, his head held too high, his stride falsely cocky, Alexi could have been the washed-up toreador entering the plaza with the shadow of doom already on his soul. Karl and I were tagging along as his undermanned cuadrilla.

When we entered the deli Moe shouted, "What the hell you doing here, boy? Go home at once. Rest. Consult with Doc as to your course of action."

"What rest?" Knocky said. "I'm not tired. I'm okay, Uncle Moe. No problem. "

He sounded punchy, like a woozy welterweight, face all bloodied, assuring his trainer that he had another round left in him. Sure, I can go out there.

Aunt Sara rushed over to give Knocky a hug, then ordered him, "You take the day off, relax, don't even think about it. I'm sending Karlie and Paulie with you, you three boys should all go up to Willow Grove Amusement Park today. Pick up some girls; enjoy the rides, school starts next Monday. Don't even think about it."

She pulled a thick roll of bills out of her apron pocket, began peeling off tens to finance our excursion. Alexi grabbed her hand, and said, "No, please, I'm okay."

With a resigned shrug Moe motioned to Sara to let it go. We put on our white aprons and went to work. That turned out to be lucky for Moe, as I had never seen the deli so crowded, customers were pouring in. I had no access to Moe's financial records but suspected that this had to be a banner morning in the history of this establishment, the bell over the door ringing, cash registers tingling, an incredible uptick in trade, people who had not been in here for years, always went to the Famous, on the corner, were dropping by for a quarter pound of white fish, a sour pickle, pastrami sandwich, any excuse to sneak a peek at Knocky, verify that this was the kid whose mother was in all the papers. Some tried to be discrete about it, other openly gawked and gaped, then nodded, they could now breathlessly report that they had seen the newly minted notorious figure with their own two eyes.

Pepe and Paco were shaking their heads in commiseration. Punchy Knocky was pretending not to be affected by this commotion; he was hustling around, determined not to show that the fuss was bothering him. Karl whispered, "I can't tell whether this is a farce or a feeding frenzy but the scene in here reminds me of a documentary I saw about piranhas devouring an animal on the Amazon River."

"How about Leinengen Versus The ants," I suggested.

"Nah, piranhas picking the bones bare." Karl insisted. "This is one of those mornings when I can't decide whether to piss or puke on the human race."

Dad entered the deli. From the started way Moe and Sara reacted it could have been Jehovah dropping by. They rushed over to him, I opened my palms to Dad, asking, 'what gives?' He signaled me to hold my horses; explanations will arrive.

Moe and Dad were consulting. Paco, the counterman asked me," Ese es tu papa?"

"Yeap. That's my Dad. Aquel señor es mi padre."

"Dicen que aparte de ser muy alto, es un gran hombre."

"Si. I am being raised by a great man."

Consultations finished, Dad came over to us, and said, C'mon, lads. Take off those damn aprons. You have the day off."

"I'm okay, sir," Knocky said. "I've got no problems, I'd rather be busy, sir."

"Nobody's asking you, Alexi," Dad told him. "Let's get cracking, troops."

Moe gave Dad a hug before we left. Mister Big and Mister Little, pounding each other on the back, it looked like a Mutt and Jeff routine. Outside, Dad glared at idiots in front of the fresh fish market who were gaping bug-eyed at Knocky, and he said to us, "I had Mrs. Jordan cancel my appointments for the rest of the say. I felt the need for some bracing fresh, a drive through the countryside. "

A new regime; this man never cancels appointments, nor takes days off. He was no Dmitri to vanish in the middle of a rush job. Of course, today was a special day. One might say, mind-bogglingly special. How often is your family number one on the Shit Parade? Dad lit up a smoke, was puffing away. I had not seen the man this agitated since that phone call in the Oyster House.

"I've parked the car in the hospital lot," Dad said. "What will it be, boys, Jersey, or Bucks County? It's a beautiful day for a drive."

"You've read the papers, sir?" Knocky asked him.

"Yes, I've read the papers," Dad assured him. "And, I've been on the phone all morning, the child welfare bureau calling, city hall, the police were by to see me, twice. We'll talk about it on the drive, Alexi. Meanwhile, take it easy. The world is not coming to an end. Neither with a bang, nor a whimper."

The nurses in the emergency ward entrance waved to Dad as we approached the Buick. Then their heads went together, they were gossiping about us, or was that my paranoia percolating away? Karl and I grabbed the back seat, letting Knocky sit up front; he was the man in the hot seat today. Pulling out of the lot, Dad asked us, "Well? Jersey? Or, I haven't been to Bucks County in quite a while?

Karl already knows Dad's style, his way of expressing preferences, and he said, "How about Bucks County, sir? I really like Doylestown. New Hope. "

We drove down Girard in silence, and Dad took a right at Broad Street. He has his own routes for going wherever we are going. Knocky was down, way down, had his chin resting on his chest. I closed my eyes, made an effort, but could not imagine what the guy was going through. We can fake it, but the arrow was not piercing my shoulder. Just to say something to break the strained silence, Karl said, "Judy has given me a new nickname."

"Yeah?" I said." What's Bloomy calling you now? Ex-fatrat?"

"No. At first she was calling me Chunky, but since I've lost so much weight she's switched to calling me Corky. Because I float through all storms and crisis."

"Congratulations, Corky." I said. "Can you float through sewers, too?

Dad almost spoke as we passed Columbia Avenue, changed his mind, not until we reached Lehigh Avenue did he finally say to Knocky, "It's painful for me to talk about this, Alexi, painful for you to hear it: on your status, I have explained the circumstances to the child welfare department, they've agreed to let you remain with us until these matters are sorted out. So you are covered, so far."

"Pardon me, I don't give a shit about myself, sir. I'm only worried about if my Mom is going to jail, sir."

"This is terribly delicate," Dad said," I will try to be delicate about it. My lawyer, Darmopray, is keeping tabs on the situation. Right now, a small piece of good news to report, it appears that Mister John Connors will refuse to press charges. If that is so it would have to be the police to press charges for fleeing the scene of a crime, or resisting arrest. I'm no legal beagle, but according to Darmopray, that's much harder for the police to nail down, so there's the possibility that your Mom may be let go, shortly. As to the other parties involved in the fracas, each seems to have prior impediments to their release."

"Pardon me again, sir," Knocky said, "The others? I don't give a shit about them; they can all go to hell in a hand basket, it's only my Mom I'm sweating out."

"Darmopray will keep me apprised of the situation, the possibilities of bail. Or being released on their own cognizance Meanwhile, what I've arranged, you boys start classes next Monday, you've worked hard all summer, should have a few days off to enjoy yourselves. Aunt Ros has her cottage in Margate, spare cots in the basement. Tonight, Boris, our handyman, can drive you three roughnecks down to the shore; either Boris or I will pick you up on Sunday. You boys can swim for a few days, pick up your chickadees on the Boardwalk, live it up a little. "

Silence, a pregnant silence where nobody is born. I was remembering the dinner with Mrs. Gottbaum when she was trying to foist Miami on us. We each have our agendas and priorities. Karl can't stand to be one day away from his Bloomy. I can't stand my Aunt Ros and her unspeakable offspring. Knocky? What was swirling through his brain now? Where do you turn, where do you hide, when your Momma is temporarily as famous as Calamity Jane and Typhoid Mary?

"Hello!" Dad snapped. "I'm not hearing shouts of glee. No rousing Huzzahs?"

Knocky said, "Sir, if it's all the same to you, I'd rather stick around town. Down the shore, I couldn't have fun. I'd be going bats, thinking about my Mom in a jail cell."

From Karl and I Knocky had picked up the habit of calling Dad sir. Dad liked that.

"You're in a pressure cooker, Alexi," Dad said. "Isn't it wiser to get off the scene for a while, not have abrasive morons gawking at you?"

"Sir, I don't give a damn about any of that. She's my only worry. Underneath it all, my Mom has a good heart."

Karl rolled his eyes without Knocky seeing that. *Underneath it all?* Viz a viz Sonya there was much to examine before you saw what was underneath it all.

Dad peered up at the heavens above our car before saying, "Let me think about this." He snapped on the radio. We were retreating again in Korea. He flipped the dial to the classical music station. Nobody wants to hear about this war. We turned onto Roosevelt Boulevard, were in another country up here, the affluent spheres where nothing happens. I had taken out girls from up here, Logan, East Oak lane, middle classy hot virgins who loved to pet but were otherwise so prim and prissy, so far removed from the crap we read about in the papers this morning.

We passed the miniature golf course at D and the Boulevard, Dad said, "Okay, here are the ground rules, to be followed strictly. You don't go into work; stay away from the schoolyard, Randolph Street, Girard Avenue, Marshall Street, you talk to nobody about nothing, especially not to strangers and reporters. I had swine calling me this morning that wanted to interview you, Alexi. Till further notice you are all to lay low, and keep your traps zipped. You got that, troops?"

"Yes, sir," we answered in almost a chorus.

Dad turned to us, and announced, "I'm counting on you two stalwarts to monitor this operation closely, and run interference for Alexi. I'm holding you responsible for keeping the crawling creeps away from him. Is that clear?"

Karl touched a finger to his temple in salute. I nodded. On the positive front Dad was sounding more like himself, forceful, in charge of the show. He was planning to retire in two years, would he make it? Will his mind accompany him on the journey? I hated to think of him toppling from his pedestal, but since that night he slumped in the Oyster House I'd seen cracks in his edifice, an unraveling in his monolithic structures. He still had not handled the Mrs. Jordan situation.

After Oxford Circle came the suburbs, countryside. Here be trees, duck ponds, cows. Screw Old Macdonald. Several barns had hex signs though not too many Pennsylvania Dutch live around here; most are further west, by Lancaster. It had been years since I'd been by this way, when Dad took me to the Bucks County Playhouse to see 'The Man Who Came to Dinner.' Karl and Alexi were the boys who came to dinner and never left. Since they moved in Dad had let our monthly cultural expeditions slide to the wayside, to the great relief of all concerned.

"Know the names of these trees? " Karl asked me, to say something because we were driving along in a morose silence.

"Search me: elm, spruce, oak, pine, Beech?" I suggested." I know bupkas from trees. My ignorance of nature could fill volumes."

"You see," Karl said, " you shoulda' gone more to summer camp, Paulie."

"Yeah, I remember how much you loved summer camp, Wronsky. Let us face it, Cossack. Our native soil is the cracked concrete of basketball courts. "

Knocky did not join in the chatter. The lad was down again, his chin resting on his chest, he might have been dozing. Dad signaled us to let him be.

After a brief tour of Doylestown Dad pulled into a farm with a roadside stand, on route Six-oh-Six, across from the National Farm School. Fat turkeys were gobbling in the pens, a sine qua no tire hung from an apple tree, the barn had the grayish-brownish scraggly façade of a let room where the wallpaper has been ripped away, and inside the barn was a rusting Model-T. Bees were buzzing over the cider presses. I prefer my bucolic serenity gracing the cover of the Saturday Evening Post but Dad said, " I think we can use ears of fresh corn for supper, and I'm tempted by those jugs of cider. Fresh food has an entirely superior flavor."

Am I a weirdo for not being a nature lover? My aunts were horrified when I told them that I disliked leisurely Sunday drives through the countryside. They think Nature is naturally good for you, like spinach, turnips, art museums.

Stepping out of the car, Dad stretched his arms up to the blue skies and said, "Isn't it glorious to get away from the stinking, polluted city every once in a while, and smell this great fresh country air."

Our trio nodded in craven agreement while our shrouded eyes conveyed that we could have done without this cantata. We were corrupt creatures, anxious to get back to the city lights, the nitty-gritty crap, back to the action.

The Evening Bulletin had a Front Page Article continued to another column on page seven, with photos of the five fugitives in the black hearse. John C Connors, the prominent banker and philanthropist, had refused to press charges, testifying that nothing had been stolen from his home; the confusing circumstances were the result of gross misunderstandings. There were no exotic strip tease acts, nor hanky-panky of any sort; he auditioned this group of entertainers with a view toward contracting their magic act for the charity benefits he organized with all proceeds going to various benevolent foundations on whose boards he served. Booker Beaumont, the estate gardener, had misinterpreted what he saw. Nor had anything of value been removed from the safe. The safe was open because he, himself, opened it to present to the ladies small tokens of his esteem. Connors also angrily rejected rumors that large amounts of cash had been filched from the safe, asserting that it only contained legal documents; the bandying around of exaggerated figures constituted canards concocted by overly ambitious reporters seeking to damage his sterling reputation; he was considering lodging suits for libel and defamation against all the publications fabricating these unsubstantiated, bizarre, and fallacious tales.

On the basis of these declarations by Mister Connors, Lawyer Morris Schenkman, representing the accused, entered a motion for the dismissal of all charges, claiming that if there had been no precipitating criminal behavior the entertainers from the Cosmo Club cannot be charged with fleeing the scene of a crime; as to resisting arrest, their refusal to pull over stemmed from the fact that the police pursuing them were in an unmarked vehicle, they feared that they were in danger of being assaulted by criminals posing as officers of the law.

Exercising his discretion, Judge Stanley M. Greenberg rejected Schenkman's motion; the accused remain in custody awaiting further actions by the office of the District Attorney based upon subsequent police reports.

That's why you need a lawyer, especially one with a vivid imagination. I had to control myself, avoid smiling while I read the hilarious alibis; an audition for future charity events? What a sweet man. The 'entertainers refused to pull over because they feared that the car trailing them contained outlaws planning to waylay them?

I could hear people chortling from the South Philly Navy Yard up to Manayunk. Karl also was suppressing grins, but out of respect for Alexi's sensitivities, neither of us could voice the caustic comments we reserved for this brand of poppycock. After Knocky read the article for the third or fourth time he turned to us and asked, "How can they possibly be holding her for a crime that never happened? And then, for fleeing the scene when my Mom can't drive, she doesn't even have a license?"

CHAPTER TWELVE

Wednesday morning, Dad changed the drill, in spite of our groans he tightened the screws, ordering us to remain incognito, in mufti, inside the house; we answer no phone calls. Pissing and moaning, we were stuck upstairs, playing chess and listening to music. Miss Pearl made a quick trip over to Feinberg's Smoke Shoppe, returned with the newspapers. It was difficult to tell which was more disgusting, what broadcasters and commentators were saying on the radio or what the press was writing about the investigations. Both sources mixed shocked, sanctimonious clucking with moist drooling over the racy material. Puritans really like to lick their lips over the lewd stuff

Karl looked up from his reading, chuckling, Knocky asked, "What's so damn funny? I aint seen nothing funny in the papers yet."

"You don't find poor Mister John C, Connors to be funny? " Karl asked." Nobody is buying his blarney that he was auditioning talent for charity events. Meanwhile, he's been asked to resign from his position at the Fidelity Trust Bank, foundations are considering severing ties with him, and his wife of thirty years has flown back from her Bermuda. Vacation. She is consulting her lawyer and Mrs. Connors has packed his bags. Mister Connors is currently residing at the Center City Union Club."

"Fuck him," Knocky said.

"Yes, that appears to be an ongoing process, with many participants," Karl said. "Other than his woes, according to the Inquirer here there's a wild scavenger hunt on the Main Line, patrol cars, also regular citizens, foraging and cruising around the woods in an Easter Egg Hunt, searching for the pouch of cash that was thrown, or was not thrown, from a fleeing hearse."

Knocky winced. The term applied, he was in denial. And he had not yet read the tabloid I was reading, where they had managed to dig up that Sonya Ratchinov was once fired from a job at a center city hotel when they caught her upstairs with a customer from the barber shop. And that Rita Demetrescu, daughter of Trixie Malloy, was incarcerated in an upstate reformatory for wayward girls, for giving knockout drops to a traveling salesman in a no-tell motel.

A wonder they failed to get the goods on our wall job up the alley. Hey! Rita was still a minor. What happened to the protection of children, the sanctity of us minors?

The upside of our being confined to quarters, Dad had sworn he would never let one of these infernal instruments enter his home, that afternoon a television set arrived: a bulky floor model chunk of furniture far too huge for the dinky twelve-inch black and white screen, I think it set Dad back a cool grand. It was installed in our third floor game room; we got to watch the Phillies beat the Brooklyn Dodgers.

Over dinner we thanked Dad profusely, then complained that after one day of confinement we already had cabin fever. He relented a bit and said that tomorrow we could go out but must follow the guidelines set forth on our drive up to Bucks County: no talking to strangers, familiar haunts will be avoided, we must only go to places where the overly curious klutzes won't be gaping at Alexi.

Thursday morning, Miss Pearl arrived with the newspapers; she did not even scold us when we read them over our breakfast oatmeal. From the kitchen she called out, "Two of my damn nephews have served time in one jail or another. Their parents were God-fearing folk but jail seems to run in our family."

"Thank you for that piece of information, "Karl called back to her, and to me he then whispered, "Maybe that is her way of conveying empathy?"

Knocky was frowning at the tacky photo of his aunt Svetla on page three of the tabloid, the Stripper Trixie Malloy with her yam-shaped knockers dangling over the pursed lips of a pop-eyed patron wearing a Shriner's fez. That must have come from the files. Otherwise we were reading about another hearing today presided over by Judge Stanley M. Greenberg. City Hall threatens to cancel the cabaret license of the Cosmo Club. Inexplicably, the Club had continued to operate after having been cited by municipal inspectors for numerous violations of the sanitation code. Both the State and Federal Income Tax Bureaus will conduct investigations into the charges that large amounts of cash had been removed from the basement recreation room safe on the Bryn Mawr estate. Mister Booker Beaumont, the estate gardener, has secured the pro bono services of the Legal Aid Society and the N.AA.C.P. to pursue his contentions that he had been unjustly discharged by John C. Connors from his employment, then viciously maligned by the racist press.

The coverage seemed to me disproportional. Why should a snafued caper on the Main Line rate almost as much space as the slaughters on the Pusan Perimeter? With a grimace, Knocky slid the tabloid over to Karl, turned to page three, featuring the lurid photo of Svetla's boobs. Wronsky, clever fellow, always know what to say. He clucked, "You're lucky, Alexi, coming from such a beautiful family. Me, and my tribe, we might be the living proof the Neanderthals are not extinct."

That appeared to appease Knocky. He glanced at the photo again, gave it one more dismayed wobble of the chin.

Dad's waiting room was packed. I wanted to pop in, ask if he'd heard anything more from his Darmopray. We had listened to the confusing blah blah on the radio, reporters questioning the mysterious silence from the courts, police, and the District Attorney's office on the status of the Cosmo Five, as the press was calling them. Dad was busy, so I just signed out for the three of us in the logbook. We will be heading downtown, destination, the movies, possibly, basketball afterwards in the Kearny yard. When in pain or doubt we go to the movies.

As we entered the vestibule the doorbell buzzed. Out on the steps was Paco from the Deli, he handed us three white envelopes while saying to Knocky, "Buenos Dias, hermano. You are too popular. After you leave on Tuesday, hey, oof, it slows so fast, no more business, nada. Customers smell through the front door, sniff, sniff, they don't see you, they go back to the Famous."

"You should ask Uncle Moe for a profit sharing plan, "Karl quipped to Alexi.

Knocky did not find that to be too funny. At times Karl misses the mark.

The envelopes contained our salaries for the entire week, no discounts for taxes, forty bucks, plus a ten-buck parting bonus. I wondered if this were Moe and Sara being so generous or if Dads sweetened the pot? While we were counting our money Paco told us about his cousin Eduardo serving time in a Florida jail for a gas station heist. People were expressing their sympathy by to Knocky gabbling about their own relatives in the clink.

We thanked Paco, he gave Karl a friendly punch, and murmured, "Hey, Don Juan, don't forget to give your amorcito a call. She's been by the deli every two hours, asking where oh where has my little Carlitos gone?"

"If you see her again, tell her I'll call her as soon as I can." Karl said.

After abrazos with Paco we headed down Sixth Street. Due to circumstances beyond our control we have the day off, the week off with full pay, plus a parting bonus. I may suggest to the Cosmo Five that they burgle another estate on the Main Line. At the Poplar corner drugstore the Daily Noose in the window was turned to page three, Aunt Svetla behaving naughty. Knocky shuddered. To distract him Karl began blathering about baseball, the Phillies chances of winning it this year, the Phillies had not won a pennant since Nineteen Fifteen, over the last twenty years had the worst record in the major leagues. Karl was doing a yeoman like job of filling the air with harmless palaver but it was impossible for him to get Knocky's mind off his troubles. Along Sixth Street, in the corner candy stores and soda fountains, half the tabloids in the windows were opened to page three, those spectacular boobs.

Knocky asked, "If she gets out today, do you think Doc will let me call My Mom?"

Obviously, Ratchinov was not worrying about baseball at the moment.

"Sure, he will," I said. "Keep a cool tool, fool. Darmopray told him that they are very close to copping a plea, getting sprung. Darmopray didn't have the inside poop yet but said strange stuff has been thrown into game. Doc will let you see your Mom once they're out, and the buzz dies down, and you can't be implicated. "

Totally familiar terrain, but streets we have slouched through all our life can suddenly seem like hostile territory. The Tenderloin was scarier today, the saloons shabbier, the hobos scabbier guitars and wedding rings in the hock shop windows ineffably sadder. Banjos twanging on the taproom jukeboxes sounded like bagpipes from hell. We, too, could end up here on this skid row. We could consult with Mister John C Connors on the subjects of the precariousness of existence and the fall from grace; from Top Dog Fatcat to Laughingstock in four short days.

Karl must have been sharing my mood. He announced, " I just finished reading 'Siddhartha' again. Herman Hesse."

"What's that got to do with anything?" I asked Wronsky.

His hands took in the panorama of puke-stained pavements, winos slumping in the doorways, and he said," Siddhartha, the Buddha figure, first left the shelter of his palace when he was in his early twenties. Gautama was so shocked by the squalor and depravity he saw that he evolved into a holy man. I'm sixteen but I've been seeing this crap for as long as I can remember, nothing shocks or moves me. This is just my daily bread, my regular scene. You, too, Paulie, and you, Alexi, we're inured to this filth, meaning we can never become saintly, never ascend to a higher plane, we are forever disqualified from becoming the Buddha."

"I don't recall ever sending in my application for Buddha" I said.

Knocky said, " I don't know what the fuck you two are talking about, "and then he almost laughed. Along Market Street he found little to laugh about. At every corner newsstand the vendors were displaying at least one copy of the tabloid folded to page three. Trixie and the Tourist. I had never thought about the vulgarity of mass production before, how much power an unknown asshole dingle bat can have. In a cruddy distant office a crusading self-righteous sleaze ball makes a decision, the switch is flipped, half a million consumers avidly consume the same hyped-up garbage, and who gives a shit if somebody's life is ruined beyond repair?

That was power. Gall had power. Bending over, Mrs. Ratchinov had power.

To distract him, take his mind off the headlights on every corner, Karl began lecturing Alexi on the Buddha and Siddhartha. I was thinking about tone and texture. On what level of paper do we live our life? Alexi had already been blasted with cheesy photos and slangy sensational headlines on this pulpy, grainy, ink-stained tabloid ignoramus level. Dad subscribes to the New Yorker, he says mostly for the cartoons. For myself I foresee a dry, wry, polished, sophisticated, cosmopolitan, witty, urbane existence on glossy, high quality paper with ads for expensive mink furs in the adjacent columns; A tad pretentious and superficial of me? What says I do not end up on skid row with the other bums?

We passed through the City Hall courtyard, the usual pigeons were flying over this somber space, a red car was pulling in with handcuffed prisoners, no one from around our way. No matter who wins the election this courtyard maintained the dank odor of shady deals, patronage, mediocrity, and corruption.

Coming out on the west side to our right was the Black Chinese Wall housing the train tracks to the Broad street station. For years they had been talking about tearing down this monstrous eyesore reaching right up to City Hall. To our left, on the south side of Market Street, were the pinball arcades and the movie houses, what the doctor ordered today, entertainment.

We were lucky, caught the Early Bird show, thirty-five cents. After One O' Clock it rose to sixty-five cents for minors. The double feature, 'Morocco,' and 'Beau Geste,' featured Gary Cooper in the French Foreign Legion. Gary had a prolonged career in the desert: 'Morocco' was from 1930, and 'Beau Geste,' 1939, so Gary must have served nine years in the French Foreign Legion.

Adios, cruel world. For thirty-five cents we board a magic carpet, leave behind draggy ass Philly and the cheapskate demanding customers on Marshall who scowl at us if we don't throw an extra slice onto their quarter pound of baloney. We land in the realm of noble deeds, sacrifices, gallantry, heroic postures, all things possible. I am the mysterious legionnaire, marching off to my certain death in the blazing sands of the Sahara, I'm so handsome and dashing I've reduced leggy Marlene Dietrich to the level of panting camp follower. The love-stricken, bedazzled gal is trailing after my doomed patrol into the desert, to die by my side.

The Magic Carpet was not working for Alexi today. He slept for a while during 'Beau Geste,' then his eyes were open though he was not seeing Fort Zinderneuf or the propped-up cadavers still manning the parapets while ominous buzzards circled over the sand dunes. His eyes glistened but he blinked away tears, he was toughing it out. He was in another picture that we might call 'Total Anguish.' What do you do after the mortar shell lands in your foxhole, blasts your life to shit and smithereens? Can Humpty-dumpty be put together again?

Knocky was slumping low, he had his elbows on his knees, was covering his face with his hands, he was sinking, Karl had to reach over, tap his shoulder, otherwise, Knocky might have fallen right out of his seat.

'Total Anguish?' If I were to write, produce, and direct a movie about the Ratchi-novs I'd have Sonya and Svetla doing tarty stuff like slipping Mickey Finns into the grog of well-heeled dupes, and lifting their wallets, but having those two dollies participate in a major burglary on the Main Line lacked credibility, was too outré. I should tell Knocky there's little chance his aunt or his momma will ever serve time. Darmopray, Dad's mouthpiece, assured me that he has never seen a pretty woman behind bars. Prison flics with the gorgeous vixens being brutally abused up the river were pure bull: desirable bon-bons were never sent up the river.

Reality was still there when we left the Fox, the bells were tingalinging in the pinball machine arcades. After a snack in the Horn and Hardart cafeteria we cut back through Chinatown toward our home turf with Karl still trying to cheer Knocky up, and not particularly succeeding with his Abbot and Costello routines.

Relief came when we reached the Kearny yard, found Boony Washington, Leroy Lincoln, and a bunch of other Colored from Franklin playing basketball on the court by the Marshall street exit. Entering the yard, Knocky received the reception John the Wizard gets when he enters Dave's poolroom; they were slapping his palm and asking him if he was revving up to star for Franklin this season.

Even though we were wearing our good go-to-downtown shoes, meaning treacherous slipping and sliding on the slick concrete, we played basketball, Leroy and Boony and our trio against five of the Franklinites. No refs were blowing whistles; at Kearny basketball was a brutal contact sport, rougher than rugby or La Crosse, basketball a la Beau Jack slugging it out with Jake La Motta in a dockside brawl, try any fancy Dan driving in for a lay-up you could get your head served up on a tray. Knocky was getting his mind off his misery; galvanized by the ferocity of Kearny style basketball, the flailing elbows, and crunching body shots he was kicking out hard at would-be defenders, playing like a whirling dervish on loco weed.

Karl glanced at me, and we shared the same thought: when we entered this yard there was no hitch in their greetings. These Franklin bruisers had not squinted at Alexi, in no way let it be known that they had seen the newspapers, were aware of his troubles. This was Cool; refinement at the yard bird level, the gentility of the Lower Depths. I should congratulate these guys; none had tried to console Alexi by telling him about their uncle Willie in the State Pen.

It was twilight time when we saw Judy entering the yard, Bloomy in her tight jeans a loose pink polo shirt. The lass was definitely developing, no more butter-will-not-melt-in-her-mouth-Miss-Goody-Two-Shoes from Girl's High, Bloomy was coming on strong as a tough-talking, ballsy colleen from Fishtown.

Time out was called for the ladies. Bloomy is our bold one. The Franklin guys hooted while Judy gave Leroy and Boony affectionate hugs, then gave Karl a smooch, sniffed at his armpit, and moaned," Uich, you're all sweaty and stinky, Corky. Go home and take a shower, or Momma will spank. But first I need to talk to you boys. You can buy me a soda. Like, now, if not sooner."

The troops roared at her Bitchy-Bossy number but understood this was the end of our basketball for the afternoon; these guys had bossy girl friends, too. We nodded our goodbyes; Boony detained me for a second as we drifted away,he whispered, "My aunt's been keeping me up about Lefty's Mom, all his troubles. You tell Alexi later that we're all with him with him all the way. Also tell him, he sure got sharp looking foxes in his family."

"Thanks, Boony, I'll be sure and tell him about your support. About the foxes thing, I may skip that."

When I caught up to my crew Karl was asking Judy, "Were you just wandering around the streets like a loose woman, or were you looking for us."

"I was searching for your scroungy hides. Went by the pool hall, Ludlow, then by Doc's office. Mrs. Jordan was snippy to me, but as I was leaving Miss Pearl showed me the logbook, where you three might be by now. "

"Theoretically, supposed to be. Sometimes we're even there," Karl said,

"Yeah," Judy sniffed. "I'm glad my folks don't know about Doc's logbook rules. If they did they'd have me accounting for every minute I'm out of the house, including when I have to take a pee."

Are girls flirting when they make unsolicited references to their nether regions or am I a scrounge for suspecting this? Another question eternally up for grabs. We entered the soda fountain at the corner of Sixth and Fairmount; Alexi winced at the newspaper racks. Aside from the now famous shot of Trixie, the afternoon papers had photos of big Wanda, looking large and scrumptious, like she could crush John the Wizard with those massive thighs. There were also more front-page articles trashing Mister John C. Connors and the Cosmo Five.

Karl sported us to four lemon Cokes, I bought the papers, we occupied the side booth. Knocky grabbed one of the tabloids. Except for the funnies and his rave reviews he had never been much into the news, now he gobbles the latest up.

"I've missed you since Monday," Judy complained to Karl. " I kept waiting for you to pass by the store window, you never passed by, Corky."

"Later, I will beat my breast, don sackcloth and ashes," Karl said," Meanwhile, I'm reading about poor Mister John C. Connors. Unbelievable what the papers will print once they get a juicy victim, the stuff they dig up from the past. Aside from the flap about auditions and burglaries they've uncovered that Connors was once arrested on drunk driving charges, and once was charged with harassment of a secretary, had to pay her off. And now, to cap it off, several of the foundations on whose boards he served announced they will conduct audits of his accounts and travel expenses."

"Boo-hoo? " Judy said. "What's that to us?"

"It's a hilarious tragedy," Karl said. "An old buzzard wants to have a little fun, ends up hit with the afflictions of Job piggybacking on the seven plagues of Egypt."

"Screw Connors," Judy said." Pay attention to poor little me, you clown."

Folding up the paper, Karl said, "You have my undivided and total attention for at least the next ten seconds. What's your problem, honey?"

"I've just had a horrible argument with my parents, you rat. They've forbidden me to ever see you again, Corky. I told them that's pretty difficult when you pass by our store five times a day but they swore that if they ever catch me with you again they'll ship me off toa boarding school up in Connecticut. I've an old aunt up there, my aunt Sylvia, I can't stand the woman, but they threaten that if I ever see you again, I'll be on the next train to Hartford, to be supervised by my aunt Sylvia"

 Karl asked, "And? Your response to that unseemly ultimatum?"

"I'm here, aren't I? "Judy said. "I told them to screw off. Just screw off."

Imitating George Sanders, I said, "Bully-bully for the gallant ladies."

Knocky glanced up from his reading, and muttered, "This is about me, isn't it?"

"You're part of it," Judy confessed. "They're using your troubles to get at me."

His face gnarling in disgust, Knocky groaned, "I knew it, goddam, I knew it."

"You're only a part of it," Bloomy assured him. "I'm so sorry for what you're going through, but, according to my dear family what they read in the papers was the last straw. They forbid me to ever see you, Paulie, or Corky, ever again, saying I'll get into bad trouble associating with delinquents like you, but that's pure fucking bullshit. They were scraping for any excuse at all to make me break it off with Corky, and they latched onto your rotten luck as a pretext, really pissing me off, Alexi."

It is not normal to see four brash teenagers fall totally silent. Not a real silence. The jukebox was playing; the radio was on low behind the ice cream counter. What to say? Bloomy's parents were not ogres or klutzes. They were acting like regular parents trying to protect their precious daughter. And, it was true, our trio was kind of gamey. If I ever had a daughter I'd hardly want her associating with a horny cads like the likes of us. Detour was playing on the Wurlitzer. 'Detour, there's a muddy road ahead, Detour, paid no mind to what was said, Detour, oh these bitter things I find, Shoulda' read that Detour sign.' Around here we called that Hillbilly music.

Not quite Milton or the Bard but 'Coming down Life's crooked road' was a great line. I looked at the photo of Connors in the afternoon edition; they won't leave this guy alone, he's the victim but the one getting crucified. Does he deserve it? He looks like a golf-playing martini swilling Republican who cheats on his taxes and pinches his secretary's behind; does he deserve his abysmal comedown? I could see Frederic March, George Brent, or Edward Everett Arnold wining an Oscar for their portrayal of the plutocratic tycoon flushed down the tube for a minor dalliance. It verges on 'Appointment in Samarra.' The spaghetti hits the fan and everything goes kerflooie.

Bloomy was stroking Knocky's wrist. All four of us stiffened as we heard through the static on the radio, already turned low, the evening news on WCAU, garbled and muffled by the static, while the whirring of the malted milk machine made it even harder to hear clearly: New Jersey authorities protesting because their requests for extradition of one Roy Bauer had been ignored. The Cosmo Five had been released earlier in the afternoon amidst confusing rumors circulating in the hallways of the municipal court about a so-called mysterious Book of John that may have influenced the Philadelphia Police Department to drop pending charges. And, now for the sports. Today, the Phillies dropped a close one to the Chicago cubs.

Knocky shot up, headed for the phone booth in the rear. Neither Karl nor I rose to stop him through we'd sworn to Dad we would monitor his activities, prevent contacts with his 'loved ones.'

"The Book of John?" Bloomy asked. "What's the Bible have to do with this case?"

"I think the announcer meant to say, 'The Book of Johns,' "Karl explained to her.

"What's that supposed to be? "Bloomy insisted.

"Kind of like a little black book about dating, hot numbers, kiss and tell. A book a gal might keep about the gentlemen paying for the hot dates," Karl explained.

"How do you know about such things, Corky? "Bloomy demanded to know.

"I wash my ears and listen to the words of wisdom spoken in Dave's pool hall. Everything you'll ever need to know you can learn in Dave's," Karl said.

Knocky was frustrated in that booth. He had used up all his nickels and dimes, none of his calls had been answered. He erupted from the booth so angrily he resembled a famished skinny bear bursting in a rage from hibernation. With a toss of the chin he implored us to move out. I may over-dramatize but Alexi looked like a stalwart squad leader indicating that we would be going over the top, to face the chattering machine guns.

Heading up Sixth, we passed the Nuts, Bolts, and Screws sign on the machine plant, nothing humorous occurred to me at this juncture. So far this had been one of the more putrid, weeks of my life. I can't imagine what it's been like for Alexi, or Mister Connors, Brothers in Pain. Strange the links that could exist between a Big Shot out on the Main Line, the dude with the carnation in his lapel, and a slumgullion urchin like Knocky, down here with us in the red brick boondocks.

Almost crouching like a simian, Alexi was slumping along, but wearing a David Farragut, 'Damn the Torpedoes, Full Speed Ahead' expression. When we reached the steps to our house Karl and Bloom began tearing into each other, as if sex might be outlawed next week. I made a tentative move to climb the steps. With a shrug Knocky announced that he was continuing on his way.

Karl broke off his ferocious kiss with Bloomy, opened his palms to the heavens. He goes to mass weekly so he has the right to invoke Heaven. It was my turn to open my palms to the heavens. Pop had given us strict instructions to control Alexi, keep him away from the bandidos, but what do you do when a buddy is in agony? Bloomy was thirding the motion. We trailed after Knocky.

With STOP and DETOUR signs flashing on my horizon, we marched on. I was feeling guilty. Guilty as charged was stamped on my birth certificate. Knocky was at point, crossing Girard we saw Buddy Baer, Burdumi, and Leon Hess entering Dave's. They did not spot us; I do not care to imagine how much snickering there must have been in the poolroom since the papers hit the stands Tuesday morning. Do I still aspire to be a journalist? Maybe not: screw John Reed, Drew Pearson, Brenda Starr, Walter Winchell, and Clark Kent.

Ludlow schoolyard was only houses past the pool hall. Dave's was always in danger of being shut down, due to zoning, tut-tutters complaining that the proximity of a depraved pool hall would have deleterious effects on our innocent, pristine childhoods. It had only been a few days since we were by here but it felt like a wide crack in time in this thickening dusk. The schoolyard was the same, yet different, hazy street lamps affording a dismal illumination; empty basketball courts were naked spaces where amputated limbs once hung. Bloomy sighed; she was also spooked by the malignant aura of the schoolyard. Karl scowled. All the dinky row houses on Randolph Street had lights on in their windows; dull yellows glowing through the shades and drapes. With the one exception of the Ratchinov house.

Sonya's front door was banging open and shut. We were far from the English uplands but the door eerily banging open and shut lent a Gothic tinge to the moment. A low rent rat hole became a deserted manor on the Moors. Bloomy slipped away from her Corky, slipped her arm around Alexi's waist as we crossed the schoolyard. A Florence Nightingale touch, I didn't think she had that in her, at her young age, to become so sisterly and motherly Reaching Randolph Street we saw the debris and rubbish stacked in front of the house, a broken down easy chair, bushel baskets loaded with rugs, cans, beer bottles, hair curlers, twisted coat hangers, rags, a broom, an ironing board, the same kind of crap you saw when the Colored tenants got evicted down there in Rubenville.

"Jesus," Alexi wheezed.

"He hasn't come by this parish lately," Karl said.

The lock was broken; this door twisting off its hinges. Knocky stepped inside, snapped on the parlor switch. A scene of gloomy devastation hit us. What jarred me most was stepping so abruptly from the pavement into his dingy parlor, the outside world wrenchingly close to your skin. The Ratchinovs had always lived too close to the sidewalk, the street. Chairs were broken, dry straw was coming out of the slashed sofa; the green icebox in the kitchen had crashed to the floor. This place had been defiled by an obscene storm.

From that blurred broadcast and static we did not know if the Cosmo Five had made bail, jumped bail, what, exactly, happened. We could only testify that Bauer trashed this dump before they took off. Roy had forgot to smear shit on the walls.

Knocky was looking around for a goodbye note.

CHAPTER THIRTEEN

Marshall Street had the word. Those retail mom and pop stores produced slews of professionals in the second and third generations, doctors, and accountants; per capita, more lawyers were born on this block than any other in Philadelphia. Top attorneys from the center city law firms and courtrooms still had strong ties to the folks with the pushcarts and fruit stands. By the week-end Marshall Street knew that a so-called Book of Johns belonged to one Trixie Malloy: aside from naming the names of street cops and police captains who had been hitting on the hookers for their free spare there were pages containing lists of prominent public officials, their nicknames, code names, the usual fees the tricks paid their escorts, also their predilections, quirks, and, in several cases, their favorite costumes.

Along Marshall Street newsy bodies were asking who in heaven might be the 'Snookums' who chose to wear the Green Hornet costumes when he was whipped?

Kids entering their junior year of high school are not supposed to know about these esoteric matters but if you attend seminars in Go-d's Bar and Dave's Billiards Parlor you learn stuff not on the standard curriculums.

Monday morning I trudge back to school, the trolley trip down Girard, the long ride on the subway, the walk down Olney Avenue passing the Widener Estate. My bail had been revoked. I was Galileo entering the Vatican where hooded inquisitors await me with thumbscrews. I made vows to control my tongue this semester; I will not peer through any periscopes, will tell my interrogators only what they wish to hear, I will keep a low profile, eat humble pie, ask only how many portions I must consume, and, above all, I will save my sardonic zingers for future audiences more receptive to over-the-top scurrilous and caustic cracks.

Good intentions, but there was my pack of jackals on the South Lawn at lunch time, we instantly resumed our contest to see who had arrived with the most obscene limerick, scummiest riddle, filthiest ditty. At our first session I earned the laurels, received the biggest howl for: What's the difference between a tribe of Pygmies and the Vassar track team? The Pygmies are a bunch of cunning runts.

Over dinner that evening Dad asked Alexi how it had gone his first day back at Franklin. Knocky said, "Not too bad but it was kind of strange. Teachers were glancing at me sideways, as if surprised that I returned. None said anything to but they sure talked when my back was turned. Guys in my classes, lots gave me punches on the arm, a pat on the back, asked if my family had really made off with a big haul or if the loot was tossed out the window, like the newspapers wrote."

"Oof," Dad said," let me know if the pressure gets too much for you, son. One solution might be, we can send you off to a private boarding school, out of town. Lots of schools would be glad to have you on their basketball team, and I can also arrange for special tutors, to help you on the academic side. You call the shot, Alexi. "

"Thank you, sir, but I'd rather stick it out here. Paulie and Karl are my brothers, and Franklin is counting on me to lead it to the championship this year."

"Okay, "Dad said, "we'll try it for a while but you've got to let me know if your family makes any effort to get in touch with you. From my sources I gather that they've left town, are probably up in Reading."

"Yes, sir, " Knocky promised. "I'll tell you first thing."

My classmates up at Central were also curious about how Alexi was handling his peculiar notoriety. Many had fond memories of Knocky, asked how come a nice guy like Ratchinov had been booted out of Central while a Shvuntz like me was still fouling up the premises. Lord, it was a drag being back. Trigonometry? Physics? I thought Einstein was covering physics. My only escape valve was our lunchtime bawdy carnivals, crowds larger than ever for our limericks, 'there once was a hermit named Dave.' 'There once was a girl from Nantucket.' We sang the more scabrous verses of 'The Ballad of Diamond Lil, and Pistol Pete, 'who came over the hill with twenty-eight pounds of swinging meat, and 'The Good Ship Venus,' where the cabin boy's name was Nipper, by God he was a ripper, he stuffed his ass with broken glass, and circumcised the Skipper. The Brains continued with their tradition of roaring at our rawness, and then scorning us as unspeakable rabble.

In consideration of the problems Dad was having, I behaved myself, did not pounce on the opportunities I had to wise off. Still, without hearing tom-toms beating in the bush, I knew this could not last. My English prof was gunning for me. Ming had received prior briefings depicting me as an insolent smart-ass, prone to outrageous remarks; I was the closest thing Central had to a juvenile delinquent. This professor shall remain as nameless as that village in La Mancha, but we will furnish his nickname: an ex-army officer with a ramrod bearing, a Chinese apple of a crimson bald school, a bellicose attitude channeled through the snarling style of a hung-over drill sergeant, and noted for his lectures on jade, Terra Cottas, and the celestial dynasties, these elements combined with his glowering Fu Manchu aspect to earn him the moniker: Ming the Magnificent.

I forgot to mention his Mongol mustache. I suspected that every morning, while shaving, Ming twirls that mustache, and says to his mirror, "I will show the little fuckers what's what today. Then he goes out and kicks the dog.

I was making a good faith effort to be inconsequential, innocuous, inconspicuous, but for our second composition assignment Ming wrote on the blackboard: 'Will the Second Half of the Twentieth Century Be Better Than the First?' Or: 'What Will the Year 2000 be like?' Choose one Topic. Forty-five minutes to complete the task, feel free to pick up extra sheets from the front desk if there is the need to expound at length. At the doorway Ming sneered at us derisively. He never actually twirls his Fu Manchu mustache as he leaves the room but we visualize him doing that anyway.

I'd been a fanatic sci-fi buff, a fan of Amazing Stories, Planet Comics, Roger Zelany, Jules Verne, Ray Bradbury, 'Doc' Smith, Richard Shaver, but thinking about the year 2000 irritated me. Will it be a Utopia, or will we be radioactive zombies crawling out of the rubble? Just to be perverse, I wrote: 'In the Year 2000 we will all wear beanies adorned with whirling propellers enabling us to lift off, fly away to romantic places without resorting to cumbersome vehicles like cars or ships, '

I might be criticized for this sophomoric humor, as I was now a junior.

Both topics irked me. Inspiration flagged. Around me, diligent slurpers were off to the races, scribbling away. I was flummoxed by the cosmic frivolity of these subjects. To consider challenging questions of this magnitude you'd need to convene a bevy of deep thinkers, heavy hitters like Toynbee, Spengler, Ortega y Gasset, not throw these themes out at us slimey-pawed teen-agers mainly dreaming about the Saturday night drive-in, caressing the toukas of Myrna Schwartzbaum.

Will the Second Half be Better? Dios Mio, doesn't Martinet Ming read the papers? In this entire putrid world the only positive news is that the Phillies might win the pennant. Otherwise, the Russkies have stolen the secrets of the hydrogen bomb, there's bloody fighting in Syria, a Civil War in Greece, massacres in India, the French are losing in Vietnam, Chang Kai Chek lost China, our army is being decimated in Korea, and, out of his ass, Ming pulls the question 'Will the second half be better?

Prolific classmates were hustling up to the front desk for more sheets of paper. Half these mutts returned this semester prematurely Joe College preppy in seersucker suits, stuck up and suck-up attitudes, already talking about Antioch, Oberlin, Swarthmore, Dartmouth. I long to go to Sidi el Abbas with my carbine and my kepi. Schatzy Marlene will trail me into the blazing desert.

My page looked bare. Assiduous rivals had finished two sheets, front and back; I had managed to eke one miserly line up there. How best to annoy Ming? He picked up his Asiatic slant stemming from a family of born again Baptist missionaries proselytizing in China before the war. Maybe I could get to him by plagiarizing the

Pepsi Cola Jingle. I wrote: 'In the year 2000 there will be mass conversions to Christianity, the number one song on the hit parade will be:'

'Christianity hits the spot, twelve disciples, that's a lot.

A Holy Ghost, and a Virgin, too, Christianity is the religion for you.'

Yeah, I was bucking for a bruising, looking for trouble. That should fairly well infuriate him. At tines, if you are into your rebel mode, you just gotta' say' Fuck it, and let it all hang out, To previous sacrileges I added a riddle. 'What's the difference between a feisty rooster and a sharp lawyer? The feisty rooster clucks defiance.'

When Ming returned with his scornful scowling to collect our compositions he glanced at the bare stretches and paucity of production on my virtually naked sheet, and asked, "What's the matter, Burris? Suffering from Writer's Block?"

Ming was locking horns with me before he even examined what I wrote,

Writer's Block, sine qua non cliché in birdbrain films where frustrated authors pull sheets from their typewriters, scrunch them into wads, toss wads into waste cans. By Hollywood authors are serene sages, spouting blowhards, braying assholes, starry idealists, incurable alcoholics, sold-out hacks or dismal combinations thereof. The wad-scrunching bit was as trite as the adorable infant peeing on whoever dares pick her up. Or was that because most writers in Hollywood were third raters who despised real authors?

"Well, Burris?" Ming insisted.

"I was uninspired, sir."

With malicious intent my classmates cackled on cue. They had wondered when I would live up to my role as the designated clown. Those cackles were designed to egg Ming on with to take reprisals against poor moi, the class wiseacre.

Ming snorted, "Not inspired, Burris? Should we regard this as a temporary affliction, or is this your existential condition?"

They cackled at his sally, too. So young my schoolmates had become faithful minions of the system, premature tools of establishment, lackeys identifying with their oppressors. They reminded me of galley slaves encouraging the whipper to lay on more lashes if any upstart in their ranks became too impudent. I upped the ante by saying, "Sir, aside from not having brought my crystal ball today I think that question- will the next half century be better- that struck me as inane. Sir. "

Classmates moaned, an insidious moan, inciting teacher to instantly retaliate. Ming countered with, "Trot down to the office, Burris, and tell Doctor Farber that you find my assignments to be inane, they do not inspire you. Add that I recommend five afternoon detentions to give you ample time to dig up the proper inspiration."

Ming took advantage of my exit to murmur an acidic aside, eliciting sycophantic chortles from my peers. I foresee that in the future there will be thousands of wise guys like me pouring out of the woodwork but in the interim it is a lonely, dolorous, and harrowing burden to be a pioneer in advance of our times. So be it. Once again, I am the abused, misunderstood, and derided rebel slouching toward my murky fate. We accept our lot. Seminal figures are often scorned and stoned during the lacteal stages of their development. They told Van Gogh he could not paint. The Wright Brothers were told that thing wont fly. If Saint Augustine had not sinned first how could he have written his confessions? I suspect that most Icons were schmucks before they ever became Icons.

When I entered the Vice-Principal's suite the secretaries arched their lashes into parabolas asking, "You again?" They did not invite me to take a seat. Long minutes passed before Doctor Farber deigned to receive me in his office. He also had his nickname: we called Farber Captain Muncie in honor of Hume Cronyn's sterling portrayal of a sadistic, corrupt, geeky prison guard in the movie 'Brute Force.'

Farber did his aloof shtick, ignoring this culprit, perusing memos while I stood there with an invisible cap in my hands, trying neither to cower nor to quiver.

Dad says never judge people by their physical appearance. Dad offers fine advice that I rarely follow. Farber, I could envision in the role of Iago, or Rumplestiltskin, or evil troll on the Asteroid Ganymede. If I were casting a movie called 'The King of the Gnomes'; he could be his majesty's treacherous advisor. Doctor Farber, of course, must cultivate his own self-image: The Torquemada with a heart of gold; when he stretches you on the rack it is for your own good and will benefit society at large.

Without bothering to look up, Farber asked, "What is it this time, Burris?"

"I was uninspired today, sir."

"I find you uninspiring every day, Burris. Give me the particulars."

I described my repudiation of the assignments Ming had given us, how I found both topics to be fatuous and inappropriate for jejune striplings.

Doctor Farber failed to bat either of his beady eyeballs at my calling our English prof 'Ming,' The faculty was cognizant of the nickname. Farber seemed to be agreeing with me that those were weighty subjects for a forty-five minute composition, then said, "Your professor recommended five detentions. I'm upping that to five morning and five afternoon detentions. That should give you sufficient time to find inspiration for a proper response. When you're finished I'd be curious to see your final product on the future as I, myself, take a dim view of any future you will be a part of. "

THE GESTAPO STRIKES AGAIN

I had vowed to eschew my gallows humor, refrain from wising off, it came out anyway. "I thought we weren't supposed to end sentences with prepositions, sir."

"Quite true, "Farber conceded. "That will be ten early morning and seven afternoon detentions. Now I am awaiting your next feeble attempt at a witticism, Burris. "

"You have drained me of inspiration, sir."

"Good. Start serving your detentions today. You know, I've known and admired your father for a long time, Burris. And, your Dad is a brilliant bridge player. It must eat his heart out to have a son like you."

Mister Warshaw was the teacher supervising confinements that afternoon. As I entered the detention room he awarded me the pained but quasi–amiable twist of the chin greeting that Wardens bestow upon habitual recidivists returning to their favorite jails. Half my rat pack was already installed in here; Seymour the Simian and Jack Kraft snorted at the sight of me. Warshaw barked at them in the abrasive sandpaper accent of teacherspeak, " Be quiet, you buffoons, knock it off, or I'll add on two more detentions for you." Then, to me, in a mocking solicitous tone he said, "Burris, you're late. We were waiting, expecting you, wondering what happened to you. We were worried, but knew you wouldn't fail us, that you'd eventually arrive."

How these teachers love to get it off on us. I did not respond, was about to plop down, grab a seat next to my buddies, Mister Warshaw pointed to a place of exile in a far corner, and said, " My policy, I think it is wiser to separate the hard core malcontents from the incorrigible miscreants. You only encourage each other."

I sat down in the nook reserved for hardened criminals, opened my looseleaf folder. My mind was a blank; suddenly the vacuum was filled with rage, a delayed reaction. I lack spontaneity. Only now was I steaming up about Doctor Farber's parting crack. He had no right to get that damn personal with me, hit me with one of those offhand remarks that can stick in your craw forever:

IT MUST EAT HIS HEART OUT TO HAVE A SON LIKE YOU

I could see that on billboards along Route 66.

Visit the cave of the Comanche witch doctor.

Buffalo Bill killed a buffalo here.

Twenty miles to the next Texaco Gasoline Station

IT MUST EAT HIS HEART OUT TO HAVE A SON LIKE YOU

Father and son relations can be tricky. According to the Brothers Karamazov, what son does not want to kill his father? Ah, that's just those morbid Russkies with their nihilistic BS, but in those anthropology texts in Dad's library I'd read chilling theories about the cavemen killing off all potential competitors, meaning their male offspring, so they could have exclusive rights to all the available fillies. That lasted until the frustrated ladies banded together to bump off the old Boy. Is that where we really come from? Is the modern home an improvement over those smelly caves?

IT MUST REALLY EAT HIS HEART OUT TO HAVE A SON LIKE YOU

"Hey, Burris!" Mister Warshaw shouted," Get cracking! You were not sent in here to drift off on Cloud Number Nine. Start studying. "

His shout almost derailed me from my train of thought. I opened a book, my mind still on Fathers and Sons; since we are much into idle conjecture and fruitless speculation, why not explore unexamined paths? I must try this hypothesis out on Ming. Many mysteries would be cleared up if Jesus were the Prodigal Son. Maybe Jesus had been behaving badly up there, kicking at the traces, and God said," Okay, Kid, I'm sending you down below, the earthlings will show you what life is all about."

'I'd Walk a Mile for a Camel.'

IT MUST EAT YOUR FATHER'S HEART OUT TO HAVE A SON LIKE YOU.

Do the teachers sit around the faculty lounge devising campaign slogans to browbeat the unruly? I must concentrate on the topics: Will the second half of the Twentieth Century be Better than the First? My pen only doodles boobs and buns, pendulous breasts with cartoonish features, the upturned and downturned lips of the twin gargoyles of Comedy and Tragedy. How can I handle the Twentieth Century when I can barely manage my paltry patch of Sixth Street?

For starters, Bloomy is threatening to run away from home. Her folks are fed up with how she picks Karl up every day at Roman, they nuzzle all the way back to Marshall Street. Ma and Pa Bloom saw fit to call the law, threatened Dad with a legal injunction, cease and desist orders, unless he takes binding measures to harness Wronsky. Dad told them to buzz off, to control their own daughter.

Knocky? Alexi seems to be okay but that aint necessarily so. His eyes are glazed. Superficially, he is in like Flynn at Franklin, loved on Marshall Street, the outlaw mystique, as if he were a nephew of Jesse James, from a family of bitchy beauties and bad-ass bandits, but it bugs the shit out of him that when he passes on by, looks over his shoulder, people are talking about him, he knows what they are saying.

Dad has problems on all Fronts. He told Mrs. Fiore he would not be seeing her anymore: he was committing himself, more or less, definitively, to Maxine Barufkin once the boys are out of the house. From eyewitness reports we received later, Carla did not go sweetly into that good night. She made a helluva' stink in Arthur's steak house, threw a twenty dollar bill on the table to cover her part of the bill, and swore to nearby diners that she would fix his wagon, get him good.

If that's not enough, Dad finally fired Mrs. Jordan, not for the reasons he should have originally booted her ass out for, conspiring with Sonya Ratchinov to do him dirt, but for disrespecting the colored patients he was seeing, gratis, Miss Pearl's relatives, and a few of the indigents from the Project. He called Mrs. Jordan in to chide her, gently, the witch spat out all kinds of venomous bile at him, and even though he gave her a generous severance pay she is also threatening to fix his wagon, sue his hide, using Mister Braxton's Walnut Street legal connections.

That is aside from Dad catching flack from unexpected quarters, catching shit from right field, and being sucker-punched from left field. The Pastor in the Negro store front church at Marshall and Buttonwood hotly denounced Dad in a sermon for undercutting up and coming professionals with his freebies, taking legitimate business away from the Colored doctors with their offices on Ridge Avenue.

Will the second half of the Twentieth Century, give me a break.

Hosts of hostiles want to fix Dad's wagon. I am seeing Dan Burris with a broken down wagon in the Oklahoma badlands. The Comancheros are bearing down on him with upraised tomahawks. Weird how stuff can gang up on you, ten days had gone by, but today there was another news item raking on John C, Connors over the coals.

What will the year 2000 be like?

I doodled more buns and bumps, my main interest in life, aside from the war, not chemical valences and binomial equations. Guys were dying in Korea to protect my inalienable right to goof off in High School. I want to go to Korea, to kill and fight and plunder. And, while I am in that neighborhood, maybe a gorgeous Communist Dragon Lady would be kind enough to seduce me.

The man snuck up on me. I was so far adrift in outer space I did not hear teacher sneaking up. Mister Warshaw snatched the sheet from my desk and then he waved it around, triumphantly, as if were a bloody sheet after the wedding night, and he snarled, "Hach! So this is how you do your homework, Burris?"

My scurrilous doodles were available for public consumption. Warshaw winced as the detained class, especially Jack Kraft and Seymour the Simian, applauded my artistic efforts. He tried to silence them with a chop of the arm, the hearty applause continued, he had to bark, "Quiet, you rabble." Then, to me, he said," Aren't you ashamed of yourself, Burris? You are being afforded the finest public education the City of Philadelphia provides, an unparalleled opportunity to learn, study, make something of yourself, and what do you do with these precious opportunities? You scrawl obscene cartoons."

"Ah, they're not that dirty, "Kraft scoffed. "My doodles are much raunchier."

"Silence!" Mister Warshaw growled at Kraft. Then he raised a menacing finger at and said, "The worst of it is, I might forgive a boy coming from a poor, troubled background, but you are a product of privilege, you come from a distinguished family. One of your uncles was my classmate, an excellent student; another of your uncles was the school valedictorian. But you, Uich! It must eat your father's heart out to have a son like you."

It could not be just a coincidence. The faculty must have conducted a conference to deal with my case; they came up with these campaign slogans.

The following morning I was sent directly from the detention room to Doctor Farber's office. He was in a testy mood, had barely finished his first cup of coffee. I said, "Good morning," he did not bother to respond. Instead, he held up a sheet of paper. From the vast blank spaces I recognized it as my foreshortened reaction to Ming's proposed topics yesterday. Farber had no good goods on me.

"You purposely seeking to be expelled from this school, Burris?" Farber asked.

"Actually, sir, that is not part of my master plan."

"This is the most abominable, disgusting piece of work I've ever seen handed in by a Central High student, Burris: snide anti-religious remarks, infantile filth. What do you have to say for yourself?" Farber asked.

He was coming on strong but I was in a good mood due to great news today. I could have dance a Boogy Woogy for such good news but suspected that Herr Farber would not countenance much levity from me at the moment.

"You've nothing to say for yourself?" Doctor Farber insisted.

"Uh, I've been a bad boy? Will that suffice? "

"Don't try my patience, "Farber snapped. " I was inclined to kick you out of here, immediately. But the Principal, out of respect for your father, all he he's done for this institution, said we should give you one final, ultimate chance. This will be it. If another teacher sends you down here, if I see you in this office again, if I hear one more sarcastic crack coming out of you, you'll be out of here. Is that clear?

Fairly clear, but I believe that was a rhetorical question; you only get into trouble responding to rhetorical questions.

"Thank you, sir."

"And, I'd advise you to tone down your lunch time activities," Farber added. "I've received alarming reports about foul, improper language heard on the South Lawn."

My inclination was to say 'Jawohl.' I chickened out, mumbled, "Thank you, sir. "

"I'm holding off on sending a copy of this filth you wrote to your father. But he will receive it, plus the entire file of complaints we 've compiled on your outrageous conduct the next, and final, time you act up. Now get out of here," Farber snapped.

"Thank you, sir."

Whatever happened to the land of the Free, and the Home of the Brave? Censorship? I could tolerate his ultimatum about no more back talk to the teachers but by what right did he stick his hooked snout into our lunchtime trash talking contests?

Instead of moping I shook myself to shuck my gloom. Not even I gave a rat's ass about my piss-ant bush league woes. I'm a flippant smart-ass being punished by detentions, threatened with expulsion; how does that stack up against the glorious news in the today's papers? At last, the worm has turned, just when everything was darkest, our troops surrounded, down to their last bullets, the Comanches about to take scalps and rape the school ma 'arms, we hear the bugles of the cavalry riding to the rescue. After a long, agonizing summer of gruesome casualties, bloody defeats, humbling retreats, came the lightning bolt out of the blue, a total surprise, the Inchon Landing. General MacArthur pulled off a brilliantly executed stroke, an amphibious landing deep behind enemy lines, leading to a total rout of the Commy bastards. They were retreating from the Pusan perimeter, fleeing in mass, and taking heavy losses.

For the next two weeks the news was mostly good. Though bogged down after the initial blitz, and facing bitter resistance, bloody fighting, and suicidal charges, the Allied forces managed to advance and retake Seoul. This was the way it was supposed to be, the smashing comeback, the Hollywood ending.

In honor of the troops I was trying to straighten up and fly right. To hell with Captain Muncie and his threats, I was striving to clean up my own act by my own liege, to quash my guilty feelings. Jody-me, back on the comfy home front, I was enjoying myself way too much: picking up Strawberry Mansion chicks in Fairmount Park, crashing parties and weddings with my Central rat pack, dating classy uptown girls, burnishing my rep as a swinger. Forget Gans, many other guys were *'looking'* for me, wanting to punch me out by now. I was living it up while G.I.'s only a few years older were getting bayoneted and dying in distant, muddy trenches.

By October we had pushed the Commies all the way back to the Thirty-Eighth Parallel, a cause for elation, but our joy was tempered if you lived in Philly. From October Fourth to October Seventh life was sheer misery. After a thirty-five-year draught the Phillie finally won the pennant, the Whiz Kids faced the Yankees in the World Series. Karl, Knocky and me watched the soul-crushing debacle on our TV: three cliffhangers in a row, three straight heartbreaking losses by one rotten run, then the final game was a five-to -two blowout.

Was the fix in? The Phillies were shorthanded in the pitching department: two weeks before the world series started the Army inexplicably drafted our second best pitcher, Curt Simmons; he had a seventeen and eight record that year. Around Marshall there was talk of conspiracies, diehard fans saying there must be Yankee Sympathizers and New York stooges on the Draft Board; they couldn't wait a goddam two weeks? What was the rush? They weren't going to instantly ship Simmons to the fighting at Pusan, anyway.

Why does Philly get no respect? Why were we condemned to provincial dreariness? Why must this always be the city of crushed hopes? Weeks later, I was still fulminating about the unfairness while running down Broad toward Olney Avenue. Near midnight, I was debating whether to grab the subway or the trolley. The subway shoots us down to Girard Avenue quicker but there are stops en route where you would not want to be alone in one of those cars when ten frustrated punks pile on, looking to amuse themselves, compensate for a draggy Saturday night

I was huffing along, after a date with Anita Green, a movie, burgers at the Hot Shoppe. You did not get to third base with prim Anita but batting it out with her on that sofa generated enough heat to thaw polar icecaps, making it hard to jog along in the specific condition I was not enduring. Then I was in luck, the 65 was pulling out of the depot as I reached Olney Avenue, the conductor kind enough to pause, to let me hop aboard. I recalled Saturday nights when sadistic swine saw me and other late arrivals frantically waving, racing to catch up, the pricks turned on the speed to leave us marooned up here. If you did not catch this last 65 departing at midnight there was not another trolley until the dawn patrol left at five-thirty in the morning.

After thanking the conductor I headed up the aisle, nodding to acquaintances. Several of my fellow travelers were slicker versions of Paul Burris, downtown hep cats up here trying to score with the uptown maidens; several faced trips longer than mine. I hopped off at Girard with four or five of them still aboard, continuing on to deepest South Philly. There was a kind of brotherhood here. Since we rarely got too far with these 'nice' girls from Oak Lane and Logan, and on this last run the 65 did not make the regular local stops, only paused at the major Avenues, this midnight trolley had come to be unpopularly known as the Blue Balls Express.

Sharpies were discussing theirs dates, I heard one saying, "Man, I couldn't get bare elbow off that Marlene," the other claiming, "I made out okay with Phyllis. She sure doesn't look it but you touch her and that girl sizzles. "

Benoff, on the rear bench, raised his hand in greeting, like a cigar store Indian. Leon went to Temple, majored in history. He faced the longest trip on this trolley, eighty blocks all the way down to Ritner Street, for him this 65 was practically a primitive space rocket connecting him to another solar system.

I sat down with Leon; let him do most of the talking. Aside from majoring in history Benoff was a cracker barrel philosopher, a barrel filled with matzoh balls; he lectured on the major thinkers of the past as if they were sidemen in his Klemzer Quartet, with scintillating riffs on Spinoza, Maimonides, Schopenhauer. No time for the trivial, Benoff might have been the first guy I'd ever smarter than Wronsky; he could turn a dull-ass trolley rides into pyrotechnical intellectual extravaganzas. Leon was as precocious in the realm of the Word as Alexi was on the basketball court.

Darkened streets out there, we were surging along, stopping every ten blocks for a stray drunk or lost soul with Benoff conducting his mobile symposium in the midst of this prosaic early-to-bed-nothingness, a few lights in a few windows. The only words I managed to get in with Leon were "Good night." I had to rectify that to, "Actually, good morning," before I hopped the 65 at Girard Avenue.

Instantly, I noted a strange emptiness. The trolley chugged off but the minimal traffic at this hour had slowed to a cautious crawl on Sixth Street. Usually, after midnight, Sixth looked and sounded like the Indianapolis Five-Hundred. A red lamp on the roof blinking, a patrol car near Fifth Street was slowing the traffic on Girard. Halfway down the block, on Sixth, another red car was parked directly in front of my house. It looked like a stakeout in preparation for a major raid. I thought about all the times Miss Pearl had warned Dad not to go out alone at night.

I lit up a smoke and drifted slowly down Sixth. Two cops I had never seen before were sitting in the parked patrol car. The driver rolled his window down, and I said, " Excuse me, officer, is there something wrong?"

"You Alexi Ratchinov?" The driver asked me.

From his tone there definitely was something wrong.

"No, sir," I said. He lives here with us. He's kind of like a brother to me."

"Then you're Doc Burris's son, " the other cop said. "Get inside the house, and stay inside. Your father's downtown."

"You can't say what's wrong, officer?" I insisted.

"Nope, just get inside," the driver ordered me.

Some of these guys forget they are supposed to be public servants. Hoo-ha.

The house was so silent even the click of my keys in the locks sounded too loud. The stairs never creak though I imagine them creaking, Dad's suite on the second floor was dark; I saw the lights in our game room. Karl was still up. As I reached the third floor, he said, "Glory be, you finally made it."

"Glory-shit, what's going down, man?"

"Too much. Doc was out for dinner with Mrs. Barufkin tonight, Knocky came home around eight, he'd just heard it on the radio, it'll be all over the papers tomorrow and they're repeating the news hourly on practically every station. The Cosmo Five are now the Cosmo Four. Roy Bauer's body was found in a garbage dump outside Reading wrapped up like a Mummy, the cadaver bound in yellow wrapping tape. From the decomposition they think it's been a while"

"Jesus," I groaned.

"I don't think he was in on this job," Karl said. "The cops up in Reading believe this was done by his lady accomplices from the J.C. Connors audition caper. They are searching for the women; believe they have skipped Reading for parts unknown. Alexi was acting frazzled and crazy, said he couldn't take it anymore, was sick of the way people stare at him. I tried to stop him but he wrote a note, thanking Doc for everything. Then he packed a canvass tote bag, pounded me on the back, told me to say goodbye to you. I tried again to block him, stop him, shit, I was actually wrestling with him but he was determined, so I ended up giving him the forty bucks I was saving up to buy Doc a birthday present."

"Where's Doc now?" I asked.

"Downtown, with the police. They wanted to hear everything Doc might know about the Cosmo Five, now the Cosmo Four. They wanted to know all about the Ratchinovs, and John the Wizard. It is really weird how our fine and upstanding family became so tangled up with theirs. I sort of see them as poison ivy infecting our garden. "

"Did Knocky say where he was heading?"

Karl sniffed, and said," He talked about maybe Gold's bar, to ask Gallagher for help in getting out of town. The Cops grilled me for an hour, I told them everything I knew but said nothing about Alexi hitting on Gall for help. God help me, I didn't say anything to Doc about that, either. "

"Oof," I wheezed. "You've had quite an evening."

"Yeah, quite an evening," Karl agreed. Then he handed me a sheet of loose-leaf paper and said, "Read the goodbye note Alexi left for Doc, Paulie. It is really a nice note, considering that Knocky is practically an illiterate. "

CHAPTER FOURTEEN

Due to the spate of sensationalistic articles over the next few days rehashing the gamey material about the Cosmo Five, the lurid auditions, the burglaries that did not happen, I had visions of John the Wizard's black hearse speeding along Route 66, with Sonya, Svetla, and Wanda counting their loot in the back seat. The Reading

Police believed that they might have been the perpetrators responsible for that bound cadaver in the garbage dump but the Four were nowhere to be found, rumors had them fleeing to upstate New York or possibly Canada. Ongoing investigations were continuing, as yet no warrants had been issued; there was still no all points out calling for their arrest.

Along Marshall Street the big mouths were speculating that the Cosmo Five, now Four, had returned to the point where they threw the cash from the safe out of the hearse window, retrieved their package, and, once up in Reading, they killed Bauer in a dispute over the division of the spoils. Conspiracy theories abound on Marshall Street. This is stuff we will never know for sure but you'd find fruit peddlers swearing to you that this was exactly how it happened.

On Friday night Karl and I told Dad we were going to catch a double feature at Ruby, on Fairmount Avenue near Franklin, two films we had already seen, 'Forty Thousand Horsemen,' and 'Four Feathers,' just in case Doc asked us what the pictures were about, since what we really did was shoot down to Go d's bar on Noble Street. They still had not repaired that neon L. We hoped to find out if Gallagher had helped Knocky make it out of town, and where Alexi might have gone.

Entering Go d's it felt like two centuries since that night we crouched in here to see the French smoker film. Eli, Schatz, Joe the Worm, Sibronsky, Dick Jardine, not only were the usual suspects present, it seemed as if none had changed their seats. For a second I had a pang of panic, Gallagher was not in his usual booth, then we saw Gall coming out of the Men's. He pointed an accusing finger at us, shifted the finger, ordering us to join him in that booth he uses as an altar. Neither Hymie nor Saul Gold were scowling, They even waved in greeting. Karl and I received a hearty welcome hardly corresponding to punk kids like us: punches on the arm, amiable slaps on the back of the head and guys wisecracking, "So you made bail, eh?" Since when had we become so charter members of this outfit? Then, I got it: the pulpy connection, noire notoriety, these wharf rats were eager to talk to us due to our links; they were only second or third hand links, but we were connected to the Cosmo Four, those sensational photos of Wanda, Mrs. Ratchinov, Trixie Malloy.

Badass Chick Gallagher never takes off his dark glasses. We sank down in his booth. Gall cracked his knuckles before saying, "Long time no see, Little Doc."

"Logical, bossman, I aint been around for you to see me."

" I see you're still a smart-ass," Gall said. "That hasn't change."

"Sorry" I agreed, " I'm trying to tone that down."

"How about you, Wronsky?" Gall asked. "You've lost around sixty pounds off that pachydermus gut you used to pack. Big Doc don't feed you in his home?"

"Big Doc treats me like I were the Prince of Wales," Karl said. "If I had any complaints about Doc I'd have to be the ingrate of the century."

"Nah, there are too many competitors for that spot," Gall said.

Behind the bar, Saul Gold opened his palms, inquiring what would we be having?

Gall answered for us, making a V for Victory and calling to Saul, " Two Seven Ups for the Katzenjammer Kids," Then he turned to us and asked, "So what can I do for the Juvenile brigade? You want somebody bumped off? If you're in here to ask me for a loan my vig rates will be way too much for you."

" I just wanted to ask you a few questions, sir, "Karl said. "If I may?"

"'Sir' me again, Wronsky, I'll smack you upside the head," Gall said.

"Sorry, sir, I mean, Gall," Karl corrected himself. "It's just that last week, when all that ugly shit came out on the radio, Reading, and all, and Knocky took off, he said he might be coming by here to ask you for a helping hand. Did he come by? "

Gall stared at me, not Karl, or he seemed to be staring; it was hard to tell with his opaque dark glasses. He said, "Big Doc sent you to ask this, Paulie?"

"He doesn't know we're here," I said." And Karl never told him about Alexi coming to see you. Nor did he tell the cops. All of this is on the cue-tee, between us."

From what I could see, gall was reluctant to talk about this. Maybe he had promised Alexi to say nothing about his whereabouts.

Saul arrived with our Seven and Sevens. Placing them down he said, "Paulie, you can tell Big Doc our baby girl is doing just fine, Jennifer is fifteen months old now, she's beautiful, and my wife, Arlene, sends her regards. "

"Thanks, Saul. I 'll be sure and tell him."

Gold was smiling, wanted to continue our chat. Gall gave him a toss of the chin, suggesting to Saul he should move on for the moment. Gallagher could be a cold, bastardly prick when he chooses to be. I raised my glass to him in a toast, as did Karl. Both of us winced in surprise when we took the first sip. Saul, without our asking, had added a goodly splash of Seagram's to the Seven-Ups.

"This will be repeated to nobody, right? " Gall said." Not even Big Doc?"

Karl raised his right hand in oath. "Honest Injun, Gypsy curse. Nobody."

"You, Little Doc? " Gall insisted.

"Likewise, scout's honor," I swore, though I'd never been a scout.

"Okay. I told Knocky to go home to Big Doc. He said no way, he could not handle living in a fish bowl anymore, needed to get to a place where nobody knows who he is. If I did not help him, he was still moving on. In memory of old times, Dmitri, what the shit, I slipped Knocky enough for a bus ticket to California. He thanked me, said he would hitchhike anyway, use the money for grub. I didn't like his hitching idea, called friends in the Teamsters, was able to get him a lift on a coast-to coast long haul, slots; gambling equipment, drivers like a body along to keep them awake. The driver I talked to said he could most likely get the kid a job in Vegas, one of their hotels. I told Knocky to drop me a post card here at Gold's whenever he settles in. So far, there has been no card. That's it."

"Thanks, Gall," Karl said. "And thanks for mentioning Dmitri."

"I don't need any thanks. You two, slurp down your sodas, which I notice have been spiked, then move out of here without gabbing too much with these barflies. They talk too much, and say too little. My orders: You do not give Arlene's regards to Big Doc. You were never in here. This conversation never happened. If and when I receive a post card from Knocky I might give you a call."

While we walked home Karl said, "You know, in a curious way it was noble of Knocky to cut out like he did, just head for the hills. Not chicken at all."

"Noble? You've pulled that *noble* out of your ear, buddy. "

"Nope. It wasn't cowardly at all. Reminds me of 'Beau Geste.' Not quite the same but Beau disappeared to join the Foreign Legion to cover up the disgrace, the shame of his aunt selling off family heirlooms. Alexi took off because he could no longer stand the humiliation of everybody gawking at him, knowing about his family. He also knew all the grief it was causing Doc. Knocky coulda' hung on. I mean, we're living a pretty damn comfortable life in Big Doc's home, but Alexi did the gutsy thing, and now he's out there all alone in the big, wide world."

"That's a scary thought," I said. "Out there, all alone, in the big wide world."

No call came. Maybe a card was sent, maybe no, maybe Gall did not bother to call. Dad was blaming himself for Alexi's vanishing act. What more the man could have done, I don't know. He went far beyond the demands of common decency, any call of duty, but he blamed himself for listening to Knocky, letting him stay on in Philly, instead of shipping him off to a private school out of town.

Dad was slipping badly, becoming fussy, impatient, grouchy. He could not find a new nurse to please him. Two registered nurses had trial periods, both qualified; he let them go after two weeks. Now he had a third candidate, a Puerto Rican, Carmen. She seemed swell to me, quick on the uptake and with a sunny disposition, but Dad was not totally satisfied with Carmen, either.

Since I was an infant I had watched hundreds of old folks tottering into Doc's waiting room, and I preferred the ostrich approach, Monkey no see, Monkey no hear, but I could not ignore the symptoms. With Dad it was incipient, the Saint Vitus shakes, trembling hands, an unsteady gait, distraction, forgetfulness, and, the most chilling telltale sign, a shorter temper. He had always been stiff, cryptic, but never unreasonably surly. Even Karl arched his lashes at his incongruous display of anger. Over breakfast Miss Pearl mentioned to Dad that girls from her neighborhood, students at William Penn High, stopped her on the streets, and asked her whatever became of Lefty? The girls missed Lefty. Instead of finding that heart-warming or amusing, Dad snapped at her, and announced he wished to hear no more on the subject, not one more word.

Day by day he had gruff reactions totally out of character. I struggled to blot the terms out of my mind: Alzheimer's, and Parkinson's. At times days he was perfectly fine, cheerful, alert, his old self, then he would shock us with a testy comeback or unwarranted complaint. He was still a powerful ox but I wondered if he would make it much further, would Mrs. Barufkin get to enjoy the company of her Dapper Dan.

Karl remained mute while observing Doc's degenerative process. That's his style, and he was formulating his own solution. Wronsky was even more obsessed with the Korean War than I was: he had set up a wall map of Korea in our games room, was following the war battle by battle, skirmish by skirmish, with tiny flags on pins to trace the main units and their positions on the shifting front lines. American forces had crossed the partition line, Thirty-Eighth Parallel, and were triumphantly approaching the Yalu River. There was fear the Red Chinese might intervene, On Marshall Street people were saying that MacArthur hoped to provoke the Chinese, suck them into the war, then use the Atom bomb on them. Injured troops returning from Korea were criticizing MacArthur, saying the great general had so far never spent one night in the country; he was running the whole bloody show from the safety of his cushy headquarters in Japan, managing the stinking war from a safe distance, as if he were flipping the levers on a pinball machine.

It was torturing Wronsky that every night we heard the scores of basketball and football games, then the tallies from Korea, two Migs down, one of our phantoms, thirty-seven dead Marines, sixty casualties over by Chosen, nobody seemed to give a damn. Karl's birthday was coming up in a few months. Against my advice, he went to ask Dad if he would sign for him, give him permission to enlist in The Marines on his seventeenth birthday. Dad was furious, said that was impossible, first he had to finish high school. Once he was eighteen he would be of age and free to do whatever he damn pleased, enlist, but there was absolutely no way he would ever sign for him to go off to a rotten, meaningless war.

After receiving that chewing out from Dad Karl asked me to accompany him on a walk. Wronsky was feeling like a stepped-on dog. That was first time Big Doc had ever raised his voice or used harsh words on him. 'Free to do what he damn pleased' sounded much like a curse.

"I told you not to broach the subject to the man," I said. "You've seen that he's not been himself, lately."

"That's part of it, too," Karl agreed. "A piece of it, but not the whole thing."

"What's the whole thing?"

"The whole thing Paulie? It's what kind of country do we live in? I can't stand this normal, banal, silly-ass, life, everybody shopping, going to the movies, complaining about diddly-shit problems, while every day guys only a couple years older than us are dying by the Yalu River. What for? Nobody seems to give a shit. "

"I'm with you on that one. But, aside from wrapping yourself in the flag, you have other stuff bugging you, Wronsky."

"True. I hate being around to watch Big Doc's deterioration, and that makes me feel ashamed, like I'm a low life ingrate. You have to stick around, and it's my duty, too, but I've got other problems driving me batty."

"Bloomy?"

"You called the shot, Sherlock. She's having a hellish time of it at home, all my fault; I'm making her life unbearable. She wants to run away, and you know she aint ready to be out in the world yet. We keep breaking it off, swearing we'll never see each other again, two days later she comes out of Girl's High, I'm there, waiting for her. We break up, two days later, I come out of Roman, she's there, waiting for me. The only way I can escape this tangle is get out of town, up, in the Marines. She shrieked when I told her about that idea. I told her to calm down. I swore to her that if I managed to come back, and she was still waiting for me, that would be it, we would be together, forever. She shrieked again. "

Trying to do the 'Honorable Thing.' I lit up a smoke, wracked my brain to identify the source; 'this is a far far better thing?' Vronsky volunteers to die in a war in the Balkans? No: too far-fetched because those mature lovers had already enjoyed a whole lot of sinning. 'Come back with your shield, or on it?' No. But the promise to return brings to mind the old World War One song: 'I'll be with you, in Apple blossom Time. ' Still, where do we find the Honorable thing? Bingo!

"Beau Geste," I said.

"What? " Karl spluttered.

"Beau Geste. You laid that tag on Knocky; said he was noble for cutting out. You want to do a variation on the theme of the military solution, march off to war to escape problems on the home front."

"Give me a cigarette," Karl said.

Thanksgiving, Dad always gives Miss Pearl the day off so she can whip up the traditional feast for her own family in the Project. Substituting, Mrs. Barufkin came bustling into our house with all the fixings to cook for us a big, fat turkey. It sat on the table as a stand-in for the Blue Bird of Happiness. Maxine was an excellent cook, also sensitive enough to note that Karl and I were not as thankful or joyous as we were supposed to be. There was horrible news along the Manchurian border, hordes of Red Chinese troops pouring into Korea, their bugles and horns blowing, once again a bruised and battered American army was retreating.

As we sat down to the sumptuous meal Karl surprised us. He has no priestly vocation but I forget how deeply religious he is. Karl said, "I know this is not the custom in our house, but might somebody please say grace?"

"Grace, "I said, trying to be amusing, but we were mildly taken aback. It was certainly not the custom in our house. Dad said, "Why don't you say a prayer for us. Karl? I know you have grave troubles on your mind."

Karl clamped his hands together in prayer, and intoned," Dear Lord, bless this food and those that eat it. But please, Dear Lord, devote most of your attention and energy today to lending a helping hand in Korea, especially in the area by the Chosin Reservoir, where the temperature is now thirty-five degrees below zero. For months now hundreds of American soldiers have been dying daily, but with the bitter fighting and attacks all along the front many more than that will be gathered to your bosom tonight. Meanwhile, we thank you, Lord, for all of your blessings, amen."

The Friday night after Thanksgiving, I took the subway uptown, to attend a 'Gathering.' Howie Toll, the meekest member of our rat pack, had arranged this 'Gathering.' Howie no longer participates in our South Law ranking contests, nor our wrestling matches. Toll was making disturbing conformist noises about going straight, hanging up his jock as a rebel.

Once again I'm the downtown boy heading north with the hopes of preying on the uptown girls. Anita Green will see me no more; she claims I'm too fresh, too grasping, too demanding. Does she expect me to tiptoe through her tulips?

My rat pack had rounded up at Steinberg's house in East Oak Lane; they were waiting for me out on the lawn, gave me lip for arriving a bit late. Donny explained that car-wise he was grounded for an infraction of the family rules, meaning that we would be hoofing it tonight. While we drifted the five blocks toward the Gathering place Jack Kraft asked me," What's your half-brother doing tonight? Still suffering?"

"Karl? He'll manage to see his Bloomy tonight. She swore to her parents that she's going to the movies with her girl friends but will sneak out of the theatre to hook up with her Cossack. Central casting wouldn't buy into this match-up but she's doing the passionate, reckless Ana Karenina role to Wronsky's Vronsky."

"Ah, you're too fucking erudite and literary for me, Burris." Kraft said. "How about Ratcho? Still no word from the Franklin Flash?"

"Nope. I've told you guys. Not a peep out of him since he disappeared."

Seymour the Simian said, "My father really drooled at the photos of the women in Alexi's family. My mother had to snatch the newspapers away from him."

"Your old man probably used them to jerk off later," Kraft said

Steinberg chuckled. He has a winning style, rarely contributes, only chuckles.

We reached Logan, white houses with the white porches, the trees were bare but the night still had the aroma of damp autumn leaves. As to the sociology, most folks up here were ex-Proles from South Philly and Strawberry Mansion into upward mobility. Poppa gets a promotion from flunky to assistant floorwalker, takes out a mortgage, and joins the Middle Class. Once they make it up here they dream of moving further out, up, further north, to Cheltenham, to have wider lawns to mow.

No Negroes in Logan. To the east was Feltonville, mostly Kraut, before the war they were singing the 'Horst Wessel' song in the Weiner World Rifle Club but Logan was still more Kosher than Jerusalem. As we approached Elaine Sangers's house on West Tabor Road, Toll warned us, "Okay, you toilet-mouthed cruds, I want you to remember that these are all nice girls. They were leery when I told them who I was bringing along tonight. You guys, except for Donny, have hair-raising reps."

"Nice Girls? " Kraft said. "You hear that, Seymour? That means no loud belching, crouch in the corner when you scratch your balls, and please do not serenade the ladies with your cannonades of explosive farts."

"Ugh, Toll groaned. "That's the kind of talk you rats better hold down on. Elaine's father, Mister Sanger, works in the same building, same floor, as my Dad, downtown, so you bastards better keep your promises to control yourselves tonight."

Kraft raised his hand in oath, and said, "I solemnly swear by all I hold holy that I will not piss in the punch bowl, nor whip out my joint before eleven o' clock."

Shuddering, Toll said, "The girls were mostly worried about you, Kraft, and you, Paulie, saying you were both notorious wise guys. I had to swear to them that both you clowns were making a conscious effort to reform yourselves."

Kraft banged me with his elbow, and said, "I've never made any such vow. What gives? Are you some kind of traitor, Burris?"

With Toll leading the way we climbed the steps of the Sanger house. Five virginal temptresses awaited us on the screened porch. The sides would be even tonight, five against five. The maidens were sheathed in tight girdles while offering up seductive scents and suggestive necklines. Based on prior consultations they were all in pink battle gear, fluffy dresses, rustling crinolines, and, of course, those tight girdles. Toll introduced them as Elaine, Francine, Janie, Arlene, and Naomi. They were all pretty, none were sisters, but they seemed to have been clipped off the same cooky cutter. Breaking the mold was our hostess, Elaine Sanger, tipping the scales for a light heavyweight bout; Seymour the Simian was instantly taken with her, adhering to the smutty underground adage: the fat one fucks.

Elaine advised us that her parents were playing Canasta on the neighbor's front porch, directly across the street; we should hold down on flagrant hanky-panky as her ever watchful parents often made surprise Gotcha' inspections.

Pretzels nestled next to potato chips with a creamy cheese dip. The punch bowl had been spiked, I believe it was with Manischewitz; we were more in danger of diabetes than getting drunk. This was to be a sedately saccharine affair. For a while we danced to the 'getting to know you' music, the Tony Bennet, Eddie Fisher, and Al

Martino records. The Ink Spots oozed a syrupy 'Sentimental Me.' Billy Eckstein crooned:' Roses, I bring you roses, with all the love their sweet blossoming encloses.'

Misty romantic music for nibbling at sweet ears, one by one the lights were turned off, hands slipped below waistlines, the girls dutifully returned our paws to decorous levels. A Gathering is a sex orgy where nobody gets laid: a Jewish variation on the Puritan practice of clamping courting sweethearts into bundling boards where they can paw at each other but not reach the realms of milk and honey

The pairing off began. Elaine and Seymour were soon going at it hot and heavy on the sofa. Toll and Janie began batting it out on the side porch. Kraft and Arlene vanished into the pantry. Francine and Steinberg were sharing the loveseat. She slapped Donny's hand away from her rustling crinolines.

Hey, I thought Donny was supposed to be our polite and well-behaved rep.

By default I found myself with Naomi on the back porch. She was a cheerleader at Olney High, one of those vixens they sent over at half time to wag their tails at us and taunt us for attending an all boys' school. The other cheerleaders on her squad had Jane Russell figures, Naomi, the slender frame of a gamin but she was the plucky athlete they flipped into the air at football games, where she could show off her exquisitely sculpted shanks. Naomi began complaining about what two-faced, catty, backbiting witches the other girls on the squad were. I listen as if totally absorbed, and utterly intrigued, part of the price of admission, there is no escape, unto each thing there is it's damn season; my face was still burning from all the rubbing alcohol I had used to tone down my adolescent complexion tonight.

My instincts were to promptly pounce on Naomi but I finesse this, deploy my savoir-faire, finally I am rewarded, I win round one: Naomi grabbed my head, gave me a ferocious kiss, then announced, "So here I am with the infamous Paul Burris."

"Infamous? Sounds like a promotion. Last year I was only notorious."

"No, I've heard that you're very Continental: Roman hands and Russian fingers."

Instant clichés receive wide circulation. I had heard this corny line at gatherings in Wynnefield and Mount Airy. But I summoned up reserves of patience. The lady must first establish that she is a tough cooky, a spunky Rosalind Russell, an indomitable Bette Davis, certainly no easy pushover.

For my patience Naomi clutched my skull and awarded me another potent kiss. I'm a turkey, recalling yesterday's turkey, Karl saying grace. That was still bothering me. I'm messing around on a back porch while it is thirty-five degrees below zero near the Reservoir. Naomi is a freckled Leprechaun type cast by nature to be a sugar plum fairy. She wants to smooch, pet, squirm and wriggle while I lick her ear; she doesn't want me worrying about distant wars on her night out, and not paying total attention to her needs. I do believe these girls are hornier than we are but they still want bloody sheets on the wedding night.

Who put that record on? The background music became inappropriate, Vaughn Monroe groaning about 'Ghost Riders in the Sky.' Kraft did us all a favor by switching off the front porch lights. Naomi was chewing at my lips, nothing will ever be steamier than batting it out with a homegrown filly transformed into a frenzied succubae when the lights are turned down low, the voraciously chaste nympho on her daddy's nearly paid for sofa. Naomi was no longer slapping my hand away from where it, theoretically, should not be; her sly hand was resting, suspiciously, near strategic locations. I was thinking about Korea, the 65 trolley, no subway service after midnight, I was currently in no condition to make a run for it, not with Naomi swishing her tongue like a cobra in my ear, while digging her nails into my wrist. Troops were fighting for my inalienable right to infiltrate my hand into her blouse.

In the brashest move I had seen a girl make since Rita did that tango with me in the back alley, Naomi abruptly rose. Up went her skirts, down went her crinolines, she moaned like an old Aunt Betsy as she shimmied out of her girdle, flung the girdle aside, and kicked away the crinolines. For one second I had a glimpse of her famous perky fanny and celestial blue panties before she rejoined me on the sofa.

Matters were getting serious around here. Her hazel eyes were dull with desire; her nails were digging into the nape of my neck. I tentatively reached down to her nether regions, intending to remove silky obstacles. This was merely a probe; I was anticipating a slap. To my consternation she was collaborating, slithering in such fashion as to facilitate the process. With a cunning twist of the chin reaffirming the evil glint in her eyes she was ordering me to get with it. Who woulda' thought it,

McGee? I had misjudged this young lady. Under her prim, butter-milky façade she was a panting Hecate, quite disposed to go all the way.

Just as we meshed we heard yelps from the front porch, screen doors slamming, more yelps, lights being snapped on. Like a genii swirling into a mist, pouring back into her bottle, Naomi vanished from my side, scrambled across the floor. Up went the skirts, on rose the blue panties, she hoisted herself into her girdle, on went the rustling crinolines. Naomi must have been a quick-change artist: this was a feat; if they had competitions she might win the cup for record time.

It had been a tactical mistake to switch off those front porch lights.

"Zipper up," she snapped to me in a frantic rasp.

This was worse than the cops busting in to ask about Joe Spinelli.

Switching off those front porch lights was like sending out a distress signal.

The Sangers had returned from their Canasta with the neighbors. In the parlor they were making parental noises along the lines of, " I trust you kids weren't doing anything we wouldn't do."

The lights were hurting my eyes as Naomi and I entered the parlor. Nobody was bleeding but it was essentially, subliminally, a scene of devastation, as if an invisible titanium bomb had dropped and scattered the debris. Kraft and Arlene emerged from the pantry; Steinberg and Francine had risen from their loveseat. Toll and Janie looked like they had crawled out of a haystack. Elaine was adjusting her skirts, she was flushed, her eyes too bright, as if she had spent two months on absinthe. Seymour the Simian was standing sideways to obscure his embarrassing condition.

The Sangers were standing there, even smiling, clueless intruders in our dust.

"Well, I'll be heading upstairs to rest these weary bones," Mister Sanger said. "I've a big day tomorrow. Early round of golf at the Melrose Club."
Not the public links at the Cobb's Creek? Mister Sanger was originally from Third and Catherine, started out with a pushcart on Bainbridge Street. This was his way of bragging to us that he was now ritzy-titzy uptown.

Mrs. Sanger said, "You kids can, of course, continue with your partying, but hold down the volume on the record player, and do, please, keep the lights on."

Her voice was sweet as she imposed these totalitarian, restrictive guidelines.

We mumbled our good nights to the Sangers as they ascended their staircase. In Spanish they would be called Aguasfiestas, meaning-wet towels, party poopers. Elaine put on her Guy Lombardo long play for desultory dancing but the presence of parents on the premises dampens Dionysian spirits. A half hour later our Gathering dissolved with the ladies supplying us with their phone numbers. Naomi murmured hints to me that on a formal date we might resume the activities so inconveniently interrupted tonight. I suspected she was pulling my string.

Snow was falling as we trudged back toward Broad Street, the sweet, fleecy snow looking soothing on Christmas cards. No doubt the girls were now comparing notes, conducting their post mortem back on the porch. My buddies were into their post-game wrap-up: Steinberg playing it mum, Kraft bragging that he had almost reached home plate with Arlene, Toll assuring us that mousey Janie was wilder than she looked, Seymour the Simian making his usual exaggerated boasts about how far he get with Elaine. As even an authority such as Rita Demetrescu (still in the reformatory) classified me as a gentleman I did not furnish my team the graphic details of my back porch grappling with Naomi.

Ten minutes to twelve, Abruptly I was glum, live downtown, and you suffer from the Cinderella Syndrome; after midnight the Magic fades, the Magic craps, snackles, and plops on you, everything turns back into rats and pumpkins.

I announced," Hey, men, I must run for it. The last trolley leaves at midnight. That's like the last clipper leaving Lisbon."

"Don't sweat it, "Donny Steinberg said." If you don't make it you can spend the night on the sofa in basement rec room, Burris."

"Thanks, Donny-man, but I'll try to make it the sixty-five. Ciao, you buzzards."

"Go gettum', Kimosabe," Kraft called after me as I took off, jogging.

My uptown pals were okay guys; I was not exactly leading a split-level life, I was no social-climbing prole sucking up to the quality folk. Occasionally I've made false noises, portraying myself as a crass wisenheimer only because I am a product of cruddy slums but that was B.S. Sixth and Girard was still a bustling dynamic area, and my Dad was well to do, at least as solvent as all my friend's fathers; there were even envious Schnurers on Marshall Street accusing Dad of being a millionaire.

The Sixty-Five had already pulled out of the depot, minutes early, my jogging evolved into a mad dash to catch up, two other guys appeared out of nowhere to enter the chase. We caught up and hopped aboard. I glanced around, no Benoff, but lots of familiar faces, my fellow travelers. While I headed up the aisle to my usual bench in the rear the usual suspects were indulging in the usual conversation, how they had made out with the ladies of Logan and West Oak Lane.

No Benoff tonight. Leon was a petite encyclopedia, storehouse of information, Benoff could lecture you on the Australians at Gallipoli, the French Foreign Legion in Mexico, the International Brigades in Spain, the Underground Man, the Anarchists and Nihilists. With Leon pontificating boring trolley trips became fascinating symposiums, but tonight our only entertainment would be provided by the pack of rowdy slobs boarding as the Blue Balls Express paused at Wyoming Avenue. They were arguing about who downed more brews at the beer bust.

A light snow drifting down, I was sinking lower, the world dreary out there. I'd taken this trolley a thousand times, why did it now feel like a hearse or a casket? Do I have the right to this glumness? I was in the dumps but relatively okay. Knocky was out there, a lost waif in the wilderness. Karl was suffering like hell with his Bloomy. And, Pop? Even Mrs. Barufkin had arched her lashes at the way his hands shivered while he trimmed the turkey yesterday. No matter his prior reputation. You'd not want to go under the scalpel of that surgeon,

Three young couples boarding at Allegheny Avenue were acting stomach turning silly up front; they were making me sick with their with their snuffling away like Elmer Fudds and Mortimer Snerds. How were these giddy buffoons admitted into the same sapient species that produces a Bertrand Russell and a Leonardo?

A snobby question but heebie-jeebies doldrums were infiltrating me, as if a foul, diseased creature across the aisle had sneezed hard and his flus, germs, and poisons were seeping into my system. No storm warning, out of nowhere black mists were swirling in from all points of the compass, tentacles gathering to whip up a raging hurricane. Hey! This was more than a standard case of teen-age growing pains. I wanted to shake myself and shout out loud, "Hey, I've no reason to feel this sad, I haven't earned these Blues. I'm too callow for this virulent attack of Weltschmerz.

At Lehigh Avenue the moronic couples from Allegheny Avenue jumped off and were replaced by a batch of braying Cretins bragging about which of them was more pie-eyed. Is it presumptuous of me to think about Korea? I've never seen a war movie that satisfied me. I've seen pictures realistic about the action, horrors and agonies in the trenches, bayonets and tear gas, screams of the wounded, but there is a huge missing ingredient; one day I'd like to write, produce, direct a film to show the whole story, flashing back and forth from the brutal combat on the front lines to the mindless crap back home, a movie asking the question, should guys die to defend those loud jackasses up front, should men be blown apart so Paulie Burris can continue to play grab-ass at Gatherings in Logan?

Motion sickness was twisting my guts, fueling a sour depression. Should I blame Naomi? What is the Latin, hooey about post-coitus tristum ist? My Latin is nulo. But if we are programmed to automatic sadness after getting our rocks off, how empty are we allowed to feel, unappeased and frustrated on the Blue Balls Express? Black phantoms swarmed around me, everything familiar suddenly seemed putrid, hateful. I'd no right to feel so alienated, even misery should be earned, but this trolley seemed to be racing along in slow motion, the ride becoming interminable, travel where you don't belong, the waters will make you sick.

Though it was not a major avenue the 65 stopped at Diamond Street. Nowhere in sight were the stinky ladies in their blue uniforms bringing the rancid stench of the cigar factory aboard but I was trapped in my mental rut. Every time the 65 pauses at Diamond Street I hear Dad saying, 'Life is unfair, ' I smell those unfortunate ladies

Big discovery, what am I, what was Dad, Columbus?

Three minutes into the home stretch, the snow still falling out there. Heading up front, I nodded to my fellow travelers continuing on to South Philly; these cats wear stylish sharper clothes, have slicker haircuts. I do not foresee them making it to uptown, permanently, but who ever anointed me as a prophet?

As I hopped off the trolley at Girard Avenue I gulped the air, hoping to fight off lingering traces of the motion sickness. For a while there I was strangely on the verge of barfing, from a mental rather than a physical nausea.

Aside from light snow drifting down, something was off, the scene eerily reminiscent of the night Alexi took off, back in October. Traffic on the avenue was creeping slowly. A red car was parked by the Linoleum store at Marshall and Girard. Traffic down Sixth had also slowed to a crawl; another squad car with a flashing red beam on its roof was in front of my house.

Maybe they had found Knocky? Or they picked up the Cosmo Four? Rumors were circulating that they had made it to near Chicago, a striptease club in Geary.

I heard Miss Pearl's familiar nagging, how would you like it if Paulie came home, etcetera? Why that morbid leap? Why instantly assume a worst-case scenario? Most likely the cops were picking up Dad because they had a hood bleeding in the Station; needed Dad to patch him up quick before reporters and photographers arrive.

The red lights signify that you are being punished for all your sins, Paul Burris. That presupposes the existence of an Almighty taking a direct interest in my affairs.

I lit a cigarette, approached my home with my guts already knotting, In spite of the falling snow two cops were sitting on my front steps. The smaller one I did not recognize, the other was Mahann, practically a member of our family. Both rose, solemnly, as they saw me. I braced for bad news; from the way they stood up this could only be bad news.

Mahann felt the need to wobble his chin before saying, "Good evening, Paul. Getting back kind of late for a kid your age, aren't you?"

"Good evening, officer. Is something wrong?"

"Very wrong," Mahann said. "We'll be taking you over to your Aunt Sara's place on Marshall Street. We already took Karl Wronsky over there; the family is waiting for you. First, you head inside, Paul, pack a toilet kit, underwear, then we'll escort you over to your Uncle Moe's house."

"Is my father okay? " I blurted out.

"No, he aint okay," the other cop said." He's downtown."

Mahann motioned to his partner to cool it, and said, "I'm sorry, Paul; earlier, your father was taken into custody. Doctor Dan is being held for questioning."

"Oof! What the hell about?"

"I'm not sure, " Mahann said. "And, if I did know I'd not be at liberty to tell you."

In a scornful tone the other cop said," Your old man's up the creek, kid. Some broad helped do him in, got him good. You can read about it in tomorrow's papers. There was a big swarm of reporters anxious to get into headquarters."

Mahann signaled to his partner to knock it off. That was enough.

CHAPTER FIFTEEN

Saturday morning Uncle Moe borrowed the Plymouth belonging to Mister Klein, owner of the haberdashery shop across from the Deli; Moe insisted on taking Karl and me for a drive. After a mostly sleepless night of tossing and turning we were both too groggy to object. First we passed by our house on Sixth Street. The front door was crisscrossed with broad strips of yellow tape, a public Scarlet Letter, a mark of shame for all to see. Moe said never mind, we needed the fresh air, needed to get away from things. Moe had never done stuff like this before, borrow cars, leave the store on the busiest day of the week, cross the Delaware River Bridge to drive through the countryside on a Saturday. Morning. Meandering around back roads in New Jersey while we were worrying about Dad felt weird, surreal, evasive, with Moe was assuring us that everything would turn out all right. He was doing his best to protect us from the news flashes on the radio. Earlier, customers had flocked into the deli to ask nosey questions. Reporters with their mikes out were trying to pick up juicy tidbits about the well-regarded neighborhood doctor, and buttonholing businessmen on Girard Avenue and the gabby vendors in the Marshall Street stalls.

Moe sought to shelter us but when we returned home, the deli was closed, and three newspapers were on the coffee table, upstairs The main headline on the Evening Bulletin dealt with the Red Chinese pouring across the North Korean border; the smaller headline to the left, dealing with local news was:

PROMINENT PHYSICIAN HELD FOR QUESTIONING

There was a gauzy photo of Pop in his prime, looking presidential, ten years younger, addressing a medical convention in Washington, D.C.

Coming in from the Kitchen, wiping her hands on a dishtowel, Aunt Sara moaned, "I should have put those away. Please, don't read that trash, Paulie."

Everybody was trying; I picked up the Bulletin and began to read:

"Tipped off by an anonymous female caller that Doctor Daniel Burris was a long-term provider of illicit medical services to Mobsters, the Police lured Burris to a staked out basement on Tasker Street and were able to film him attending to the wounds of the notorious Mafiosi, Vic, 'Three Fingers' Bastiano. In return for grants of partial immunity from charges of loan sharking, extortion, and labor racketeering, Bastiano had agreed to become a witting informant. Special unit police were positioned to film the ostensibly reputable obstetrician receiving a five-hundred dollar cash payment after patching up superficial wounds on Bastiano's shoulder and right arm while planted microphones recorded jocular remarks about previously well-remunerated services Burris had performed for top South Philadelphia Capos, and lower level thugs. Among the names bandied about on the tapes were those of Bernie 'the Bat' Bartolo, Gaetano, 'Tootsie' Tomasino, and major figures such as Sam Sacco, and Salvatore 'Big Sal' Bonafaccio.

Rumors had it that Doctor Burris, highly respected in his center city community had fallen into the thralls of the South Philly mob due to his pressing gambling debts and a high-flying lifestyle featuring the company of many glamorous women. Burris will be arraigned Monday morning at ten AM in Superior Court, the hearing to be presided over by the Honorable Judge Stanley C. Greenberg

Don't they have any other Judge working that court?

I handed the paper over to Karl, watched his face age as he read the article.

"I told you not to read that slop," Aunt Sara said. Then she wanted us to eat supper, had prepared her special brisket of beef with roast potatoes, for desert, her pineapple upside down cake with the walnuts and the whipped cream. I had zero appetite, Karl less than that, but Sara insisted that we sit down with Moe, eat. No matter how bad things are you must keep your strength up, boys.

Food had never seemed revolting to me before. The fact that it was delicious made it obscene. After we rose from the table Karl requested permission to go to Saint Pete's, to light a candle and pray for Doc to come through this safely and well.

Sara said, "You'd better stay in here, Karlie dear. We already had people from the Child Welfare Agency come by this afternoon, talking about taking you back under their wing. I persuaded them to hold off for a while, told them you'd be all right with us. They were reluctant but said they'd be checking back."

"So fast the vultures swoop down? " Karl said." In adventure movies they always circle around for a while before descending to gnaw on the remains."

"Hey," Moe complained, "Think of it this way: they are just doing their job for the City. They are authorities concerned with your health and welfare, Karlie."

"Too fast," Karl said. "Doc has been arrested but has not been found guilty of anything yet so why are they jumping the gun? Something else is going on here. I suspect they might want to use me as another pressure point on Doc."

Neither Moe nor Sara seemed quite to understand what Wronsky was saying.

From the second I hit the sack In the third floor bedroom I knew it would be another sleepless nigh. Karl was talking in the darkness about not letting himself fall once more into the clutches of the clergy or social workers. I was wondering which of the ladies in Dad's life might have been the anonymous caller: a parade of slinky candidates slunk by; Mrs. Jordan? Fired. Sonya Ratchinov? Doc took away her boy. Svetla might have called from long distance? Mrs. Minnie Gottbaum? He rejected her. Mrs. Carla Fiore Dumped. One of his Beryls or Rifkas from the Broadwood dances; many ladies thought he had done them wrong. Dan Burris had slews of irate females pissed off at him for fifty-seven varieties of reasons.

"What's bothering me is the tapes, "Karl said." The newspapers claiming that Doc talked blithely about gangsters he has stitched up. That doesn't sound like Doc."

"He hasn't been himself lately," I said, defensively, though since that morning when I asked Dad about firing Mrs. Jordan and he answered with that mumbo-jumbo about 'in time,' I had begun to question his judgment.

"True, "Karl agreed. " There's still something that doesn't jive here. Doc is off his game or he'd have never let Bastiano joke with him about mobsters he had previously patched up. That should have been the prime tip-off that treacherous shit was going down. The man has an encyclopedic knowledge about many things, from what we've read, Bastiano joking about that crap should have rung bells for him."

To defend Doc, I said, " The problem is, my father is an intellectual, read serious stuff, Mann and Zweig. He never read detective novels, police procedurals, the noire stuff, or saw cheapy grade B crime movies. Remember my theory about the paper texture of a life, the pulpy and the slick? Big Doc never caught on that regular life is mostly crude slop at the Confidential Magazine level."

"Who you trying to snow with that bullshit?" Karl asked. "Me? Big Doc knows more about the docks, and bang-bang, and back alleys, and what's going down than any man in this city. Face it. Something else is the problem, Paulie."

Sunday morning I discovered that I have more flaws, gaps sins, defects, and shortcomings than I had suspected. According to the rules, we are supposed to love our relatives. As they bickered away in the parlor over the deli, I concluded that, with the exception of Moe and Sara, I was not too enamored of loved ones. My other aunts and uncles were spouting off about the disgrace, the articles in the papers represented a humiliation, a black eye for the entire family. They were giving themselves too much credit. My uncles did not know Jack from bupkas but were mouthing off about the Underworld, illegal arrests, entrapment, sting operations, set-ups, frame-ups, and agreeing that the charges could be a politically motivated gambit by the publicity hound District Attorney seeking headlines for his re-election. Aunt Ros said that this was a prime example of blatant Anti-Semitism. Uncle Burt boasted that he had often warned Dan that he was playing with fire. Uncle Phil and Uncle Max were in a shouting match. Phil had suggested that they call Daniel's brother, Jonathan Burris, semi-retired but still a heavyweight in the legal arena. Sara shrieked that Dan would murder them if they dared to call Jonathan; the brothers detested each other.

On the sofa across from me, Karl was reading the papers, trying to stay calm, stay out of this. Sunday editions had fresh garbage about the arrest of the prominent physician; the Daily Noose with an old photo of Dad back when he was a high school basketball star. The gist of today's article in the Bulletin had Dad walking into a well-executed set-up on a soundstage where Three Fingers Bastiano sang like the lead soprano in the South Philadelphia Boys Choir. The phone rang. Moe grabbed it, and signaled everybody in the packed parlor to please hold down on the noise. His plea availed him little, the family insisted on jabbering away while Moe squinted at whatever he was hearing on the phone. Karl tried to keep a neutral expression but his eyes finally rolled as he endured the downside on being adopted by a noisy, bumptious clan.

Moe hung up, and announced, "That was Darmopray, Dan's lawyer for financial matters and real estate. He said that none other than Milt Soll, the sharpest criminal lawyer in town, agreed to take on Dan's case. Soll is downtown with Dan right now. They will be claiming that the cops were over-reaching, that Dan was planning to report Bastiano's wounds to the appropriate authorities, but the police charged in, never gave him a chance, they were too eager to hit Daniel with hokey charges because of inside shit Daniel knows about sleazy police antics."

After a five second pause to absorb the fresh information the clan erupted in arguments again, Uncle Burt repeating that he had often warned Dan that he was skating over thin ice, Uncle Max shouting at Burt to not be such a smug 'I –told-you-soer.' Aunt Rosalyn whimpered something about "Leonora must be turning in her grace." Aunt Ethel waved a finger for Ros to knock that off.

Who the hell were these people? True, I'd been to their homes, eaten their food a hundred times, the pinched my cheek a hundred times when I was a tyke, but they meant little to me. Now they had invaded my life and taken over center stage. My old man was in the calaboose, locked up with the scum of the earth while these clueless old fogies were babbling nonsense about matters they did not grasp at all. Karl winced as my Uncle Phil said, "If Dan really patched up all those big shots in the mob that means the Italians, in gratitude, will pull strings to get him off." Aunt Fanny was asking Ethel who the anonymous female caller might be? Sara whispered to her," Such things should not be discussed in front of the children."

Wronsky raised his hand, and asked, "Do you think it would be possible for Paul and me to go downtown and visit Dad?"

They gaped at us, Karl's question triggered a hubbub of negativity, everybody jabbering back at us that it was impossible, the authorities will never permit it, Dan would die of same rather than let us see him behind bars. Relax children, Milt Soll; the sharpest criminal mouthpiece in town is handling his case. Our Dad will be out by tomorrow; everything will be all right.

Oohs and ahhs greeted Paco and Pepe as they arrived with heaping trays from the deli downstairs: lox, white fish, cream cheese with chives, rye bread, Danish pastries, Russian Coffee cake. My family hunkered down to enjoy an enormous brunch. With all this scarfing of the goodies this catastrophe became a social occasion where they, without bothering to request our ideas or input, determined how they would handle 'the children' for the next few days: Ros and Phil would take care of us for the afternoon, then hand us over to Burt and Aunt Fanny for dinner tonight. Tomorrow morning Sara and Moe would decide whether we should go to school or not. It might be best if we laid low for a while.

An hour later we were driving through Fairmount Park. Karl lit up a Lucky, Aunt Ros stirred, preparing to object, Uncle Phil motioned to her to let it slide, he was sucking on a Corona cigar himself. We were in the rear seat of their station wagon, a vintage Ford with a wood chassis; our destination was the antiques fair in Lancaster County. The adults decided that it would be best for us forlorn children to escape the corrupting influences and foul fumes of the evil city.

Phil had the car radio badly tuned to Kate Smith. Through the static I heard more appropriate jukebox music, Rhythm and Blues matching my depressed tone:

'Your momma's in the graveyard, your poppa's in jail.

Your sister's up the corner, shouting 'pussy for sale,'

Singing hey bobba-rebop.'

I had no sister but otherwise that ditty summed up our situation. Dad was in the clink, a clean and meticulous man locked up with lice-ridden scum. I'd read that in India they grade the prisoners, by social status. Even if they are felons they don't lock the upper caste Brahmins up with the lowly pariahs. Screw Democracy. Even in Heaven there is hierarchy. Not all Angels are equal.

Over his shoulder, Phil asked. "So you've heard nothing from your buddy still?"

"Nope. Knocky, him done gone, as the saying goes," I said.

"I don't know," Aunt Ros sighed." I don't know. I was dead set against Daniel ever bringing that boy into his home in the first place, then it turned out more horrible than my worst expectations: his mother, his aunt, sex shows, robberies on the Main Line. And now, maybe they were murderers. I simply don't know."

Since you don't know why don't you shut up was what I could not say to the lady. Besides, half of it was cheesy B.S., like the jazzy hype about Pop's life style in the company of glamorous women, making him sound like a swinging Porfirio Rubirosa squiring around Lana Turner, not Yetta Goldberg from the Broadwood dances.

"Ah, all of that is water under the bridge," Phil wheezed. "Water under the bridge. What we must think about now is what's next. And, while we are on this subject, let us speak of something else. Either of you guys have any idea of who the female caller might be?"

"You shouldn't ask them such questions," Ros snapped. "They're only kids."

"Hey, kids know a lot these days," Phil assured his wife. "You'd be surprised."

Without them seeing it Karl surreptitiously counted on his fingers, like Alexi did when he was totting up his conquests under the Boardwalk. Karl glanced at me and I nodded in agreement, a line could form for that position.

"I was talking to Miss Pearl, she dropped by the deli," Aunt Ros said, " Miss Pearl believes it was one of her own kind that secretly squealed on Dan to the police."

"How's that? " Karl asked, wincing in disbelief.

"According to Miss Pearl," Aunt Ros said," the pastor's wife from the Buttonwood Street church was peeved about Daniel seeing poor colored patients for free, taking business away from Negro doctors, she threatened to fix Dan good."

"Jeez, in this fucking world, you can't win for fucking trying," Phil said.

"Don't talk like that in front of the children," Aunt Ros chided her husband.

Karl glanced at me, nominating me to answer for the family. I said, " I don't believe the pastor's wife would be the likely source of that phone call. Miss Pearl has a tendency to see matters through her own intramural, parochial binoculars."

"Hey," Phil exclaimed," you're getting real edjumicated at Central, Paulie, learning to talk high-fallutin. I went to Gratz, myself, and did not shine there."

We were passing tobacco fields. We don't think of tobacco in the same stale breath with Pennsylvania but these fields produce a fine harsh leaf for cigars and corncob pipes. Mental associations are terrible; tobacco made me think of Carmen, the new nurse, crying on the phone, asking what's to become of her. She thought she had a job locked in, now everything was up in the air.

Dad, Dad, Dad, you were leading the charge, carrying the banner of decency, had so many people depending on you, and you dropped the ball, Dad.

As if reading my mind, picking up my vibes, Phil began talking about the Eagles, the season, Steve Van Buren carrying the ball, Chuck Bednarik at Center, only hard man left still playing both offense and defense. Phil talked sports to distract us because he saw how glum we were. Sports are a great escape hatch when you don't care to confront the fact that you're dangling over a precipice. Screw my woes and troubles, let us yack away about the hot stove league.

Aunt Ros interrupted her husband to point out the Amish family trotting along on their horse and wagon. She said, " Aren't they picturesque?"

Karl scrunched his lips. He did not find them to be particularly picturesque. After he moved in with us Wronsky had broken his bad habit of mumbling to himself but today his lips had moved as if he were deciphering ancient Aramaic texts.

Phil turned to Karl and asked," How come you never say anything, kid? I mean, every once in a while you raise your hand to ask if you can go pee, otherwise, we don't get much out of you."

"Because he's a deep thinker, trying to win a popularity contest," I suggested.

"No," Karl said," I was pondering, concentrating on a smelly mystery."

"Don't get a hernia, Kid. Lighten up," Phil said.

Karl thrashed in his seat as if he were a tadpole touched by an electric spark, and he groaned," That's it. I've finally got it."

"What's your big discovery?" Phil asked.

"What's so off-key. Too much information," Karl said." Way, way too much information, so much it stinks from high heaven to the gates of hell."

"I don't getcha, kid. " Phil said." You've lost me."

"The cops have talked too much," Karl explained. "Why would they leak to the press they have recordings of Vic Bastiano and Big Doc joking about wounded bambinos Dad has sewed up, and also throw in names like Sam Sacco and Big Sal? That's the kind of conclusive, vital evidence held in reserve, the crushing material to be sprung at a trial, not broadcast right off the bat to Mister and Mrs. America, and all the ships at sea."

Phil mulled that over for a moment, then asked Karl, " What, you some kind of Perry Mason or Ellery Queen, big expert on this crap?"

"Whatever I might be the police are bastards," Karl said, " and, they've already screwed Doc, made it impossible for him to return to a normal life. If he makes bail the streets will be more dangerous for him than a jail cell. They leaked this to force him to talk, give testimony, rat on the Mob. Dad can't ever go back to his regular routine after this. Either way, the cops have him by the… short hairs."

Karl censored himself out of respect for the old folks.

Aunt Ros scowled at his language anyway, she was intending to reprimand Karl, Phil cut her off by saying, "You might have something there, Kid. I hadn't thought of that. In any event, Daniel will have a real legal eagle like Milt Soll representing him. From what I've seen and heard it hardly matters what you did or didn't do, the only real crime in this country is to have a klutzy incompetent mouthpiece."

"How this will end, I just don't know," Aunt Ros sighed." I just don't know."

"Congratulations," I said to Karl. "I was feeling fairly rotten, you've managed to make me feel shittier."

Phil and Ros gave us permission to wander off, not stick around for the antiques auction. Inside the duded-up barn there were knotty spindles, kerosene lamps, brica-brac, faux Tiffany lamps, foot looms, and truly awful paintings of horses. How collectors could bid for this junk was beyond me but to each his obscure own. Karl and I tramped down a backcountry road. Mocking our sadness, a glorious autumn afternoon was unnaturally warm for late November, time filched from the Indian summer we did not have this year. To shuck off my gloom I began singing " What a difference a day makes, twenty-four little hours." Then I said to Karl, "How weird, on Wednesday my main concerns in life were not getting expelled from Central, and finally finishing a composition for Ming about the second half of the Twentieth Century. Now I have to blot away images of Dad in a striped uniform, a ball and chain around his ankles, he's swinging a rusty pick, slaving away in a chain gang. "

"That won't happen," Karl said. "That was Paul Muni in the chain gang. Our great State of Pennsylvania has no chain gangs; they are for the hayseed, hillbilly rednecks and noble Negros wit basso voices. You're back to Wednesday? I'm thinking what a lousy Thanksgiving weekend this has been, feeling guilty for saying that grace on Thursday. I asked for the blessings of the Lord upon our house and in response he hits us with the afflictions of Job and the plagues of Egypt."

"Do you think HE really pays that much attention to us, Wronsky?"

Karl did not answer that question. He peered up at the flock of crows cruising by, and, for whatever reason, murmured" Judith."

"As in your Bloomy?" I said. "

"No, as in myth and scriptures. As in Judith cutting off the head of Holofernes."

"As in anonymous callers?" I said.

"Yes. As in Jezebel and Delilah clipping hair, and Lilith in the shadowy garden. "

"We could go all the way back to Miss Eve handing the apple to Mister Adam."

Karl shrugged and said, " Doc munched on many apples. Munch on enough on them, and you'll to hit the jackpot, a really vile worm coming down your throat. "

We were passing a scraggly spread that had to be the disgrace of the county, a trashy rural slum amidst all these manicured gems, transplanted from God's Little Acre two miles south of Tobacco Road, Out on the shorn cornfield a raggedy-ass scarecrow drooped; the battered barn had fading hex signs on the roof, ominous sixes and malignant nines in the murky depths.

Karl stared at the run-down farm for a while, said, "You don't believe in the Bible, Paulie. Do you believe in hex signs?"

"I don't know what I believe in. Friday night, before I ever hopped off the trolley, I was spooked for no reason at all. Before I was aware of any of this crap awaiting us I was hit by omens, portents, whatever the fuck they are called. Sadness sloshed through me. Evil spirits, goblins, demons were forewarning me that bad shit was coming down my pike. I thought I was just a horny kid brooding on the Blue Balls Express. I have no explanation for that weirdness."

Dad's downfall was generating a social whirl for us kiddies. As per the arrangements Ros and Phil turned us over to Burt and Aunt Fanny that evening. They took us to dinner at Schoyer's, still on Arch Street. Thank God they did not drag any of my cousins along to cheer us up. Schoyer's was half empty, not offering a notably jolly ambience. Sundays, even in your posher restaurants, no spirits are served, Philly's Blue Laws. Burt circumvents these obstacles by packing along his pocket flask and lacing his tall glasses of Seltzer with double shots of Kummel. He offered us kiddies a quick slug, Aunt Fanny nixxed that, then recommended the excellent meatloaf.

"Everything will turn out alright" Aunt Fanny assured us." You'll see."

What did that mean? Tomorrow morning Dad will be sprung and greeted on Girard Avenue by string bands and minstrel singers from the Mummer's Parades. A banner over Marshall and Poplar will proclaim: WELCOME BACK, DAN.

Uncle Burt began reminiscing about the good old days when Dan drove over to Strawberry mansion, rolled up his sleeves, and sat down to play gin rummy with the boys. Dan was such a regular guy, so modest, but after Dan left the other Berman sisters berated their husbands as Schlumps, asking how come Leonora managed to latch onto a successful professional who drives her around town in a black Buick while they were stuck with Zhlubs who could barely afford a Schwinn bicycle.

Fanny said," Dan was modest, but Leonora was always our princess. Not once did Leo offer to help Mom with the Sunday cooking. Ros, Ethel, Sara, Me, we all pitched in while her majesty, Leo, sat out in the parlor, reading her fashion magazines, and then, at the last minute, acting surprised that there was still anything left to be done, she would pop into the kitchen and ask, 'Oh, can I lend a hand here?'"

Do not criticize my sainted mother, you wrinkled bitter witch. Why the hell were we here, anyway? All this gorging was making me nauseous. I'm on teeter hooks, waiting for the surgeon to emerge from the operating room to give us the word, does the patient survive; these two are busily munching on their breadsticks.

Karl glanced at the empty chair at our table, then looked at booth where we had dined with Mrs. Gottbaum. No need to say anything. Knocky was gone, loads of regrets, roads not taken, woulda-coulda might-have-beens came to mind. If Dad had accepted Mrs. Minnie's proposal of marriage everything would be different now.

Uncle Burt swerved off his good old days tack to talk basketball, how great Joe Fulks was with the Warriors, and the college point shaving scandals in New York. Sports fill in for when you have nothing to say. Then Burt and Fanny began arguing because he was bringing out his pocket flask again, sneak off little nips. Burt is what the Jews call a Schicker, an uncontrollable tippler. Jews despise a drunk more than they do a thief because you more or less know what the crook will do, he will steal, but you never can tell what a drunk will do.

No wine tonight, neither the chardonnay Blanc nor the Bordeaux. We drank Seven-ups sans the Seagram's. The meatloaf was actually not that bad but hardly in the same league as the Porterhouse all around that Mrs. Gottbaum had ordered for us. We could have been on her yacht in Miami tonight, Dad retired, and fishing, reeling in a big Marlin. Sun and Sand down there, it was already freezing outside on Arch Street, the people strolling by had Jack Frost vapors coming from their mouths

Picking at the meatloaf I reached the conclusion that *Life* is a poorly edited, shoddily plotted, disorganized novel. In proper novels we stick to the narrative, cut away extraneous crap, irrelevant figures do not pop in out of nowhere at dramatic junctures, but I was condemned to *Life*, spiked here in this banal scene with Uncle Burt and Aunt Fanny, tangential extras, inauspicious characters having nothing to do with nothing, but they insist upon existing, and cluttering up my purview.

Burt wanted to order desserts all around. Fanny said that since we were going to spend the night over the deli Aunt Sara would surely serve us her apple strudel or cheesecake for a midnight snack, so we limited ourselves to the complementary mints. Burt flinched at the bill when it arrived. Not too classy of him. I am spoiled and a snob; I'd never seen Dad publicly wince at a bill in his life.

Burt paid in cash; Fanny filched two dollars back from the tip he was leaving. Once outside, Burt was fuzzy, they argued over who should drive the car. Aunt Fanny won this argument by giving him the okay to take one last swig and he finished off the contents of his flask, then she drove. We chugged up a dark, deserted Fifth Street. Karl again thanked them for the gracious invitation, Fanny once again assured us that everything would turn out all right.

Sunday nights in Philly were, historically, the night for fishcakes, and leftovers, tuna casseroles, macaroni and cheese, traditionally, a night for suicides. 'So, Tata, why is this dreary Sunday night different than all other draggy, soul-killing and mind-numbing Sunday nights?'

'Your father is in the clink, you schmuck. That might be a factor.'

'Yes, excuse me for asking. That might cloud the picture. Couldn't we just go back to dull and draggy? '

'A tough and demanding customer, you certainly are, kid. You want boring again? Suddenly, your life has become too interesting? '

"You'll see, boys," Fanny announced. "It's not the end. Everything will be fine."

Flash: this just in from A.P., U.P., Reuters, and I.N.S. Everything will be Fine. The prominent Walnut Street law firm of Silverstein, Diamond, Goldberg, Pearlman, and Cash has handily won a million dollar summary judgment against abusive police tactics. Tomorrow the Mayor, District Attorney, and Chief of Police will apologize to Doctor Daniel Burris, and publicly kiss his ass in a star studded ceremony at Independence Hall. The beloved physician will have a gala float with hula-hula dancers in the New Years Day parade, and, accompanied by the Mormon Tabernacle Choir, Josephine baker and Sammy Davis Jr. will sig a duet of 'My Yiddishe Momma.'

On extremely dreary Sunday nights the only thing that keeps us trucking is imagination. Aunt Fanny pulled up at the corner of Marshall and Poplar across from the fish market. Burt saw that the lights were burning in Moe's second floor front, and said, "Okay, boys, they're up and waiting for you. You can hop out here, but no messing around, you head straight to the deli and straight upstairs to Moe and Sara."

"No sweat, Unc, " I assured him while thinking that once they are out of sight Karl and I can zip over to Sixth, check out our home; and, I knew Karl was dying to pass by the Sweet Shoppe, see if by chance his Bloomy came into view.

We are not graceful in my family. It was a clumsy moment. Fanny gave me a too fervent kiss on the cheek. As an afterthought she gave Wronsky an awkward kiss. Burt shook our hands and as we climbed out of the Plymouth we again expressed our gratitude. They were doing their level best, I am basically a carping ingrate, feeling like a soldier who just survived a mission with a squad of inept slew foots.

Instantly our teeth were chattering. Since our stroll through the warm Indian summer the temperature had plummeted, a malignant technician flipped a switch out on the tundra, sent these chill blasts of winter as a warning, another cruel omen.

"Woof," Karl said, possibly to express his relief that Fanny and Burt had pulled away, or maybe as a protest at the frigid winds snapping at us. To the 'Woof' he added," Man, what a miserable fucking day."

"I won't argue with you on that score," I said.

Too cold, by mutual consent we did not check out our house on Sixth, headed up Marshall toward the deli. Sunday night, the taproom, fish and chicken markets were closed, the stores shut, most with their metal curtains rolled down, the stands and pushcarts were locked up tight. Lights were burning in the second or third story windows, Momma and Poppa watching television over their Mom and Pop stores. Few pedestrians out, Marshall Street was a vibrant Bazaar designed for bustling crowds, haggling, raucous arguments, noise. Shadowy dark and empty like this, it was tinted with sadness, depressing as a deserted Coney Island.

A stirring by Klein's Haberdashery, movements in the darkened doorway, for a second I thought it might be muggers lurking in there. Then I saw Judy stepping out of the shadows, running in our direction. Even at this distance I could see that she was trembling, with goose pimples puckering her arms. Arctic weather out here, and the nutty girl was charging at us wearing only skimpy denims jeans and a pink polo.

Judy collapsed into Karl's arms for a kiss, then grabbed me, kissed me hard on the cheek, and moaned," Paulie, it's so fucking disgusting horrible. This all must be a terrible mistake. I'm so sorry for what you're going through."

Sweet and kind of Bloomy to be so emotional; I was trying to maintain my equilibrium, no blubbering, whimpering, no complaining, trying to emulate Dad. When everybody else thrashes in a tizzy he turns on the phlegmatism

Karl took off his jacket, wrapped it around her shivering shoulders. Bloomy was distraught, over-excited. Through her chattering teeth and trembling she rasped, "Doc was all they were talking about in the store today. Most customers were saying it's a big crock of shit, they want to draw up a petition, have all the neighbors sign off on what a wonderful man Doctor Dan is, a credit to the community, but a few sickening sonsabitches had the nerve to down your father, Paulie. They said he was stuck-up and had his come-uppance coming to him. I told them to fuck off and my father ordered me to leave the store, calm down, relax, to go watch TV. "

"Yeah," Karl said," telling valued customers to fuck off might alienate them." Then he scolded her, saying, "What the hell you doing out here with no jacket on, girl, when it's so damn cold? You want a double pneumonia?"

"I'm not feeling anything except furious and nauseated, "Judy said. "To top everything, just when you guys need all the love, and support, and help you can get, my parents said that Doc's arrest was the last straw. They forbade me from ever seeing either of you guys again. They said if I ever saw Karl again they'd ship me out of town, to that private school. I told them to fuck off."

"Easy, easy, girl, " I said." You don't have to be a better patriot for me than I am for myself. Your folks are trying to do their best for you."

A freezing gust slashed at us. Judy's chattering teeth sounded like skeletons screwing on a tin roof, before she gave me another hard hug, and said, "I'm with you, Paulie. This is so lousy. Anything I can do for you, or Big Doc, you let me know. "

"Thanks, babe. I appreciate that."

"Can I talk to Corky alone now for a few minutes? Our personal stuff?" Judy said.

I gave Bloomy a brotherly smooch on the cheek, moved along to let them have their privacy. Karl pincered a bull's eye at me, indicating that he'd catch up with me, soon as he dealt with the personal stuff. He put his arm around Bloomy's waist, guiding her back toward the Sweet Shoppe. Adults can scoff, dismiss them as two crazy, mixed-up kids, but I'd never had seen two lovebirds so nuts about each other.

I paused by the deli and lit up a smoke. That was touching of Judy to offer her help, anything she could do. When a girl is for you they become more passionately involved than a guy but in practical terms what would that translate to? Could she throw a monkey wrench into the majestic machinery of the law? Seduce the jury foreman; get a hung jury, a mistrial declared? Ach, I'm a swine for stooping to such putrid thoughts but taking in the desolation of shutdown Marshall Street it was hard to hear detect any silver lining. I was almost angry at Wronsky for being so damn smart, opening his trap today about the cops hamstringing Dad with their leaks, mentioning Big Sal and Sam Sacco; the thought had occurred to me but I am superstitious, I never say forbidden words out loud, never unseal sealed tombs.

Me, freezing my gonads off, Karl spent another ten minutes saying good night to Bloomy. When we went upstairs Moe asked if we had had a nice day. Sara insisted on serving big slabs of cherry cheesecake because she knew that cheapskates like Burt and Fanny would skip ordering any dessert. Moe told us that Darmopray had called earlier with a message from Dad. Darmopray had been in to see Dad, along with Milt Soll, and Dad said that we were not to worry, he should be out by Tuesday at the latest, and everything would be all right.

I recalled corny jokes about the Captain trying to calm the passengers on the Titanic, telling them there was no need to panic at a little bump.

"So," Moe said, " I have to consult with you guys. Give it to me straight. Sara and I were arguing before you boys came in. I think, tomorrow, you boys should just hang around here, maybe I could take a day off, and we go downtown to a double feature. Sara thinks otherwise: that you should make an effort to lead your normal lives, go to school as if absolutely nothing's wrong. I'm figuring that could get pretty hairy."

Karl glanced at me before answering, "I'd prefer to hang around here until we have the word on Dad but I've no problem with going to school. Except for a couple of priests and my Confessor nobody at Roman links me to Doctor Dan."

Links? Wronsky was already using station house blotter lingo.

"How about you, Paulie? " Sara asked. "I know it could be awfully embarrassing for you but if you didn't show up your classmates could get the idea that you are ashamed to show your face, and the charges against your father could be true. But if you attend school, acting like it's a regular, normal day, that would show everybody you fully support your father and there's nothing to the accusations."

"I don't think we should put the boy through this, "Moe said. "You know how cruel high school kids can be, capable of saying any kind of nasty shit to hurt Paulie."

"How about letting him decide this himself?" Sara snapped." Paulie is almost a man now, and can make manly decisions."

Well, since you put it that way, what would Gary Cooper say? 'I must go back for him, Clem. The scumbag may be a swine but the script says I must go back for him.'

"School, tomorrow," I said, "but you must promise to call me the minute you hear anything about Dad. I believe the hearing is at ten AM."

"Wonderful. Would you care for another slice of cheesecake? " Sara asked us.

Karl smacked his gut and said, " No, thanks, I've had my fill."

Upstairs, after two consecutive nights without enough sleep we should have simply passed out but we continued bullshitting till well after midnight. I had the hard cot, Karl was on the lumpy sofa, we said goodnight, minutes later we were yacking away again. In the darkness Wronsky repressed what sounded like a gulp, or it could have been a sob. I asked, "Now, what the hell's the matter, Wronsky?"

"Bloomy."

"She's having a rough time of it with her folks," I said.

"It's actually worse than that," Karl assured me. "Cosmically worse."

"What might that be?" I asked, though already suspecting where he was going.

"She has the oldest problem in the world," Karl said.

"Jesus. Wouldn't that be a bit premature?"

"Jesus had nothing to do with it, Paulie."

"So, you two were actually doing it?"

"Yeap, a couple of times. Then we hit the jackpot."

"Do her parents know?" I asked.

"They do. According to her they are plum roaring bonkers out of their minds."

"What do they propose as a solution?"

"They are insisting that she see a doctor, Paulie. The kind that does excavations, not any obstetrician."

"Ugh. And, what does Judy say?"

"She says nay, nope. No way. She wants to have our baby."

"Jesus."

"I swear he had nothing to do with it, Paulie. It was all me and Bloomy."

"So, what are you going to do?"

"Whatever we do, we will do it together," Karl said.

I did not like the sound of that. Last year there were articles in magazines about G.I.'s in Japan not allowed to bring their Japanese wives back to the States, desperate couples committing a double Hari-Kari. Karl and Judy did not have the stature for that level of tragedy. Come to think of it, that might make it even worse.

"Don't do anything stupid," I said.

"We already did," Karl said. "I'm stunned, not thinking too clearly. What really stuns me, Bloomy is tougher, more decisive, than I am."

What he said it took me back to our dinner at the Oyster House. It began as an inauspicious dinner, turned out to be an historic event, the war starting in Korea, Dad picked up by an 'ambulance' to sew up a Goombah. Judy had chattered about her classmates at Girl's high getting knocked up. That was only supposed to happen to underprivileged slum dwellers at William Penn High.

"So, you going into school tomorrow?" Karl asked.

"Most likely. I'll decide that in the morning."

"It was funny, "Karl said, "the role reversal. In the movies it is usually the ladies, the preacher's wife, the school ma'arm, the whore with a heart of gold, urging the hero to cop out, avoid the showdown. Tonight it was Moe doing that, while it was Sara implicitly demanding that we stiffen our backbones, show what size balls we carry, strap on our guns, and ride into town."

"You've got it, Wronsky. Our grand mission tomorrow is to have a *'normal'* day."

CHAPTER SIXTEEN

At dawn the shrill cockadoodling of roosters saluting another sunrise in their chicken coops woke us, the rustic racket you'd expect to hear in remote Mexican Villages, see peons greeting bandidos returning from a successful raid against the Gringos but out the windows of this third floor front we saw tangled telephone wires, smoke rising from brick chimneys, ugly unpainted roof tops.

Dad will be waking up in his cell. I stared at the cracked plaster in the ceiling above me, wondered why we try to fool ourselves? I'd always known that one day everything would go kerflooie, waves would wash over our sand castles.

Karl rose to take a shower. After he moved in with us the ex-slob became a one shower a day man, since Judy got her hands on him he became a three shower a day fanatic. People can and do change. As he dried off Wronsky said, "I'll be skipping breakfast. Dropping by Saint Pete's first, to pray for Doc, and pray for Bloomy."

I considered suggesting that the Almighty might not be too receptive to prayers channeled through Saint Pete's about the hanky-panky of a naughty Jewish maidel but figured Karl might not cotton to my abrasive sense of humor at this early hour.

Wronsky dressed in the new clothes had Moe picked for us in Klein's. Weird, our justice system, Dad not yet been convicted of anything, but we still were not allowed into our own house. According to Miss Pearl, who had been let in there to retrieve some of her things, the cops were tearing our home apart.

Karl touched his finger to his temple in a salute before clomping downstairs. I lit up a smoke, listened to him arguing with Sara on the second floor. She was insisting that he eat her breakfast of home fries and scrambled eggs. He said he needed to pass by the church first, to light a candle. Later he would grab a coffee and a donut on Broad Street. Sara believes that food is the solution to most problems.

Smoke rose from the factory stacks by the river, black crows were flying south, overcast skies promised dismal rains, smog smudged the waterfront, the gloomy panorama out the window fit my mood. Thank you, Lord, for a glum, gray morning, but why can it not be Friday night again, when my main goal in life was to insert my hand in Naomi's blouse, and not this bleak down where I am called upon to defend the family honor, and do not feel up to the task. Lord, do me one more favor, turn back the hands of time, turn the clock back to Friday night, to sheer old stifling normalcy. Make Dad be home; he growls at me for arriving late.

No, Burris, the moving finger writes, and having writ, is shoved up your rectum.

The new clothes Moe bought for me did not feel right as I dressed. Aside from not being a perfect fit, they were alien skins; I felt like I was donning a disguise.

Sara served scrambled eggs with chives and her special home fries, and asked if I had slept well. I assured her that I was okay but she said, "You know, I was thinking this over more, maybe it's not such a good idea, Paulie. Perhaps you should just hang around here, and wait until we get the call from downtown, from Mister Soll."

"School," I said. "No sweat. I wouldn't miss my classes for the world."

Coming out of the bathroom, Moe said, " You've got guts, kid. More guts than I ever gave you credit for."

"What are they gonna' do to me, Unc? Stone and pillory me?"

"You haven't seen the morning papers yet," Moe said." The sonsabitches are really giving Dan a working over. Maybe you should give this more consideration."

What happened to Korea? According to the radio hundreds of thousands of Red Chinese troops were pouring in from Manchuria and all the tabloid could think to feature as a the full-page headline was: NABBED MOB DOC ALSO WANTED BY FEDS.

The Inquirer had a more discreet heading in a left hand column about the F.B .I. seeking to broaden the investigation, question Doctor Daniel Burris about purported links to the New Jersey and New York Mobs.

Munching at breakfast I scanned the article in the Inquirer. 'Over the weekend anonymous tipsters, both men and women, had called into police headquarters to provide supposedly inside dope on the controversial figure of Doctor Daniel Burris, unsubstantiated allegations that the much admired pillar of his community was leading a double life as a high rolling gambler and inveterate womanizer, while supporting his opulent lifestyle with illegal abortions and a lucrative side practice of attending to bullet-ridden fugitives from the law.'

Opulent? Suddenly I am Ali Kahn, son of the Aga Kahn; yearly they give Pop his weight in gold. And, what was this crap about a womanizer? If a man likes the ladies he is a dastardly womanizer? Would they prefer he be a flaming fruitcake? All men are would-be womanizers; some turkeys just don't make out.

'It was further reported that Doctor Burris used his seaside vacation home in Cape May as a clinic to attend to mobsters from New Jersey and New York. Among the many female anonymous callers, several requested his private phone number and Doctor Burris received three marriage proposals.'

Moe touched my shoulder, and said, "You see? Now even Sara agrees with me: That it might be better if you just stick around and we wait for the call."

"Nah. I'm heading into school, Unc. But one question, Miss Pearl said that the police were tearing our house apart. Why would they be doing that? "

"Uich," Moe said. " I don't want to even think about that one. The cops claim that they are searching for evidence but there have long been rumors that Daniel had loads of cash stashed away in his home. The cops might believe in those rumors."

After one more cup of hot cocoa I headed downstairs. The deli opened at Eight AM, customers were already waiting outside. Paco and Pepe had prepared the urns of coffee, both rushed over to give me Latin abrazos. Paco again told me about his primo Eduardo serving hard time in Florida. This was to make me feel better. Moe glanced out the window. Aside from the regular customers ready to pour in for their morning Java and bagel stray onlookers were attempting to look casual, gathering by the taproom and the fresh fish market, look nonchalant. They are just there by chance, nonchalant vultures perching on a branch, waiting for carrion-me to emerge.

Knocky went through this the morning that crap came out about the *'audition.'*

"Seeing those noodnicks hovering out there makes me I feel like I'm throwing you to the lions, "Moe said. " You sure you don't wanna' change your mind, Paulie?"

"Don't sweat it, Unc. Screw the buzzards. I'm off to the races."

"If the load gets too heavy, drop it," Moe called after me as I stepped outside.

Triggering an instant stirring by the taproom and the fish market. As if on cue the casual by-standers were blatantly gawking at me. The clicking flash bulbs were lacking but I might as well have been Capo Frank Costello leaving the Federal Court Building. A few of the spectators waved. Hey, fans were showing support.

Once, on one of the few trips I ever made with Dad, we traveled up to Boston, I saw a residential block near Beacon Hill that might have been as long, otherwise this block, from Poplar up to Girard, had to be the longest in the U.S., Marshall Street stretching even longer today, this was the domain of the yachnas and the yentas, the bigmouths, gossips and busybodies, Every soul, both living and dead, standing in the doorways along this street, knew who I am, knows who my dad is.

Mister Klein waved from his haberdashery shop; I wave back. Be courteous, and correct, Paul. Today we are carrying the flag for the entire Burris clan. Stores are open, metal curtains rolled up, tarps had been pulled off the pushcarts, and fruit peddlers were waving as if I were a beloved celebrity, Milton Berle, passing through the neighborhood. There are also antipathetic squinters wincing, as if I were a leper with pussy fistulas strolling by. Inside shops, husbands were calling to their wives, 'Quick, honey, come and see the Burris kid go by.'

Knocky had been through these ordeals, had it worse. First, he was the adored fledgling toreador, then, he never quite sunk down to the level of shunned pariah, but he sure became the scorched target of morbid curiosity. So far I was getting off lightly: Mister Schutzbank, from the bakery, gave me a thumb's up sign; Balaban from the Linoleum outlet, a 'V' for Victory sign. Marty Katz, from the record shop, stepped outside, thrust his forearm at the horizon, imitating the agitprop posters of Stakhanovite tractor drivers; Katz was pledging his solidarity with Doc, loyalty to our neighborhood, screw all outsiders. We are receiving defiant signs of residual support, Big Doc has his hardcore fans. For a moment I felt better, then I passed the Sweet Shoppe. Mister and Mrs. Bloom were scowling, shaking fists at me: they must be both horrified, sickened, delighted: 'We told you over and over, Judy, the Burris are riff-raff, you must never go near them again.'

Had Karl run through this harrowing gantlet earlier, or had he shot over to Fifth Street to avoid these condemning eyes? Was he still in Saint Pete's? Will his candles, prayers, and supplications generate action upstairs? Will the Almighty say out of the side of his mouth, "Gabe, let us give this Burris guy a break; the Doc walks."

Walt Stein waved to me; I waved back, only then realized I was floating in a daze. What the hell was I thinking, I'd imagined my mind was clear but my hands were empty. How can you go to school with empty hands? I'd brought my textbooks and looseleaf folder home last Wednesday, not touched them since. My books were still back at the ranch. Wednesday? Wednesday was one thousand years ago. Screw books, today will be highly educational without books.

It had stopped drizzling so there was merchandise on display in the stalls and carts: bras, girdles, droopy long Johns, and cotton bloomers. Peddlers reached out to touch my shoulder, whisper words of encouragement. Up ahead was the only structure on this block not dedicated exclusively to commerce, the small yellow brick synagogue. A bunch of the Alta Cockers, the stern old boys in the beards and black hats and black and white prayer shawls were filing into the synagogue for the morning service. They paused to stare at me. Ten seconds passed. They said nothing, then entered the Shul. Well, that was a fairly eloquent statement.

I braced, beyond the synagogue was Feinberg's Smoke Shop. The establishment with its stock of humidors, clay pipes, pricey Cuban cigars, and Turkish, Gauloise, Players, exotic imported brands of cigarettes, had always struck me as too Ritzy fancy-shmancy for Marshall Street. The newspaper racks outside offered up the woes of the world, as if our local calamities were not enough to sate our appetites.

I braced harder before daring to glance to my left, at the racks. Feinberg's was an accursed spot on earth for us, a poisoned well in an oasis. It seemed impossible that it was barely three months ago that our happy trio had come out of the back alley to read that headline: STRIPPERS NABBED IN MAIN LINE HEIST.

Everything has been in a downward spiral since. Though, that's not true either. Why do I lie, even to myself? Poisoned seeds had been planted way before that.

When I finally screwed up enough courage to peek at the racks, there it was; aside from the inquirer, the tabloid. Dad had always hated this Daily Rag, said that reading it burned away brain cells. No, the headline had not changed since I read it over the breakfast table: NABBED MOB DOC ALSO WANTED BY FEDS.

Linked to South Philly slayings. Article on Page Three

What's this *nabbed* shit? The semi-literate morons can't come up with another verb like arrested, apprehended, caught? They've only got *nabbed* in their grab bag?

I did not want to touch this paper, to me it was a soiled rag, but I was unable to resist, picked the top copy off the rack. It was slightly damp from the previous drizzling, I turned to page three, and the title over the article was:

FBI SEEKS FIRST DIBS ON MOB DOC

First Dibs? Where did they acquire this vocabulary, from the sandbox? 'I get the first lick at the ice cream cone.' There was a small corner photo of the handcuffed physician, flanked by two burly policemen. Why had the cops arrived with photographers in tow that night? Was that the custom and the practice?

I looked up. Mister Feinberg was giving me the evil eye from inside the store. He rubbed his fingertips together; his gesture for reminding freeloaders that this was no public library. Recognizing me, Feinberg awarded me a dismissive wave. Today, boy, you can carry off a paper for Free.

How do you like that, sports fans? Fringe benefits, every time there is a calamity in my family we get free newspapers. I drifted toward the corner, looking straight ahead, heard comments of support and sympathy, did not turn to see who made them. The pressure of so many eyes boring into the nape of my neck felt like a kinetic force clamping down to crush my brain. Across Girard was Himmelstein's. The restaurant should evoke images of its great Weiner Schnitzel Specialty, with the gooey fried egg topped by an anchovy, but when I see Himmelstein's what comes to mind is the Gang Bang, the horrid mermaid in reverse. I try to resist but that filth pops into my mind like a pinball machine blinking a 'Tilt.'

A Trolley was heading west, I took off, running, hoping to catch it in front of the Capitol Restaurant at Seventh Street. The conductor saw me almost get hit by a speeding, delivery truck; he kindly paused, and then nodded as I hopped aboard. He knows me, but doesn't know who I am. I dropped my token in the slot, was instantly sorry for racing like that, taking off like a banshee. Snoopers might think I was fleeing, cracking up, because of this headline. So far I had flubbed the first test. These things get distorted. My intention had been to stroll up the block cool as a cucumber Gaylord Ravenal; I'm the Man who broke the back at Monte Carlo. I spoiled it all by running for this trolley as if I were a bawling baby. Man, you tear yourself apart if you worry about what people think.

One person aboard was reading a newspaper, the Inquirer. The other passengers were maids and workers, heading in for their shifts. I had taken this trip so many times travelers with familiar faces were nodding to me. But they did not know who I was so, for the moment we were okay. I was traveling incognito.

Winds whistled in my ears when I stepped off the trolley to grab the subway at the Broad and Girard Station. I reject psychosomatic B.S, seconds later I was underground, below could not recall coming down the steps. How did I get from there to here? The roar of the arriving subway was painful to my ears.

No escape. Stepping aboard I saw that two passengers in this car were reading the Inquirer, five others holding up the tabloid. I thought about switching to another car, just sat down, another might be worse, might contain people who knew me, guys from Central, or passengers familiar with my face, at least on this car I was incognito. The Daily Noose I was clutching was loathsomely alive in my hand. I had that sickening sensation that comes when you reach for a box in a darkened pantry, suddenly realize you have picked up a squirming rat.

Contradictions, I needed to see what garbage they were spewing while trying to control myself, not look. Like picking at a scab when you know you shouldn't pick at it, your tongue darts helplessly between your teeth when you're aware that will only make the soreness worse.

NABBED MOB DOC ALSO WANTED BY FEDS

Three of the cleaning ladies and two workers heading uptown were turned to page three, absorbed, and fascinated. I had to dip into this cesspool myself, began reading about 'the fast-living Doctor Jekyll and Mister Hyde using smoke and mirrors to cover up his illicit activities, honing his public images as civic-minded contributor to charities and saintly Albert Schweitzer-like physician attending gratis to impoverished slum patients in his crime-ridden waterfront area while simultaneously collecting succulent fees from notorious underworld figures. '

My Dad? Blow it out your ass, Mister Reporter. How many gross inaccuracies can you cram into a single paragraph? He even gets the context wrong: what waterfront? There are denizens of Fifth Street who've never seen the river except on post cards. Slums? Sixth and Girard and Marshall Street have a vibrant, pulsating dynamic beat.

I'll bet the hack who scribbled this tripe had been around our way maybe one time once, and he probably never read 'Doctor Jekyll and Mister Hyde."

Maybe he saw the flic with Spencer Tracey?

'Doctor Daniel Burris had long been the target of an investigation by State and Local Police, their surveillance intensifying after the well-connected Physician was observed keeping company with Mrs. Carla Fiore, widow of the notorious Anthony 'Tony Flowers' Fiore, and sister of Jersey mobster, Jimmy 'the Cat' Pardolino. Their on-going probes were impeded by stubborn interference from lower echelon officials in headquarters where, according to sources refusing to furnish their names for attribution, it was widely rumored that Doctor Burris had performed sub-rosa services not only for major underworld figures but had also been called upon by members of the police department after station brawls and internal incidents they wished to cover up. '

'Spokesmen for the District Attorney's office have refused to comment on other rumors that Doctor Burris was the Mastermind behind the mysterious dropping of charges back in September when the Cosmo Five were inexplicably released on their own cognizance. Burris had the son of one of the accused strippers residing in his home, and was also reputed to have been in a romantic relationship with another of the strip tease artists 'auditioning' in the Main Line mansion.'

How could they get it so totally wrong? They added two and two and out came twenty-two. And, if you write a letter to them, it makes it worse;

I was feeling punchy, pummeled and clobbered by left jabs, right hooks. First I had a taste of what Knocky went through for months, now the papers were giving Dad the full John. C. Connors treatment. Say, whatever happened to our dear Mister Connors? Three months ago he was all the rage, pictures in the paper, his finances, private life, and kinks available for public scrutiny. Now, except for an item a few weeks back about the Feds after him for taxes, he has vanished. After they brand you, stomp on you, crap on you, and shove you three times through the meat grinder you are no longer of much interest unless they can get a photo of you rummaging for your lunch in a garbage can.

The subway jolted me back to reality with a crunching halt at the last stop, Olney Avenue. I tossed the Daily Noose aside. The power of the press: it can turn a man into a stain on the bottom of the toilet bowl while simultaneously magnifying him enormously: at the moment there could be a half a million people in this city reading about Doctor Daniel Burris, chuckling, sniffing, tsk-tsking; always mucho fun to read about the miseries of others.

Apparently I was still having psychosomatic difficulties; when I reached street level I turned right. Why the hell would I do that when I've made this trip a thousand times, must always turn left to head down the hill? When did I step off the subway? I must have, I'm up here, but I in a soupy trance.

Passing the Widener Estate I tried to shake off the dizziness but thousands of questions were swirling in my mind. What were his colleagues and the nurses at the Northern Liberties saying? Dad had over two hundred patients, what would they do without their Big Doc? A dire question: maybe a half a million people were reading about him today, the ones who'd be paying the closest attention to his situation would be Sam Sacco and Big Sal. What were they thinking?

At Harry's luncheonette I considered ducking in there, hiding out for the rest of the day, pass the time playing the pinball machine rather than face the music in school, I was sick of the eyes on me. Cancel that. Dad always accused me of a Vitamin C deficiency, a shortfall in the character department. Today, though he may never know it, I will run interference for him, will be his blocking back, take down all tacklers coming at him. The man had always gone the extra mile for me.

Central perches on a green hill. Most high schools in this city resemble National Guard Armories, or medium security reformatories. Central had the aspect of a suburban pharmaceutical lab or headquarters of an insurance firm. I had never done anything outstanding, noteworthy, or meritorious but was fairly famous around this campus due to our scabrous, salacious obscenity marathons. While climbing the front path to the main entrance seniors who'd never spoken one word to me nodded in sympathy. Quick Conferences behind my back confirmed, "Yeah, that's him."

We discover what it is like to be a half-ass celebrity. Strangers nod; twittering erupts the second you pass. Though these students were behaving discretely. I detected little infantile brashness. These boys were uptown bred, middle classy, more urbane than my slack-jawed bug-eyed green horns down by Marshall Street.

The din in the hallways was the usual din yet a thunderous roar to my ears as I headed upstairs, the first bell shrieking like it could shatter rocks. I received more nods; a few outright assholes did double takes at the sight of me. I would not classify him in that category but my homeroom advisor, Mister Dishman, would not have been a good poker player. His grimaced in surprise when I entered the room, had not been expecting me today. From his startled expression he was the corrupt Governor of California, I am Zorro, swinging across his balcony with drawn rapier. Dishman instantly covered his gaffe with a sheepish grin, and chirped," Good morning, Paul. Please take your seat."

Our name is our fate. I'm with the Bees because bureaucrats divvy us up in homerooms by alphabetical order; up front there is Barr, Batt, Baumann, in the back row I am with the three Browns, penultimately me, and finally, Sheldon Byatt, last of the Bees. As I headed toward the rear a few Bees had blank expressions, puzzled as to why other Bees were shocked at the sight of me. Prima facie, these were not newspaper readers. Otherwise, I imagined the gabbling in two thousand homes yesterday, all over town, from Kensington to Wynnefield, from the Navy Yard to Germantown: "Hey, Dad. There's a wise guy named Burris in my physics class."

Taking my seat, I wondered what kind of breakfast they served Dad in the can. Did he have a tray, was he allowed to eat privately in his cell, or was he obliged to stand in line, mingle with the general locked up population, Sunday night's haul of muggers, dregs, and rapists? Dad was fussy about breakfasts. Miss Pearl serves spicy compotes of stewed apricots and figs with ginger and cinnamon, fluffy omelets, and she had her own secret recipe for superlative sticky buns. I doubted whether they would cater to his whims, downtown.

Reginald Brown, to my right, whispered, "Sorry about your family problems, Paul. My Dad knows your Dad and said he could not believe that stuff in the papers,"

"Thanks, Reggie. Tell him to keep the faith."

Reggie was the son of a funeral parlor director and one of our prim Colored who came to school in knickers and neckties. We had been sitting next to each other for almost two and a half years now without becoming bosom buddies. Reggie was sort of scandalized by our South Lawn who can be slimier derbies.

Sheldon Byatt, to my left, whispered," They clammed up when you entered, Paul. Some were saying you probably would not be in today."

"Yeah, I sure fooled them, didn't I?"

Stirring at his desk, Mister Dishman was about to growl, "No talking back there," then saw it was me, changed his mind. He went back to his task of taking attendance, pretending this was a routine morning, black roll book open, he is glancing around as if it were a complicated task to note down the absentees. Dishman is making amends for that faux pas wince when I arrived.

I've made teacher uncomfortable, also, my classmates. Unfair of me to come to school today, subject my worthy peers to this ordeal. I'm an apprentice pariah, and must learn how to lay low, learn not take my sackcloth and ashes act out to busy intersections and annoy bystanders. The thirty-five Bees were straining to face forward; I could see tension in their necks, invisible periscopes peeping out of their hairy heads to peer at me. Only two overt buffoons, Bass and Blumenthal, could no longer control themselves, looked back over their shoulders to directly fix on me.

The Nine: Fifteen Bell rang. All well trained Pavlovians, my classmates are rising in unison, gathering up their books, we are off to the races. A weird sensation, my naked hands, if one of my teachers dare ask why I can answer that my textbooks have been sequestered as evidence, are currently sealed behind police barricades.

Bees touched my shoulder on the way out. There are sponges who relish being objects of sympathy, centers of attention, the designated victim, I'm not one of them but confess I was glad to see my sturdy crew of outcasts awaiting me out in the hallway: Jack Kraft, Steinberg, Toll, Seymour the Simian. They poked at me, pounded my back, while babbling that I was crazy to have come into school today, I should have laid low, relaxed, stayed away, taken a walk in the park.

Seymour said, "With my father I drove by your house yesterday. Miss Pearl, your cleaning lady, was our front, arguing with the cops, cursing them out. But they said they can't let her in until after they finish the investigation."

Toll said," Yeah, I passed by yesterday with my Dad, too. There were patrol cars parked outside, the cops had the place cordoned off, were bringing out boxes and files, and what looked like medical records, My Dad tried asking them what's going on but the cops snarled at us to move along, get the hell our of there."

Can they really do that before the arraignment and the hearing? What happened to the constitutional amendment about unreasonable searches and seizures? Cheez, if the sonofabitching cops were ransacking my house they might have rifled through my room and found my hidden cache of pin-ups from the girlie mags and Amazing Stories. I could see the headlines tomorrow:

ARRESTED MOB DOC'S SON A CLANDESTINE PERVERT

Steinberg said, "Anything we can do for you, Paul. My father says your Dad is one of the finest men he's ever known, he'll be glad to be a character witness for him. He believes the charges are trumped-up bull to cover up police misconduct."

"Thanks, man," I said to Steinberg though I experienced a disturbing twinge. Loyalty is fine and dandy, even when it is not entirely warranted.

Jack Kraft was wearing his scornful, superior expression. He punched my shoulder, and said," You'll make it, Paulie. You will make it. Fuck em 'all, the long, the short and the tall. You will come out of this, too, smelling like the roses."

That sounded good, just happened to be silly. It is presumptuous of me to invoke such terms but since Friday night there was a split in time, a rip in the fabric of my universe. The hallways were quiet, almost empty now. Runty Mister Warshaw, on corridor patrol, turned the corner and thrashed, theatrically, at the sight of us gathered here. He growled in his *sandpaper accented Teacher-speak, "What the devil is this? Are you scoundrels* planning to run a crap game out here? Get moving to your classes before I haul the whole lot of you down to visit Doctor Farber."

My troops touched my shoulder, assured me that they would catch me after the next period. Warshaw again rasped, "Now get a move," to them, me, he signaled me to remain in place. When my buddies were out of earshot he squinted up at me, and said, "Burris, today you can skip your afternoon detention class.

More fringe benefits? First I get a free paper, now I can skip a detention class.

"Thank you, sir. Very kind."

"Tomorrow, Burris, we will see about tomorrow "

"Thank you, sir."

And, Burris, if you talk to your Dad tell him we believe in none of this crap. We are behind him. Now you get a move on, and take care, son."

'Son? Wow, that was a wild upgrade.

Hey, an insight: harsh little Mister Warshaw must prove he has a heart, too; one more of these gruff top sergeants with the tapioca pudding heart. One cause for relief: the flinty fuddy-duddies of the faculty would not be able to use that line on me again. "It must eat your father's heart out to have a son like you.' At least they would not be able to say it with a straight face.

Physics was my first class. Mister Kruger would be a better poker player than Dishman. He merely blinked when I entered the room, ordered the class to shush. Kruger spared me his usual caustic wit, made no comment on the fact that I was arriving several minute late; he pointed a finger to my seat in the rear of the room. Friends, acquaintances, enemies were nodding, basically in support; a few oafs were gaping as if I were a three-eyed Martian stepping out of a space capsule.

On the blackboard were chalked diagrams of ventilation ducts with arrows pointing hither and yon. The only thing I ever learned in my physics class is that I will never be a rocket scientist. Kruger resumed his lecture on flows and pressures, the class started scribbling away. I strummed my fingers on my desk. Look Ma, no books. I felt a tapping on my right shoulder; nice guy Gary Kelman slipped me a few sheets of blank paper. There was tapping on my left shoulder; nice guy Ronnie Neu passed me his spare fountain pen. We are supposed to take notes on these lectures where the confusing arrows point every which way but why would I give a damn if the wheel of fortune were no longer turning my way?

Flows and pressures? According to the Evening Bulletin more informants were calling into police headquarters and their editorial offices, squealers and snitches with fresh poop, scoops, and hot tips about the Doctor Jekyll from Sixth and Poplar. Karl had talked about the Cosmo Five provoking a feeding frenzy, it does not take much for a large life to shrink to fit tabloid clichés. Dad has become a punching bag, an object so scrutinized he is no longer recognizable. The more they write about the man the more he vanishes into a void.

What are the Physics of a life in dissolution, a bug swirling around, being sucked down the drain? Nine: thirty. Will he make bail? Right about now Dad should be leaving his cell for the hearing or arraignment, whatever it is. I'd seen so many tough guy crime movies I could write scenarios, beefy guards making dense wisecracks escorting the accused to the courtroom. A huffy judge presides. Starched-ass District Attorney rattles papers, objects to bail being granted. Shrewd defense attorney asserts that the accused is an upstanding citizen with deep roots in the community, and no prior criminal record. Crusty, white-maned judge calls the antagonists up to the bench for a whispered conference. While the conference takes place the accused culprit is tugging at his collar. The only thing wrong with this rotten movie is how did my old man wander onto this farkacta fucking farshtukene set?

I'm not sure if I heard one word of Mister Kruger's lecture on hot air rising. When the period was over my gang of four was waiting in the hallway, I did not recall hearing the bell ring. It must have rung. When did I rise to leave the class?

Howie Toll grabbed me around the shoulders and said, "Head home, Paulie. You're ashen gray. You're looking like death on a bicycle."

"Nah, I'm okay," I assured him. That's what you're supposed to say.

"If you want," Kraft said," we can both cut out, let's get the fuck out of here."

"I'm in," Steinberg said. "We can go to my house and shoot some pool."

"Some other time," I said." Today I have to carry the stick."

My uptown buddies would not catch the meaning of that phrase. What the Winos in Franklin Park used to say when they were out all night, broke, no roof over their head, no place to go. We had reached the door to my English class, Sylvan Gans bore down on me, he was radiating a purpose. My rat pack stirred, immediately had their backs up, fearing or anticipating that Gans might say something vindictive to me. They were about to order this lump to shag ass, but Sylvan leaned over, touched my shoulder to convey support, then he briskly moved on.

How do you like them apples, Emma? Even a feckless dingus like Gans can step out of role, display a smidgeon of decency, and manifest positive qualities, hitherto unsuspected attributes. Does being from the same neighborhood trump personal venom?

"Know how my father views this sloppy mess?" Seymour the Simian said." He said what's the big deal about your Dad bandaging up bleeding mobsters? Your Dad took the Hippocratic oath. He'd be a hypocrite if he did not attend to bleeding men, and naturally he gets to charge for his services, he's a professional. "

"Jeez, Seymour, Tell your Dad thanks for me."

Kraft seemed ready to bash Seymour for that contribution but Mister Warshaw was siddling up, preparing to bark at us. My troops touched my shoulder and said they would catch me at noon, out on the South Lawn. With a toss of the chin Warshaw ordered me to get into the class. Coach Schneyer was coming down the hall. He paused, scrunched his lips, was preparing to say something, apparently nothing crystallized; he merely shook his head, and continued on his way.

Well, that was a fairly eloquent statement, Coach. Come to think of it, a repeat of what the old boys entering the synagogue said this morning: nothing.

Even on the most routine of days there was a touch of theatre and drama when I enter the den of Ming the Magnificent. I entered, striving with all my might not to be making an entrance, just to slouch in as if everything is hunky-dory. My classmates did not collaborate with my interpretation of my role, their reactions ran the gamut from surprise and dismay to consternation. Hipper guys gave me furtive signs of support. Ming was wearing the strained, forbearing expression he usually wears for me; with a tilt of the skull he asks the universe what can we do with schlock like this, and why was I assigned this Burris creature?

His Fu Manchu mustache twitched in such fashion as to order me to take my seat in the rear. Ming and I have excellent communications. It is just that we deplore the messages sent by each other. I also suspect that Ming enjoys the challenge of dealing with a buzzard like me. Or maybe I am just flattering myself. As I sat down, Joe Rizzo, to my left, whispered, "Paulie, my old man also knows Sam Sacco, and Sal Bonafaccio. We go to the same church in South Philly."

"No shit? Congratulations, Baciagaloop."

"Yeah," Rizzo said, enthusiastically. "They get a bad rap but my Dad swears that down deep both of them are real swell guys."

"Great, Three Hail Marys. Three Pater Nostros, and let's all go to the seashore."

Ming was about to growl 'no talking back there.' Instead, he sniffed.

It is book report day. I ignored the impertinent staring, sank lower in my seat as Ming called upon Sidney Greenblatt to deliver his review of "The Mill on the Floss.' Floss my teeth, momma. I was waiting for the call from the office, Moe calling in to say that Milt Soll had been able to spring Dad. By now the Honorable Judge Stanley C Greenberg should have reached his decision, verdict, ruling, One day one of these pimple heads sitting around me might well be a judge. These are all bright, clever lads but how does anybody dare become a judge? Where do you acquire the brass balls to don the robes and stand in front of a mirror and say, 'I am the Judge.' Some of these guys will be surgeons, too. Would you consent to go under the knife if you personally knew the eminent surgeon back when he was the slimey pawed dingus dissecting the frog in your biology class?

Sidney Greenblatt was droning on about 'The Mill on the Floss.' A snoozer of a bore they cram down our throats. Don't the birdbrains in the Board of Education know that sixteen-year-old boys are savage beasts? Feed us raw meat, bayonet charges, cavalry charges, sex orgies, 'The Chinese Room, I, the Jury, give me that steamy scene in Anthony Adverse where the beautiful mature governess Faith Paleologus seduces adolescent Anthony. What droning Mill on what snoring Floss?

A few pimple heads can no longer resist the temptation to peek back my way. When I catch them in the act they at least have the courtesy to gulp. Ming the Magnificent was now offering his scathing critique of Greenblatt's critique, noting that Sidney failed to detect at least three motifs and four symbols. This chewing over of sodden tests struck me as redundantly incestuous to no discernible purpose. My next class was trigonometry: I did not believe I could productively engage with any logarithms today; exponentially, I have been off base for a while now.

My classmates swung around, craned their necks, Ming said nothing as I rose and left the room. We really do have clear communications. Out in the hallway I waited for the usual bursts of laughter. My departures customarily elicited sarcastic asides from Ming followed by the obligatory cackling of his captive audience. Today we were hit by the silence.

Congratulations, Ming. He had refrained. I was hearing no chortles.

Wall posters are still exhorting us to buy extra tickets for the traditional Thanksgiving football game against our perennial rival, North-East High. We had already lost that game, we always lose, ancient history in four days. The hollow clopping of my heels sounded desolate in the empty hallways. To punctuate the moment as I left the building the sun vanished, the skies swirled bleakly gray. Thank you, Mother Nature for providing a color palette to match my mood, pastels and primary tones would be intolerable today. Cutting across the south lawn I was on unexplored terrain. Where am I going? What am I doing? I was inclined to clamp my hands over my ears like the creep on the Munch painting. Wronsky and I endlessly debated sources, scenes, which novel, what movie, was this from? I'd read hundreds of books, seen a hundred movies about the travails of poor saps unjustly accused, abused, harried, vilified crucified, but I'm trudging along our here as the son of a man guilty as charged, guilty as sin. I'm guilty of being his son, with no guidebook as to how to behave in these circumstances. Send me a script, Lord. So far, I've flubbed playing this role, flunking all the tests, chasing after the trolley this morning, now cutting out of school because I can't take the shrouded straining not to peer my way.

My wolf pack will not forgive me for not showing up on the south lawn for our competitive vocal bowel movements. Along Ogontz Avenue I find this panorama to be Snoozeville sterile, stultifying, redundant row houses with monotonous trimmed lawns, screened porches, uptight inhabitants drained of vital fluids, wrung through three strainers pasteurized and homogenized before they're allowed to move uptown, are issued the deed. Down my way the Irish still look like Murphys, the Hebes like Moishes. By the time they move up here they can pass for the bland denatured Wasps in ads for low-cost insurance policies. What the hell were you doing, up here, Burris, trying to pass? Trying to suck in with the quality folk?

On Broad Street, trying to hear news about Dad, I ducked into the doorways of bars, stores; anywhere they had a TV or radio playing. A long time since last I played hooky. At ten I cut school, hid out on the docks with books, curled up in my hidden niche on the wharfs with the great action novels like Captain Blood, The Prisoner of Zenda, Scaramouch, Pellucidar, The Chessman of Mars. I was only ten but refused to be imprisoned in stifling classrooms run by old biddies with corks up their asses. It's supposed to be an education but felt like a four hundred pound Aunt Martha sitting on your face. Yes, your honor, I was a troubled child. Dad sent me to Doctor Schwartz, th coot had not a clue, I had to swear to the psychologist that I would straighten up and fly right, never play hooky again, two days later the patrol cars would again be picking errant truant me up, dragging me back to reality, not a place where I care to spend much time.

Down by Allegheny Avenue I passed an ice cream parlor. For flickering seconds there seemed to be flashes about Dad on the TV, then news about Korea, I was ashamed to go in there, ask what the news about Doctor Burris might have been. Could they really send Pop Up the River? He was such a fastidious individual; I can't visualize him in prison togs as one more jailbird. Could he buy his way out of it? Find a volunteer to serve his time for him? During the Civil War the scions of the rich paid bounties to Paddy immigrants just off the boat to perform their military service for them. That seemed like a sensible arrangement, an eminently logical solution. What benefit could this society derive from throwing a valuable man like my Dad into the clink? They could send him to work on an Indian reservation, to the impoverished hollows in Appalachia, make practical use of him.

Pausing in the entrances of luncheonettes where radios were playing, I heard snatches of the news: a two-car accident on Passyunk Avenue, Marines staging gallant retreat in Korea, new shooting incident in the Sinai Desert, massacre in India, stick-up in a Frankford Avenue gasoline station, dock workers threatening a strike in Camden. What had they just said? They mentioned Dad but it came across as an unrecognizable blur. On WCAU they just talked about Doctor Daniel Burris: At the request of the Federal Government the Judge Greenberg refused to grant bail to the accused physician, another hearing is scheduled for tomorrow.

Did I hear that or is my over-active imagination playing tricks on me again?

In the distance the Statue of William Penn stands atop City Hall. Traditionally, in our town, no structure may soar higher, sort of stunting our growth, like smoking cigarettes or jerking off. I staggered along Broad Street, as if a swinging load on the docks had smacked me, knocking me silly and senseless. Yes, I had heard that. Why play games, why this mental masturbation? Why am I sending Dad to work on Indian reservations? They might scalp him. Why is Broad Street not broad enough, and not an elegant, distinguished thoroughfare? Why is it not a Fifth Avenue or the Champs Elysees? Why no mystery, the beauty? Where is it writ that Philly's main drag should be drab, dull, mediocre, lifeless, third rate, when Philly is older than Leningrad, founded before magical Saint Petersburg was built in the marshes.

Why am I blowing steam out of my ass about Philly to avoid thinking about Dad spending one more night in the Hoosegow? I cannot imagine what must be going through the man's mind by now. As much as I know him I know nothing about Daniel Burris,. Only thing I knew certain sure at the moment, I was not yet ready to run that gantlet on Marshall Street, the somber eyes, the clucking, insidious comments with the hands covering the mouths.

Limbo, it is lonely out here, spending time out of mind, time off the clock, on unexplored terrain, Frankford Avenue. I 'd never known it was this peppy under the El Tracks, I needed to suck in life at the moment, fight off the crawly creeping deadness. After wandering around I found myself in the Jumbo Theatre. I did not recall buying the ticket but must have purchased a ticket because I was definitely sitting here. Inexplicably. I'd never been in this cavernous dump before. At Front and Girard, only six blocks from my home, so close, but this was my first time in here. I'd been to the Poplar, the Ruby, Astor, Girard, hundreds of times, even been to the Booker in the project when Miss Pearl took me to see Lena Horne in 'Cabin in the Sky', but this was my first visit to the Jumbo. This place is huge, easily a thousand seats, but large sections were roped off, closed. There were maybe fifty other spectators in this audience. Then I recalled why the Jumbo was unofficially off-limits for me. The Fishtown Kellys and Murphs did not appreciate it when ginks of the Marshall Street persuasion strayed onto their turf. Only Six blocks from my home but this was like dropping by the wrong pub in Belfast.

With the Jumbo so empty on a Monday afternoon I felt like an outcast, marooned on an isle of deserted nothingness. What kinds of weirdos go to the movies on a

Monday afternoon? Only dropouts, lost souls, nobodies who do not count can enjoy a movie on a Monday afternoon. Let us put the onus on me: In which of those categories did I fit?

Far from the Madding Crowd we are catching a double feature for only a quarter: 'Gunga Din' and 'Four Feathers.' British Imperialism. Months ago we did French Imperialism downtown. Beau Geste and Morocco could not save Alexi. Knocky covered his face with his hands, almost collapsed out of his seat. I've caught up with him fast but let us stop all this extraneous B.S. and concentrate on our future, lay contingency plans: what happens if they send Dad away?

'Allons enfants de la Patrie.'

Ah, that's B.S., too. You're not joining any Foreign Legion; it is currently jam-packed with ex- Nazis right at the moment, fighting over there in Vietnam.

Au revoir, Mon Cher Amie. No legion for me this time around.

Maybe I can look up my three half-brothers in California? 'Hello, I'm your Dad's Winter Wheat. Not an impressive crop, but I am what there is.'

Caution! The authorities will try to divvy you up between your aunts and uncles. All your gall will be divided into three parts.

No damn way, Jose. I'd rather become a reclusive hermit in Southern Argentina.

Caution! They don't pay much attention to your druthers. So, Are you going to be passive? An orphan tossed by the storm?

No! I will seize the reins, be the captain of my ship, master of my fate, hopefully, because I've always been loosey-goosy silly putty, letting others shape me.

The opening credits were rolling for 'Gunga Din. ' I rose, headed down the aisle. I'd seen this movie maybe five times; they never change the ending. If they promise to fix the ending I might give it another look-see.

Leaving the Jumbo Theatre it seemed like just left Ming's class. I waited. Would there be an acidic aside followed by sycophantic chortling? No. It was the silent treatment. Nobody was paying attention to my scurrying hither and yon.

Dusk, crepuscular shadows were spreading under the El Tracks. I'd often seen similar gray shadows at this hour, never called them crepuscular before. Crepus cular sounds so muscular, does the object change when you change the name? The early edition of the Evening Bulletin was displayed at the corner kiosk, nothing on the front page about Mob Doc. The headlines dealt with the so-called 'Police Action' in Korea. That was another downer, name-wise. It seems déclassé to die in *a 'Police Action,'* We at least want to die in a legitimate, dutifully declared, authorized war.

Hopefully, the papers are weary of the Mob Doc by now. They can devour some other victim. Me? Had I behaved like a squalling infant demanding attention today? In a snit, are we, having our little tantrum? The tribe is waiting for me back at the ranch. It was bad enough they had the news that Dad would not be sprung yet, they've probably spent the entire afternoon worrying about my whereabouts, and what great thing did I do today? I went to the movies, momma.

Up Girard Avenue, this bedraggled stretch was near my auld sod but I'd never had the common courtesy or the idle curiosity to explore these blocks so close to my stamping grounds, nail them down in my mental landscape. From what I could see I had not been missing much, flyspecked luncheonettes next to seedy little businesses on the first floors of what were once homes. I had wanted to write about the great wide world, was not even conversant with my own bailiwick.

Until we reach Saint Pete's. Had the candles Karl lit in here his morning helped any? Helped Bloomy? What, exactly, do you pray for in their situation? I was staring at Saint Pete's, Fifth and Girard. A famous church, built like around 1843, a Saint associated with it. My associations tend to be raw, ribald, perverse, unfit to print. Himmelstein's? Bingo! 'Gangbang!' Saint Pete's here triggers recall of Wronsky telling me about buxom Rosie, the birthday present he never received, Are my trials and tribulations due to my congenital, innate crudeness? Lord, please send me a can of cerebral Dutch Cleanser to help me clean up my act.

Traffic was slowing as it crosses Girard, Ut oh, another telltale sign; I am the crafty urban beast, attuned to the snap and crackle of every twig in my asphalt jungle. I looked to my left, had instant feedback. Halfway down the block on Sixth a red light was flashing, a patrol car was parked smack in front of my house.

An optimist might leap for the thought that Dad had been released; they had driven him home, now they were abjectly apologizing to him. But I believe I heard the radio say were holding for another hearing. Had I heard that?

Reaching the linoleum outlet at the corner, I turned Down Marshall; will these people never close their stores? Shoppers were swarming through the stalls and pushcarts, every window had signs, liquidating stock, two-for-one, fire sale, half–price, special bargains, incredible discounts, must sell, going out of business sale. Some of these dumps had been going out of business for decades now. The old joke; 'two more bankruptcies and I can retire, Abe.' The Burris family is going out of business, medical monkey business.

The delivery truck paused at Feinberg's smokes shoppe, the helper tossed a bundle of Evening Bulletins down by the fireplug. A familiar sight from one hundred black and white gangster movies; avid readers eager to snatch up copies hot off the press. Hear yee, hear yee, read all about it, you pus slurpers, little happening in your own wormy lives so you need to suck in your daily dose of printed venom. Mister Feinberg stepped out of his shop to retrieve the bundle; one brief lifetime ago he awarded me a free copy of the Daily Noose this morning.

The patrol car in front of my house on Sixth was the first hint that things had taken a turn for the worse; that dismal sensation deepened, twisted two notches deeper from the way Walt Stein waved to me, adding a sad toss of the chin, convey-ing sympathy, pity, grief. Had there been more shit on the radio, more crap coming out in the papers. Fruit peddlers, neighbors, patients I knew from Dad's office, were giving me the same kind of tentative wave, struggling with mixed emotions, the expressions contained more pain than they had this morning, like they wanted to rush over, give me a hug, pat my back comfort me, while they were hesitant, afraid I might not welcome their approach.

Down the block vans were blocking traffic, a commotion in front of Moe's deli. Before I could check on what that was about the Blooms came rushing out of their sweet shop, Mister Bloom grabbed me, almost knocking me over as he groaned, "Paul, we're so sorry to hear about your father, but have you seen Judy or Karl today? We're sorry about your father but concerned about Judy."

People who never spoke to me, had never been great admirers of my father, they even threatened to sue him , what was this crap about sorry. Removing his hands from my shoulders, I said," Good evening, Mister Bloom. Judy, not at all, sir, and Karl I have not seen since dawn this morning."

"We're frantic with worry about them," Mrs. Bloom said. "Judy hasn't come home from school. This is not like her. We went to your uncle's deli. Moe swears he 's not seen hide nor hair of the Wronsky boy since this morning and it's almost eight now, no Judy. We don't know what happened to her, where those two could be."

Under other circumstances I might have wisecracked about Karl and Judy not having the means to rent the honeymoon suite at the Bellevue Stratford. I limited myself to saying, " They no doubt have lots to talk about but I wouldn't worry, they are two homing birds, they'll be back by and by."

"Look, Mrs. Bloom snapped, "I know you've suffered a terrible tragedy in your own family, young man, but there is no need to get fresh with us. This is not like our Judy. She'd have called by now. Our daughter is out there and we don't know where she is. We are crazy with concern."

A snoopy crowd had gathered around us. Folks on Marshall always enjoy a good car wreck. I was wondering what tragedy Mrs. Bloom was talking about. Sure, Pop had awful problems but she was jumping the gun already calling it a tragedy.

"I'm not being fresh," I said. " Did you check to see if clothes or luggage was missing? Had she packed a bag, or anything like that?"

"We checked her room, her piggy bank was smashed, "Mrs. Bloom said.

I had to control myself to not laugh; a smashed piggybank? That sounded like the props for a Kindergarten melodrama; a Gotterdammerung in the Sandbox.

"Later this afternoon we discovered that money, a substantial amount, was missing from our cash register, "Mister Bloom said.

"You didn't have to tell him that," Mrs. Bloom snapped at her husband.

"I told him that, and that's what I'll tell the police," Mister Bloom growled. " That Wronsky boy influenced my daughter to steal. She's never done anything like that in her life. Judy's a wonderful girl, a top student, obedient, well behaved, until she took up with that farshtukene Chazerai Cossack. I'll have that little weasel nailed to the wall if he's damaged my daughter."

To the best of my knowledge, damage, if what some would call a blessed event can be called damage, had already been done. I limited myself to saying, "Karl is no thief, sir. He's deeply religious and may be the most honest guy I know."

"I don't give a shit what that little gonif is," Mister Bloom shouted. "My daughter is missing, she's out there, somewhere in the night. I will see that little wart in jail and have his balls on a platter if he's touched her."

Aside from being enraged and hysterical Mister Bloom was lying. He knew she had already been touched. Mister and Mrs. Bloom began shouting at each other; these were exactly the kind of people you did not want to have around in an emergency. I turned to move on, Mister Bloom blocked my path and snarled, "You, too. You're involved, too. You must have been in on their planning. In spite of the tragedy in your own family I'll have your ass in jail, too."

Still coming at me with the tragedy crap, was this not premature? I again removed Bloom's hands from my shoulders. Mrs. Bloom shook a tiny fist at me, and shouted, "You, too, you arrogant snot. You must have been in on the robbery. I'll see you in jail with that scummy Cossack. You must have been his accomplice."

Lately everybody is throwing legal lingo at me. An accomplice? Why not? I am an unindicted coconspirator and will submit an amicus curiae brief for the accused.

I broke away from them. Spectators were shaking their heads ruefully as a commentary on Mister and Mrs. Bloom's overwrought antics. Other street vendors reached out to touch me. For a moment I thought that was to display sympathy for the lambasting the Blooms had just given me. Then I saw it was another matter. Down the block, past the clutter of carts and stands, dresses hanging from high hooks, flash bulbs were clicking, reporters were seeking statements from volunteers in the crowd around the deli, Uncle Moe was being interviewed. Aside from the patrol car there were vehicles from radio and TV stations, KYW, WCAU.

Friends, neighbors began calling out to me, "Sorry to hear about your Dad, Paul."

Leon Hess shouted, "That was no suicide. Your father was murdered in there."

"It was probably the cops, themselves," Buddy Baer shouted. "The fucking cops."

"What suicide?' Art Balaban called to me. "The mob wanted to shut him up, Paul."

From the door of the bakery, Mister Schutzbank shouted to me, "How come he had a belt in his cell? They always take your belt away from you. What is this crap that he hung himself with his belt? "

Moe spotted me, thrashed, and elbowed his way free of the reporters surrounding him, he came charging toward me like a miniature Bronco Nagurski plowing through traffic, knocking aside bystanders. Tears were streaming down his cheeks; this man gets emotional. For a second it seemed as if he might rear back and sock me one. Instead Moe grabbed me around the shoulders, shook me hard, and groaned," Where the hell you've been, kid. We've been crazy nuts with worrying, the red cars were our looking for you all afternoon."

A pack of reporters had trailed after Moe, they began shouting, "Is this the boy? Is this the son? Can the boy give us a statement?"

Fifty people crowded around us, jabbering away. A reporter thrust a mike at my mouth. Moe knocked it away and snarled," Get the fuck out of here, you asshole."

Flash bulbs were clicking. Moe turned to me again and wheezed, "We were so worried about you. Where the hell have you been, kid?"

"I took a walk, Unc."

CHAPTER SEVENTEEN

A mortar shell landed directly on my foxhole, blew me apart, smashed my little world to smithereens, every thought I ever had must be re-examined, otherwise, nothing had changed. The family reunion in Moe's parlor seemed a sequel to the Sunday meeting, next episode in the soap opera, Karl had been cut as member of the cast had been cut, the raucous arguments were about how to handle young Paulie over these next few days, with nobody soliciting my opinion on the matter. After acrimonious debates they decided to ship me off to Aunt Ethel's place in South Philly, to hide me away from the reporters still hanging around on Marshall, still clamoring to interview the son of the deceased.

Burt and Fanny drove us down to Porter Street, arguing as to which it was: Burt was sure it was a murder, Fanny was voting for suicide, Burt told her she was crazy, the only question doubt was whether it was the cops or the mob that put the belt around Dan's throat. Ethel and Uncle Max scolded them for discussing these matters in front of the boy, provoking a shouting match. I wanted to clamp my hands over my ears, scream at them all to please shut the fuck, When we reached Porter Street Fanny patted my wrist before I slipped out of the Plymouth. She assured me," You'll see, Paulie. Everything will turn out alright."

Excellent. What does that mean? In three days Pop will rise from the dead?

In spite of my protests Uncle Max and Aunt Ethel insisted that I eat. They heated up a pizza, we listened to the late-breaking news on the radio: Informed sources suggesting that the gang war erupting this evening, a bloody shoot-out on Snyder Avenue, reminiscent of dramatic Hollywood style slayings, was no doubt linked to the ongoing investigations of the suspicious circumstances surrounding the demise of the Mob Doctor, Daniel Burris, earlier this afternoon.

Uncle Max winced at the 'Mob Doctor,' and he rasped, " The rotten Mumsers. No trial, no evidence, not a thing proven, but the stinking bastards dump more slop on Daniel's grave even though he is not yet in his grave."

"They are plying their trade, Unc. " I said. " Trying to make a living,"

"They should only drop dead making a living that way," Max said. Then he turned to fix on me and added," What surprises me is, not a tear out of you yet, kid? You're kind of a cold fish, aren't you, Paulie?"

"I'm trying to be one, Unc. Dad hated hysterics; people became sloppily over-emotional and beating on their breasts. I'm trying to honor his reserve."

"Paul inherited his coldness from Leonora," Aunt Ethel said. " Leo could be very cold when we were excited and hot and bothered, she bristled like an ice cube.   For a while we gave her the nickname 'Our Ice Queen.' "

Over fourteen years gone by, none of the Berman sisters forgive her an iota.

"It's alright for you to cry," Max said. "Let it all hang out. We're all family here."

Dad was a snob. Apparently Momma Leonora was, too. From which side did I inherit my arrogance? We are not allowed to be our own product. Every trait must have been supplied to us, fifty-fifty, sealed in the initial package, where the sperm meets the egg.

The rules say if you do not cry you are not grieving properly. Learn how to mourn, you grub, at least an audible sniffle. One tear came to my eye that night. Was that a tear for Dad, or for me, poor me, recidivist as an orphan, stretched out, trying to sleep, in my cousin Barry's old room. Max and Ethel had three grown sons, out in the world. Their model airplanes still dangled from overhead strings. On the walls were fading photos of athletes past, from way back when the Phillies played in Baker's Bowl, and slugging Chuck Klein was in his prime.

Barry was supposed to be my 'nice' cousin, the prick was a sneaky snake, used to sucker punch me. Maybe the tear was from my fury at those long ago sucker punches, not a farewell toast to Dad? I'd always known this was coming. The afternoon Karl and I jogged to the Art Museum I envisioned the cops clicking the cuffs on him. Or had I shed this tear for Miss Pearl? She imagined she was set up for life; her world had fallen apart, too. His thinking had been a bit fuzzy these last few months. What had Pop been thinking: Après moi l' deluge?

Over breakfast, I listened to Aunt Ethel gabbing away with Sara over the phone, both angry because Mrs. Barufkin and other ritzy-titzy ladies from the Broadwood dances were seeking to horn in on the funeral arrangements. Aunts Ros and Fanny were also vehemently opposed, insisting that the rituals be the exclusive domain of the Berman Sisters. Who the hell were these interlopers to stick their two cents in at a time like this. Max scowled in agreement as he listened to the conversation while I winced inwardly. Do I get involved? Apart from his last will and testament, Dad provided me with a folder containing explicit instructions on how to handle his affairs and remains if he precipitously popped off: KISS was the code word: no pomp and circumstance, please. Cemeteries were an egregious waste of precious land; the most modest of tombstones was a Pharaonic pyramid. He was to be cremated, and should be naked under the sheet; it was idiotic to burn up a perfectly good suit some poor devil down in Franklin Square might well need. His clothes were to be donated: half to the Baptist Church at Marshall and Buttonwood Streets, half to the Catholic Charities at Fifth and Spring Garden. Any reception should be simple, modest, food and drinks at an austere minimum, no feast, no gorging in his honor, no flowers, please. Why should his passing on represent a bonanza for Florists?

From what I was hearing, Aunt Ethel and Sara, et al, were planning exactly the kind of three stars de luxe extravagant Shindig Dad would have abhorred.

Reluctantly, Uncle Max passed the morning papers across the table to me. Doctor Burris was still front page but lower case, relegated to the third paragraph. The main news was the gangland style hits at a Snyder Avenue gasoline station where three henchman of Victor Bastiano were gunned down in a suspected retaliation for his spilling to the Law. There were gory photos of the bullet-ridden car, blood staining the gas pumps. Meanwhile, the local police and the Feds were in a public pissing match: the Philadelphia cops had classified Doctor Burris's official cause of death as a suicide; the Feds suspected foul play, were demanding that an autopsy be conducted by FBI forensic experts.

Further complications stemmed from the public feud between Darmopray and Milton Soll, both lawyers contending that they had exclusive jurisdiction over the unresolved legal affairs of the deceased. I was reading this while listening to Aunt Ethel explain to Sara that the rabbis from both the Marshall Street and the Sixth and Green synagogue were disputing who would conduct the funeral services. There were also doubts as to whether Daniel could be buried in the plot next to Leonora. It was an orthodox cemetery, if he was murdered it was okay but if it were a suicide that was a sin; sinners cannot not be interred in that sacred soil.

Page seven offered photos of Dad at long-forgotten civic events, the man natty in a tux and bowtie, a photo of Dad playing basketball, and a boxed note explaining that due to the ongoing investigations no final obituary would as yet be furnished.

Passing the newspaper back to Uncle Max, I asked, "Why would Milt Soll be claiming that he is still on the case if Dad is dead? I thought Soll was only brought in to defend Dad on the strictly criminal charges. "

"You might as well ask him why he became a lawyer. The case could drag on for years. Soll will do his best to absolve Daniel. The bill will go to Daniel's estate. Meaning you, Paul. The fees would be coming out of your pocket. Be careful if and when Soll asks you - don't you want your father cleared, young man?"

Of course, and if I answer no I'm a lowdown rat and a heartless ingrate.

"That's gross," I said.

"Sure is," Uncle Max agreed," Death is gross, too, never simple. Death cuts off many complications, and creates batches of fresh complications."

Aunt Ethel had finished her call to Sara. Sitting down at the table with us. She said, "I'll second that motion. You should see how complicated these arrangements are getting. We're still sorting out the location, which funeral home, which rabbi will be the main speaker. Priests and protestant pastors from local churches want to participate. Sara is going crazy trying to coordinate things up on Marshall Street. So far, it's a big tizzy, people running around like chickens without a head."

Everything Dad had hoped to avoid. In spite of his generous donations he had zero use for organized religion, could not abide preachers, pastors, rabbis. He said it forever puzzled him how hairy flatulent bipeds could offer up their services as standard bearers, representatives, and spokesmen for a divine almighty Lord.

Slapping his hands to his knees, Max rose from the table, and said, "Well, I have to go into work. How about yourself, Paulie? There's a Shul a couple of blocks from here; I can drop you off there, if you feel an early Shiva, a prayer for your dad."

Should I suddenly get religion? Does it require a miracle or divine intervention? Sergeant York sees the light when the lightning bolts strike his rifle?

"I think not, Unc. If it is all the same to you, I'd like to go for a walk. I need to organize a few matters inside my skull."

"But, you'll be back in time for lunch," Aunt Ethel said, anxiously.

"Sure. In time for lunch," I assured her, not necessarily lying but with no intention of returning for lunch. I hoped to drop by police headquarters, or the morgue, wherever they had Dad laid out, for our own private goodbye.

"I'm driving to the Navy Yard," Max said. "Can I drop you off anywhere, Paul?"

"Nah. Thanks, Unc. I just want to wander around for a while."

"Okay." Max said, dubiously, "but you be back before noon, Paulie. We still have tricky technical details to work out, like the release of Dan's cadaver from the authorities, and the question of the cemetery plots. They're still up in the air. Dan was paying for several plots next to Leonora's stone, but apparently he had no intention of occupying any of them himself. There's still the threat of a delay from Uncle Sammy wanting an autopsy. We're juggling lots of balls in the air here."

I raised my hand in oath while saying nothing. Max and Ethel both stared at me, suspiciously. They knew that Dad had to send me to see a psychologist due to my deplorable tendency to fade away, fink out, and vanish. Yes, I had this habit of wandering off into the mists. I plead guilty to that, your honor.

Five minutes after Max drove off I gave Aunt Ethel a kiss, and left, swearing that I'd be back by noon. Chill winds were whipping up the dust as I hit the streets; wads of newspaper sheets were rolling along like urban tumbleweeds. Do narrow homes produce narrow minds? Folks down here were squished together in cramped row houses. The local Jews aspired to make it uptown, have a real lawn, a lawn mower. The Italians were more stick in the mud, not too prone to move or they only moved to larger places a few blocks away from La Nonna's meatballs. By what right do I put down these honest, upwardly striving Tonys when I'm the offspring of the reputed Mob Doc and should be skulking around like a cur with a stepped on tail?

Pardon me, your honor; I have not internalized that identity as yet.

In just one day Daniel Burris has lost his top billing. The headline in the corner candy store window screamed:

SNITCH PALS SLAIN

Fabled South Philly on a raw end of November morning; a different world-view down here. In lore, legend, to a degree, even in reality, South Philly is tough. Even the Jews here were supposed to be gutsy fighters like Benny Leonard and Lew Tendler. South Philly oozes mystique, breeding grounds of musicians, comics, Capos, hit men, boxers, greasers, crooners, hepcats, sharpies. You wouldn't know it from this lackluster barren panorama. Mystifying how rows after drab rows of dull row houses could grow so many exotic sprouts: great guitarists, chefs, rock and rollers, tenors. Up at Central we had an English teacher whose main claim to fame was that Mario Lanza had punched him in the kisser back when Lanza was a practicing juvenile delinquent at South Philly High. Viva Mario! And these streets are safe. There is no petty crime around here, no muggings, no purse snatchings; the Mafia will not stand for it.

SNITCH PALS SLAIN

The same headline graced the stand by the grocery store across the street, while a smaller headline on the side column asked Murder or Suicide? The tune will not change from block to block; I will see this all over town today, grasping how Knocky must have felt when he saw Aunt Svetla's knockers featured the length of Market Street. A question, your honor, in fact, several questions: suicide is classified as a crime, will that be added to the charges against Dad, will he be tried in absentia, or will all charges be dropped? Can the Law seek to drag Dad back from Hades, or his white cloud, wherever he may be, attempt to tack another five years onto his sentence because with his suicide he is guilty of obstructing justice, and impeding ongoing criminal investigations? Sorry for my silly questions but the next one is-how strong was that belt? Dad had been slimming down but he was not exactly a shadow of his old self. At our Thanksgiving Feast on Thursday he was still tipping the scales at around two-eighty so that must have been a mighty strong belt they used to hoist him up there, dangle him from that pipe.

SNITCH PALS SLAIN

Corner pharmacies and candy stores offer the same headline. Like Gunga Din, they never change the ending. According to the Inquirer, it was another horrible day in Korea, the First Marine Division creamed and smashed with many casualties. Young guys were dying in those snows to preserve these wonders back home so should I stop my wailing? Dad had certainly lived a full and rich life. A question, your honor: how many apes did they need to grab him and string him up there?

Reaching the Italian Market at Ninth and Washington I was back on my familiar turf of stalls and pushcarts, and chickens clucking in coops. This bustling stretch was a Nea-politan version of Marshall, delis selling prosciutto rather than pastrami. The Italian nonnas carry the same leather shopping pouches the Polish babushkas carry up my way. Several women tending to the stands were vivacious sparrows with sharp, darting eyes, reminding me of Mrs. Carla Fiore. Shoppers were arguing about the news flashes on the Italian language station, saying that Bastiano would never make it to any trial. Others were talking about how the mob strung-up the Jew doctor. Yeah, they shut that Hymie up good.

South Philly, a distinct place where they have local pride. Up my benighted way nobody says Northern Liberties.' Newspapers use the term and there's the hospital with that name but I've never once heard a neighbor say 'I come from Northern Liberties.' Back when I wanted to be a journalist I did research and discovered that our area was once a thriving industrial area and also had a throbbing Red Light District. Voila! That may explain why I'm horny all the time. I can blame it on the lead in the paint, the priapic ingredients in the soil and water,.

You wretched Toad! How dare you lightly muse about sex, when yesterday your father was strung up from an overhead pipe?

I can't control what crap pops into this rotten radio station between my ears; what snakes slither up the drainpipes. I can only censor my tongue, fool people into believing I'm halfway serious, and only I will know that I'm a spaced-out goofball.

SNITCH PALS SLAIN

Yes, we got the message; stop kicking dead horses. There's no need to glance at every store window and paper rack. How about a little comic relief, man? Send in the clowns. Dance a Charleston. Sing the Blue Bird of Happiness or, vaudeville style- drop your drawers. That always gets yucks from the yokels.

But what the fuck do you do on a day when absolutely nothing is funny?

Look for the Silver Lining. And try to find, the sunny side of life, young man.

Oh, bullshit. Our fault, dear Brutus, is not in our stars, but in our name. Since the name of Burris in this city will forever be a curse perhaps I should change my surname to something uncontroversial: like Burr. Bingo! Burr! Nitty-gritty grass roots dow- home hominy grits all–American: Inconspicuous Aaron Burr.

I'm cracking up out here in my silly season. Drifting east, over to Sixth, I reached South Street, a disappointing commercial strip that never lives up to its billing but the clothing salesmen here were brasher than the barkers in front of strip joints, aggressive types brandishing their tape measures like weapons. They could be Thugees with nooses to strangle you, rushing right at you on the street, pressing the tape against your neck, and wheedling, "Have I got a suit for you, Boichick, a Double- breasted gabardine that will turn heads and you'll knock the maidels dead at the Y dances. This suit is you, boy."

We will all have to wear suits to the funeral. What would my aunts say if I told them that Dad gave explicit instructions that he did not wish to be buried in a suit? Ethel would say-who asked him? This is no longer any of his business.

A block further up, Sixth and Lombard, passing Levis's, I was shocked to observe that they raised the price of their renowned hot dogs from ten to fifteen cents. A Schnook might say that this is a nominal increase, a radical might object that a fifty percent hike is galloping inflation, So nothing is what it is but rather what you call it, a crepuscular shadow is more foreboding than a dim shadow. If Karl and Bloomy can find a Justice of the Peace willing to hitch them the flight of two harebrained mixed-up kids running off hog-wild blossoms into a formal elopement.

This is a Sara Bernhardt final wrap-up tour. I wallow in premature nostalgia because I suspect I'll never see these places again. Back when Wronsky was into his slimming down for Bloomy phase we jogged all the way down here to Levis's. Karl made noises about possibly, perhaps, treating himself to a hot dog, as a reward for his accomplishment, and buying one for me, too (trying to bribe me). I had to moan, "Hey, fatrat: that would wipe out all the benefits of your exertions. "

We argued when we jogged by Independence Hall, him huffing and puffing, he'd start reciting, "We hold these truths to be self-evident," then turn to me to ask, "You realize that our entire country is predicated on a crock of shit? That all men are created equal?"

"It means, Dumbo, equal under the law," I would explain, patiently.

"That's bullshit, too. Aside from that, if we're all created equal why am I not beautiful like Ratcho? Why do I not have the powerful physique of a Billy Schmitz? Why am I sentenced to spend my one and only life like it 'd take little effort from the make-up department for me to portray the Hunchback of Notre Dame?"

"You've no right to bitch, Wronsky. When the Almighty was divvying up the attributes he gave you a sharp mind. That should be enough for a crud like you."

"Well, bless his benevolent hide, but I'll let you in on a secret, Burris, he did me no big favor. Smartness is pretty much a curse. How many geniuses are happy? I believe that the truly fortunate people in this world are clueless, handsome oafs stupid enough to believe they deserve all their good luck."

I told him that Einstein looked happy; at times he even looked daffy. Jogging by here we had endless variations on that debate. I'd contend that the unexamined life was supposed to be not worth living, Karl answered," Suppose you examine the sloppy mess and say, 'Take back this paltry trifle, Dear Lord. Return to sender.'"

Not exactly the Lincoln versus Douglas debates but we really went at it during those long jogs. This morning there were only a few tourists snapping pictures in front of Independence Hall. A yellow bus paused on Chestnut Street, boisterous brats disgorging from the bus, one of those class excursions where they will stand in rapt attention in front of the Liberty Bell while teacher will reverentially read off the words, 'We hold these truths to be self-evident.'

There are plans to eventually build a park here. Meanwhile, Independence Hall was a gem in an undistinguished setting, ringed by insipid banks and insurance companies. One block down, at Market, is the used bookstore with the sealed porno pamphlets in the rear. As usual I flinch as I pass by and pompously ask- What would the Founding fathers say of the decks of dirty cards with the nude Casbah houris, and the two by fours comic booklets of Dick Tracey planking Lady Luck, and Batman doing Sheena of the Jungle?

Ben Franklin might say Tut-Tut. Ben was a bit of a swinger, reputed to have driven the French ladies wild. Sorry Dad, I know I should be thinking saintlier, more elevated thoughts but under hostile skies I feel useless. Is there anything I can do for you? You were worried about your legacy, they've done a smear job on you. What is my task now? How do I handle the spectacle they are preparing? Do I just follow their script, just read their lines? In your own way you were a tremendous rebel, Dad: portraying Mister Solid Pillar of the Community while doing your own strong, private Don Juan outlaw thing.

It had never been my custom to sit down in Franklin Square. I surprised myself by flopping down on a bench. With the skid row 'Tenderloin' as a backdrop the trees and lawns in this square seemed like plastic artificial props, the park a spoofing diorama of depleted nature. When I was hanging out with the gang from Buttonwood Street several times we drifted up here to play football on the grass, instead of the concrete in Paxton schoolyard. The park guard ran us off, preserving the grass, I guess, for esthetic considerations. His other duty was to harass the bums, hobos, vagrants, winos, and derelicts occupying these benches. They are allowed to sit or slump low, but if they try to sprawl or stretch out flat the guard comes rushing out of his bunker, chases them off with his billy club. Jeez, what a mean and lousy job. What can the man possibly talk about to his wife at night? 'Today, honey, I ran off fifteen of the scabby- nosed dregs. The low lifes actually had the audacity to try to take a nap in my park.'

Four blocks north of where they read off that declaration about all men being equal, in this year of our lord, 1950, it is a humdrum day. Down by Vine Street the winos are lining up for their afternoon bowl of mush in front of the Sunday Morning Breakfast Association. Traffic is pouring across the bridge to Jersey, passing the big yellow sign over the Whitman Chocolate Plant. The none-too-bright Dodos from around our neighborhood consider themselves lucky to get a job in that factory; they punch in, and are never heard from again.

If all men are created equal, why are the winos lining up for their mush over there while the fatcats are enjoying their cigars in Rittenhouse Square? Two years back, pretty girls strolling by, squirrels begging for nuts in Rittenhouse Square, me reading "The Mucker,' I never imagined I'd find myself on a bench in Franklin Square, and making a big mistake by bringing out my pack of Luckies. Four shabby, poorly attired gentlemen by the gushing fountain instantly stirred, were hurrying my way, evincing socialistic inclinations, signaling that they wanted to share in the bounty. Serves me right, I knew better than to do this.

Scrounges mooched four smokes from me before I escaped from Franklin Square. Nothing was happening, this will be a long day, minutes seeming like hours, then you wonder where the time went. In the drugstore at Sixth and Callowhill I used up all my nickels calling headquarters and different police stations, then the morgue, trying to find out where they were storing Dad's body. Who? What? A huge run-around, nobody seemed to know, care. I also suspected I was hearing lots of lies.

Disgusted, I drifted over to Fifth Street, passed the SKF plant at Noble and the Baptist Church and wood cabinet factory at Buttonwood. Across the way York

Avenue was a fairly forlorn cobbled side street to be called an Avenue. It had the Russian Orthodox Church; next to the church was Roses Ivanovich's dinky pink Hansel and Gretel cottage. Naturally, I must think of Karl, unreceived birthday presents. Knocky, where are you, man? Karl, what's happening? What the fuck happened to my right and left flanks. Where is the life that once I lead?

York Avenue was instrumental in creating the miniature triangular park at Fifth and Spring Garden. It contains the pigeon-stained bronzed statue commemorating the World War One infantryman holding high his rifle and bayonet over a plaque listing all the brave doughboys from this area who died fighting over in France. Dad had been part of a committee hoping to erect another statue honoring the G.I.'s killed in World War Two. That idea never got far. I lit up a smoke in honor of Dad's project, and examined the plaque: inscriptions so worn, rusting, and weather-beaten you could hardly make out the names of the fallen. Was that a Joe McGurk, an Isidore something or other? Provincial inhabitants of tabloid territory vanish in the rust. Every twenty years or so they march off to die on foreign Fields. In Flanders Field the Poppies grow, now they will grow in Korea but we will smoke the poppies. Yet I found this rusting plaque to be sending a soothing and comforting message of 'No big deal, Burris, all your troubles, kid. Everybody dies. This, too, shall pass.'

Nothing has passed for me yet; my wounds are still bleeding. I thought about crossing over to the Diner but saw Betty and regulars from Gold's bar at the counter. I needed a coffee but if I drop in there well wishers will offer me consolation and stilted condolences, well-meaning people will say, "I know how you feel, Paul."

No, you don't. Nobody knows how I feel. I'm not even sure myself, yet. I drifted toward the Third and Brown poolroom. On a normal day about now I'd be entering my Spanish class, conducted by Doctor Del, a stern, authoritarian pedagogue of the Old School, a legend in his own mind, believing that he is a magnificent instructor, while teaching Spanish as if it were a dead language, ancient Greek, or classical Latin, he really doesn't much care if his students are subsequently unable to order a taco in Tijuana as long as they are up to snuff on the subjunctives. Del especially dislikes guys like me, vivarachos who can actually speak Español, I'm picking up the lingo from Marshall Street, Xavier Cugat records, and Mexican Ranchera films at the

Ruby. Which shows which shows what a frivolous tonto I am, worrying about pendejadas, babosadas, and estupideces on a day where I cannot even locate my father's cadaver. Mi padre está muerto y no sé donde tienen guardado su cadaver.

No grammar drills and subjunctive today, I'm climbing the back stairs to the Third and Brown billiards parlor, a joint near the waterfront that makes Dave's seem like the Ritz-Carlton. Clientele here are stevedores from the Steel Gang, and bullshitting ex-seamen, rickety old rummies still bragging about the cheap rugs they bought in Istanbul and the virgins they deflowered in Algiers. But no hustlers patronize this dump. Hustlers would not make it past the first dark alley.

As I reached the second floor I was hit by the comforting stench of stale cigar smoke and the music of clicking cue balls. From behind the cash register, Mike, the manager, did a double take at the sight of me, implicitly asking what the hell was I doing here when I should be elsewhere, lighting candles, engaged in reverential activities. Mike waddled over to touch my shoulder, and used the tone reserved for funerals to say, "There's nothing to say, Little Doc. I was destroyed to hear about your Dad. Big Doc was something special. But, what's there to say."

"Nothing. But people will say it anyway."

"Yeah, that's all we were talking about all day. What they did to your father and the shootings down on Snyder Avenue, the Dagos going at it hot and heavy, and the word is already out on the street, Paulie."

"What word?"

"Ah, it's tough for me to talk about it, but that was no suicide, kid. There was no way your father could ever go home. Not with what he knew. And, certain parties in there, for their own reasons, they went along with it."

"You know that for sure, Mike?"

The manager shrugged, and said, "Kid, on a deal like this you could have ten eye witnesses swearing on ten stacks of bibles, and you'd still never know for sure what truly happened. Mahann was in here earlier. I asked him, all he said was that he taking his early retirement from the Force, hanging up his jock, said he couldn't handle the underhanded stuff anymore."

Mahann? I suppose I should be deeply touched by his early retirement.

"Want a Coke or a coffee, or something?" Mike asked.

"Nah, I'm okay. I just thought I'd run a few racks, get my mind off things."

"Good idea," Mike agreed." I won't be chalking up any time on the blackboard. Shoot a few racks, and get your mind off things."

"Thanks, Mike."

Fringe benefits. For one dead father you get free newspapers and free time in the pool hall. I headed to a table in the rear, chalked up, began banging balls around. Nothing dropped. Some days nothing will go in. I was off, missing shots that were normally duck soup for me, like Knocky was, off that afternoon in the schoolyard. The main thing I had to concentrate on was not feeing sorry for myself, none of that poor Paulie crap. I hate the saps that suck up sympathy.

The afternoon news on the fuzzy TV behind the counter showed shots of patrol cars tearing down Snyder Avenue; the announcer was talking about the police informant, Vic Bastiano, ongoing controversies over the death of the mob physician, Doctor Daniel Burris. Like waiting for the other shoe to drop. Mutt and Jeff, Abbot and Costello, Laurel and Hardy, Alphonse and Gaston, Bastiano and Burris, their names will be forever linked. Though, nowadays, forever last maybe three weeks.

From behind the cash register Mike could not help but glance my way at the mention of Dad's name. He tried to fake it but this was the way it would be from now on. I must learn to live with my scruffy notoriety and adversity: words of wisdom from an Occidental fortune cooky.

My pool shot was off, my mind seized by infantile phantasies about heading down to South Philly, taking up a position as a sniper on an adjacent roof, peering through my sight, and picking off the capos as they came out of the church. This was puerile Walter Mitty bullshit, hardly me. I'm not even handy with my mitts, why am I dreaming of being a half-baked Avenging Angel. Bang! Bang! What?

Sibronsky and Joe the Worm came through the side door. They lived confined, circumscribed existences: the Diner, Go d's bar, this poolroom. I braced for crass-ness. They were approaching with the woeful expressions of mourners and this pair was not especially known for their dainty and and exquisite refinement. They both shook my hand, gave me manly pats on the back, it sounded like a chorus as both told me how sorry they were.

"Thanks a lot, you guys, " I said.

"I'll really miss your father," Sibronsky said. "Big Doc had a great sense of humor. He musta' cleaned up three cases of the clap for me, and the last time I was in his office he said the next time I came in there dripping, he'd cut it off on me."

"That's the way he was," I agreed. "Great sense of humor."

We were already into the myth-making process. Dad was not a funny man.

"There gonna' get Bastiano, " Joe the Worm assured me. "The Feds can hide that slime ball snitch out at the North Pole but the South Philly Wops will get his ass before he ever gets to a trial. The Mob will never let that fucker shoot his mouth off."

"Yes, that would be appreciated, " I said.

"We couldn't believe it, Friday night," Sibronsky said. "When Dick Jardine burst into Gold's, babbling about how Big Doc had been taken in. I mean, man, fucking unbelievable, like hearing that Eleanor Roosevelt was picked up for street walking."

No, I could not see her pulling tricks, either. I did not want to continue this conversation; so far I had escaped unscathed. Joe continued blabbing away about all the grizzly things the Mob would do to Bastiano and his cohorts, that was okay, acceptable. Then Sibronsky said, "It aint gonna' be the same without Big Doc around. He was a man you could trust; you could confide in him, tell him your troubles, he would give you the shot you needed. In Gold's and the Diner, it's been Big Doc we've been talking about since the shit hit the fan Friday. "

"Yeah," Joe the Worm said. " Some were saying that it's awful, disgusting, and how down in he dumps you must be but there were also dinks clucking about the big money, and insinuating that you are one lucky kid. "

"Lucky?" I spluttered.

"Sure." Joe said. "It's sad, and terrible for you, but on the other hand, look at it this way: you're kind of in the money now, Little Doc."

It had not yet occurred to me that there was an upside.

Joe touched my shoulder, and said, "You're probably still out of it, on cloud six, but in the Diner guys were saying, 'you're one lucky kid.' I mean, you aint even seventeen yet, and how many sixteen year old kids are suddenly rich, big house, beach front property down the shore, real estate in Florida, all your old man's loot coming to you, and with nobody around to ride your ass. Everybody knew Big Doc had a busy practice, but if all that crap in the papers about him being the sawbones of the Mob, is true, man, he must have had bigger moolah than we ever imagined. Cheez, you've got the world by the balls now. With all the big bread you've got coming your way next year you could be driving your Cadillac down the streets of Paris, France, Little Doc."

Sibronsky said, " Yeah, after the funeral, and all that stuff is over, drop by Gold's and we'll buy you a drink, Paulie."

"What the fuck do you mean, we will buy him a drink?" Joe the Worm snapped. "With all the fucking money he's gonna inherit, he can buy us the drinks, man."

I finally found out why Joe had acquired his nickname.

Later, drifting along the docks, I wondered if I were supposed to dance a jig, do a high-stepping kicking routine from the Rockettes line, sing, 'We're in the Money, I'm the man who broke the bank at Monte Carlo.' I'd been so occupied feeling sorry for myself it had not occurred to me to think in terms of dinero coming my way. I had read that too Easy Money was a curse; it was a major catastrophe to win the Irish Sweepstakes, winning the prize a prelude to horrid calamities. My windfall already stank of sulfur, already spooked, cursed, tainted, the treasure you do not dare remove from the Egyptian tomb. Workers were always getting scalded and maimed in the mint. On every dollar that might come my way I'd not be seeing George Washington but the image of Dan Burris hanging from a pipe. I still had a knot in my guts from that chat with Sibronsky and Joe the Worm. Their jaws were dry but I'd not seen such envious drooling since the Demetrescu sisters entered Knocky's house with the old geezer.

Speaking of Knocky, there was the alley with the hallowed trashcan where Rita parked her butt and initiated me into the joys of sex. Actually, batting it out with Naomi was more fun than that but you can't confess stuff like that to your buddies.

The subway rumbled by on the overhead-elevated tracks, I stared at Camden across the river; Philly's corrupt, stunted, and slightly retarded little brother. Why was I worrying about geography when I should be concentrating on how to put the pieces back together? Humpty-dumpty had a great fall.

"What do I do, Old Man River?" I asked the Delaware. The river was brown, rather than blue, polluted, contaminated, stinky, they have plans to clean it up. "What do I do, Old man River? You're not the Mississippi but over there by the wharf is the secret niche where I hid out to read my books, Point Counter Point, Ben Hur, Brave New World, Eyeless in Gaza, After Many a Summer, All Quiet on the Western Front, Siddhartha, absorbed while freighters sailed away to distant places, hundreds of books I consumed in that Sanctuary, half of me is Sixth and Poplar, Marshall Street, the rest is those books. What do I do, Old man River? Send me words of wisdom from your depths, Gramps.

'Donate all your inheritance to charity, a foundation, in honor of your father. Then go to India, take vows of poverty, become a Trappist monk, work in a Belgian coal mine, become a taxi driver in New York."

'Wise guy, that aint me; that sounds more like Larry in 'The Razor's Edge.'

Probably we tell ourselves what we'd like to hear. I drifted over to Second Street and entered Dirty Gertie's. Their coffee was rank but the café had a scruffy coziness, was a place where you found bosses from the upstairs offices at the same counter with uniformed janitors from the boiler room. Around me loud stevedores were arguing whether the Eagles could beat the Bears Sunday.

Dad disliked football, said that for a sport to be truly gipping it should be a paradigm capturing reality: in real life a man must do it all, confront all situations, play both offense and defense, no substitutions, you cannot bring in some Clyde off the bench to kick a field goal for you at the last minute.

After a second up of coffee I went to the phone booth, dropped my nickel into the slot, dialed the deli. This was for the off-hand chance that by now they knew where the police were storing Pop's body. I still wanted my private goodbye.

Paco, the counterman, answered the phone, when I said it was me, Paco groaned, "Ay, carajo! Que lios! Todos te estan buscando, Pablo. La maldita policia ha estado aqui cuatro veces preguntando por ti, y hablando mucha mierda por el radio."

"The police looking for me four times? Por que? "

"Tiene que ver con Carlos, Pablo. They are after Karl."

Coming on line, Moe groaned, "Paulie, is that you?" Unc had obviously snatched the phone away from Paco. He rasped, "Where the hell have you been, kid. We've been frantic with worry that you might do something crazy."

"I've been meandering around. Now I'm over by Second Street, calming down."

"You're calming down, everybody else is going nuts around here. Police were in here four times, searching for you. They had driven by Ethel's; she thought they had arrived to say they had fished your body out of the river because you had wandered off with a strange look on your face this morning, and you didn't come back for the lunch she prepared after swearing you'd be back."

"Yeah, I'm funny that way, Unc."

"The cops think you're hiding out. They don't believe me when I say you're a moony kid who drove your father nuts with your vanishing acts. Meanwhile, they demand to talk to talk to you because you're accused of being Karl's accomplice."

"Oh, Jeez. Accomplice to what?"

"The Blooms have gone batty. That rotten Meshuganah Bloom has accused Karl not only of kidnapping his daughter but also influencing her to steal money from the cash register in the store, and cash from their safe in the cellar. The Blooms accuse you of being his partner in these crimes; they say you know where the kids have fled. The cops know that's mostly bull but they still have to question you. Mahann was apologetic but he said that's the way it is, they need to talk to you. "

I had nothing I wished to say. Would the cops take 'no comment' for an answer? The coin dropped, Moe groaned," Don't hang up on me, kid. I've good news, too. "

"Good news?"

I dropped another coin into the slot, and Moe assured me, "Good news. The cemetery has relented. Rabbi Green came out with the opinion that since there are lingering doubts as to whether it was really a suicide, they will give Daniel the benefit of the doubt. Two other rabbis have consented to conducting a service at the funeral home, and later at the cemetery. Tomorrow. Kinahera, your father will have a proper funeral and proper burial."

The benefit of the doubt; and, that was the good news?

Troubled by my silence, Moe asked," You still there, Kid?"

"Yes, I'm still here, tentatively."

"It was touch and go, all the way, the FBI still wanted to delay the funeral, insisting on their own autopsy, it became a political football. Then your Uncle Jonathan got into the act, used his political clout, got on the horn with the mayor, and Muckety-mucks he knows in Washington. He warned those Faigeles that there could be severe consequences in next year's elections if the religious vote is ignored, repercussions in South Philly, Logan, Strawberry Mansion, Oak Lane, and Oxford Circle. That turned the Faigeles around. Tomorrow you'll have to give a special thanks to your Uncle Jonathan."

"Jonathan? What Uncle Jonathan? "

"Dan's brother. Your Uncle Jonathan."

Out of nowhere people come crawling out of the woodwork. Suddenly, I got me an Uncle Jonathan.

"So you're coming right home, Paulie? Or, if you like, I'll grab a taxi and pick you up. Then we'll call the police , and tell them you're coming in voluntarily."

"Hold your horses Unc. I'll be there by and by."

"Paulie," he pleaded, but I clicked off.

CHAPTER EIGHTEEN

That evening I wore my dark glasses when Moe escorted me to the Buttonwood Street station. The cops kindly sent a red car to pick us up, so we saved on the taxi fare. Last time I wore these specs was at the Dell, to hide the florid shiner Gans gave me, the night Dmitri was shot, I wore them again for Dmitri's funeral. I was seeing things through a glass, darkly. Who wrote that? I believe it was John Donne, I'll check it out. For the funeral tomorrow I will wear these specs as shields, not to be stylish, just to ward off the probing eye picking me apart.

When we reached the station Darmopray and Milton Soll jumped up from the bench by the Sergeant's desk, charging at me, both of them babbling that they were uniquely qualified and better equipped to protect my rights. Darmopray grabbed my shoulders and burbled "Paulie, you know I've been your Dad's attorney for thirty years, handling all of his personal and legal problems, estate and financial matters. Dan and I go back a long way. I know Dan would certainly prefer me to be handling all your affairs, too. I've been practically part of the family, an Uncle to you."

My family is growing by leaps and bounds, new uncles all over the map. Milt Soll shouted, "Get your hands off the boy, you Schlemiel, I'll have you disbarred for molesting a minor. You know that you're a hopeless hack when it came to criminal matters, you have zero expertise in the field of criminal law."

Shakespeare came to mind, ' A plague on both your houses.' I thought that these two adults should spare my tender sensitivities but Moe and I watched a braying match with the adversaries bumping puny chests and accusing each other of being unprincipled shysters, both threatening to lodge complaints to the Ethics Committee of the Bar Association. It appeared that the flabby butterballs would actually get phys-ical, start swinging their brief cases at each other's heads. They resembled bellicose Bubbas on Marshall Street in a tug of war, about to do battle with their leather shopping bags after reaching for the same cantaloupe on the fruit stand.

The desk sergeant was rising to intervene. Other cops in the lobby were amused bystanders, glad to see a free show. Captain Mulroney emerged from his office and spoiled the fun by stepping in, and announcing, " That's enough. Fight nice, children, or we'll send you to the cooler. "

It unnerves me when professionals, teachers, coaches, figures with clout and authority, supposed to have breeding, class, decorum, act like shits. Moe showed that he was no Shmo; he ordered both lawyers to stand down, said that only he would accompany me into the Captain's office.

There was a stenographer in there, a psychologist, Mahann, and a lady from the child welfare agency. They were apologetic about subjecting me to an interrogation at such a painful moment in my life, then proceeded to do so. After perfunctory questions about Karl and Bloomy fleeing the coop they began asking about Dad, visitors to our home, what about Mrs. Carla Fiore, had Joe Spinelli ever been one of Dad's patients? Though my brain was fuzzy after sleepless nights I caught on that Mob Doc was the real target here, this piffle about Bloomy and Karl was a smoke screen. Moe picked up on that, slapped his palms to his knees, rose, and said, "Hold it up, that's enough. This boy is under a great deal of stress and pressure. You can talk to him in a few days, meanwhile the boy has to rest."

"We only have a few more questions for him," Captain Mulroney complained.

"Enough," Moe snapped. "In a few days you can talk to him while he has proper representation. His Uncle Jonathan will be here to protect his rights."

In the taxi back to Marshall street, I asked Moe," What was that crap about an Uncle Jonathan intervening? I want nothing to do with the man."

"Ah, I just said that to scare them off your case. He's a hotshot lawyer, lots of pull, it makes the cops nervous when they can't push you around."

Sara was waiting for us with a huge supper. To my disgust, I ate, and then was ready to collapse from exhaustion. Or thought I was. Upstairs, in spite of my weariness, I was painfully awake, worrying about my act tomorrow. Since we packed Dmitri off on his trip to eternity I'd been to five funerals. Dad, damn his slippery hide, hated funerals, sent me as his surrogate. They always ask if anybody wishes to say a few words over the departed. I will no doubt be asked to speak, was struggling to compose a speech in my mind. Curse my lewd, stupid, silly hide, why must I be such hapless birdbrain, hacking my way through thorny hedgerows of profane, vulgar, cruel jokes reserved for funerals. Instead of clean elevating words sickening jokes were swirling through my brain like demons rising from asphalt pits.

Dad, I'm sorry, man. You did your best but you raised a clown.

Out loud, I said, "Doctor Dan was..."

Already stilted, and off-key I never once called him 'Doctor Dan.' I was groping around in the dark, and all we have is words, only words, but every word in the language is defiled by use, we are working with soiled instruments. If forced to speak tomorrow maybe I will pull a Sampson, an outrageous breach of the protocols, topple the pillars, bring the entire hokey production crashing down by telling them that Dan Burris wanted no ceremonies, pomp, no circumstance, the man believed that grave-yards are temples of vanity, even modest stones were arrant pyramids.

When the cockadoodling of the roosters woke me at dawn a new dark suit was spread out on the sofa. Klein's must be running a special: white shirt, dark tie, the complete ensemble of going-to-a-funeral togs. I showered and the aroma of fried potatoes reached me, Sara was whipping up a batch of her super spuds mixed with crispy onions and hot peppers. I soaped again for a second cleansing, needed to shed the stink from the police station. That was sleazy of the cops to try to grill me about Dad, using the flight of Karl and Bloomy as the pretext. That will forever be a mystery to me; had Karl gone with the purest of intentions to light a candle at Saint Pete's, or did he already have a pact with Bloomy? I visualized them as dusty waifs with their thumbs out on Route Sixty-Six. A light snow is falling in this image.

Sizzling noises were coming from the kitchen when I went down for breakfast. Moe was in his gray pinstripe reserved for the high holidays and burials, not his natural outfit. Catching Moe in a suit was like spotting a military officer you are accustomed to seeing in uniform with medals, and shoulder boards, vacationing in a Hawaiian shirt and Bermuda shorts. The morning papers were spread over the dining room table. Moe looked up and said, "Morning, Paulie. You sleep okay, kid?"

"No problem," I said. Who wants to hear my whole weather report?

"Don't read the papers this morning," Moe said. " It's nauseating how they dig up old slop and get it all back asswards, add two and two, out comes twenty-two."

"Actually, I had not planned on reading the papers this morning, Unc. "

"They got it all faschimalt mixed-up here. They tie together Vic Bastiano and the Mob, the shootings on Snyder Avenue, and connect that with Roy Bauer's body in the Reading garbage dump, and Alexi once living in your house, and your father was once seen in Arthur's Steak House with Trixie Malloy, so he must have been in cahoots with the Cosmo Five, and maybe even planned the screwed-up burglary on the Main Line. To them it 's crystal clear, case solved."

Why had he told me not to read the papers this morning if he was insisting on giving me a full Presidential press briefing? I wanted to hear no o crap today. Could this day not be, please, set aside, reserved for the reverential?

Shunting the papers aside, Moe growled, "In the Inquirer there's controversy, critics are complaining about the lack of an in-depth autopsy before the funeral, and claiming this is a transparent cover up, there is politics involved."

In-depth autopsy? Without trying, Moe really knew how to hurt a guy

"That's enough already," Sara called out from the kitchen. " Enough to burden the boy with." She came bursting into the dining room with a gorgeously depressing tray of goodies: fluffy scrambled eggs, pyramids of crispy home fries, Danish pasties, onion rolls, and a fruit salad featuring strawberries, totally out of season.

I held up my hands in self-defense, and Sara exclaimed," You look so handsome in your new suit, Paulie. But you're going to take those dark glasses off, later, no""

"Maybe later." I conceded."

After serving us heaping portions Sara plunked down at the table, announcing, "It's going to be a wonderful funeral, Paulie, such a response, you wouldn't believe it. So many people want to speak over the casket: patients, colleagues from the hospital, supporters, and aside from the rabbis who will officiate, Father Conlan from Saint Peter's and the Pastor from the Baptist church at Randolph and Buttonwood, a priest from the Rumanian church at Fourth and Brown, they have all asked for permission to say a few words and add a prayer."

Snide remarks occurred to me: 'Have you checked with the mosques to see whether they will send an Imam over?" But, I was swearing off my snotty Shtick today. Sara gushed on about how splendid the funeral would be. Originally, the plan was to invite the mourners over for the traditional nosh after the cemetery to Aunt Fanny's home on Thirty-Third Street, Fanny has that huge parlor to accommodate guests, but so many people had called saying they would show up Uncle Burt changed the plan. Out of his own pocket he had arranged to rent the basement recreation hall in Sixth and Green synagogue for the reception.

Last time I was in that hall was for a charity bazaar, where they had Baccarat, blackjack, and craps tables, and miniature roulette wheels. The cops dropped by but said nothing, as per their practice of not messing with the bingos of the Nuns in the church basements.

"Shelling out dough like that is out of character for Burt," Moe said. "Can you imagine how many cobwebs he broke on his wallet?"

Sara shushed her husband and said, "Better Paulie should imagine how many distinguished figures have offered to be pall bearers. For doing the picking and the choosing, I'm making so many enemies. The other wonderful news, Paulie, for the reception Moe and I were intending to a send over loads of food from the Deli. Out of nowhere, Himmelstein's calls. Without ever being asked, in honor of Doctor Dan, all he has done for the community, Himmelstein's will cater the entire affair, hot and cold food. For free. No charge. They said it was the least they could do."

"A tax write-off," Moe said. " They'll probably deduct double of what is sent."

The worst of it was, Moe and Sara meant well, were doing their best in a trying situation. Or maybe that was not the worst of it: knowing how my mind works, the implacable machinery of my associations, when I remember this wretched day the equation will always read funeral equals Himmelstein's equals gangbang.

As we were about to head downstairs the phone rang. It was Ethel on the line to say that she was already uptown at the chapel, viewing the body, an immense crowd was gathering, we'd never believe the amount of flowers pouring into the chapel, she was sorry, we should please grab a taxi. Max and Ethel had promised to pick us up at the deli and drive us uptown. This was a betrayal, necessitating a quick change of plans. It is wrenching and discombobulating when suddenly the plan changes. As we passed through the deli Moe told Paco to mind the fort today, he was in charge. Then we hurried up Marshall, waving pack to vendors and neighbors waving to us, grabbed a taxi at the Girard Avenue cab stand while Sara continued to grumble and kvetch about her sister. "We could even be late for the prayers and the speeches. I'll kill Ethel if we're late."

"What late?" Moe said." Nothing important can happen till Paul arrives. He is like, if I may say it, pardon my French, Paulie is the main attraction at this ceremony."

I'd not quite thought of it in that fashion but I finally get to overshadow Dad. After they check out the casket, eyes will turn to me. The figure in the coffin becomes a prop, a Magoffin, a mere detail; I will be center rink.

"She will see," Sara said, ominously. "The next time she calls, the next time Ethel needs something desperately from me, she will see how quickly I come running."

"Ah, let it go," Moe said." Today should not be a day for petty thoughts and spites. Today should be a day for large thoughts and real sentiments. Even though I know that Dan did not hold me in the highest of regards, I was hardly the kind of relative he could proudly introduce to his high and mighty bridge partners, I still had a great admiration for Daniel, and he is no longer with us."

Except for the limp euphemism tacked on the end that was a fairly articulate statement from Moe. Cancel that thought, Burris. No more gratuitous sotto voce put-downs of Moe and Sara, that was too much like shooting gefilte fish in a barrel.

"I am trying to contemplate holy and elevated things but the next time my sister calls she will get an earful from me, " Sara said. "Ethel will get a piece of my mind."

I had to censor sarcastic thoughts about not giving away pieces of your mind if you do not have much to spare. Last night, trying to draft my speech, I became snarled up in the question of clichés and shopworn set formulations prevailing on these occasions. Was it my duty to break the mold? I could think of no anecdotes I cared to share with strangers, nothing catchy for public consumption, certainly no bon mots. I would probably come off as a real stumblebum dunderhead today.

For Broad Street this was just one more normal Wednesday afternoon, traffic flowing, buyers buying, sellers selling, the usual dogs peeing on their regular fire plugs. The only difference, my father awaiting us in the chapel will not hear the results of the Eagles Game on Sunday. Not that he had any interest in football but Dad tried to be a regular fellow, talking football with Knocky, Karl, and Me back when we were the rogue quartet. Could I use that as the opening line? 'Daniel Burris was a regular fellow?' Hardly. That would be chemically pure, unadulterated Bull; Dan was certainly not your run-of- the-mill regular fellow.

"One more wonderful thing, I forgot to tell you, "Sara said." Your Uncle Jonathan called. Of course he'll be at the funeral, with his wife, but, aside from that, he'd heard that poor people from around our way will be attending the services in the chapel but have no transportation to take them to the cemetery. So, out of the goodness of his heart, Jonathan Burris has chartered two buses to help out. Isn't that grand?"

The goodness of the heart is abetted by the thickness of a wallet.

"I'm not aware that I have any Uncle Jonathan. For me, no such creature exists."

"C'mon, Paul," Moe coaxed. "Today's a day for forgiving and forgetting. Give the man a break, he wants to be a part of your life."

Ech, this was sticky and icky, and also a bit late for that. I never quite swallowed the Dickens melodramas where previously unknown benefactors belatedly appear out of nowhere. It was also anti-aesthetic, a character popping in out of nowhere.

What do I do, Dad? Could your spirit still be hovering overhead because the Grim Reaper hasn't yet arrived to harvest you? You know my problem has always been that I see myself as the protagonist of novels not yet written, hero of movies not yet filmed. Today I cannot detect any thread of a plot. I am rudderless, without a script.

We reached Olney Avenue. To my left, a few blocks down, was Central, where I should be entering my Spanish class about now. Adios, Colegio Central, creo que no te voy a ver mas. I cannot see myself entering my homeroom next Monday, with all the Bees looking up in surprise. To my right, past the trolley depot, the Esquire movie house, where I had tugged at many a bra strap. Adios, lovely ladies of Logan, East, and West Oak Lane. We bid farewell to a bunch of depraved virgins, Myrna, Arlene, Anita, Sandy, Barbara, Elaine, Zelda, and Marlene Kay.

Next landmark is the Hot Shoppe, semi-deserted on a slow Wednesday afternoon. Strange local customs: Friday nights the Hot Shoppe seethes, packed cars arrive from all over the city, girls in duos, trios, and quartets to see, be seen, flirt, picked-up, or scorn rejected losers who approach them. Saturday nights, no girl would be caught dead in this place. It would mean she had no date.

Sorry, Dad, for frivolous ruminations but I'm in a wrap-up mode, can't get off this kick. I'm in the B.C. and the A.D of my life.

So far the cab driver had been respectfully mute, due to the address we gave him, and the tenor of the conversation he could not help but overhear, but as we passed the Hot Shoppe, pulled into viewing range of the chapel, the driver yelped, " Holy Shit! All that really going on? "

His yelp was in honor of the implausible spectacle, enough police around the funeral home to make it look like a convention, or at least a job action by the cops, and for chapels you expect sedate assemblages, this could the be starting time at a football stadium, crowds swarming around the buses, delivery trucks arriving with more floral wreaths, photographers snapping pictures. There were black limos parked across Broad that could only belong to mobsters or prelates and the chapel was surrounded by so many patrol cars, and mini-vans from the TV and radio stations it look like a besieged fortress.

Moe slapped his palm to his head and moaned, "My aching ass, Gib a teet. Just gib a teet. Look at what we're stepping into."

Sara muttered," it's already a circus already!"

Complete with unfunny clowns, Aside from the snarled traffic and throngs spilling over into the streets, there were shoving matches in the parking lot. The frenzy around the chapel was a pulsating parody of a Breughel Feast, Death rather than Food as the motif. We had to pull up short, at the corner.

The taxi driver surprised us by saying, "You folks haven't been listening to the radio. The cops were saying that because of the shootings down by Snyder Avenue, and bang-bang yesterday on Passyunk Avenue, they feared there could be violence here today. Because of who might show up from South Philly. "

A well-informed cabby, Moe said, "Thanks," paid the fare, with an extra large tip. I slipped out of the taxi to help Aunt Sara. Panting reporters came charging in our direction, not much collegiality, they were jockeying for position, elbowing their rivals, and jabbering, "Is that him? Is that the Son? Is that the boy?"

How did they know my secret? Of course: Me- boy. My uncles were hurrying over to rescue us. Flashbulbs were clicking, photographers calling on me do take off my dark glasses so they could get a clear shot of my face. One fatso reporter, he looked like an out-of -shape ex-linebacker, was bulling his way through the crush, and bellowing, "Press. Make way for the Press. Press. "

Uncle Burt stuck out his foot to trip him, and Burt snapped," Press my pants, you

Asshole goon. Get away from us. "

We were trapped in a vortex of butting, pushing, jostling bodies. Uncle Phil smashed through the crowd to join Uncle Burt in doing heavy duty blocking for us. As we broke free of the crunch Phil said out of the side of the mouth, "Crumby bastards. Wanna' go in and see your Dad now, Paulie?"

Churned through a cement mixer, gashed, scratched, my dark glasses knocked askew, I was inclined to kick these gentlemen of the press in the balls but all I said was, "Not yet, Unc. I'm heading up the corner, to have a smoke, if you don't mind. "

"Suit yourself. But no talking to these mother-humpers, give them nothing, Paul." Phil growled, then spun around throwing haymakers at the press corps to block their pursuit and facilitate my escape. They were threatening to sue him. Cops were watching this confrontation but yet making no move to intervene. I don't think the cops like reporters much. A few cops nodded to me, seeming to say that they were here for me.

Mourners, friends, neighbors, strangers, and Dad's patients were reaching out to touch my shoulder, I had to nod, and bow my head, before making it to the corner where I adjusted my glasses, and lit up. Phil caught up to me, spun around, raised a warning finger at the press trailing after us, warning them to back off.

"Shit, " Phil groaned," it's a nauseating carnival."

I could hardly disagree with him on that score, Meanwhile, I was doing my best to respond to greetings, waving back to Officer Mahann, practically unrecognizable. I'd never seen Mahann in civilian clothes before, as out of uniform as Moe. Across Broad Street, Mrs Carla Fiore was stepping out of the same Cadillac as Mrs. Maxine Barufkin. Dear Lord, when had those two hooked up? Had they been comparing notes on their old beau? Questions flitting through my mind while persistent reporters bombarded me with questions: Did I care to make a statement about my father's death? Had I ever met Roy Bauer? What was my opinion of Vic Bastiano? Was it true that my father had been raising two other boys in his home, and they'd both gone wrong, and were now in trouble with the law? Did I believe that my father's death was a murder or a suicide?

"Phil snarled," Will you bastards get the fuck away from us? He's just a kid. Why are you torturing this kid with your moronic questions on a day like this?"

I waved back to our handyman, waving at me. I'd never known Boris owned a suit. No more off-the-books job for our jack-of-all-trades. Dad, you have let lots of people down. Like Carmen, my wave took in the new nurse, out of a job so fast. The sweet, capable, competent woman had been with us only weeks but still felt impelled to make it to this farewell party.

Phil turned to me, asked, "Will you be okay? I need to go inside, straighten things out. The rabbis are arguing, everybody got their own ideas on how this operation should go, and who gets to shoot their mouths off over the coffin. I've never seen anything sacred so screwed up. C'mon in with me."

"I'll be all right here. Unc. You go in and organize things."

He patted me on the shoulder and said, "Okay, keep a stiff upper lip, and do not talk to these Mumsers. They're out to get you to stick your foot in it."

"They'll get nothing from me, " I assured Him.

With a disgusted toss of the head, Phil left, wind milling his arms menacingly to open a path through the crunch swarming around us. I lit up another smoke, heard clucking from bystanders disapproving of smoking on solemn occasions. Who asked them? A photographer quickly snapped a shot of my breach of protocol. I should smile; I'm on Candid Camera: a heavy contingent of photographers here, aside from pros from the papers and TV the cops had stooges snapping shots of the mobsters showing up, and there were volunteer amateurs present hoping to get lucky, make a fucking buck. They will be in luck if there is a shoot-out day, as per what the cabby said. The clicking continued. For the history books I will be the skinny sullen smoker in the dark specs. Reporters were still babbling questions at me: Had I ever met the stripper reputed to be one of my father's girlfriends, Trixie Malloy? Was it true that the high school basketball star, Alexi Ratchinov, was also missing, and believed to be in hiding with his fugitive family? Had my father ever discussed his underworld clientele with me?

Taxis and cars were arriving, familiar faces joining the assemblage: upper crust and patrician faces from the Robin Hood Dell and Academy of Music, tough faces from Dave's and the Third and Brown poolroom, plump Evas from the Roll Out the Barrel Dances at the Broadwood, Black faces from the Project, store keepers and peddlers from Marshall Street, Doctors, nurses, waitresses from the Oyster House, the Spring Garden Diner, so many familiar faces I half expected Dmitri to be standing behind Betty's shoulder.

Silence is a weapon that frustrates the sonsabitches. Infuriated by my silence, most of the reporters stalked off in search of gamier meat but a few stubborn hold-outs insisted on clawing at me with obnoxious questions: What were my feelings at the moment? Had my classmates in high school commented on my troubles? Did I know that Mister Bloom from Marshall Street had accused my Father and me in being complicit in he disappearance of his daughter?

Of course: Dan Burris massacred the Indians, and then killed off the Buffalos, besides those lynchings in Mississippi. Sideshows were taking place. Milt Soll and Darmopray were arguing in the parking lot, seemed like they might start bumping chests again. Their crass act reminded me of engravings Dad had in his library: French Eighteenth Century Cartoons satirizing all the professions, for the Law a merchant and peasant were fighting over a cow, the merchant was grabbing the ears, the peasant had the tail, and in between was the advocate, milking the cow.

By the lobby entrance rabbis were disputing which rite prevails today, Orthodox, Conservative Reformed, I'm not into the fine points of theology, will not go near such explosive stuff, it's a major mental struggle not to recall all the jokes about three Rabbis entering a saloon. Across the Street, Mrs. Jordan had slipped out of the Lincoln. She was with her Mister Braxton. After doing her best to harm Dad, was that nasty bitch here to pay her respects? I have sworn off humor for the occasion but could not help but remember the old Hollywood joke about a well-attended funeral for the much hated Mogul, mostly enemies showing up to certify that he was dead. Inappropriate, Burris. This large turnout shows how loved the old Boy was.

Cousins, I had them by the dozens, were arriving, waving to me. Idah, Myrna, Joel, Sydney, Michael, Joanna, etcetera, I suspect that they had a prior meeting to agree on terms on how to deal with difficult me. So many cousins, I didn't want to think about the Circus, Volkswagens arriving, twenty midgets disgorging, but the image came to mind. Boony Washington and Leroy Lincoln were slouching up the street. Nice of them to show up; I didn't want to be cynical like Moe over breakfast this morning, talking about Burt's wallet and tax write-offs, but it occurred to me that this was a school day, these two were delighted to skip classes.

Why is my mind so foul? Why, on this day of all days, could I not give the foulness a rest? I lit up another smoke. A first; I'd never before chain-smoked three cigs in a row. Flashbulbs clicked. I considered removing my dark glasses. For the record I will come off as the despicable duck-tailed smart-ass hiding behind dark specs though only fledgling South Philly Mafiosi can wear these shades with any degree of authenticity. I am not now, not have I ever been, a cool daddy.

The last of the reporters hovering around me left, snorting, "You know, you're pretty arrogant; you could at least have said, 'No comment,' to us, kid."

My only comment to him would have been 'fuck you' which I could not say at the moment. Uncle Burt was picking his way through the crowd. When matters drag on this long there is definitely a screw-up in the making. Burt reached me, and I asked, "What's holding up the proceedings, Unc?"

Burt groaned, " Too many cooks spoiling the soup, while nobody can decide who's in charge, Usually, it's the Funeral Parlor Director who's the behind the scenes Master of Ceremonies in these productions, but today everybody's sticking their two cents in, the list of candidates wishing to be speakers has become ridiculously long. One of the rabbis is objecting to priests participating. The Reba says a funeral where you consign a soul to eternity is not an ecumenical civic affair where you bring in the whole team of clergy to bless a new fire engine. So far, about the only thing we've agreed on is that you should be the last to speak, Paul. Incidentally, your Uncle Jonathan has been negotiating, he also insists on speaking."

"Oh, shit."

"Be careful, " Burt snapped.

"Of what?"

"You don't want to talk dirty on a day like today. But then, I am gathering that you are you violently against letting your Uncle Jonathan speak? "

Remembering that night in the lobby of the Academy of Music, the two brothers staring at each other, coldly, then going their separate ways, I suspected that Dad would have put his foot down. Just guessing. We will never know: the dead do not opine on a posteriori situations. And then, why should I continue ancient feuds? With a shrug, I said, "Why not? Sign him up. The more the merrier."

"Woof, that's some rotten attitude you've got there, kid, " Burt said.

"Right now, Unc, I do not give a flying flute if President Truman pops in to say a few words. Invite The Mayor and Archbishop. Roll out the barrel."

A sigh went up from the crowd in front of the chapel; in appreciation of the immense floral wreath being unloaded from a delivery truck, so outsized as to be offensive, with a red, white, and green banner indicating that it came from Sam Sacco and family. I did not know you were allowed to do promotional advertising on these occasions. Max and Phil were waving to Burt from the steps; they needed him for urgent consultations. Burt gave me a quick hug, and said, "Okay, I'll say it's okay with you. Good thinking. I'll be right back."

As Burt rushed off an affectionate arm slip around my waist, I thrashed in anger to fling the intrusive arm away, fortunately, caught myself in time. It was Miss Pearl. Flashbulbs clicked as she gave me a maternal hug and a kiss on the cheek. Good: there will be heart-warming human-interest stories for the early editions:

SLIM AUNT JEMIMA EMBRACES WHITE ORPHANED PICKANNINNY SHE RAISED

"This has been horrible, Paulie, " she whispered. "You okay, son?"

"No, but I'm handling it. How about yourself, dear?"

"I've been miserable. I loved that man. Times like this can make you believe in the devil and demons and curses, all kind of evil things."

"Moe said the cops finally let you into our house."

Her voice cracked as she said, "After I went by there five times, just wanting to do my cleaning, they finally let me in to bring my own things out. The cops took me downtown, asked me hateful questions about Doctor Dan. They could not believe the vile language was coming from a church-going woman like me when I answered them back, told them Doctor Dan was no saint but he did more good for more people in his life than the whole fucking Cracker police department of Philadelphia all put together."

For that beautiful answer I gave her a kiss, flashbulbs clicking as she hugged me and whispered, "Don't you go home yet, Paulie, until I've had a chance to clean the place up, straighten things out. The cops have been tearing everything apart, saying they're looking for evidence, the sonsabitches are looking for money."

Another whoop erupted from the crowd milling around the entrance. Sam Sacco had sent an enormous wreath but that was Sal Bonafaccio's black Cadillac parking across Broad Street. Cops were snapping to attention, I noted that at least ten of these ostensible mourners were plainclothesmen and detectives, and they were all packing, Photographers were scrambling to position themselves to get at Big Sal. Then there were sighs of disappointment from reporters as only minor henchmen, lead by Big Vinny Cannoli, Big Sal's main bodyguard, emerged from the Limo. Miss Pearl squeezed my wrist. Boony and Leroy were having trouble getting past the ushers; she had to hurry to the chapel entrance. I blew her a kiss, then saw my pack from Central coming up Broad Street: Jack Kraft, Steinberg, and Seymour the Simian. No Toll. I guess Howie was worried about missing an important chemistry exam. Billy Schmitz was approaching; in lieu of a suit Billy was wearing his jacket from the Wilmington Clippers. In this crowd huge muscular Billy looked like an alien athlete from a harsher galaxy dropping in on the twelve tribes of Israel.

Except for Knocky, Karl, and Bloomy, just about everybody I knew was showing up today. The chief absentee would be Rita. Last I heard she was still upstate but getting her act together, elected, 'Inmate of the Month' by her fellow felons.

Turning around I received another kiss on the cheek. This was from Mrs. Barufkin. She was with Mrs. Fiore. Handing me her card, she said, "Paul, I don't even want to imagine how horrible this has been for you, and we wont go into it now. Please give me a call next week. I'll have you over for dinner; I know how you must be feeling. I'll cook your favorite dinner with the brisket and garlic mashed potatoes."

"Thank, you Ma'am." Was that in another lifetime? It seemed impossible that Thursday she had cooked a turkey for us.

"You know I was crazy about you father." Mrs. Fiore said, handing me her card. "The minute you're feeling up to it, give me a call, Paulie, and I'll take you out for dinner." She sealed her promise with a kiss.

Dad's death was triggering an impromptu gastronomic festival. Comfort me with brisket and veal parmigiana. I'm an ingrate, so many people were doing cartwheels and being kind to me, I churlishly bristle at their attentions. I've been trying to ward off maudlin mawkishness today. The women held hands as they headed toward the chapel lobby. A curious pairing off: once they were competing fiercely for the affections of Big Doc.

Ushers were signaling from the steps for the audience to please enter, the show is about to begin. Vinny Cannoli was standing over me. Flashbulbs were clicking as he touched my sleeve and said, "They told me you are Paul Burris, the son. Mister Bonafaccio extends his sympathy, and condolences. Mister Sal said that he really liked your father and deeply regrets Doctor Dan's passing. He ordered me to give you his private card, and said that you should definitely give him a call next week, to his office, where we will see what we can do for you, Paul."

Reporters were scribbling away as Big Vinny handed me the card, So many cameras were clicking it sounded like the frenzied oratorio of crickets at nightfall

"Thank you, sir," I said, wondering what this card might entail: Blood money? Most in my family firmly believed it was the Mob that did Dad in. Or was it an offer of steady employment instead of straight cash? I wasn't suited for dockside stompings, possibly Big Sal could use me in his white collar scams, The cops were noting that Big Vinny was giving me the down country Sicilian style pat on the back. On the Chapel steps Uncle Phil shuddered, slapped his hands to his skull, horrified by the photos that might appear in tomorrow's papers: notorious hood paired with the Son of Mob Doc. In a town like Philly this could nail down your rep for life.

Well-wishers reached out to touch my shoulder and arm; I mushed along with the crowd shuffling toward the portals. My pack fell in beside me. Kraft, Seymour, and Steinberg nodded, saying it all; with buddies there is no need for windy speeches. They were in their school clothes, not suits, maybe cutting classes this afternoon, maybe they had received permission. The thing was, they were here.

Organ music was groaning as I entered the chapel lobby, sonorous morgue chords; the organ plays a big role at both weddings, and funerals. Pop was never a great fan of the Brandenburg Concerto. I spotted Uncle Burt sneaking a nip from his pocket flask, the poor Schicker could not wait till they served the alcoholic libations in the Sixth and Green basement. Fresh scuffles were taking place by the fire exit doors, burly ushers were blockading cameramen and TV technicians hoping to infiltrate and film these sacred proceedings. In the parking lot, Mob chauffeurs were tangling with the police lackeys snapping photos of their license plates.

The man waving to me from across the lobby looked more like my father than my father had lately, taller and stouter but the same Teutonic features, Uncle Jonathan, recently excavated and reactivated. The petite woman with him was exactly the wife he'd have, a comely, gray-haired matron reminding me of the lady rushing to kiss Alexi in front of Wanamaker's. My new aunt, whatever her name is.

Why do these apparitions insist on popping in, unsolicited, out of nowhere? I don't go mucking around in anybody else's story. I had nothing against him. I had nothing for him.

Uncle Jonathan waved again, flashing the smile used for greeting acquaintances at cocktail parties, necessarily toning it down due to the gravity of the occasion. His smile transmuted into a semi-reproachful pout as I signaled back might they kindly keep their distance, my dance card was filled for the moment. My new aunt scowled: they had been admiring a puppy in the pound, thinking of taking the stray mutt home with them, the ungrateful cur has snarled and bared his fangs. She managed to erase the scowl with a forced smile as I pincered my thumb and finger together to assure them I would eventually be over to chat with them, by and by.

That seemed to placate them but Uncle Jonathan is probably thinking, 'I lay out all that bread for two chartered buses, and don't even get an honorable mention?'

That moment in the Academy of Music Lobby was awful; two brothers staring at each other, in silence, then going their separate ways.

"You okay, man?" Jack Kraft asked.

"Super, I am being raked over the coals, but thanks for asking,"

Uncle Max took my elbow, hustled me into the line of mourners entering the chapel to view 'the Remains.' A busybody noodnick plunked a black yarmulke on my skull, and white yarmulkes on the skulls of my pack. I'm not sure how I came off, Kraft, Seymour, and Steinberg looked like they were suiting up for a disguise party. Kraft whistled at the massive overkill of floral wreaths inside this hall, whispered to me, "Nobody else better die today in the Delaware Valley today; all the flower shops must have run out of stock."

Muchas Flores, a full house, standing room only, powerful organ music, precisely what Dad wished to avoid, and, in spades, a send-off for a Capo de Tutti Capi.

Mrs. Jordan was toodalooing to me, trying to get my attention. She did not get it. Billy Schmitz waved to me. No more odd mugging jobs for Billy. With this turnout, they could have charged for tickets, premiums for scalpers. My aunts were beaming, thrilled, taking pride in having pulled off a 'wonderful' funeral, and the best was yet to come, a ceremony in the cemetery, and all the goodies from Himmelstein's awaiting us in the Sixth and Green basement.

Up ahead, by the pine casket, there were rumblings, protests, the ushers wanted a faster clip, they were noodging the mourners to speed matters up, several were dawdling up there, taking too long to view the 'remains.' The ushers want them to behave like respectful tourists in the Art Museum where each gets thirty seconds to admire the famous masterpiece on loan, and then must toddle along. Move on out, next, please. Productivity Efficiency; maybe we had rented this facility for only X number of hours; management has another cadaver scheduled to arrive today. You can get insensitive if you're too long on a job like this.

My buddies dropped out of the line, signaling that they did not necessarily care to view remains. I could dig that. They slipped into a pew on the second row, next to Boony Washington, Leroy Lincoln, and Miss Pearl.

With the stark strains of the Brandenburg Concerto blurring into the comforting strains of the New World Sympathy, I reached the casket. Why do weddings and funerals resemble all other weddings and funerals? I listened to the haunting, ever poignant 'Going Home ' melody. What's that, you say, eh? You are going somewhere, are you? This theme should be a touching tug at the heart strings, but played on these nerve-scratching pipe organs 'Going Home' made me think of Saturday afternoon double features, grade B westerns, shoot-outs, Gabby Hayes.

Not thoughts you care to entertain when you are looking down at your father in a pine box. Be it a murder or a suicide, they had done a job on the man, the mortician was a magician, had managed to eliminate visible traces of the strangulation, this was an impressive and distinguished corpse. For his journey outward they dressed Dad in his number one blue pinstripe suit with matching red and blue University of Pennsylvania tie. He would have been enraged. I recalled insignificant minutiae; Dad arguing with Mister Donovan in the Oyster House. They had attended a funeral for one of their poker partners; Donovan said it was a 'splendid funeral. Dad said, "Baloney, why the hell did they bury Murph in a perfectly fine suit some ragged Schlump in Franklin Square might have appreciated? It's a primitive, savage, pagan idiotic custom to plant a body beneath the earth as if the deceased were going off to an important job interview."

Dad was never one to mince his words, or am I already into the myth-making process? I hated to think of the critique he'd give this affair today.

An usher by the altar was shifting impatiently, from foot to foot, like he had to pee; he was conveying the message that I'm being discourteous here, lingering too long over the casket. No loitering permitted; move along, fellah. Another usher shushed him, with a 'Zei shtill." A third whispered, "That's the son, leave him be."

Right, I'm the son, so leave me be. There is one thought here I must not think. Dare not think. One question pending that I can discuss with no one.

As much as I knew him, I never knew this man. Maybe he wanted it that way.

I murmured an, "Adios, Dad, " turned around to find every eye in the chapel on me; I'd never been a center of attention like this before. Tears might have helped but I had none available for public consumption.

A conundrum, I'd never faced one before, hardly knew what a conundrum was, suddenly I was facing one. From all corners of this packed chapel mourners were inviting me to come over, sit with them: Mrs. Barufkin and Mrs. Fiore were waving hankies. Darmopray, why would that schmuck have the audacity to wave at me? My cousins were occupying two whole pews on the left; they were inviting me to join the kiddy brigade. The logical place for me to sit down was up front, my aunts and uncles were beckoning, expectantly, Die Ganze Mishpulcha, Phil, Burt, Max, Moe, Ethel, Fanny, Ros and Sara, but I froze in mid-step as I saw Jonathan and what's her name barging into the pew with them, taking seats, opening up a space, reserving it for me, next to them. Since when had these arriviste party crashers became charter members of the clan, taking over, getting to determine where I sit?

Bowing deferentially, ignoring gasps, and frowns of protest, I ducked into the pew with Miss Pearl. She had not been one of the competitors for the grand honor of my proximity but she surreptitiously squeezed my wrist. Her smile may have had a touch of the triumphant.

From the murmuring sweeping through the chapel I may have to later distribute leaflets explaining that I am not now nor have I ever been an Abolitionist, do-gooder, provocateur, activist, or outside agitator: this was not a political statement; this is private. Miss Pearl just happens to be the person taking care of Dad and me since I can remember, and the person in this world I currently most love. Aunt Sara, you are the close runner-up in this contest.

Rabbi Green will kick off these proceedings; he signaled to mourners still in line that they can view the remains later, then glanced at me, seeking my acquiescence, complicity, the okay to get this ball rolling. I nodded. I'm game.

The organ music ceased. Thank you, Lord. Music is the most beautiful creation of Mankind except when used as an instrument of torture. Rabbi Green tapped the microphone; three taps, sounding thunderous. Why am I such a Kvetch? I find electronic equipment to be off-putting at religious ceremonies. Medicine men should not come jitterbugging out there with RCA mikes, Except for coughs, sneezing, shuffling noises, the crowd in the chapel fell silent. The moment reminded me of olden days in elementary school, teacher opens the bible, instantly unruly squirming brats sit up straight, clasp their fingers together, put their feet under the desk, don seraphic and beatific expressions.

Silence, then a shock, grunts of surprise, ripples of protest, as the rabbi began his eulogy in Yiddish. Half the assemblage in here were Goys, pardon me, Gentiles, and of the Jews in this congregation probably most didn't speak Yiddish either. I could get by, from my German, and my stretches in the trenches on Marshall Street, but many beatific expressions were fading to blank, and puzzled. The uninitiated folks will need sub titles to catch this show.

Pointing lovingly, theatrically, at the pine box, Rabbi Green became the Hamlet of Second Avenue, eine richtege Maurice Evans, asking, rhetorically, "Daniel Menachem Ben Burris, who were you really? We want to know? Who were you, Daniel Menachem Ben Burris, when you were with us? What did we know of you?"

Across the aisle my aunts and uncles were telegraphing me messages to slip over, sit with them at the first opportunity. Burt, the most socially awkward member of the clan, was flagrantly pointing at Jonathan Burris, I should sit next to my new uncle. Miss Pearl squeezed my wrist, granting me permission to transfer over there if I so chose. I remained where I was. Dad had taken care of Miss Pearl in his will. She had ten years of salary coming to her at the upgraded rate that included the bonuses and increases for Karl and Knocky.

"Daniel Menachem Ben Burris, who were you really?" Rabbi Green asked for the fifth time. Then he proceeded to tell us, at least those of us who could understand him. It was hideously unfair of him to go exclusionary parochial Balkan ethnic on us. My buddies were staring up at the ceiling, as were Leroy and Boony, and half the mourners present. I was hearing about my father in a botched translation. He was a complicated man, a difficult man, a complex man, whatever his faults he had a huge heart. So far it was pure treacly boilerplate, Rabbi Green describing a generic 'one of my most unforgettable characters' from the Reader's Digest.

For a moment I was moved as the Rabbi offered recollections of the brave Doctor Dan during the Influenza epidemic after World War One, when many other physicians were shirking their duty, nowhere to be found, but young Doctor Dan fearlessly made house calls with his black leather bag to attend to the ill and dying. Back then it was a new black bag. Over the years that worn leather kit came to personify and symbolize Doctor Dan's loving nature, his devotion to healing, and dedication to the community.

That sanctified black leather bag again? The cliché had been beaten to death, had become the worn leather equivalent a peace pipe or Cigar Store Indian.

Hey, Rabbi, it was the same bag he carried to yank bullets out of wounded Baccagallups. When and if it became my turn to Hail Caesar should I disabuse the audience of this buttermilky, vitamin-deprived, condescending portrait, tell the congregation that Dan Burris was an immense iceberg; only a tenth of his tonnage was above the surface. You cannot pick a man apart and preserve only the choice tidbits. The Saint you are describing was also a hardnosed swinger and randy old goat. He enjoyed his food, liquor, poker and women; he relished exercising power, sending bruisers around to do little tasks for him. He liked hanging around with the bad guys, and he was comfortable with all of his hypocrisies and contradictions.

Rabbi Green was so moved by his own performance that he touched the back of his hand to his brow, and then said in English, "Let us rise, and pray. Please turn to page thirty-two in your hymnals. "

The congregation dutifully rose. My buddies were staring off into space; Boony and Leroy did not loo happy, either. Once I went with Karl to a mass at Saint Pete's to see what a mass was all about. Just like synagogue services, Simon says sit, and Simon says rise. Dad would have hated this. The man in that pine box was not a believer; he believed in the Mystery, the Mystery of Creation. And, what he believed hardly matters now. The saying in Spanish is that the old cock ends up getting his neck wrung by the crone in the kitchen. Likewise, the priests will sprinkle their incense on the cold hides of the agnostics.

Uncle Phil took advantage of the prayer recitation to slip over to my pew, whisper, "Paulie, we know you love your Miss Pearl, but you really should come over and take your place with the family. Especially sit next to your Uncle Jonathan, and Nora. They were talking to us, have big plans for you, talking about taking care of you, becoming your guardians, adopting you."

I rose. What impelled me, I'm not sure if it was the threat of my newly minted Uncle taking command of my life, or seeing who the next speaker was; the S.O.B, approaching the altar was our local ward heeler, Dubinsky, a loud-mouthed would-be Big Macher who was one of the most disliked customers entering Moe's Deli. Dad had detested this politician. Why this Genzil would horn in here was beyond me unless he was trying to drum up votes for his next rigged election. I finally understood Pop's maxim: funerals are never for the dead; funerals are for the living.

Miss Pearl gave me a puzzled squint when I kissed her brow, and whispered, "Goodbye, dear, be well." I motioned to my buddies to rise; Uncle Jonathan scowled, as if he had recently acquired scowling rights. No doubt I looked like a willful, distraught, nutty kid trudging up the aisle with my pack trailing after me, As indicated by the arched lashes, dropped jaws, and wall to wall shocked expressions in the pews, this is not done, but I had to get out of here. This was a bit more outrageous than leaving Ming's class, or the Jumbo movies, but leaving early is my modus operandi lately,

As I hurried through the lobby Uncle Phil was tugging at my elbow. It seemed he might even swing at me out on Broad Street. A black hearse was arriving. I suppose I was supposed to ride in that in the trip out to the cemetery. Another detail that bugs me; the fanciest vehicle most people will ever travel in pulls up a too late for them to enjoy it. Patrol cars, TV vans, reporters and photographers were still hanging on. The cabby had called the shot. What with the mobsters in attendance they were hoping for another shoot-out a la Snyder Avenue. Reporters recognized me, rushed over to pounce again while Uncle Phil blocked my path and shouted, "What's wrong with you? What's gotten into you, Paulie? "

"I need a smoke, Unc."

My buddies were pale, concerned. I seemed to be acting irrationally.

Eighty things I could have said, nothing I wanted these reporters to hear, nothing that Phil would have understood. I just hugged Phil around the shoulders and said," I love you, Unc. Goodbye. Please say goodbye to everybody for me, tell them I love them all, but I'm taking off for a while."

Phil grabbed me and groaned, "What kind of garbage is that? You can't walk out in the middle of your father's funeral. "

Again the cameras were clicking, reporters scribbling away.

I broke free of Phil's grip, said, " Say goodbye to the tribe for me, Unc. "

"Hold it up," Phil ordered me. "I'm going inside, I'll be back with all you uncles."

What was he going to do, bring a whole posse out to corral and hogtie me? I faded down Broad Street; my buddies hurried to catch up with me.

Steinberg asked, " What's the matter, Paulie? Was it too hard on you hearing all that praise they were heaping on your Dad?"

"He deserved that, and more, but there are still sixteen people wanting to shoot their mouths off. I'm not inclined to hear more yapping."

"So, what the hell you doing? " Seymour shouted. "You just can't walk out on a father's funeral. That's the grossest, most insane thing I've ever heard."

"It's not his funeral, it's their funeral; he will never know about it."

"Wow, you are really off right in the head right now," Seymour growled.

"You guys don't have to go back in there," I said. "Unless you want to. Thanks for coming, really. I'm taking off, taking a walk, a long walk. "

"You mean you're not going to the cemetery with the casket to bury your Dad?" Seymour yelped. "Or to the reception, afterwards?"

"Right. I am donating my share of the chopped liver and apple strudels to the needy who need it."

Steinberg said," You sure you're not sick? Even with those dark glasses on you're looking shaky, Paulie."

" I'll be all right but I had to get out of that place. So, thanks for showing up, you guys. Maybe I'll see you in school, Monday. Maybe not."

Jack Kraft asked, "Are you sure don't want us to tag along on this walk?"

 It was a kind offer but I did not want company on this walk. I'd also hate to sound like Greta Garbo complaining, 'I Vunt to be alone,' There are moments when words spoil things, only make them worse, there had been too many words today. Looking back over my shoulder I saw that Phil, Max, and Burt had come out of the chapel, were arguing with the cops, trying to persuade the cops it was their duty to zip down here and pick me up. I shook hands with Kraft, Seymour, Steinberg, and said, " Thanks for all the support, troops. I'll see you guys around."

 As I reached the corner Kraft called after me," Don't make that walk too long, Burris."

Jack knew something I did not know as yet. I hurried along, it was getting colder, so far it had been a bright, clear *'wonderful'* day for a funeral. The Hot Shoppe was virtually empty; otherwise it offended me that the passing parade on Broad Street was resolutely routine, no black birds, no ominous portents, background music. no somber dirge by Franz Waxman as I drift through the Valley of Desolation. I've failed to show a decent respect for the opinion of Mankind; assembled grievers will be appalled and flabbergasted by our sacrilegious flight, To myself, I said, "Sorry, Pop, I don't intend to spend the rest of my days driving over to Strawberry Mansion to play pinochle with the in-laws."

The gray skies answered back: "Good for you, boy. You show them."

That was most likely wishful thinking.

A patrol car was slowly trailing after me, hovering about half a block behind. I suppose that was to protect me, but I did not care for their protection, and ducked into the subway station at Olney. Protection also means control.

As I hopped onto the subway pulling out there was swirling not only in my brain but also in every atom, corpuscle fiber, and cell of my body. If I doze on this car might I wake up as a transformed unrecognizable creature for skipping out on my family, a rat, snake skunk, wart, worm, fink. Varmint, or that famous roach, you name it, but I had to get out of that bathetic movie starring me as a woebegone victim. Dad: the funeral was no longer about you.

Why did Mrs. Jordan show up? How dare she? How come a nobody politician like Dubinsky comes crawling out of the woodwork? It's a wonder that Mrs. Ratchinov and Trixie Malloy did not pop in. Uncle Jonathan suddenly wishes to adopt me? That was a mirthless circus with twenty sideshows.

Getting off at Girard I peered at the headlines in the cigar store window: gory stuff about South Philly, then, lower case, vultures still picking at the bones of Mob Doc. I never did find out if Mister Connors had a son to be humiliated back when his Daddy was the metropolitan laughing stock and punching bag of the month.

Drifting down Girard to the elevated tracks at Ninth, my atoms were swirling wildly again, change is a sickening sensation; we were becoming somebody else, had been enjoying a golden age, living it up brown in the Sixth Street Follies, while Golden Ages exist only in retrospect, beneficiaries waste them grousing about petty-ass crap, our insight of the day: Paradise exists mainly as Paradise Lost. Till Friday Night Paul Burris was leasing a cabin in Nirvana.

After the expulsion what happens? So far we have been the insidious carper lurking in the corner, getting our rocks by putting down the scene with corrosive comments on the foibles and flaws of everybody else. Now we may actually have to do something real, old buddy. Possibly fleeing the funeral was step one in becoming who the hell we really are.

Beyond the railroad tracks where trains no longer run, at Eighth and Girard is the family style Night Club. Knocky's Momma tried to latch onto a job as hatcheck girl. The manager wanted to put her on but had to turn her down, because his wife said that Shiksa was way too beautiful, you cannot have a home wrecker checking the hats of gullible bug-eyed hubbies. At Franklin Street is the Astor movies, I will miss the girls no longer discreetly tittering at our ribald wisecracks on Friday Nights. Gansky's luncheonette is to my left, I never really stiffed Rita on the malted mild shake but that is the way she will forever see it. Neighbors waved to me from inside the Ambassador dairy restaurant. Where Moe Tanner kicked Buddy Baer's ass, almost threw him through the plate glass window. Considering the many fistfights around here I enjoyed a pacific existence. Yeah, I had my periodic punch-outs with Sylvan Gans but he hardly qualified as an enemy, Sylvan was more of childhood malady, measles, mumps, acne, jerking off.

Business as usual on Marshall; banners stretch over the stalls advertising discounts, and pre-Christmas bargains. Is it possible to both love and hate the same place? Every corner, sign, and storefront evokes grainy newsreels of long ago fisticuffs, girls whooping in embarrassment when the winds lifted up their skirts. I love this cruddy spot on earth like a hunchback comes to love his hairy hump.

Hawaiian Jack was gimping into Dave's poolroom. Imagine what the gossip must have been like in that dump this week. Down Sixth Street there was no longer patrol cars by my house but tapes was still crisscrossing our front door, bringing to mind cobwebs in the cavern where the tarantulas lurk, bandages on a sore rump, a mark of shame, our public Scarlet Letter; Herein dwell Dregs.

Instead of drifting down Sixth I entered the back alley appearing on no map but dissecting our block, an uneven cobbled pathway between the rear yards of the town houses facing Sixth and Fifth. The sour smell of damp laundry mixed with the dank odors of trash cans. Soggy girdles and unmentionables dangle on clotheslines over barren gardens. Flanked by cinderblock and rickety wood fences, it is our Slumgullion Junction back here, a hodgepodge of shingled ticky-tacky additions, slumping tin sheds, sagging back porches, and cluttered garages; a ready made set for filming gang rumbles, merciless stompings. Taking into account how proper are the facades of the houses facing Fifth and Sixth Street, this festering tapeworm of a back alley is like a grand dame getting dolled up to attend a fancy Ball while wearing stained and ragged underwear.

Most of these tilting fences were adorned with rusty barbed wire. Other diligent homeowners opted for upraised nails and broken bottle chips in cement frosting to discourage uninvited gusts. Pop was content to have chicken wire sweetened by strands of the barbed to protect our rear yard. Since I did not foresee having much need for a dress suit in the near future I took off my jacket, smushed it into a ball, used the jacket to protect my hands as I leaped for the fence, tugged, scrambled upward, vaulted, and tumbled hard into our back yard.

My butt hurt, I was seeing the stars and shivering asterisks from landing on my funny bone, which is rarely funny. The Buick was missing; the cops must have sequestered it, *evidence,* to check for bloodstains. A pity, I had been considering using the Buick for my getaway, envisioning a shoot-out on the turnpike.

Finally the comets and zephyrs stopped dancing, I checked for other damages, my suit jacket was ripped, my left cheek bleeding, I had imagined that I toppled over this fence, unscathed, you rarely escape these drills unscathed. Pop had bandages and Iodine and Mercurochrome in his glass cabinet. Unless the cops sequestered those materials as '*evidence.*'

I congratulated myself, which I rarely do; all my push-ups and pull-ups had finally paid off. For that gymnastic feat of vaulting over the fence I rated an A. With prejudiced Mister Schneyer doing the judging I'd be lucky to get a B minus.

Apparently the Law had secured this back door from the inside, I used my keys to no avail, so I scrunched my jacket into a ball again and punched out panes of glass in the rear kitchen window, crawled in, over the green and yellow metal table where Miss Pearl ate her breakfast. Weird, spooky, eerie, I was creeping back into my own home as if I'm a sneak thief burglar; if I wanted to get literary, I was a phantom fliting back to the haunts of my past.

No cops were around, my house was simmering with faint creaking noises, falling plaster the pitter-patter insects or rats mixing with the beeping and rustling of the traffic out on Sixth. I stiffened at the sight of sickening devastation, furniture turned over, scattered around in the dining room and parlor, holes punched in the walls. The cops had done a better job of trashing my home than Roy Bauer did with that warren on Randolph Street.

I almost had a tear welling, it never quite dripped out; but it is odious how the sight of material destruction can produce as strong a reaction as the sight of a bleeding, physical wound. Miss Pearl must have cried when she came in here; she took care of this place as if it were the Taj Mahal and Buckingham Palace. Now it was a mess, potted plants smashed, dirt all over the rugs, parquet floors ripped up, straw was curling out of torn sofas, the marble slabs were cracked on our faux fireplace, shelves dismantled. Somewhere, over the rainbow, bluebirds crap on those below, cops were searching for *evidence,* or the Pot of Gold these cunning, rich Hebrews must have hidden, somewhere.

The waiting room was another scene of devastation. Could they really wreak all this havoc before the accused was officially charged? That made no sense. Who would hide ill-gotten lucre in a waiting room? In Dad's office the filing cabinets had been ransacked, were open, empty, his fading, curling anatomy charts were torn off the wall, I guess that would make Mrs. Jordan happy. Dad's framed certificates of merit, and diplomas, and degrees were scattered over his desk, ugly holes had been drilled in the discolored spaces where they once hung." That Loot and booty must be around here somewhere, Mack." Ut-oh, the shelf where his glass bowl of spent bullets was empty. The cops must have loved latching onto that incriminating item. "Hey, Zeke, we finally got the goods on the tricky sonofabitch!"

For old times sake I stepped on his antique scale with the balancing rod and metal doojiggers. Then it stung like hell when I sprinkled rubbing alcohol over the slash in my cheek. Pop would have probably wanted to knit a few stitches into this cut but I figure the hell with it, a day like this should leave us with a few mementos, and I can tell the ladies this scar comes from my dueling period at Heidelberg, I have my black belt in the sabre. The burning subsided and I dabbed on what was left of the red Mercurochrome. For a few seconds those stars danced again.

Expecting the worst, I headed upstairs. My trepidations had been inadequate. The shambles in Dad's suite made it look like they had gone easy on the first floor. Bookcases were wrenched loose from the library walls, floorboards ripped up; the medicine cabinet had been torn away from the bathroom wall. For the cops to dare to trash our home like this they must have been pretty sure they had Dan Burris by the balls, unless thee main carnage took place after Monday afternoon, when they were sure he was safely extinct. Or, maybe they did not give a damn, they were so anxious to find the coffers of gold in our grotto they figured they could handle the investigations and law suits later.

Three cigarettes remained in the pack of Luckies left on Pop's nightstand; a wonder the Law had not confiscated them as circumstantial *evidence.* I lit up one of the cigs Pop never got to smoke, then headed up to the third floor. We had received equal treatment up here, everything turned over, ransacked, torn apart, smashed, and scattered around. As a malicious parting shot, to tweak my nose if not my balls, the cops had discovered my treasured cache of pin-ups; spread the collection across my bed, the Betty Boops in tight lingerie, spicy covers of Planet Comics and Amazing Stories. "Yeah, we gotcha', kid."

I considered formulating a headline but screw that, we have left the journalism trade. Then I discovered the meaning of the word *chagrin.* I had never used it before but when I checked my night stand for the hidden envelope where I always kept a hundred dollars in cash as an emergency fund I found t only two twenties. Some scumbag minion of the Law had made off with sixty bucks. Or maybe I should thank the Sport for leaving me a forty-dollar nut to begin my voyage around the world. But. hey, the cocksucker took more than half, reminding me of the old joke about the Jewish saloonkeeper spying on the Irish bartender he suspected was ripping him off, opening the slot when he catches him slipping the entire five-dollar bill into his packer, and he says, "What's the matter, Ike? Aint we partners no more?"

Chagrin, may I never use that word again. After changing into Levis and a sweat-shirt I examined the luggage situation. There was my old valise from happier days at summer camp with lots of stencils of smiling bears and grinning foxes, too cute for current needs, I'd look like a real goofball trying to travel with this item. Next to it was the dinky cardboard suitcase Karl had shown up with as part of the Wronsky legacy. More promising was Knocky's blue and yellow team tote bag from Ben Franklin. Why not? From now on we will be winging it, flying under false colors.

After stuffing the tote bag with winter gear, long johns, dungarees, flannel shirts, my shaving kit, I checked around for items of value I might be forgetting, wavered, her image was branded into my brain, would go wherever I went, but then I slipped the mother of pearl framed portrait of Leonora into the bag. I might have kids one day who will want to know what grandma looked like. There she is, forever young and beautiful. I could almost here the Ink Spots singing, "Sentimental Me."

"Leonora, according to you sisters you were bossy, egotistical, self-centered, and manipulative. You sound like an interesting lady. A shame I never got to know you."

My voice in this empty house sounded like an unrecognizable echo in a void. All the sounds were grating and off-key. After putting on my heavy winter P-coat I clopped down the stairs, for the first time detecting faint hints of creeping noises. This place had always felt like an established fact, a solid, rooted, impenetrable castle; with a few pokes it has started dissolving, become like a collapsing thingama-bob no longer held together by thumb tacks, band aids, and chewing gum.

My idea had been to crawl back over the rear fence but I saw mail scattered all over the floor in our vestibule: letters, magazines, pushed through the low slot in the door. What does the Law say about your correspondence if you're being held for questioning but have not yet been formally indicted? Can they open your mail? I had not the foggiest? If I call Milt Soll he'll charge me by the hour. Or Darmopray might give me a heaper rate. I sank to my knees, began flipping through the accumulation, maybe hoping to find a check in here I could cash. According to Pop he was owed over seventy thousand dollars in bills he never collected during his long years of practice. One of those statistics of no use to nobody,

Medical journals I was tossing aside, bills to be paid, requests for charitable contributions, real estate prospectus from Florida, a reminder to renew a subscription, nothing too sexy in this pile. In my sloppy heart of hearts, grinding out pulp we can never say aloud I was hoping for something meaningful, symbolic, a gesture, sign, token, a dog at the feet of a slain hero, like a post card from Knocky, or a post card from Karl and Bloomy, saying 'you know what Big Doc always had to say about funerals, that he did not plan to even attend his own.'

Nope, there was nothing like that. If there are going to be any poetic or romantic gestures here, I will have to supply them.

I spotted our logbook open on the table by the waiting room door. There was Knocky's last entry, before he took off and went to see Gall. And Karl's last entry, Friday evening, will go to the 333 movies on Market Street, with friends, be back before midnight. And my last entry, Paul, a gathering in Logan, be back by One AM.

On a whim I picked up the pen, deciding to sign out one last time, one of those meaningless gestures that tie the loose threads of a story together. Even with no audience I strut on stage while I wrote my last entry in this log: "Paul, 4:00 PM, Wednesday, November 31, 1950. Destination: The South Seas."

Then, I surprised myself. Doing lots of that, lately. The idea had been to slip out through the back yard, instead I found myself opening the front door, kicking, flailing, thrashing, using my tote bag to smash my way through the tape sealing the entrance to my house, resistant, tough, and sticky tape, strips clinging to my Levis, face, and shoulder like spider webs, With all the struggling I had the sensation of being a wee chickadee, punching and clawing my way out of a yucky shell and yolk.

Or was that Yoke? And now there will be pooty-Kats out here to devour me.

Control yourself, Burris. Dad hated exposing emotions, displays of impotent rage. Just because you did not find any icky-poo bittersweet postcard is no reason to lather yourself into a public dither. Look at the way the drivers speeding down Sixth are gaping at your unseemly spectacle.

Peeling the last strips of yellow tape off my knees I drifted down Sixth, The Poplar Movie house, near the corner, was now the Second Bethel Baptist Church. Instead of the rumble of Russian tank battle we will now hear fervent hymns coming from this theatre. Why are movie houses turning into churches a sign of decay?

About now, up on Broad Street, they should have finished with the eulogies and prayers, the pall bearers should be carrying the coffin out to the hearse, perhaps there is an all points alarm out to retrieve this Prodigal Absalom, though some might be saying good riddance to bad rubbish. Like that stranger who decided to suddenly parachute into my life. What might my new Uncle Jonathan be thinking? "Daniel raised a neurotic, ungrateful cur!"

In the grayness of dusk neighbors were waving, mournful and respectful waves: Mister Freed, from the butter and egg store, the pharmacist from the drug store, Mister Shor, waving. Well, Dad had sent a lot of business his way. Knock it off, Burris. You're beginning to sound like Uncle Moe.

The protective cocoon of familiarity, are we leaving all this behind? Dear Philly-Cream Cheese? Scrapple? I puked the first and only time I ate scrapple. But no place else can you get a more succulent hoagie. Pat's, out in Strawberry Mansion, invented the cheese steak. As to sports, our teams will break your hearts: our fans are the surliest fans in the universe; they'd boo the Roman soldiers for not knowing how to drive nails in properly. Boxing–wise, we have the Philadelphia Decision, and the Philadelphia Bleeder. Our Police Force will break your head, our Mayors tend to be corrupt dimwits, we compensate for them with colorful string bands in the New Year's Mummer Parades. According to Hollywood no mouthpiece is slicker than a Philadelphia Shyster. We also export our prim school ma 'arms to civilize the beasts in the western boondocks. Stepping off those stagecoaches it is our Quaker Ladies who become hot numbers when they tame the well-slung gunslinger.

My hometown, the Fops live on the Main line, the Wops in South Philly. Also part of our rep: vets returning from the army say that drill sergeants in boot camp have a special hatred for this city. The barking Sarges claim that Philly produces the snidest smart-asses in the nation, Philly spawns the cocky wise guys whose butts they would most love to kick during basic training.

So we are not breaking any new ground here, not creating precedents; I am hardly unique and verge on being a prototype, possibly a standard product. In this blustery twilight Colored kids were still playing basketball in the Kearny yard, another bunch playing touch football with a wad of wrapped-up paper tied with strings as their ball. If you are really into the spirit of the thing you don't need genuine pigskin. Make believe is as real as it gets: forget the lack of uniforms, that is the rugged Eagles versus the Chicago Bears in this murky dusk.

At the corner of Fairmount I hesitated. The synagogue is further down Sixth, near Green, and a patrol car was parked there. Early arrivals for the reception were passing by the A and P store. They might spot me; attempt to buttonhole me into rejoining the festivities. Why call it a reception? The grim reaper receives the main morsel. I have no appetite to nosh delicacies in honor of my father's departure. "Will it be the luxion kugel or the latkes? For dessert would you care for one of the chocolate brownies or the apple strudel, Paul? "

Naturally recalling Dmitri's funeral, my need for an Alka Seltzer afterwards, I faded down Fairmount to Slovak Hall, then turned onto quirky Randolph, this street appearing and vanishing like a meandering underground river in the desert. You could buy a house damn cheap on this block if you did not mind the overwhelming stench of the horse manure. City Hall is talking about shutting down these stables; eventually they may get around to it. There are plans to expunge the Tenderloin, and upgrade or get rid of Marshall Street. Pity me.

Randolph shifts yards to the left at Green, and the Oyster House on the corner is, of course, shut down. This was the last two blocks for Randolph before it comes to a dead end at the empty lot on Buttonwood Street. This stretch from Green to Spring Garden had once been the Poles working in the quarry, Irish cops and firemen, the smells coming from the kitchens were of Mulligan stews and kielbasa, now you were hit by the aroma of tamales and arroz con pollo.

Across Spring Garden the Wronsky gas station had finally been demolished after lingering on for two years as a festering eyesore suppliers were using as a drop off spot for their local dealers. Booze was old hat. We had always had our contingent of hopheads puffing on their Maryjane, small time; drugs seem to be the next big thing.

Funny if this were remembered as the age of innocence I considered hitting the dinner for one last cup of coffee flavored with Auld Lang Syne but spotted a trio of the gang from Go-d's Bar at the counter, they might hit on me for a loan now that I am reputed to be heir to a hidden fortune and a wealthy young man about town.

Instead I passed through the mini-triangular park. They rarely mow the grass here, or scrape the guano off the bronzed infantryman holding his Garand on high. Since an *'ambulance'* picked Pop up at our famous last supper in the Oyster House thousands of soldiers have died in Korea, their names will not be added to the worn weather beaten plaque under the Infantryman as the city plans to eliminate this memorial park, and install this statue elsewhere. The wood cabinet factory, Baptist church, the Russian Orthodox Church, cobbled York Avenue, Berger's grocery store, everything I'm gazing at is scheduled to be demolished, gone with the bulldozers.

By now the burial rituals at the cemetery must be over, the caravan heading for the reception. Today we did not go to school, but the day has been instructive. So what has our dedicated scholar learned today?

Today, teacher, I learned that I find reporters, photographers, lawyers, priests, rabbis, cops and robbers to be obnoxious. It may be that I was not designed for this society. Also in doubt , do I really belong on this planet?

Tough shit, daddy-o; this is the only world you've got. You must deal with it, if only, tangentially; play it cool hover in orbit around the fringes. Besides, this world will soon vanish, anyway. Gone with the fumes.

Too early for the neon sign to be lit at the corner of Fourth and Noble: the dull plastic letters advertised the joint at Gold's Bar. When they drove by at night bemused drivers must have chuckled at the sight of Go-d's Bar. 'Step right in, Mister, for divinely celestial martini.'

My entrance raised eyebrows. Dick Jardine and Sibronsky were occupying a booth; Schatz and Eli were playing darts. Hymie Gold was polishing his shot glasses behind the bar. The TV was turned to the Roller Derby, brutal looking broads throwing aggressive elbows as they skated around in moronic circles. The scene in here was so frozen and static I might have been viewing an anthropological diorama at the Franklin Institute: 'Neanderthals chipping stones in front of their authentic paper maiche caves.'

Gallagher was stationed in his usual back booth, working on his racing form. With his dark glasses on I could not vouch for what his reaction might be but he was fixing on my tote bag, I sensed that he was glaring in disapproval.

Schatz, Eli, Jardine, Sibronsky surrounded me to touch my shoulder, touch my back, tell me how sorry they were about Big Doc's death. Hymie came from around the bar to give me the hug an uncle might give, then said, "What you doing here, Pauli? My brother Saul drove out to the cemetery in West Philly to pay his respects to your father, and all day long we've been catching news flashes about incidents marring the funeral."

"Many incidents," I said, instantly using his words to cook up an excuse and logical alibi. "I had to escape from the photographers and reporters. Sonsabitches trying to stick a mike in front of my mouth."

Hymie gave me another hard hug, and agreed, " Bastards, a few of them were snooping around here yesterday, trying to dig up stuff on Big Doc."

That back booth was slightly elevated, maybe only two inches but a high two inches. From his throne Gallagher tossed his chin in disgust at the sight of this tote bag in my hand. He sensed that I was shucking and jiving here.

"Care for a stiff shot, Paulie?" Hymie asked me. "Drinks on the house this evening. If the cops come in, screw it."

"Thanks, sir. I could use a Seven and Seven. With emphasis on the Seven."

"Coming right up, kid," Hymie assured me. "Coming right up."

I headed toward Gall's booth, Schatz and Eli shuffling along with me, an entourage. Gallagher motioned them to back off; he intended to conduct a private audience. I extended my hand for a shake. Gall ignored my extended hand. With a toss of the chin he ordered me to take a seat.

A minute went by before he said, " Take off your dark glasses. You've no right to those things yet. I need to see your eyes cause I've an inkling you're ready to come at me with dippy-ass kiddy crap I don't care to hear. "

I obeyed orders. Gall stared into my eyes, then glanced at the cut on my cheek, the blue and yellow Franklin tote bag. He tilted his chin at a scornful angle before saying, "Going somewhere? The Coast? Oil Fields of Oklahoma, Tee jay?"

"All, possibilities. I dropped by hoping for a helping hand, boss-man."

"What the fuck do I look like? Your friendly travel agency?"

"C'mon, Gall. You helped Knocky leave town."

"Knocky is Knocky; you're in a different category."

Hymie arrived with my drink plus a large bowl of peanuts and potato chips. He was about to join us, Gallagher said, "Please, Hym, hold it up a bit, Paul and I are in a private conference; we are conducting serious business here."

With a shrug, Hymie said, "Catch you in a bit, kid," and then spun away.

Hey, we were catching a modicum of respect now. Gall just said Paul, not Paulie.

I sipped at my Seven and Seven. Gallagher strummed the tabletop, his fingers expressing disapproval. Then he said, "Alexi, the kid is beautiful, but doomed: a basket case losing proposition; mother, a whoor, father, a stewpot, Uncle, a Con. Alexi will be lucky to not end up spaced-out sprawled in a gutter, strangling in his own puke. You? You come from money, family, pack a brain. You have to study, graduate, make something of yourself."

"Hey, Gall, " I protested, " how come a hard man like you, walking on the raw side, preaches at me to stick to the safe, straight and narrow? Sure, you're not my fucking friendly travel agent but I also didn't expect you to sprinkle holy water on me and hit me with this Moishe-the-kindly-social-worker Shpiel."

Gallagher chuckled, first time I'd ever seen him remotely amused. He removed his dark glasses, looked older, sinister eyes, two gray chipped arrow points. Putting the dark specs back on, he said, "Yeah, I am a hard man, you are not. I'm not inclined to help a kid running away, hauling tail, ashamed of his father. That bugs me. Get one thing clear in your mind, Paul. You've nothing to be ashamed of. Big Doc was one of the few men around here we admired, a stand-up guy; the crooks loved him as much as the cops did. Whatever the whimps, snivelers, and pussies of this world say, whatever the cuntlapping politicians and jerk-off newspapers say, you had the luck to be brought up by a great man. So, don't let loudmouthed assholes who don't count run you out of town. This is your town, Paul. Philly is you, kid."

I raised my hand, asking teacher for permission to speak. Gallagher nodded, and I said, " I don't give a shit if I have to spend the rest of my life as *'The Son of Mob Doc,'* that aint the problem, it's just that at the moment my mind is elsewhere. There's no way I'll take the subway Monday to go sit in a classroom. That will not happen."

"Sure," Gallagher said, " you'll be running off hunched over, tail between your legs, ashamed of your father, that 's your bad sess, I'll not lift one finger to help you."

"I'm not ashamed of the man," I snapped. " If anything I'm pissed off at him."

"Pissed off? " Gallagher sat up; I finally had his full attention. He repeated, "Pissed off? That's a new one."

"Yes, sir, we had our family philosophy, the first Commandment was: Don't get caught. Do your shit, whatever it is, and your main duty will be to not get caught. Dad fell down, he got caught, his butt out to the wind, when he came tumbling down, he took others with him. Until I work that out in my mind I can't see myself toddling off to school."

Apparently my being 'pissed off' had struck a chord with this hood. Or was it the 'Don't get caught' mantra? Gallagher folded his arms across his chest, rested his head against the wall, was taking his time while formulating a response. If I did not know the man I might have said he was meditating. Rarely was it so clear that a man deciding my fate was sitting across from me. I took a long sip of my Seven and Seven.

On the TV they had switched off the Roller Derby and were showing the evening news, scenes of scuffles in the parking lot up at the funeral parlor, then scenes of similar confrontations at the cemetery in West Philly. All the guys in Gold's turned to stare at me. Except for Gall, he still seemed to be concentrating with his eyes closed, until he said," Yeah, I could certainly buy into that. Don't get caught. Everything else is bullshit. But I still think you're not ready to face the world yet. What if I told you out of me you'd get nothing; make like Hank Snow and drift, Kid. "

"I'll live with it, Mister Gall. I was hoping to ship out, if I can't maybe I'll head down to the docks, sneak aboard as a stowaway. If that doesn't come off, plan B, I buy hokey papers, enlist. Korea would be interesting right now."

"Korea? "Gallagher scoffed. "What is this Korea shit? From what I hear you've got big money coming to you. Right now you don't see it but you are waltzing down Easy Street. And, you are talking Korea and stowaway shit."

"Would you believe, sir, I don't give a flying flute about money right now. Don't want to touch it. Maybe it'll be here when I get back? Maybe I'll never touch it."

Gallagher sat up and shunted his racing form aside, almost knocked over his bottle of Schlitz. He said, "What I wanted to hear. Proof that you are nuts and have jumped off the deep end. Yeap, you are ready, ready to join all the other messed-up drunks, bonehead crazies, and fuck-offs out there on the bounding main."

"Is my tide turning?" I asked him.

"Yeah, " Gallagher said, "you're a danger to yourself and others. We might as well get you out of town before you hurt anybody." Then he cupped his hands around his mouth, called out, "Hey, Hym, do I have to stick nickels into your suck-ass telephone booth or can I use the horn in you back office. I've important calls to make."

"My office," Hymie called back, " as long as it's not to your Bookie in Tokyo. "

Rising, Gall said, " Hold down on the alky while I make my calls."

These guys were the same, like Dave in the poolroom, live depraved lives while offering sensible advice. I waited till Gall closed the office door behind him to finish my drink with one long gulp. Hymie was switching channels, the Big Doc show was monopolizing the airwaves, afternoon shots of when the Bonafaccio caddy arrived and Big Vinny stepped out. There seemed to be a live feed on Channel Seven, at the Green Street synagogue, protests about photographers taking shots of the mourners arriving for the reception. Again, everybody in Gold's turned to stare at me. No comment would be my only comment.

Hymie saw that my glass was empty. He arrived with another drink, and said, "This will be your last on us, Little Doc. You're too young to be hitting it this hard. But here are some slugs for the jukebox and the pinball machine. Put on some music and forget about your troubles, kid."

"Thanks, Hym."

The troops at the bar nodded as I faded over to the Wurlitzer. Hymie had given me quarter-sized slugs for the jukebox, nickel-sized for the pinball machine. For dead fathers you receive free newspapers, time at the pool table, shots on the house, and free slugs. On this Wurlitzer they gave you six songs for your quarter. I selected, Cool Water, Caravan, Song of India, Sixth Minute Man, the Blue Bird of Happiness, and a big surprise, a recent acquisition: Detour.

I stuck a nickel slug into the pinball machine, sent the first ball into action while 'Detour' was the first song to click on. Grass roots poetry, I picked up the verses from those Hillbilly joints on Eighth Street, all those plinking banjos and scratchy violins:

'Headed down life's crooked road, lots of things I never knowed

And cause of me not knowin', I now pine

Every damn channel was offering slices of the Big Doc Show. At the bar the regulars were squinting me, unasked questions in their eyes; what the hell was I doing in here when I should be part of this black and white breaking news story?

I was never good on pinball machines, tended to shake them too hard. 'The Song of India ' followed 'Detour' on our little Hit Parade here. So distant and mysterious but India probably stinks worse than our Carmens from the cigar factory. As long as India remains distant she will be exotic and romantic, a temptress with her clicking castanets. Only when you get too close do you learn what you don't want to.

Gall seemed to like my 'don't get caught adage.' While there is stuff we cannot say, dare never tell another human being. Dad was failing; the proud man was slipping. Had he been spared the indignities of decay, dementia, and decline?

Am I a swine for thinking this? One more conundrum I will have to work out.

'Night Train' was playing on the jukebox when Gall came out of the back office. He touched my shoulder and asked, " Know any Spanish, Pablo?"

"Claro que si, amigo: El Español de la Calle Marshall. "

"Bueno, " Gallagher said. "How about dishes? Know how to wash dishes?"

"I believe you use soap and water," I said.

"Great," Gallagher said. "Qualified, you passed the test. A Panamanian freighter leaves at dawn tomorrow. Needs a messman. You're it."

Not a deckhand? Well, nothing is ever perfect.

I extended my hand to thank him, Gall waved it off, saying, "You won't be thanking me when you're sweating your cojones off in a tropical hell-hole. You'll be cursing me out for not talking you out of this."

Thinking about practical matters, suddenly, I was in a panic: I had no papers, no passport. Gallagher read my mind and said, "Get on the fucking ship and sail away, kid. Everything will work itself out. I'll slip you a few buck so you can buy yourself documents down in La Zona. They have Chinese job shops down there that do a nice job on passports and social security cards."

"Thanks, man. Really,"

With a shrug Gall said, " I like to bank in heaven. One day, when you're a big shot Muckety-muck, I'll drop around to collect, in Spades. Finish your games, then sit down with me for one last drink, and we'll take you aboard. I don't know whether to pity or envy you. Leaving Boolah-Boolah days to enter the real world."

Hymie, behind the bar, gave me a thumbs up sign and Gallagher returned to his elevated station in the rear booth. I had two balls left to finish this game, and could not decide whether I were elated or scared shitless. Things get scary when you get what you want. Horrible as it was, this was the most important day of my life, and this a crucial moment, I was giving a major spin to the sands in the hourglass. There should be clever wrap-up lines, famous last words with a lapidary effect, demanding customers might require a whole epiphany. it was only fitting to consecrate this moment with burnished, ringing memorable phrases but the options flitting through my mind were corny, childish stinkeroos. I felt a pang of pain, a Corsican Brothers style sharp stab of pain, was not sure whether that was for Knocky or Karl, but one of my brothers was suffering out there, Ready or not all three of us were now out here in the world. Meanwhile, I had shaken this machine too hard, ending our game with a loud plink and flashing tilt sign.